Poodles at Dawn

Also by Tara Manning

Seducing Adam

Poodles at Dawn

TARA MANNING

POOLBEG

This edition published 2003
by Poolbeg Press Ltd
123 Grange Hill, Baldoyle
Dublin 13, Ireland
E-mail: poolbeg@poolbeg.com

1 3 5 7 9 10 8 6 4 2

A catalogue record for this book is available from the British Library.

ISBN 1-84223-022-0

Typeset by Patricia Hope in Palatino 10/14
Printed by
Litografia Roses, Spain

www.poolbeg.com

Acknowledgements

Some people lay a great deal of store by three little words – I lay a great deal of store by two – The End! And now that I've come to the end of *Poodles At Dawn*, there are a number of people who deserve my heartfelt thanks for their ongoing love, support and encouragement. Star billing, once again, must go to my always-there-for-me parents, Col. G P and Emily Manning, both of whom have worn out a ton of shoe leather doing 'reccy' on the streets of Dublin – ever since *Seducing Adam* hit the bookshops last year, in fact. You are now officially on the payroll!

Thanks again to my brothers and sisters Ger, Niall, Mark, Angela and Sharon, my sisters-in-law Ann, Frances and Joan, and my brother-in-law Wil – I hope you all enjoy this book too.

Thanks to Gaye Shortland, Boadicea of editors – Gaye, you wield a mighty red pen and to great effect. Thanks for all your hard work – I hope I didn't drive you to the Prozac – but if I did, you drove me to the drink – so, that makes us quits!

A huge vote of thanks to Paula Campbell and all the crew at Poolbeg, who organised such a terrific marketing campaign for *Seducing Adam*. Did you personally hang up all those apples in Eason's, Paula? Special thanks to those responsible for writing out the royalty cheques! Could you add a few more noughts, do you think?

Thanks and appreciation to all the terrific booksellers who made my first book launch such a joy last year, to all the journalists who were so kind, if a bit terrifying, and especially to all the wonderful and intelligent readers who bought *Seducing Adam*. I can't tell you the difference it makes to know that somebody somewhere appreciates and identifies with my own slightly mad brand of humour.

Well deserved thanks to the creative souls at Slatter-Anderson who have made such a great job with the covers of both *Seducing Adam* and *Poodles At Dawn*. I can't wait to see what you come up with next!

And so to my colleagues at Anthony Gold in London, endlessly encouraging, supportive, interested, and for putting their money where their mouths are. Thanks guys for the pension instalments!

Sue, you keep me going with the emails and the chats on the *gufan* which, let's face it, is the job of a best friend! Some chocs wouldn't go amiss though!

A special mention for the man from Achill Island – you know who you are!!!

Lastly, like the wine at Cana, I have saved the best till last. Tarek and Emmet, two mammy's boys in the making, my reasons for living and inspiration in all things – I love you with all my heart!

Poodles At Dawn is dedicated to
women friends everywhere
Because we know cellulite is out to get us
Chocolate is good for the brain cells,
And life without support underwear would be
totally unbearable!

CHAPTER 1

"So, Gemma, any sign of you getting married?" No sooner was she in the door than Aunty Kay fixed me with a 'half-joking, wholly in earnest' eye. "Isn't it about time that young Tony McCann fella made an honest woman out of you?"

I flinched. The woman had about as much tact as a pig at a bar mitzvah. "Don't hold your breath," I snapped. "Tony and I are history."

"Oh? But I thought you were betrothed, so to speak."

I'm sure I detected a kind of morbid satisfaction in her voice, which wasn't surprising considering she had never liked me, the old bitch, even though she and my mother were twin sisters. Unidentical, thank the Lord! If Mammy was small and birdlike then Aunty Kay was brick outhouse material.

"She was, until he bethrew her over! For Primrose Barry, would you believe?" This, from Orla, my younger sister, a cow if ever there was one – a cow who

1

knew exactly which buttons to press to wind me up. "Imagine the shame of being thrown over for a heifer like her!" She buried her face in her hands. "Jesus, if it was me I'd never set foot outside the house again as long as I lived, so I wouldn't."

"Well, it's not you, so shut your face!" Speaking of faces I could feel my own beginning to spontaneously combust. "Anyway, Primrose Barry is welcome to him."

At a nod from my aunt, my mother poured a cup of tea, added a splash of milk and two heaped spoons of sugar, gave it a good stir and pushed it across the table.

"There, get that inside you, Kay." And turning to me, "Personally I never *could* see what you saw in him, Gem. We knew his father from school, didn't we, Kay? Not a shoe to his foot and that's no lie."

Aunty Kay dug in her capacious handbag and produced a box of Rizla papers and a small square tin of Sweet Afton. "That's true. Not an arse to his trousers but full of wind and piss all the same." Almost ceremoniously, she laid one of the Rizlas flat on the table, prised the lid off the tobacco tin and, extracting a good pinch of shag, laid it the length of the paper. Then, rolling it into a miniature sausage, she licked all along one edge to stop it from coming apart, lit up and inhaled deeply. "Not that you'd know it to look at him today, puffed up as he is with his own importance, the big galoot!"

"Oh, he made good all right!" Mammy nodded sagely. "Pulled himself up by his bootstraps and owns

half of Ireland now if the press is to be believed."
Musingly, she shook her head. "Mind you, you've got
to admire the man and when all's said and done, Gem,
you could have done worse than to hook up with young
Tony. I mean, he *is* an only child. It stands to reason that
he'll inherit the lot."

I shot her a filthy God-you're-a-right-hypocrite look.
"I thought you said you didn't like him?"

"I know, but he was beginning to grow on me."

"He was beginning to grow on Primrose Barry too,"
Orla giggled. "And now he's all over her like lichen."

"Shut your face, you!" I snapped again. "Before I shut
it for you."

Aunty Kay sucked hard on her roll-up. "So, what
exactly did he say when he gave you the big E?"

Christ! Talk about cold as a witch's tit – the woman
was unbelievable! Not only did she want to humiliate
me but she wanted *me* to humiliate me! As if! As if I
could ever tell anyone about the evening my world had
tipped over on its axis and I found myself sliding right
over the edge. I shuddered internally. The mere memory
was enough to bring me out in a cold sweat, burning
face notwithstanding.

* * *

It's funny, but looking back I don't know what I
thought when I first heard the noises coming from the
bedroom of the flat Tony and I shared. That he had the
telly on, maybe – although the last time I looked we

3

didn't have a TV. That we were being burgled? Again! The reason we *didn't* have a TV! That he was having one of his asthma attacks, which would go a long way towards explaining all that heavy breathing, snorting and thrashing around? As I hurried towards the bedroom I remember praying he hadn't gone and lost his Ventolin pump, knowing from past experience it would mean another marathon hospital job with him playing Darth Vader on a nebuliser all night long and me getting a numb bum from the uncomfortable hospital chairs. At no point do I recall thinking, hey ho, that's my Tony, having it off with someone else. Only it *was* my Tony having it off with someone else! I couldn't see with whom at first due to my never before having made the acquaintance of the king-size pimpled ass hovering like a UFO a couple of feet above the mattress. Believe me, it put the ass in massive and there's no way I wouldn't know if I'd ever met it before. Unforgettable, that's what it was. So was Tony's face when he suddenly twigged me standing by the bedroom door like a Dark Avenging Angel. To say his head came clear of her mouth with the same sort of sucking noise a sink-plunger makes when it's yanked free of the plughole would be an understatement.

"Gemma!" Half-struggling up in bed he grabbed a sheet and pulled it up around his nipples. To cover his modesty, presumably, as if having lived with him for the past two years, I couldn't have read every inch of him by Braille if I'd wanted to. The thicko!

"That's me!" I said, amazed that I had time for conversation before following my baser instincts, shooting across the room and bludgeoning them both to death with the nearest blunt instrument. "Who were you expecting? The Pope?"

"But you're supposed to be at work!"

"Yeah, sorry about that." Even my pores exuded sarcasm. "I thought I'd nip home early, rustle us up a nice meal and surprise you." I raised my eyebrows. "Only it seems great minds think alike and you had a bigger surprise for me – with the emphasis on the *big*!" My eyes moved to where the 'ass' had made an about-turn and showed itself to be possessed of a front, as well. More front than Banna Strand, actually! I mean, her boobs were so big you'd run out of oxygen miles before you reached the summit.

"Hi, Gemma."

Hi, Gemma? If I hadn't heard it with my own two ears I'd never have believed the gall of her. Hi, Gemma! As if she'd just met me in a bar or something and was observing the social niceties. As if she wasn't stark bollock naked in *my* bed having just experienced *coitus interruptus* with *my* fiancé.

"Oh, hi yourself, Primrose," I said, sarcastic as hell when I finally recovered from the shock and recognised her as one of Tony's work colleagues. "Still working in the bonk – er sorry – bank?"

Knowing my ability to raze whole forests to the ground with my tongue in a matter of minutes, Tony

5

jumped in to put an end to the chit-chat before Primrose was wood pulp. "Primrose was just going, weren't you, Primmy?"

Solemnly I shook my head. "No, no, she wasn't, Tony. She was just coming unless, of course, she always leaves with such fanfare."

"You're disgusting, Gemma."

"That's rich coming from you," I snapped. "I'm not the one with my accoutrements hanging out all over the place. I'm not the one cheating, lying and deceiving." I took a threatening step forward although there wasn't an inch of me that wasn't trembling and that went double for my voice. "So how long has it been going on for, then? Eh? How long have you been making a fool out of me?"

"How long is a piece of string?" For a woman whose butt made the bounty of the loaves and fishes pale into insignificance, Primrose Barry was looking remarkably composed. "I told him he should finish things. I told you you should finish things before they got out of hand and something like this happened, didn't I, Tone?" Suddenly her composure vanished. Her mouth trembled like a giant, red-lipped mussel. "And now it *has* happened and I'm not happy." Tony slipped an arm around her. Correction! Tony attempted to slip an arm around her but being of average length, it only went round halfway.

"I'm sorry, precious."

Bloody hell! I couldn't believe my ears. *I* was the

6

victim here, the legitimate girlfriend, the love casualty. *She* was the intruder, in *my* home, in *my* bed, in my sodding plans for the future. Yet there was Tony, *my* boyfriend, soothing *her* ruffled feathers and sending me the evil eye without benefit of gift-wrapping.

"Get out, Gemma!"

"What?" For feck's sake this was too much! "What did you say, Tony?"

"I said, get out!"

I can only assume he was trying for masterful as he climbed out of the bed and stood like a human signpost, one hand pointing to the doorway behind me, his dick pointing towards Australia and his balls pointing east and west. I could have laughed were it not for the fact that the bile in my throat was threatening to choke me.

"You cannot be serious," I yelled with a quick transition into John McEnroe mode. "This is my flat too. Half of everything in here is mine."

"Except me!" Tony grabbed his trousers from off the floor where he'd obviously discarded them in a hurry. "Nothing of me is yours any more. Come on, Primm. Let's get out of here." Obediently, Primrose plopped off the bed and began squeezing herself into a pink lycra condom-dress which, if there was any justice in the world, should have cut off her air supply and left her dead in seconds.

"Don't forget your knickers," I sneered, watching her squeeze her Miss Piggy feet into impossibly high, red stilettos that simply had to have been reinforced with girders to withstand her weight.

"Don't wear any!"

The brazen cow! I thought, remembering the old saying 'Red shoes, no knickers!' Or maybe it was 'Fur coat, no knickers'. Anyway, knickers or the lack of them featured largely in it whatever it was.

"I'll be back for my things," Tony said coldly, a minute or so later as, hand in hand, they practically bowled me over. "Soon."

"Oh, will you, now?" Mad as hell, I tore after them, ran down the stairs that led to the pavement below and, hands on hips, roared after their retreating backs like a fishwife on a megaphone. "Well, you'd better take this now, you shite you, because if you don't it's going down the bog!" Tearing at my engagement ring I ripped it off my finger and flung it after him. Too late! By the time it hit the pavement the pair had already disappeared round the corner. A pensioner got lucky though. Stooping down as far as her dowager's hump would allow, she picked it up and jammed it over an arthritic knuckle. Then, flashing me a toothless smile she burst into song. Something about ding-dong, bells chiming and getting to the church on time.

"D'ye want it back, luuve?" she asked, drawing level with the bottom step upon which I was standing. "Only, it's a nice bit of a trinket. He didn't get that in no Lucky-Bag in Woolies."

"Nah!" I shook my head. "You keep it. It's no good to me where I'm going."

The pensioner looked mildly interested.

"Ah, you're not thinking of topping yourself?"

"No. I'm off to join the nearest convent."

"Same thing, luuve," she said sadly. "Same thing!"

* * *

So, as you can imagine, there was no way I was going to regale Aunty Kay or anyone else for that matter with the sordid details of my break-up with Tony. Besides which, in my more cowardly moments, of which there were many, I still hankered after him and dreamed he'd come back begging for forgiveness. Then we could move back into the flat which I'd had to give up on account of not being able to afford the rent on my own.

"Primrose was a *big* mistake," he'd say.

"*Big* is right," I'd say, and we'd laugh like a couple of drains at the wit of it all. Of course, in my more lucid moments, I knew there was no way on God's earth that I'd ever have him back – roasted, baked, boiled or even with an apple or a sprig of parsley shoved up his ass. No way! Like the Battle of the Boyne or last week's All Ireland final, Tony McCann was history. From now on I was finished with men. I was going to concentrate on my career as a veterinary nurse and search hopefully for signs of latent lesbianism.

"From now on I'm going to concentrate on my career," I told Aunty Kay, which didn't sound very convincing even to my own ears. I thought I'd keep quiet about the lesbianism bit though. No point in giving too much away! Besides I'd have to research that particular topic a bit more, ask Sophie, my workmate, for some pointers although, according to her, a lesbian's lot was not a happy one – principally, because they didn't *get* a lot! Well, not in Ireland anyway!

Aunty Kay dragged on her roll-up. I swear I never saw anyone get so much mileage from one cigarette. "Well, it's always a good move to bury a broken heart in work, though I'm not sure I'd call shoving your hand up a cow's backside work, as such."

'Well, the cow likes it,' I said, but only in my own mind because smut like that doesn't go down well with my mother.

"Ah, Gemma doesn't be doing that, Kay." Maternal instincts ablaze, Mammy galloped to my rescue. "Gemma does be holding little kittens and rabbits and things still, so the vet can give them their vaccinations. Isn't that right, Gem?"

I nodded. There was no point in going into the nitty-gritty and talking about the shit, piss, vomit and entrails that pervaded a normal day at *Vetz 4 Petz*. Let her keep thinking it was all adorable kittens with ribbons and bells round their necks and fluffy bunny rabbits like Thumper from *Bambi*.

"Still, it's no class of work for a girl." Aunty Kay tipped about an inch of ash onto the table, completely missing the ashtray that had been provided for her exclusive use. To make matters worse, when she tried to retrieve it she only succeeded in rubbing a big black mark into my mother's cherished Irish linen tablecloth. (Personally, I loathed the tablecloth. Talk about twee. It had little shamrocks all over it and bits of old Irish sayings like 'May the Roads Rise with You' and 'Top o' the Mornin'. Real American souvenir stuff!) "Why don't you go off and be a model like Orla?" She gave a speculative look at my hands, which were big and capable and better suited to the end of bakers' shovels than arms. "Although, maybe not!"

Orla's plucked eyebrows made the countdown from ten and lifted off into space. "That one, be a model? Do me a favour, Aunty Kay! With a shape like that?"

"There's nothing wrong with Gemma's shape. We can't all be beauties, you know." Mammy came to my rescue again, though I wished she hadn't bothered. "In my day, men were queuing up for girls like your sister – a good armful is what they wanted – someone who could heft a sack of spuds, put their back to the plough and bear a football team of children."

"All at one go!" Orla giggled, as well she might, the skinny bitch! "Listen, Mam, we're not talking about the Dark Ages when people were still evolving from the apes. This is the new millennium. They have machines now to heft the spuds and do the ploughing and –"

Mammy cut her off. "Are you calling me and your father, God rest his soul, apes?"

Orla giggled again. I hated the way she giggled. A cross between the tinkling of bells and the high notes on a piano, it enchanted everyone who heard it but just made me sick to my stomach.

11

"It's 'your father and *I*', Mammy." Orla had been to elocution lessons.

"I don't care if it's *The King and I*," Mammy snapped, getting annoyed. "Don't you dare call me and your poor dead father apes!"

Orla looked innocent. "I was talking about the *Dark Ages*, Mammy. I didn't know you and Daddy were around then. I must say *you're* wearing well for your age!"

Now if I had said something like that I'd have ended up tarred and feathered at the very least, but not Orla! Instead, Mammy laughed and called her a card.

"Oh, she's a right card, isn't she, Kay?"

"Oh, she is, May, a right ticket! It's a shame your Gemma couldn't be more like her."

So it was back to me again the 'fine, big, rump, sthump of an Agricultural Irish Girl' as the song went.

"Look," I said, before Aunty Kay got into her stride again. "Get off my case all of you. I'm perfectly happy the way I am. I'm not in the market for a cure. Still, if you feel you've got to find a solution to something, why don't you turn your attention to curing cancer, or finding an answer to the Northern question." Okay, I admit it, I was on a roll here. If I'd had a soapbox I would have stood on it! If we lived anywhere near Speakers' Corner, I would have haunted it! "And what about the pandas in China? Aren't they threatened with extinction or something? Then, there's the Brazilian street children." Now, I thought I was being fairly witty, much more so than Orla and her Dark Ages bit but Aunty Kay shook her head and it must have been catching because, one by one, Mammy and Orla did the same.

"Well, it's no wonder he gave you the push." Aunty Kay nodded sourly. "Sure, men are only interested in having a clean pair of socks and their dinner on the table when they come home from work. Pandas in China are probably the last thing on their minds."

Mammy nodded her agreement. "Your Aunty Kay's right, Gemma. Leave the pandas in China, why don't you, and go get a nice perm put in your hair?" Then, to Orla, as the telephone rang a timely interruption. "Answer that, love, would you? It's probably for you, anyway." The inference being, I took it, that nobody in their right mind would bother ringing me!

"That was my agent." Orla returned beaming. "I've got the *Sensuelle* lingerie job – subject to losing half a stone."

"That's great, pet." Mammy got up and gave her a hug. "But half a stone sounds like an awful lot to me. I mean, you're only a little snip of a thing as it is. A puff of wind would blow you away."

Earnestly, Orla shook her head. "No, I've got a big bum. Losing half a stone won't kill me."

I rolled my eyes wishing to God a puff of wind *would* blow her away. If that one had a big arse then mine was right up there alongside Kilimanjaro.

"Your mother's right, Orla," Aunty Kay frowned. "It

doesn't do to be too thin. Look at them heretics you read about in the papers – nothing but skin, bone and a hank of hair."

"Anorexics, Aunty Kay," I corrected her, delighted to get one over. "Joan of Arc was a heretic. Well, she wasn't really – at least Catholic Ireland wouldn't have thought so. Mind you, she did end up burnt at the *steak* so I suppose with a bit of lateral thinking there was an element of foodism there." Oh, I was witty all right. Expectant, I waited for the sound of, if not exactly applause, then laughter anyway. It never came. Instead, Aunty Kay fixed me with a baleful eye and sucked on her cigarette in a way that told me she was determined to get the value of every last drop of nicotine.

"Is that right, Gemma? Well, I daresay it's not something you'll ever need to concern yourself with anyway. Too fond of your food, aren't you?" *She* could talk. That one could eat a horse from the hooves upwards and start in on the jockey.

Fondly, Mammy tucked a stray wisp of blonde hair behind my sister's ear. "Well, nobody could say the same about Orla. She eats like a bird, so she does."

Yeah, a vulture! I thought, wondering how they could be so naive as to believe that. It wasn't through eating like a bird that Orla kept her size-eight figure but by chucking up in the bathroom after every meal. I knew that for a fact. I had heard the sound effects. And man, let's just say it wasn't church music!

Aunty Kay rose, retrieved her coat from the peg in

the hall, came back and stuck her head round the door. "Well, I suppose we'd better be going, May, or we'll be late for the bingo. Are you ready?"

"Mm, I'll just get my handbag." Mammy gave us the same anxious look she'd been giving us since the day we were born. "You'll be all right till I come back, girls?"

"No!" I said sarcastically. "There's a mad axe-man waiting outside till you've gone and then he's going to come in and chop off Orla's head and extract her brain, if he can find one."

Orla shot me a filthy look. "Don't mind her, Mam. Of course we'll be all right. You just go and enjoy yourself and, remember, be lucky!"

"Yeah, don't forget to call house," I yelled after them, looking pointedly at Aunty Kay's rump. Big-as-a-house!

CHAPTER 2

"So, who's rattled your cage this morning?"

"Excuse me?" Honestly, for a girl who was supposed to be my best friend, Debbie Dunn didn't half get up my pipe sometimes.

"Well, it's just that you look like you lost a condom and found a sieve."

I made a face. "For God's sake, Debs, it *is* Monday in case you haven't noticed. You know, start of another long and boring week at *Vetz 4 Petz?*"

Debbie hoisted a mock-sanctimonious look on her face. "Well, personally, I find I get great job satisfaction. And Friday evening was particularly edifying, if you get my drift."

I gave a reluctant grin. "I take it we're talking about Friday after hours here? Only, the last time I saw you, you were out back in the kennels knee-deep in doggy-do."

"Yes, well that was nothing a quick shower, a fresh

16

pair of knickers and a splash of Impulse couldn't cure."

"I'm surprised you bothered with the knickers," I said, "considering you probably dropped them not five minutes later."

"Less," Debbie admitted. Then, on a serious note. "Look, I know you don't approve but I really love him, Gemma."

Switching on the computer, I settled back for the five-minute wait it took, amidst much whirring and self-important clicking, to boot up. "I wish to God you didn't. Lord knows you're worth more than a married man with three kids."

"Don't start."

There was a warning in Debbie's voice but undeterred I waded in. "Oh, come on, Debs. Guy Evans is a tosser. If he can't be faithful to his own wife, and *she's* a supermodel *and* loaded, what chance have you got?" Realising I'd been a bit tactless there, I hurried to gloss things over. "Not saying that you're like the back of a bus or anything but, honestly, when it comes to a bit of skirt, that fella's only trotting after Bluebeard."

Flicking the switch on the office kettle to 'On', Debbie shot me a killer glare.

"Rubbish! It's not his fault if he's trapped in an unhappy marriage. He got married too young. Besides, these days they're more like brother and sister. There's nothing like *that* between them any more." Rummaging in a cupboard she produced two mugs – mine in the shape of a pig, hers in the shape of a sheep – and ladled a good spoonful of coffee into each. There was no need to ask if I took sugar. We'd been making drinks for each other long enough to know each one's personal preferences in coffee as well as in men.

I quirked an eyebrow. "And, if you believe that, you'll believe there's fairies down the bottom of the garden and they all talk like Graham Norton."

Debbie ignored the jibe. "Besides, Brigitte's father has invested heavily in the practice and until Guy can save enough to pay him back, he's more or less stuck in the relationship."

"How convenient! After that, I suppose he'll be telling you that he has to stay just long enough for the kids to start school/finish school/start university/start a family etc etc. Then, by the time his wife finally kicks the bucket and he is free, you'll be like a dried-up prune and he'll leg it with the nearest available twenty-something having stolen the best years of your life."

"And you're such a good judge of character, I suppose. I mean, that's rich coming from someone who came home to find her boyfriend in bed with the town whale." She grinned nastily. "Mind you, Tony *was* a member of Save the Whales, wasn't he?" Giving the coffee a good stir, she pushed mine across the counter with such force that a tiny tidal wave crashed over the side of the mug and slopped all over the morning's list of appointments.

"Oi! Take it easy, would you!" Grabbing a tissue from my pocket I dabbed at the appointments book which had turned a most attractive shade of sepia and, with every passing moment, was looking more and more like the Gettysburg Address. "There's no need to get vicious."

"There's every need, Gemma. None of this is easy for me and, as my *friend*, I expect you to support me – not preach at me from a height and especially not from the less than secure position of your very own glasshouse."

I tossed the soiled tissue in the bin, and rummaged about for another."As your *friend*, I'll continue to reiterate that Guy Evans is a pig masquerading as a human being, till the cows come home, if necessary." Frustrated, I grabbed her by the shoulders and turned her towards a mirror hanging on the wall. "Oh, take a look at yourself. You're beautiful, intelligent, young and witty. You have the world at your feet. Guy Evans must be cock-a-hoop at finding someone as gorgeous and willing as you to be his bit on the side. Someone *so* undemanding! So innocent!"

She shrugged me off. "I am *not* his bit on the side." Her voice was forceful but there was a distinct tremble to her chin. "We're getting married, Gemma, whether you believe it or not – just as soon as he leaves Brigitte." Fishing beneath the neck of her green veterinary nurse's uniform, she pulled out a thin gold chain on which a ring was suspended. "See, he gave me this. It's supposed to be our secret but –"

I cut her off. "I bet it is! And not one he'd like to get

out to his wife!" I abandoned my attempts at mopping the appointments book. We'd just have to be surprised at what came in the door this morning. Besides, if push came to shove, we had a back-up copy somewhere on the computer. "In any case, Debs, he had no right to give you a ring. He has no right to give you anything except instructions relating to your work here."

"Ah, the penny drops! So that's what's at the back of all this, is it? You think I'm getting preferential treatment just because I'm screwing the boss. All this concern for my welfare is nothing but a pretence really. Perhaps you think I'm getting more in my pay packet than you and Sophie!" Belligerent, she brought her face so close to mine I was tempted to land her one but settled instead for a light push.

"Don't be ridiculous! I wouldn't mind if you *were* getting special treatment. God knows, you deserve it! Unfortunately, from where I'm standing, far from singling you out for any privileges, he treats you with the same contempt as he does the rest of us."

Still on the defensive, Debbie took a sip from her coffee which in her annoyance she'd made far too strong, grimaced in disgust and tossed the rest down the sink. "Well, he's got to be discreet."

"Discreet?" I drained my own mug – I like strong coffee. If you can't have a strong man, have a strong coffee – well, that's my philosophy, though a nice big box of Butler's Handmade Truffles has the edge. "That's not discretion," I said. "That's pig-ignorance. I mean, where's the harm in 'good morning,' or 'thank you'? They're only common courtesies, something you'd accord to strangers let alone to your work colleagues."

Debbie tossed her head. "Oh, you haven't a good word to say for him, have you? No more than Sophie! To hear her on the subject you'd think he had 666 tattooed on his scalp and his second name was Lucifer."

"Someone mention my name?" Almost on cue the door had opened to disclose a very wet, very dishevelled Sophie who took one look at Debbie and threw up her hands in horror. "Lord have mercy! Don't tell me! Man-trouble!"

I grinned, pleased as always to see her. "Got it in one, Soph, although strictly speaking you couldn't really call him a man. A turd, maybe!"

Debbie rounded on me. "Oh, shut up, Gemma, and you can shut up and all, Sophie. I mean, it's not as if *you're* an expert on men, is it?"

"No. No, I wouldn't say I'm an expert." Sophie shook herself like a dog, spraying water everywhere, then took off her scarf and coat and hung them up. "But I do have a father and brothers and as approximately fifty per cent of the world's population are male, I wouldn't say I'm entirely ignorant, Debbie. Like, if I was to see one with no clothes on, I wouldn't mistake him for an alien or plant life."

Debbie blushed. "No, I mean in the sexual sense. You don't know men in the *sexual* sense!"

"If you mean I haven't had one jump my bones and

21

vice versa, then you're right. But that doesn't make me a bad judge of character." Sophie was perfectly at ease with her lesbian status. She picked up the kettle, weighed it in her hand to judge how much water was left and satisfied that there was ample, switched it back on again. "As far as I'm concerned, if something looks like a turd, smells like a turd and squelches like a turd, chances are it ain't a diamond! Ditto Guy Evans!"

Whatever response Debbie was going to make was lost as the door opened again and the first client of the day came in, towing a large Rottweiler behind her.

"Good morning, Mrs Birch." My heart sank as the woman approached the desk, wearing that confidential look I had grown to dread. "Brought Kilroy in for his enema, have you?"

Oblivious to Debbie and Sophie tittering and making rude gestures behind her, the elderly lady smiled.

"I have that, young Gemma. Sure the constipation is terrible bad. I can't tell you the last time he had a good dump for himself. Isn't that right, Kilroy?" The dog gave a pained, half-hearted thump of his tail.

"Well, no doubt Martin will sort him out quick-smart," I said, knowing that as Martin Shanahan's nurse I would have the unenviable task of holding the brute still, then following him around to make sure he didn't crap himself to death. So much for my mother's idea of cuddly little kittens and puppies! "Now, if you'll just take Kilroy and go through to the waiting-room, Martin won't be too much longer."

"Thanks, dear. Come along, Kilroy." Mrs Birch urged the Rottweiler up from where he'd taken up residence on the floor then, as a kind of afterthought, turned back to me. "By the way, I was sorry to hear about your young man and that Primrose Barry hussy. Maybe you should have tried dressing up as a French maid or a nun or something. You know, kept him happy in the boodeewar the way he'd have been less likely to stray." She gave a broad wink. "Mind you, from what I've heard that Primrose young-one does things that haven't even been invented yet. A right little goer, by all accounts."

"Thank you, Mrs Birch!" I said pointedly, shooting a daggers look over her shoulder to where my two so-called friends were in hysterics. "Just take a seat in the waiting-room, please, and Martin will be with you shortly." Bugger! I thought, watching her stagger away on bowed and varicosed legs. Bugger! Damn and blast! Clearly the skeleton was out of the closet. The whole of Ireland must be sitting at home rubbing their hands in glee, chewing over the ignominy of my break-up with Tony. I could feel myself starting to sweat, the tell-tale prickling breaking out along my forehead and spine as if a million fleas were Riverdancing up and down along my skin.

"Jesus! Not starting the menopause, are you?"

I whirled around as Martin Shanahan, having sneaked in through the rear entrance, came up behind me.

"No, I am not!"

"Only the wife's got it," he continued, unabashed by

23

the ice in my tone. "And honest to God, she's like an Antichrist so she is and I don't think I could cope if you had it as well." As though the menopause was a communicable disease or something, the cretin!

"Well, I haven't got it," I snapped, "but come back in another twenty-odd years or so and I'll see what I can rustle up. In the meantime, Mrs Birch's Rottweiler is all bunged up again. They're waiting for you now."

"For my sins." Martin nodded dolefully. "For my sins and me with a delicate stomach this morning. I swear, I've a good mind to ram a truckload of strychnine up his jacksey and see how bunged up he'll be then. Now go get the treatment room ready and break out the irrigation hose. There's a good girl." He patted my shoulder and all but shooed me away.

Patronising git! I thought, wishing I could ram something up his own jacksey.

"Hold the fort, you two," I called to Debbie and Sophie who were still convulsing over by the kettle as, dead-woman-walking, I headed for the gallows. "And mind you don't break your holes laughing."

"We won't." Debbie wiped her streaming eyes, enjoying her revenge, the bitch. "But watch out for your uniform, although I think there's a spare nun's habit knocking round somewhere if you get stuck."

"Ha, ha! Very bloody funny." I stuck my tongue out. "But just remember, she who laughs last laughs loudest!"

* * *

24

As I followed Kilroy around the yard outside a short time later my mind turned once more to the 'the break-up' and the fact that I hadn't seen it coming. Honest to God! *I hadn't seen it coming!* Even looking back there were no telltale signs, no lipstick on his collar, no exchanging his T-shirt and jeans for Armani three-piece suits, no silent phone calls – nothing to put me on cad-alert! As far as I was concerned everything in the garden was pest-free. I mean, we still did *it* together – okay, maybe not quite as much as at first and maybe with less shifting of position but from everything I've seen, heard and read, that's par for the course, right? Like even insomniacs get tired of twisting and turning all night. All right, all right, so admittedly, in the months leading up to 'the break-up', he was more likely to find me with my hair in Molton Browns, Cyclax all over my face and wearing flannel jim-jams as opposed to a basque and stockings but, the way I see it, that was a compliment to him. I mean I felt so comfortable, so relaxed with him, it was almost like we were extensions of each other. And so, by baring my face I was also, in the metaphoric sense, baring my soul. Being honest – taking off the mask and letting him see the real me, letting him in on the secret of my oily T-zone and penchant for flannel pyjamas in a nice paisley pattern. Big mistake! Obviously Tony liked war paint and in a past life might even have been Sitting Bull.

Primrose Barry wore make-up. Correction, make-up wore her and it's no exaggeration to say that you'd see

25

it coming from miles away. If some people had the X-factor then, boy oh boy, Primrose Barry had the Max Factor!

"Life," I told Kilroy, as I trailed him round and round the yard, "is crap!" His agonised expression as he sat down and strained and strained only to find it was all effort and no production told me clearer than any words that such had not been his experience which, in turn, set me to wondering about that pain/pleasure principle thingy. Could it be that because I was getting so much crap, poor old Kilroy was getting so much constipation? Which led me off on yet another tangent, namely Tony's toilet habits. The best I can say about them is, they weren't nice. For God's sake, he took the newspaper into the loo with him *and* library books. I'll tell you that was enough to have me taking the scissors to my own library card. I mean you don't know where your library book has been, do you? In whose hands! I know for a fact he read all the classics while sitting on the crapper. Talk about *War and Piss* and *A Tale of Two Shitties*. But, sad cow that I am, I still loved him. Even when he took off *his* mask, the veneer of controlled respectability he wore all day at the bank, I didn't diss him. Even when he farted in bed and fanned it over to my side with the duvet, I still didn't diss him. No way! I loved Tony McCann farts and all and wanted his babies. Hell, I'd even put their names down for the best local schools already! Samantha Jane and Daniel James McCann – real classy!

26

"Hurry up!" Upset by all this introspection I nudged the dog with my foot but, as with everything else in my life, my timing was also crap and in another moment so were my shoes as the enema finally kicked in full throttle and Kilroy pooped all over them. As I cleaned up the steaming mess I wondered if Aunty Kay might not be right and if I might not be better off in some other class of a job but, then again, working in an office or shop didn't necessarily guarantee you wouldn't be shat on. *And*, say what you like about animals, at least they were grateful. "Come on, you," I said, tugging on his collar a short time later. "Let's get you back to your mother."

"Ah, look at him!" Back in the waiting-room Mrs Birch fondled his ears. "Did you have a good dump for yourself, eh? Did you have a good dumpy-wumpy?" She turned to me for confirmation. "Did he have a good –"

"He did," I assured her hastily. "He's as empty as a kettledrum, but lay off the sweets and chocolates, Mrs Birch, would you? Dogs' digestive systems aren't the same as ours. Just feed him on a normal dog-food diet and he'll be as right as rain."

Mrs Birch rolled her eyes. "Ah, don't be starting that again, young Gemma. How many times do I have to tell you he loves his Curly-Wurly of an evening, so he does? And, sure God knows, we all need a bit of a treat now and again." She closed an eye, winked salaciously. "And now that he's too old for a bit of rumpy-pumpy,

27

you wouldn't deny him the odd Curly-Wurly, would you?"

"Give him a nice big juicy bone or a pig's ear or something," I told her, immune to the 'enlisting support' looks she was darting round the waiting-room. "And remember, Kilroy is a dog with a dog's needs and not a human being."

Mrs Birch took umbrage, took Kilroy's lead and took her temper out on me. "God, you're a hard class of a young one, Gemma Murphy! It's no wonder young Tony took off with that Primrose Barry. A big soft armful like herself must make a nice change from a hard-faced strap like you!"

"Next for Martin Shanahan," I called, resisting the primeval urge I felt to pound upon her dowager's hump like on a pair of bongos.

"We're next, aren't we, Bella?"

I groaned internally as I recognised the poodle held up for my inspection as Bilious Bella, the vomiting Wonder Dog!

"Hello, Mrs Hughes. What has she eaten now?"

"My nephew's school tie." She looked around. What was it about these blue-rinse types that they felt they had to play to an audience? "Honest to God, I came into the kitchen and there was the tail-end of it disappearing down her throat like one of them sword-swallyers in the circus."

"Right, you'd better bring her through," I said, completely unsurprised by Bella's dietary excesses which to date had included a pair of wellington boots (size 10s, belonging to Mrs Hughes's husband), a set of house keys, two sets of dentures (his and hers) and an entire combine harvester. Okay, so the latter *was* made from Meccano and stood only one foot high – but you know what I mean? Like, could you see yourself eating it? It was a standing joke in the practice that Bella's throat was the canine equivalent of the Black Hole of Calcutta.

And so, Bella having been despatched but not before she added vomit stains to the shoes Kilroy had already crapped on, the day wore on in a progression of wormings, vaccines, de-fleaings and mange treatments till, by home time, I felt fit only for the knacker's yard myself.

"God, there must be more to life," I told Sophie who had joined me at the bar of the Fox's Retreat.

"I know." Sophie took a long drink of her Holsten Pils. "I've just had the day from hell myself. I swear, Gemma, some people should never be allowed to keep animals. You should have seen the farm Rob and I visited today. God, it would give you nightmares."

"Really?"

Sophie nodded, clearly upset. "There were about fifty cows, some already dead and rotting in the fields and the byre, the rest so malnourished and diseased they were like walking skeletons and had to be put down. We couldn't save any, Gemma. Not one!"

Shocked, I drained my bottle of lager and signalled

for another one each. "Jesus, that's desperate. Where was the farmer?"

"Drunk! Drunk as the proverbial skunk. And do you know what he said to us when we confronted him?" Indignant, Sophie's voice rose. "He said they were his animals, bought and paid for by him and he could do what he wanted with them. The bastard!"

"So is the ISPCA going to prosecute?"

"You bet! They're going to nail his ass to the Cross and by the time they're finished he'll be banned for life from owning so much as a toy hamster."

"Proper order too!" For emphasis, I banged my fist down on the counter, earning a black look from a patron further down the bar whose pint of Guinness had come dangerously close to losing its head. "I don't know how you do it, Soph. I mean, go out on the farms and with the ISPCA and that. Agricultural animals scare the living daylights out of me. They're so, you know, big!"

"Well, the horses and cattle, maybe. The sheep and lambs are gorgeous. Anyway, you know me – I like to be out and about. I couldn't be stuck in the surgery all day like Debbie and you. Dogs and cats aren't really my scene and certainly not snakes and spiders."

"Well, snakes and especially not spiders aren't my scene either. No, I'm happy enough to leave the 'exotics' to Debbie. She finds them fascinating or maybe it's just Guy she finds fascinating. I mean, she's always going on about how gentle he is with the iguanas and tarantulas and things. In any case, she's welcome to them *and* him. No, I'll stick to Kilroy and Bilious Bella – at least I know them both inside out!" I stuck out my shoes. "Behold, proof positive!"

"Anyway," Sophie changed the subject, "when are you going to come down to Wicklow, for the weekend? After all, you're a free agent now; no Tony to tell you not to do this or not to do that." A wicked glint came into her eye. "Besides, there's a fox-hunt on near Blessington next weekend and I know you'd love it." She gave me the hard sell. "Think about it, Gemma, all those riders, hunting-pink and smart black jackets, jodhpurs straining over taut thighs and buttocks, the passing of the stirrup cup, the thrilling, rallying sound of the horn – the even more thrilling sound of a well-placed sod of turf finding its mark and knocking them, one by one, like ninepins off their horses!"

I laughed disparagingly. "Do me a favour, Soph! What do I know about being a hunt saboteur? The only thing I've ever managed to sabotage so far is my own love-life."

"Not a problem! I'll teach you. Come on, what do you say? Think of the fox. Think of the cubs waiting for their mother to return to the den – only she won't. She can't, because somewhere she's being torn apart by a pack of marauding hounds while the hunters stand around, comrades in murder, overfed, arrogant and high on the scent of the poor vixen's blood!" Crikey, talk about passionate! Sophie's whole face was lit up like the Ringsend Power Station.

31

"Yeah, all right, I'll go then," I said, having thought briefly about it. After all, what had I got to lose? It wasn't as though my social diary was chock-a-block with invitations. It wasn't as though I even *had* a social diary any more. That went when Tony went. It's funny but I never realised how much I'd made him the centre of my universe, depended on him to provide me with interests, conversation and sex. Mind you, I'd learned my lesson. From now on I would always hold a bit of myself back. No matter how much I loved somebody. If they didn't have all of you – they couldn't hurt all of you! And that resolution lasted all of about five minutes!

"Are you serious?" Sophie punched me on the shoulder. "You really will come? You're not just yanking my chain?"

"I'm serious." Reaching out, I clanked bottles with Sophie. "Watch out, Wicklow, here we come! But, be warned, I've a terrible aim."

"Now she tells me," Sophie joked. "Now she bloody tells me!"

CHAPTER 3

"Mammy," I roared downstairs, knowing full well she'd gone out. "Furbee's left a bleached bone in the bathroom!"

"Ha, ha, very bleedin funny." Orla, clad only in bra and pants stepped off the bathroom scales and made to push past me but I caught her arm, carefully for fear I'd break it, and held on.

"No, Orla, looking like something out of a concentration camp is definitely not funny. Tell me, how much do you weigh, now? Three stone? Four?"

Her lip trembling, Orla yanked her arm away and rubbed it where my fingers had left red marks.

"Too much! I weigh too much. I've only managed to lose three pounds this week. I can see the *Sensuelle* contract flying away on wings and short of chopping off a few limbs I don't know how the hell I'm going to lose the other four pounds."

I closed the bathroom door, kept my back to it so she

couldn't escape. The way I saw it, someone had to try and talk a bit of sense into my cow of a baby sister.

"And I suppose you *would* chop off a couple of limbs except that that would be even more likely to put the kibosh on your modelling career – even more so than weighing a couple of pounds over the regulation quota of skin and bone, I should imagine?" I fixed her with a steely eye. "Listen, Orla, this has got to stop. Don't think because you've got Mammy and everyone else fooled, I don't know what you're up to." Grabbing her right hand, I pointed to where the knuckles of her first and middle fingers were split from banging against her teeth. "This is what comes of sticking them down your throat to make yourself sick. It's very hard to be a silent puker, you know. *Someone* is bound to hear you. Like me for instance!"

A skeleton in denial, Orla shook her head. "So, I've had a few cases of food poisoning lately, a few gippy tummies, so what? Is that a crime?"

"Gippy tummies, my arse," I said, which, all things considered, was hardly anatomically correct. "You're bulimic, Orla. You're chucking your food. Everybody thinks you eat like a bird but I know about the big stash of goodies you keep at the back of your wardrobe. I *know* because I've been in there and done a raid and just so you know for the future, I prefer milk chocolate to plain."

Orla paled beneath her perma-tan. Sunbed – not natural! "Don't tell Mammy, Gemma. Pleeeze. You

34

know how she is. You'll be responsible for sending her to an early grave. You will!"

God, it felt good having her in my power, pleading with me, grovelling, giving me the same face she gave to her boyfriends when engaged upon the serious business of charming the blank cheques out of their pockets. It felt good, or rather it would have done had I not felt a bit guilty about the whole thing, as if I were profiting from something rather sordid.

"Well, you've got to stop, Orla. I mean it! Even if it does cost you the *Sensuelle* contract. I mean there's no point in being the best-dressed corpse in the morgue, is there? Centrefold in the *Undertaker's Gazette*? Imagine the caption: *Dead Gorgeous! Out of this world! A Spirited Lass!*"

Orla sniffed. "It's all right for you. You're used to being big and I suppose that's fine for *your* chosen career where you're handling bull elephants all day long but modelling requires a more delicate physique."

"Don't be disgusting," I snapped, deliberately misunderstanding her. "I don't *handle* bull elephants. What sort of perv do you take me for? Besides, being a veterinary nurse wasn't my chosen career. Acting was!"

Orla abandoned all attempts to get past me and, plonking herself on the side of the bath, burst out laughing. "That's right! How could I forget? Hamlet!"

"Yes, Hamlet!" Somehow, since the Tony and Primrose episode, the Hamlet episode didn't seem quite so bad and although it still brought a blush to my face, I could see the humour in it now whereas before all I could see was the sheer humiliation. Nonetheless, the whole thing was horrible, the stuff of nightmares and then some. I was twelve years old back then, a budding actress on the brink of a great career treading the boards, or so I thought. Mind you, I'd wanted to play the part of Juliet in the school play but due to a technicality, wrong play or something, I couldn't. And so I ended up playing Hamlet, Prince of Denmark. Anyway, with the exception of one or two glitches things were going reasonably well till it got to the part with the skull scene. So, picture this, I pick up this skull – we'd borrowed it from the nearby medical school. Every second tooth was missing and it had Walter and 666 tattooed on the back. I swear, the audience was mine, spellbound by my thespian abilities! I'm sure they thought they were looking at the next Vanessa Redgrave. You could have heard a pin drop. Turning the skull over and around for dramatic emphasis, I patted its poor bony protuberance of a forehead and turning to the audience uttered the immortal words:

"Alas, poor Yorick, I knew him . . . Fellatio!"

Fellatio! Imagine it! Honest to God, the entire audience pissed themselves. Oh, I recovered quickly though. "Horatio!", I cried into the pitch darkness of the auditorium lit only by the flashing of a thousand bared teeth. "I knew him, *Horatio! Horrr-ash – eee-oo!*" But it was no good. The words fell on barren ground. The bastard audience had the bit between their teeth

36

and there was no way they were letting go. I wouldn't mind only I didn't even know what fellatio was and, at twelve years old, it still amazes me that I could even get my mouth around it. Still, the audience enjoyed themselves hugely and gave me, for want of a better word, a standing ejaculation at the end of the night.

Suddenly suspicious, I turned my attention back to Orla, knowing her tactics of old and how she tried to distract me whenever I confronted her with something about which she did not wish to be confronted. "Anyway, Hamlet's in the past. A bit like your dinner although, strictly speaking, that's more in the pan than in the past."

"Look," Orla drummed on the side of the bath with her heel, "I said I'll stop. Now, what do you want? An undertaking in blood?"

"Don't be facetious. This is for your own good," I told her, hating my sudden metamorphosis into my mother. "You've seen the documentaries the same as I have. You've seen what happens to people with eating disorders if they don't take themselves in hand. They end up dead, stuffed sideways into envelopes because they can't fill a coffin. Is that what you want, everyone standing around and saying 'My, isn't she thin!' and 'I hope the worms aren't after a banquet tonight!'? *And* you get hairy," I added as an afterthought, thinking that this might be enough to sway someone as vain as Orla in the right direction. "It's the body's way of trying to conserve the heat that's lost when you don't have enough fat in your body." I thought of something else, a real stroke of brilliance. "*And* all that puking rots the enamel on your teeth so that not only do you end up a hairy toothpick, you end up a toothless hairy toothpick."

"Rubbish," Orla snapped, forsaking her perch on the side of bath in favour of examining her near-perfect reflection in the mirror over the sink. "There's nothing wrong with my pearlies and my hair is exactly where it should be – on my head!" Slyly her eyes slid down to the substantial gap between where the hem of my skirt ended and my ankles began. "Which is more than can be said for you. Tell me, Gemma, have you never heard of the *razor*? It's a far more recent invention than the wheel. Most people possess at least one. They use them to dispose of unwanted hair, you know. Maybe it's something you should investigate."

"Oh, shut up, Orla!" I snapped, beginning to get really annoyed, not least because I knew she was right. My legs really were a disgrace. Since Tony'd slung his hook, there hadn't seemed too much point to the whole preening routine. As for my bikini line – suffice it to say, if ever I had the misfortune of being stranded at the North Pole, I could always pull it up over my shoulders like an extra blanket. "Face up to it. You've got a major problem. Now, what's it to be? Do you get help yourself or do I tell Mammy and let her deal with you? Come on, it's your call!"

Orla sighed hugely. "I said, I'll stop. Okay? You can follow me round the house twenty-four-seven if you don't believe me. Just give me a chance, Gemma. Just a chance!"

"All right then, just one more chance!" I agreed, caving in against my better judgment. "But just remember Big Sister is watching you. Now do one, would you? I'm desperate for a pee."

* * *

"I still think you should have told on her." As usual, Debbie played mother, and made the morning coffee.

"Oh yeah? The way you'd want someone to tell your mother about you and Guy the Sly?" Sophie cradled her mug. Hers was in the shape of a horse and if you tipped it over, which wasn't a very good idea when it was full, it neighed.

"It's hardly the same thing." Debbie's voice was dry. "I mean, our little love affair is hardly life-threatening, not like bulimia."

"Oh, you reckon, do you?" said Sophie. "Only, you might change your mind if Brigitte ever twigs what's going on between you and her precious husband."

"Oh, get off my case, Sophie!" Debbie shot me a look of appeal. "Tell her, Gem, would you? I'm not in the mood."

"Bet you didn't say that last night." Like a dog with a bone, Sophie was reluctant to let it go. "More's the pity."

I threw her a speaking glance. Actually Debbie *didn't* look too well. For a few days now I'd noticed she looked really tired and washed out. This Guy business was obviously getting to her a lot more than she let on.

"Leave her, Soph. Besides, we were talking about Orla. I swear I don't know what to do for the best. I mean, she is twenty-two, an adult. Part of me feels that if she wants to chuck up left, right and centre then I should just stand clear and let her get on with it. I mean, trying to stop her might be interfering with her human rights or something."

"No way!" Debbie shook her head. "Bulimia is as much a mental disorder as a physical one and it goes without saying that people suffering from mental illness are not *compos mentis*. Therefore, *you* have to take control and do what you think is right for her. Personally, I'd have no hesitation in getting the whole family involved. Really, Gem, it's far too much for you to carry on your own."

"And how come you know so much about it?" Honestly, sometimes Sophie was so belligerent I wondered if she secretly fancied Debbie. A kind of 'lady protesting too much'?

"I know," Debbie said, slowly and with emphasis, "because I've been there, done that and, puked all over the T-shirt, and if it weren't for the support of my own family I might well be six foot under now and pushing up the daisies."

Sophie and I were shocked. I mean, you think you know someone, work with them day in and day out, never guessing that they're only allowing you a glimpse of their real selves, that what you actually see is only a thin veneer of the real person.

"No! No way," I insisted. "I'm your best friend. How could you have kept a secret like that from me? I would have known."

"No, no, you wouldn't. We bulimics become very deceitful. We've all sorts of little tricks up our sleeves to put people off the scent. Literally!" Debbie shrugged. "As for why I didn't let you in on it – shame, I suppose, or maybe the fact that you always seemed so in control yourself, Gemma. Also, if I'm honest, I thought you'd probably take the mick."

Completely thrown, I didn't know which allegation to answer first so I tackled them on a first come, first served basis.

"Me? In control? You've got to be kidding. I was never in control. I can't even control the temperature of my bath water. And, as for taking the mick, I've always been protective of you. Who was it thumped Breda Hennessy when she told the teachers about you smoking in the loo? Me, that's who. *And* I got half an hour's detention for it five nights on the trot."

"And never let me forget it," Debbie grinned while Sophie looked impressed.

"God, I never thought you had it in you, Gemma. I couldn't imagine you decking anybody. I thought you were a pacifist."

I gave her my best cynical look. "Which is why you're dragging me off on one of your hunt-saboteur weekends, I suppose? For my United Nations peace-keeping abilities. Anyway, this is not about me; it's about Debbie. And I swear, I feel terrible, Debs, like I've really let you down."

"Well, you didn't and besides my problem was too much for you to cope with, which is exactly my concern about Orla."

"All right, point taken," I said. "But, before I call in reinforcements, I really think she deserves a chance to get herself back on the straight and narrow. But, I promise, at the first hint of a retch, I'll rally the troops. Will that do?'

"It'll have to, I suppose." Debbie still didn't look too happy. "But don't say I didn't warn you."

Sophie checked her watch. "Okay, girls, it's door-opening time. Get ready for the stampede."

* * *

There was no point in denying it, I thought later, as I was feeding a tiny kitten drop by drop via a pipette, I wasn't happy. Oh, I was putting on a good show, no doubt about it. To hear me talk you'd think Tony had been nothing more than a notch on my one-night-stand belt instead of a serious relationship – *the* serious relationship – the biggy! Alone at night though, back once more in my schoolgirl, virginal bed, with no one to bolster me up, no one to tell me what a wanker he was, what a complete and utter shite, I had no option but to admit the truth. I was hurting. I was hurting like a half-healed cut from which the scab has been ripped. I mean, he'd been so – well – vicious. I just couldn't get my head round that. There was no call for it. Like, if I pissed him off that much all he had to do was say so. You know, plain speaking!

"Gemma, you piss me off!"

I would have understood that. It's not like I'd have needed a degree. Mind you, I'm not saying I'd have liked it and that I wouldn't have taken his head off but I would have understood – eventually. What I didn't understand was why he felt the need to shag Primrose Barry to get his point across unless, of course, it was his very own interpretation of sign language – a sign I was dumped – a sign I couldn't possibly miss! The kitten mewed and reached up a curious paw as I shifted it into a more comfortable position, squeezed the bulb at the top end of the pipette and delivered another drop of milk into its tiny pink mouth. Primrose Barry of all people! Talk about adding insult to injury.

"Ah, there you are, Gem!" The sudden appearance of Sophie at the door startled me out of my musings. "Your Aunty Kay is at reception."

"Aw no, you're joking!" If my hands had been free I would have made the Sign of the Cross. If time had allowed, I would have armed myself with a sharpened stake or a silver bullet. "What does she want now?"

Sophie held her hands out to take the kitten. "You know very well what she wants or rather, who she wants."

43

I groaned. "Yeah, Rob. Wouldn't you think she'd have got it into her head that having reached the wrong side of fifty without benefit of a wife he's unlikely to break the habit of a lifetime for her. I mean, it's not as if she's Miss World – Miss Other World, maybe! The Thing from the Deep!"

"Well, maybe you should tell her about the sheep," Sophie suggested, a wicked glint in her eye.

I laughed, thinking back to the time Sophie had first told *me* about the sheep. Of course she'd been mouldy drunk or she'd probably have been a lot more discreet – given that, at that time, I was the new kid on the block, so to speak.

"Rob, that's my bossh, you know," she'd slurred, the first time I'd ventured down the Fox's Retreat. She knocked back what, judging from the collection of empty bottles on the bar before her, was probably about her tenth Holsten Pils. "Goesh with sheep." She banged her fist on the table for dramatic emphasis. "Honesht to God, he goesh with sheep."

Naive as a nun in a knocking shop, this disclosure puzzled me somewhat. I mean, where does anyone go with sheep other than to a farm or to the butcher's? It's not as though they'd make riveting conversationalists unless, of course, you were Scrooge and they could go 'baah' and you could go 'humbug'! For instance, I can't imagine linking arms with one down Grafton Street hell-bent on a spot of retail therapy or heading off with one done up to the nines for a bop down the local nightclub.

"Where?" I gave in to the puzzle and asked Sophie. "Where does he go with them?"

Sophie'd burped, laughed and made wild and graphic gestures with her lager bottle. "Not, *goesh*, shtupid, ash in the shense of *going* anywhere. You know, he *goesh* with them!"

I remember the feeling of light dawning, my eyes growing big as saucers, the slightly sick, fascinated feeling pooling in the pit of my stomach. "You mean he *goes* with them? As in . . ."

"Got it in one!" Sophie laughed uproariously. "Ash he probably shaid lasht night!"

"But that's disgusting! He should be defrocked or whatever it is they do to vets."

"Fleeced," Sophie announced drunkenly. "He should be fleeced. Given the lamb-chop!"

And to think my Aunty Kay was in love with a sheep molester!

* * *

"Aunty Kay, what are you doing here?" A few moments later I accosted her in the waiting-room where, sandwiched between a gigantic Doberman and a Vietnamese pot-bellied pig, her face didn't seem at all out of place.

"And good-morning to you too, Gemma." Sarcastic as shit, her glance bounced all round the room much as to say: See that little guttersnipe, that's my niece – now watch how I put her back in her box! "Got out of the wrong side of the bed this morning, did you? Left your manners in the sink along with the dirty dishes? I hope that's not how you greet all your clients because they must be really impressed. They must be overwhelmed. They must be –"

I rolled my eyes quellingly. "Look, Aunty Kay, I'm very busy this morning." Letting my own glance roam around the room I put a lot of telepathic meaning into it. See this silly old cow, I telepathised. It's thanks to her that you're all waiting so long. Look at her taking up my time just because there's a tenuous blood link between us. And that's not my fault either! So go on, feel free to tear her apart with your bare hands. There's quicklime out the back. No one need ever know!

"It's Furbee!" Aunty Kay came suddenly to the point. "He's got rabies."

"Don't be silly!" Furbee was *my* dog. I'd bloody know if he had rabies, and noticing him for the first time, crouched on the ground patently planning an assault on the Siamese cat peeping from its cage across the room, I knew he no more had rabies than I had Kate Moss's figure and men propositioning me on street corners. Nonetheless, Aunty Kay stood firm.

"He has," she announced. "He was foaming at the mouth this morning. 'Rabies,' I said to your mother when she phoned in a panic. 'Definitely rabies!' The poor woman was distraught which is why I'm here."

Foaming at the mouth? Suddenly suspicious, I bent down and sniffed the air around his muzzle. Just as I thought! The silly sod had been at the toothpaste again. He had a thing about fluoride which, I suppose, to him was the canine equivalent of a big bar of Fruit 'n' Nut.

"Toothpaste, Aunty Kay." I made my voice deliberately bored just to show her up in public for the stupid old mare that she was. I mean, rabies! Pulleese! "He can't resist it, especially the one with the red stripe."

But Aunty Kay was not one to be consoled by common sense. "I still think Rob should have a look at him. I mean, you could be wrong, Gemma. *You're* not a vet, are you? You're just the oilcloth, not the mechanic. It could be he's been at the toothpaste *and* has rabies." Around her, heads were nodding. Obviously, the old saying 'there's one born every minute' still held true.

I shrugged with an oh-well-if-you-will-insist-on-making-a-bloody-nuisance-of-yourself look on my face. "Suit yourself but it won't be Rob who has a look at him though; it'll be Martin. Rob only deals with agricultural animals – especially sheep. Apparently sheep just flock around him."

Unfazed, she patted her hair, freshly washed and set in Thelma's Hair Emporium earlier that morning. Thelma herself was around seventy and a confirmed proponent of shingle hairstyles and corrugated perms that smelled like ten-year-old eggs. No fear of her hooking up with Louise and driving over the Grand Canyon!

"Well, I'm sure Rob will make an exception for me. We do go back a long way. His grandfather was a distant relation of ours, you know."

Around her the nodding heads, with a swift change of allegiance. took to shaking instead, accompanied by sundry disgruntled mutterings at this first hint of nepotism.

"Sorry, Aunty Kay, no exceptions." I swiftly put their minds to rest, seeing how one man was frantically trying to unleash Tyson, his German Shepherd, a particularly nasty brute with a fetish for traffic wardens, though aged spinsters would, apparently, do equally well. "Besides, Rob is out on a job somewhere and won't be back till some time this evening. Still, I'm sure, Martin will fit Furbs in. Won't he, baby?" Bending down, I tickled the dog behind his ears – as a concession to me, he closed one eye in ecstasy, the other remaining firmly fixed on the Siamese cat. "Mind you, there's quite a wait. You could always go away and come back later, I suppose."

Plainly miffed by the dismal failure of her little ruse, Aunty Kay rose and yanked Furbee to his feet. "I don't think I'll bother, thank you very much. And you, Gemma, should learn to keep that dog of yours more under control. Honestly, the trouble I've been to this morning! I mean, toothpaste! Whoever heard of a dog eating toothpaste?"

I smiled wryly, thinking of Bella the vomiting Wonder Dog. "Believe me, there's worse things than toothpaste." Bending down again, I gave Furbee one last pat. "And you must admit, he has a lovely smile." Across the room, the Siamese cat with a hiss and a spit

48

begged to differ and in another instant Furbee had closed the distance between them, towing Aunty Kay behind him like a water-skier.

So Aunty Kay was making waves! Oh well, I thought, heading back to reception, nothing new there, then!

CHAPTER 4

"Someone's moved into Gothdere, that big house up the road – you know, the one with the big long drive and the electric gates." Debbie took a well-deserved bite of her sandwich. "Some big noise or other, Guy says."

"Well, he'd know all about big noises," Sophie snorted, fresh back from some farm or other and carrying the distinctive whiff of Eau de Cow Poo about her person.

Curiosity getting the better of me and unwilling to spend my precious lunch-hour refereeing between the two, I waved a placatory hand. "Shut it, Sophie. Who? Who's moved in? Male? Female? Rich? Eligible? Quick, I want to know if I should do the neighbourly bit and pop round with a fresh-baked apple pie like they do in those middle-America feel-good movies, before they find out the neighbour is really Hannibal Lecter."

Debbie giggled. "I shouldn't bother, not if your

attempts at baking are still as poisonous as they were at school. Anyway, I'm not too sure who's moved in. Some writer or artist, Guy said. Johnny Cashel, I think. Although, isn't he the one who's into country-western and burning rings of fire?"

A glorious thought struck me. "Not – not Rocky Cashel?" I asked, scarcely daring to breathe. "Not *the* Rocky Cashel, *the* very good-looking, very wealthy, very famous musician? Ireland's most eligible bachelor! Denizen of my bedroom walls and erotic dreams?"

Maddeningly slowly, Debbie retrieved a bit of parsley from between her teeth, examined it on the tip of her finger and unhygienically wiped it off on the pocket of her uniform. "Hmm, I think so." Deliberately she took another bite of her sandwich, masticating so intently that I wanted to stuff it whole down her neck then stamp on her stomach to hurry the digestive process along. "Oh, that's right. I'm sure Guy said something about some musical or other he wrote based on the Irish Famine."

In the grip of excitement I nodded furiously. "That's right, *Rotten to the Core* – a kind of double play on words," I told them. "On the one hand it referred to the blight of the potatoes and, on the other, to the English for shipping out what was left of all our other crops and shipping in Indian maize, which as anyone will tell you is of little or no nutritional value at all."

"Thanks for the history lesson." Sophie's voice was dry. "Anyway, how come I haven't heard of this Rocky Cashel fella?"

Probably because he *is* a fella,' I said, but only in my mind because I'm not homophobic although I'd be lying if I said I wasn't kind of curious about the whole thing. I mean, you can't help imagining what they get up to and I must say when we all went out to dinner one night and Sophie ordered oysters, it did leave me with a very odd feeling. Like I couldn't keep my eyes away from her mouth. All that slurping!

"Probably because he doesn't have four legs, a bushy tail and a fox-hound snapping at his arse." Debbie, thank goodness, had her own theory. "Besides, you're tone deaf, Sophie! Your karaoke rendition of 'To All The Girls I've Loved Before' at the Christmas party proved that."

"True. True," Sophie nodded, always slow to take offence even where offence was intended. "But I take it he's what you 'straights' take to be a bit of all right." A note of cynicism entered her voice. "This man who sings about rotten potatoes?"

"More than a bit of all right!" I could feel my eyes growing dreamy, clouding over as I brought the vision of Rocky Cashel in full flow to mind. "And it's not so much the subject-matter as how he sings it. I mean, the man's a poet. Talk about Byronic!"

"More like moronic," Debbie sniffed. "Oh, it's coming back to me now all right. Wasn't he the one who went to number 50 in the charts with something daft like 'Where Have All The Young Spuds Gone'?"

"Jesus!" Sophie regarded me with something akin to

horror. "That's desperate. Tell me you couldn't possibly fancy a man who rips off Bob Dylan, Gemma. Gemma! I'm talking to you, Gemma!"

"Oh, don't mind, Debbie! I snapped. "That's not what it's called. It's called simply, but appropriately 'Hunger', which if you spent any time at school at all, you'd know is what the Irish famine was all about. And, okay, certain factions have remarked on a certain similarity between the chorus and Dylan's 'Where Have All The Flowers Gone', but that's just coincidence – pure and simple. Besides, when it comes to ripping off, I don't care who he rips off so long as he rips off my clothes and gives me the best seeing-to of my entire life."

Debbie giggled. "As if. He's probably got a different girlfriend for every night, you know, like those seven-packs of knickers you used to get with the different days of the week embroidered across the bum."

"Maybe, but whilst he's not married I reckon I'm still in with a chance." I shot a speaking look at Debbie. "Not, mind you, that some people would let a little thing like a wedding ring put them off."

"Oh, get a life!" Debbie snapped. "Then, maybe, you won't be so interested in mine. Anyway, it's door-opening time – time to let in the hordes of great unwashed and their stinking animals."

"Stinking animals?" Sophie raised both eyebrows, which considering each one was the size of a miniature rainforest, was a feat equivalent to a circus strongman pulling an articulated truck along by his teeth. "That's not very PC, Debs."

"No? Well, I'm not feeling very PC, actually."

"Guy!" Sophie and I guessed simultaneously

Debbie sniffed and dabbed at her eyes, which had suddenly become very moist. "Well, you know I said I couldn't go away with you both on this hunt-saboteur weekend thingy?"

"Yes," Sophie nodded. "Because your Uncle So and So is coming over from the States and you haven't seen him since you were knee-high to a tadpole."

"Well, I lied. The real reason was because Guy was taking me over to London for the weekend. We were going to stay in the Savoy, go shopping in Harrods and Harvey Nicks – you know – do the whole Abfab bit and then he was going to take me to Stringfellows or Lamplighters."

"Only?" I prompted.

"Only something's come up. He's got to go away on some Animal Welfare junket or other and now he can't."

"And you didn't think you could tell us? You didn't trust us?" I was hurt. There was a time Debbie would tell me everything or so I'd thought. What with the bulimia episode and now this, I was rapidly beginning to re-evaluate our friendship.

"Well, look at it from my point of view." Debbie bit her lip. "You and Sophie are always banging on about Guy –"

"Which we wouldn't," Sophie interrupted callously, "if you weren't always banging him full-stop!"

"Yes, but that's *my* choice and, while I know you think you're only doing it for my own good, it does get a bit wearing."

"Okay, point taken." I gave her arm an affectionate puck. "We'll lay off – but you're right, it is for your own good. Still, what can I say, time will tell."

"Yes and then you can pat yourselves on the back and say I told you so. But until then – it's my life!"

"So why *don't* you come away with us after all?" Sophie's eyes lit up, so much so that I couldn't help wondering once more if she wasn't trying to get into Debbie's knickers. I mean her eyes didn't light up when I said I'd go along. She just had one of those mildly pleased looks, the kind you reserve for your favourite nephew when he draws a picture of you with a massive head and a stick body, or when you win ten pounds on the Lotto. Obviously I wasn't her type. Now don't get me wrong. It wasn't that I particularly wanted to be her type. I wasn't gone so far beyond the pale that I wanted to climb on board the Tampax Express but I couldn't help feeling a bit miffed all the same. I mean, everybody knows lesbians are sex-mad and will go with anybody. So what was wrong with me, for Heaven's sake! Left in the lurch for a whale and dissed by our friendly neighbourhood lesbian. It didn't exactly inspire confidence.

"Maybe I will go." Debbie pinned a valiant smile on

her face. Frig's sake! Anybody would think she'd been asked to walk across the Atlantic blindfolded on a tightrope! She'd probably come back expecting the Victoria Cross.

"Oh, do!" Sophie almost clapped her hands. "You can have the tent. Gemma and I don't mind sleeping out under the stars, do we, Gem?"

"Yeah, sure, whatever blows your skirt up!" I said dryly as, behind Debbie's back, Sophie made a vicious ear-to-ear throat-slitting motion. "Besides, I hear rain is very good for the complexion!"

* * *

"Of course I knew Furbee didn't have rabies." Mammy lavished half a ton of butter onto a slice of bread and pushed it across the table towards me. "But your Aunty Kay has a bit of a thing about Rob and so I thought I'd give Cupid a hand."

"Look, you could give Cupid an arm, a leg and all the tea in China as well," I told her, "but it wouldn't do a blind bit of good. Rob Kilbride is not the marrying kind and if he were I doubt if his fancy would lead him in Aunty Kay's direction." I took a bite of bread. "I mean, let's face it, Aunty Kay is to beauty what the Spice Girls are to classical music!"

"Don't speak with your mouth full." Mammy grabbed up another slice of bread, showed it to the butter and took it away again. That was for Orla, of course, because unlike me, Orla was figure-conscious and *ate like a bird!* "Besides there's nothing wrong with your Aunty Kay. She could have had her pick when she was young . . ."

"So, why didn't she?"

"Because there was something the matter with them all." Mammy gazed off into the middle distance, her eyes looking back on something only she could see. "Although, to be fair, there was really nothing wrong with them at all, except maybe John-Joe Dooley who had a hare-lip, a hunchback and a withered arm. Oh, and he was blind in one eye." With a swift return to the present, she glared at me. "No, too fussy, that was her trouble and look where it got her – on the shelf, that's where. And you be careful, Gemma Murphy, that you don't end up there alongside of her."

I shook my head. "No way! I'll make sure I've got my own shelf."

"Ha ha, very funny!" Mammy wasn't amused. "One of these days you'll pass yourself out with smartness and meet yourself on the way back."

"I'm not being smart. I'm just not getting married. From now on I'm going to concentrate on my female friendships and men can go screw themselves."

"Gemma!" Mammy ignored her own strictures on not speaking with your mouth full. "That's no way for a lady to talk. And while we're on the subject of friends, I'm not sure I entirely like the company you're keeping." With a surreptitious glance from side to side, to check for Cold War spies presumably, she leaned across the table waving a lettuce leaf to give weight to her argument. "There's an old saying, you know. Show me your company and I'll tell you what you are." She popped the lettuce leaf into her mouth and mangled it with her incisors. "You'd do well to bear that in mind."

She meant Sophie, of course. For a long time, like Queen Victoria, my mother refused to believe in the existence of lesbians but the evening Beth Jordache snogged another woman on *Brookside*, she'd been forced, despite herself, to wake up to reality. Still, I suppose, seeing a lezzer on the box was one thing; having your daughter consort with one was another matter entirely.

"You mean Sophie?" I challenged her head-on. "Just because she's unconventional –"

"She's bloody unnatural!" For my mother to use even the mildest of swear words was indicative of the strength of her feelings. "It goes against all common decency, so it does. The way this world is going it'll soon be Sodom and Gomorrah all over again."

"Who's that? Sodom Hussein's younger brother?"

"You see!" Mammy picked up and banged a teaspoon on the table. "Smartness, that'll be your downfall. That, and the company you keep!"

"Look." I put on my best talking-to-an-imbecile voice. "Lesbianism isn't catching. It's not like the common cold, you know. It's not spread by coughing and sneezing. It's a genetic predisposition, like blue eyes or a big nose."

"Oh yeah? Well, if that's the case, how come that young nanny in *Brookside* was all right till that Beth one came along?"

I snorted. "Soaps, Mammy! Real life is a different kettle of fish and, let me put your mind at rest, I haven't the remotest interest in Sophie. Not in that way, anyway." An imp of mischief entered my soul. "No way – her boobs are far too small!"

"Gemma Murphy!" Mammy was shocked. "Go and wash your filthy mouth out with soap. Then, take yourself off down to Confession."

Confession! She'd be lucky. I hadn't been to confession since the first time I confessed I'd slept with Tony McCann and been chucked out of the confessional. Well, it had been a slow kind of a week – what can I tell you? I hadn't told many lies, stolen anything, worshipped a false god or coveted my neighbour's wife. What did that leave apart from fornication and murder? And, since I hadn't murdered anyone, the options were further reduced to just one. Mind you, I'd dressed it up as a euphemism of course, in order to try and slip it past Fr Eugene's guard.

"Bless me, Father, for I have sinned. It's been six months since my last confession. Last night I had it away with Tony McCann."

"What did you have away, my child?"

"It! Father."

"Can you be more specific, my child?"

"Yes, Father. Tony McCann and I had it off."

"And what exactly did you have off, my child? Was it the day? Did you have the day off from work? Were you on the skive, my child?"

"No, Father. What I mean is, we did the dirty deed."

"And which dirty deed might that be, my child?"

"Oh, for feck's sake, Father, do you want me to draw you a picture!"

I grinned now at the memory although, at the time, the humiliation had been dreadful as the Lamb of God turned into a fully-fledged lion, erupted round my side of the confessional, grabbed me by the back of the neck and frogmarched me out onto the street.

"Ah, hello, Orla, love." For once in my life I was grateful for the timely interruption of my younger sister and not in the least resentful of my mother jumping up and fussing about her like she was the Queen of Sheba. "Here, give me that coat, sit down and get a bite of tea into you. I made some of your favourite potato salad, extra chives, just the way you like. And there's a nice bit of ham there too. God knows you could do with a bit of meat on your bones. Gemma would make two of you!"

Orla sank down on the chair opposite and sent me a filthy look. "Thanks, Mammy, but I'll just have a cup of tea." I made a what-the-bleedin'-hell-have-I-done-now gesture with my eyebrows, backed up by a bit of deep shoulder action, as my mother bustled back, placed the side of her hand against the teapot, clucked, and bore it off for replenishing.

"So, love," she called over her shoulder, "did you get the modelling contract?"

"No! No, I didn't. Karen Rogers got it instead because *she* was a half-stone lighter!" Ah, now I knew what the filthy look was all about. "Honest to God," Orla complained, "I felt like the Michelin Man in comparison to the rest of them in there. I almost died when they said I was too fat."

"Too fat? You?" I could hear my voice rising like Aled Jones on Viagra. "Well, if you're fat the rest of them must be like something out of a Lowry painting. That's all I can say!"

"You say too bloody much!" Orla hissed. "If it wasn't for you threatening to open your big gob to Mammy in the first place, I wouldn't be in this position now. You've ruined my career. Ruined it!"

"Ha! If you can call walking up and down with the cheeks of your behind falling out all over the place a career!" I returned the hiss with interest.

"Ah, you'll have a bit of salad!" Mammy returned, plonked the teapot in the centre of the table and covered it with a revolting knitted tea cosy in violent shades of red and purple which some nun with cataracts in both eyes had knitted for her years ago. "A bit of lettuce won't hurt. Sure there's nothing in lettuce! As for that old contract, *que serà serà!* It wasn't meant to be and you can bet your life there's an even better one just round the corner with your name written on it."

"Yeah, but what corner?" Dispiritedly, Orla pushed

her food round and round on her plate. "One in Timbuktu?"

"Ah don't be like that, Orla. Your star is still in the ascendant. Every dog has its day . . ."

"Mammy," Orla and I said together. "Shut up!"

CHAPTER 5

"Isn't this great?" Sophie beamed, looking around the field, although I use the term field loosely. Quagmire would be more apt.

"Oh, yeah, brilliant!" I couldn't keep the sneer out of my voice. "If cow-dung is your bag!"

"Don't moan," Sophie was brusque. "Just help me get this tent set up."

Grabbing two poles and a tent peg, I did a quick reconnoitre around the place. "So where's Debbie disappeared to then? Can't she give us a hand?"

"She's gone off to get provisions from that village shop down the road. Anyway, she doesn't look too chipper these days and we can easily manage without her."

Dismayed, I gazed at the yards of Army surplus canvas strewn across the ground, the hundred and one poles of assorted lengths, the ropes and tent pegs that in some magical way were supposed to slot together to form something resembling a tent. "Oh, you think so, do you?"

"Nothing to it!" Optimistically grabbing a tent peg, Sophie whacked it into the ground, tested it for solidity, then tied a piece of rope around it.

"And that's supposed to be . . . what?"

"Well, for Gawd's sake, Gemma, we have to start somewhere. Now stop whingeing and give me a hand."

"What's that supposed to be?" With one accord, Sophie and I swung round to find ourselves face to face with what I could only imagine was an eco-warrior – either that or the Missing Link. "You one of them modern artists or something?" He wiped his nose on the back of his hand. Green snot. I wondered if he'd ever thought to recycle it. "I suppose you'll put a big plaque on that and call it something like *Conundrum* or *Field with Rope and Tent Peg* and charge people an arm and all three remaining limbs to view it."

Sophie took umbrage. "Listen, mate, instead of standing around taking the mick, maybe you might consider lending a hand. After all, I suspect we're on the same side – you know – the side of the fox?"

"Oh, yeah, right. You're here for the hunt, then?"

"No, for the good of our health!" I snarled.

"Shut up, Gemma," Sophie snapped. And to the eco-warrior, all matted dreadlocks and unravelled jumper, "That's right. Well, we've all got to do our bit, haven't we?" She fluttered her eyes. I mean, get this, she actually fluttered her eyes. I mean, what on earth does a dyke want to go fluttering her eyes for? It wasn't like he was a Madonna look-alike or anything. To tell the truth I felt a bit annoyed, like she was moving in on my patch or something. Not, mind you, that I'd touch him with a fifty-foot bargepole. Still, she'd no right to go fluttering her eyes at a man. Any man! A moment later I forgave her as it became apparent that the only erection she was interested in was getting the tent erected. "I don't suppose *you* know anything about these things?" Digging deep in her repertoire of rarely used feminine wiles, she fished out a coy look, dusted it off and slapped it on her face.

"Me?" He thumped his chest, which action produced a hollow malnourished ring as if he hadn't been fed for a year and then only on alfalfa and sprouted seeds. "Not a clue. Still there's a spare tree two fields along. You could always sleep in that. Very comfortable, a tree. Symbolic – Mother Earth, shelter and all that!"

"Do I look like bleedin' Tarzan?" Indignant, Sophie wasted no more time on flutters or coy looks. She jerked her head towards me. "Does *she* look like bleedin' Jane?"

"No, you both look like bleedin' cheetah!" Delighted by his wit, the eco-warrior folded himself in half so that his arms hung down past his knees and with a series of chimp noises and a bent run took himself off, dreadlocks swinging, presumably to his tree.

I rounded on Sophie. "Well, there was no need to be so bloody adamant. In a dim light I could easily pass for Jane."

"Yeah, right!" Grimly, Sophie kicked the mishmash of canvas that littered the ground. "I'll bet he would have turned himself inside out to help if Debbie had been here, though."

"Well, thanks to you, she wasn't!"

"Yes, well, like I've already said, she hasn't been looking too great recently. Besides, we're going to need something to eat, aren't we?"

"Yeah, but you let her take Wanda. How come you never let me take Wanda?"

"Duuh!" Sophie's head rocked. "Maybe because you can't drive!"

I had to admit she had a point. Nonetheless I was rapidly beginning to feel like a gooseberry and more convinced than ever that she fancied the pants off Debbie. "So that's all that's stopping you? I mean, you'd let me drive her if I had my driver's licence?"

"Sure," Sophie said, but her voice was at least two octaves too high for sincerity. "Oh, talk of the devil, here she comes now." Her head spun round as a sudden almighty clatter punctuated by the sound of a cranky exhaust pipe filled the air.

"About bloody time," I muttered as Sophie's beloved, ancient Honda Civic farted and rattled its way across the field before grinding to a halt in a spray of mud. My voice was sulky, almost an accusation, as laden with Spar carrier bags, Debbie almost fell out of the car. "I never saw you go."

"Well, it wasn't top secret, Gemma. Not an MI5

matter!" She picked up the disapproval in my voice. "Besides, you were peeing behind a hedge on the far side of the field and you might as well know all the trees overlooking you were occupied." She grinned wickedly. "And I don't mean by birds either."

Appalled, I had visions of my bare behind exposed, my off-white belly-warmers on display to the elementals. And I *mean* elementals! *And*, a horrible thought struck me, they would have seen me jump up swearing as my butt came into contact with an over-zealous nettle. "You're joking!"

"Yeah, okay, but admit it, I had you going."

"Cow!" Good humour restored, I reached out and took one of the bags and stood there with no idea of where to put it. Like I could hardly put it in the tent, could I, considering there *was* no tent?

"Where's the tent?" Echoing my thoughts, Debbie looked around, almost jumping ten feet into the air when her eye alighted on the huddle of canvas still in exactly the same place as when she'd left. "Christ Almighty! You should have had the bloody Taj Mahal built by now let alone a poxy tent. Honest to God, a pair of more useless articles it would be hard to find!"

"Huh! Listen to Miss bloody Krypton-Factor 2000!" Sophie snapped and I was glad to see she'd traded in her cow-eyes for two pieces of flint. Not, let me reiterate here, because I was jealous or anything – it's just that the thoughts of trailing around after a love-sick Sophie all weekend was more than flesh and blood could bear.

And, let's face it, lovesick hunt saboteurs just don't cut the mustard!

"Here, put the shopping back in the car." Amazingly, Debbie took charge and belatedly I remembered why she had been elected Head Girl in our final year at school. Talk about hurrah hurrah and jolly hockey sticks! By rights she should have been christened something like Mabel or Gladys. Something capable, gymslip clad, with a penchant for lacrosse, ginger beer and macaroons. Enid Blyton would have loved her! "Sophie, you pick up that long pole over there. That's right. Now that, if I'm not mistaken, should slot into this one, like so. Gemma, don't just stand there with your mouth open catching flies – give me over that right-angled joint. No! Not that! *That* thing over there! Thank you! Sophie, take your size nines off that guy-rope and loop it round here. Now, we're motoring!"

"Well, frig me!" Sophie muttered, as before our bewildered eyes the muddle of canvas and poles on the floor assembled itself under Debbie's expert directions into a pleasing, triangular structure that, to my relief, looked like it could easily house three people. The rainwater complexion test, thank God, would have to wait.

"Way to go, Debs!" My own admiration knew no bounds till I went to unpack the shopping and pulled out two large tubs of HB vanilla ice cream, a box of glacé cherries and a bottle of malt vinegar. A cursory inspection of the second bag yielded more of the same only this time the vinegar was balsamic.

Sophie looked as perplexed as I felt as one by one I laid the purchases down on a scanty patch of grass. "Debbie, you do realise this is a camping trip, don't you? Only, we don't *have* a fridge. Where are all the tins of baked beans, sausages, ravioli, stewed steak and Cup-a-Soups – you know, standard fare of happy campers?"

"You never said anything about Cup-a-Soups." Debbie was belligerent. "Besides I had a yen for a nice dollop of ice cream with a good splash of vinegar."

"Oh, my God!" Sophie's hand flew to her mouth, an action immediately mimicked by me as somewhere there was the unmistakable pinging of a dropped spermatozoon.

"Oh, my God . . . Debbie, you're pregnant!" This time, we achieved unison.

"You're bloody pregnant!" Sophie felt the need to repeat herself, as did I but a lot more euphemistically.

"Debs, you're bloody preggers! Up the duff. In the club! Up the spout! In the shit!" Groping about behind me for an invisible chair, I let myself fall to the ground, jarring my coccyx against a piece of rock, shock rendering me insensible to any pain.

"Oh, my God!" Debbie crumpled down beside me, the penny not so much pinging as clanging like Big Ben and reaffirming what we'd already told her. "I'm pregnant. I'm bloody pregnant! I don't even like vinegar! And ice cream brings me out in hives!"

Sophie sank down beside us, knees jutting outward,

ankles crossed one over the other, Red Indian style. "No wonder you've been going around with a face like Clancy's corpse. Still, I would have thought you'd have had enough sense to go on the pill."

"I *was* on the pill, although I did have a recent bout of food poisoning and I suppose that could have prevented it from working." Debbie's hand moved slowly to her stomach, caressed the still flat material of her jeans. "Little Guy," the earlier fright was quickly being replaced by a note of wonder. "Imagine it, little Guy – little Guy inside of me."

"And not for the first time neither!" A sarcastic Sophie was obviously rapidly reviewing the situation. I suppose fancying Debbie was one thing but fancying Debbie big with Spawn of Satan – well, that was another matter entirely.

Debbie ignored the jibe. "He'll have to marry me now. He can't not!"

Unable to take any more, I leaned over and knocked soundly on her head. *"Earth to Mars, Earth to Mars, come in Mars!"*

"Do you mind!" Debbie caught my hand and flung it away.

"Oh, have a word with yourself! In case you don't remember, the man is already married *and* he's not exactly a stranger to fatherhood either. At the last count I believe he had no fewer than three sprogs and those are only the ones we know about. Let's face it, he's not a man to scatter his seed on barren ground."

Affronted, Debbie threw me a dirty look. "Oh, shut up, Gemma. You're just jealous."

Sophie sprang to my defence. I hoped it was simply a reflex action and not because she was on the rebound from Debbie. "Don't be such a moron. Nobody's jealous. We're just worried."

"Well, don't be. Guy will take care of everything." There was a look of the egg that got the sperm about Debbie as imperiously she motioned to the tubs of vanilla ice cream thawing on the grass. "Now, bung me over one of those and break out the vinegar." Lazily her palm made concentric circles across her stomach. "Pity we've no champagne to celebrate. Although, I don't suppose drinking, in my condition, is such a good idea, do you?"

"Debbie," Sophie's voice was quiet, deadly in its timbre, "I've never hit a pregnant woman, yet. Don't make me start now!"

* * *

In the morning I awoke to the dawn chorus or more accurately a dawn solo which consisted of Debbie puking her guts up on the grass outside. Damn! I shot a filthy look over to where Sophie was still sound asleep, her mouth wide open and cavernous, solving the mystery, once and for all, of the fate of the Marie Celeste. Crawling out of my sleeping bag I batted away two earwigs and a piece of dried cow-dung.

"Hey, you all right?"

"Jesus!" Debbie halted mid-puke as I stuck my dishevelled head out of the tent flap. "I thought you were Cat Weazel!" She resumed vomiting, heaving and coughing with such force that I thought the embryo would shoot right out of her mouth. "Here, take it easy! Sophie's still asleep."

"Piss off, Gemma!"

"Piss off yourself," I retaliated, immediately feeling sorry as she went off into another spate of retching that brought every eco-warrior from miles around down from their respective trees.

"Up the duff, is she?" This helpful contribution was brought to us courtesy of yesterday's Missing Link. Stepping forward he examined the pool of puke on the grass as if sizing up the breakfast potential.

"What's it to you?" Aggressively I dragged the rest of my body clear of the tent and stood up.

"I was only asking!" The ML shook his dreadlocks and a million fleas jumped clear.

"And I was only saying! Now clear off, all of you." My gaze swept from one to the other but clad only, as I was, in thermal vest and long johns, I was dimly aware that my attire detracted somewhat from the note of authority for which I was aiming.

"Arrowroot! That's what she needs." A female eco-warrior-type person stepped forward. "Arrowroot has anti-emetic properties."

"And ginger-root." She had brought a clone along with her.

"And Bisodol."

Once was not enough. She'd cloned herself twice. I wouldn't have bothered!

"Hi." The prototype decided it was time to formally introduce herself. "I'm Earth."

"Wind." Clone number one followed suit.

"Fire!"

"Earth, Wind and Fire?" I could feel a giggle rising.

Awakened by all the commotion, Sophie crawled out and pulled herself upright by dint of grabbing onto the ML's knee. "Pleased to meet you," she beamed, shaking hands all round. "We're the Three Degrees!"

Around us sundry heads bobbed, some dreadlocked, some shaved and tattooed, all unwashed and all united in their approval of our collective name which they obviously thought brought communal living into a whole new dimension. "The Three Degrees? Cool, man!"

Squinting at the sky, the ML pronounced that, judging by the position of the sun, he reckoned there was an hour to go before the fox-hunt started, and they'd better take themselves off to prepare some missiles.

"What sun?" Glumly, Debbie stared after them, her face white as curdled whey. "I don't see no sun!"

"Ah, never mind him!" Sophie was bracing. "He was only putting on the agony. That fella couldn't tell time even if he'd the speaking clock nailed to his butt. Isn't that right, Gemma?"

"Hmm," I replied absent-mindedly, my eyes riveted to a spider that was busy draping its lace smalls all across Wanda's right wing-mirror. If only everything in life was as simple as nature – everything playing out its prescribed role. A time to be born. A time to mate. A time to eat your mate. Only, in my life, nothing was simple – my family – my friends – my job. Everything was complicated, upside down and topsy-turvy. And to add insult to injury – even my smalls were big!

* * *

"Everyone ready?"

"Aye, aye, Cap'n!" I saluted Sophie, then turned to where Debbie was dragging her heels. "Come on, slowcoach. It's time we saw some action!"

Debbie sniffed and hung back a bit. "I don't know if this is such a good idea. I mean, what with me being pregnant. Like anything could happen. I could get trampled by a horse, kicked by the fox, anything!"

Exasperated, Sophie sighed. "Gimme a break, Debs! As you've rightly pointed out for half the night and most of the morning, you're pregnant. Not terminally ill! Besides which, we'll be well hidden behind a big hedge or something. No fear of you getting so much as a split end. *And I'm talking hair, here!*"

I added my support to Sophie. "Yes, and think of the kid. Everybody knows kids learn while they're still in the womb. Look at all those babies that pop out doing the breaststroke or humming the theme tune to *Match of the Day* or *Coronation Street*. Yours will pop out with a well-developed social conscience and, hopefully, a terrific over-arm swing. Mind you, on the negative side of things, it could turn out talking like Vera Duckworth!"

Debbie giggled. "I must admit I hadn't thought of it quite like that but, okay, I'm up for it! Yeehaw! Let the games commence!"

Leaving Wanda behind we walked the short distance into the nearby village where the hunt assembled for the traditional drinking of the Stirrup Cup. Looking around at the medley of Hunting Pink (though, call a spade a spade here, it was actually red!) and black jackets it was hard, in some cases, to distinguish between the rider and the horse. To add to the confusion fox-hounds milled about everywhere, weaving their way in and out between the horses' legs and snapping indiscriminately at anything that had ankles.

"Isn't that Camilla Parker-Bowles?" Debbie nudged me excitedly as a particularly equine-looking woman, her hair looped up in a net, trotted past on a bay hunter. "Imagine, Royalty in Wicklow!"

"Don't be daft," I nudged her back. "That's not her. Besides *she's* not royalty – just screwing it!"

"I'm all for screwing royalty!" Sophie, who had disappeared a few minutes earlier, came back and shoved a can of Coke and a doughnut into each of our hands. "There, an army marches on its stomach, men! Tuck into that!"

"Thanks." I pulled the ring out, took a deep drink.

"Thanks to Debbie and her ice cream and vinegar lark last night, my stomach thinks my throat's cut."

Ignoring my complaints and with a slightly green look about the gills again, Debbie waved the doughnut away. "I'll just have the Coke."

"All the more for us." Unsympathetically, Sophie broke the doughnut in two and gave me half. "Look, they're marshalling the hounds – looks like they're just about ready to move off, the murdering bastards."

Across the way a rag waved to us. Embarrassed, we pretended not to notice but we weren't getting off that lightly.

"So," Eco-man made his way over, Earth, Wind and Fire trailing at his heels, "are we ready for the off?"

Nervously we exchanged glances. Obviously he thought a couple of words exchanged over a pool of puke was the equivalent of blood-bonding and was now ready to amalgamate us into his harem of planet-savers. Probably expected to get his leg over us en masse too if the truth be known.

"Er . . . I'm not feeling all that great at the moment, actually." Debbie, with lightning-quick thinking, did a great impression of coming over all unnecessary. "You lot go on ahead and we'll catch you up. Okay?"

"Yeah, okay. But you'd better have these in case you run out."

"What's this?" Suspiciously I took the sack he thrust into my hand. I mean, it could have been full of severed heads for all I knew.

"Ammo. Rotten everything. Eggs, tomatoes, potatoes – you name it."

"Heads?" Well, I wasn't going to leave anything to chance. Like, for all I knew he could have been a second Charles Manson and there was no good reason I could think of why I should take the rap for mass murders he'd committed. I mean, I could have been looking at life.

"Heads?" He grinned wolfishly. "No, but you never know – after the hunt we might be able to rectify that little omission."

"Whoah!" Sophie held her hand up. "Now listen here, my peculiar manikin, we're not into violence per se. A few rotten eggs, fine! A few dollops of manure, finer! But anything involving the spillage of essential bodily fluids, count us out!"

"Alphonsus is only joking!" Earth grinned and I was fascinated to see she had organic stuff growing on her teeth. Talk about living the cause!

"Alphonsus?" There was disbelief in Debbie's voice.

"Nobody calls me that!" The Missing Link looked outraged and seemed somehow, in the light of our recent knowledge, to shrink before our very eyes. In another minute, like the Wicked Witch of the West there would be nothing left but a steaming bundle of rags and a curly sock.

"We call him Al," Wind informed us helpfully. "It's Al, all the time."

"Isn't there a song that goes like that?" I asked, bursting out laughing.

"Ha, ha!" Al, looked firstly as if he might knife me, then grateful as the sound of the hunting-horn filled the air. "Well, that's our signal to manoeuvre. Be lucky, yeah?"

"Sure thing . . . Al!" Grinning, I tossed the sack over my shoulder almost dislocating it in the process and, after waiting a good five minutes to make sure the coast was clear, we set off ourselves in search of a good vantage point.

CHAPTER 6

"Look!" Waving wildly, Debbie almost fell off the five-barred gate we'd settled on as a prime location from which to view/launch missiles at the hunt. "There goes the fox. Oh, poor thing, he looks exhausted."

Grim, Sophie nodded vigorously, staring after the fleeing animal disappearing into the distance. "So would you if you'd fifty bloody fox-hounds snapping at your rear end. Hurry up, Gemma. Break out the missiles. The hunters can't be far behind."

"Here they come now," I yelled excitedly, spying a vivid red flash through the trees. Hurriedly delving in the sack, I grabbed a fistful of unidentifiable well-composted something or other and let fly just as the first horseman appeared in our line of fire. "Murderer," I roared, really getting into the swing of things and totally off target. "Pick on somebody your own size, why don't you? Not a helpless little fox!"

"Shit-arses! Wankers! Bollixes!" Sophie bellowed,

her insults a little more graphic, her aim a hell of a lot more accurate and in a relatively short period of time a number of pristine black riding-hats left their owners' heads and embarked on a second career as a fleet of UFOs.

"Bingo!" Debbie made the victory sign. "Way to go, Soph!"

"Yeah, well done, Soph!" Scrabbling in the sack I refuelled over and over again, sometimes getting lucky, missing more often than not but finally hitting the bull's-eye with the very last rider and landing him one which knocked him clean off his horse.

"Yeehaw!" Beside me, Sophie and Debbie went wild. I almost expected to be lifted up on their shoulders and borne triumphant into the middle of a cheering crowd.

Dashing over and bursting into her own version of a rowdy football anthem, Sophie did a Red Indian war dance around the rider's prone body. "You're not hunting! You're not hunting! You're not hunting any more! You're not hu-u-un-ting en-ee-more!"

"Jesus!" A sudden note of anxiety entered Debbie's voice. "Stop, Soph! He's not moving. I think he's dead."

"Dead schmed!" Contemptuous, Sophie continued to whoop around the body. "Old fox-hunters never die; they only get the brush-off!"

"No, stop, Soph!" I could feel myself turning a whiter shade of pale. "I think she's right. Oh bugger! I think I've killed him! Trust me to get the one with the chicken's neck."

"Quick! Get his helmet off!" Debbie yelled, all her first-aid training flying straight out the window.

"No! Don't!" I screeched. "Don't move him – he could have broken his . . ." But it was too late – Sophie had already removed his riding-hat and carelessly tossed it to one side. Leaning over, she placed two fingers beneath his jaw-line, feeling for his carotid artery. She seemed to be taking an eternity.

"Dear God," I prayed, staring life imprisonment in the face, "don't let him be dead! Please, don't let him be dead!" Not a moment too soon, a weak and pain-filled groan signified that my prayers had been answered. With a bit of luck I might get away with ten to fifteen – out in five, on good behaviour. Struggling to sit up he pushed feebly at Sophie but, as Sophie had been likened more than once to a Sherman tank, the movement did little more than dent her sleeve.

"Move, would you? I'm not bloody dead, you know!" His voice was weak but he wasn't dead! He *wasn't* dead! I could have done the Highland Fling. He wasn't bloody dead!

"Hallelujah! Thank you, God!" Racing over, I threw myself across him, caught his head between my hands and began kissing the face off him. "Thank you," kiss, kiss, "for not being dead, although, you should be bloody ashamed of yourself," kiss, kiss, " for chasing a poor little defenceless fox like that!" Kiss, kiss, a flurry of kisses!

"Yeuch, get off!" As his consciousness came back, so did his strength and in another moment I found our positions reversed with me on the bottom, my arms pinioned above my head and him sitting astride my stomach.

"Oi!" Picking up a broken branch, Sophie advanced menacingly. "Get off my friend before I knock your block off!"

"No!" Debbie stayed her arm, a sudden note of excitement in her voice which, under the circumstances, I thought was pretty out of order. I mean, just catch me dialling 999 the next time *she* was attacked by a raving lunatic. "Don't you see who it is? Don't you recognise him?" Her voice was rapidly nearing the frequency where only the fox-hounds had a chance of hearing her. "Gemma, you eejit! It's Rocky Cashel!"

I took a closer look. Buggered if she wasn't right! It *was* Rocky Cashel. A bit battered, a lot pissed-off but indisputably, undeniably him! *The* Rocky Cashel, Ireland's 'most eligible bachelor, musician extraordinaire and writer of *Rotten to the Core*' as the newspapers dubbed him, and I had felled him with, appropriately enough, a rotten potato. Unmasked and presumably fearful of the sudden lust lighting up my eyes, he tried to get up. Big mistake, as I wrapped my newly released arms around his knees and pulled him back down astride me, enjoying the warm feeling permeating my pelvis from the heat of his buttocks. Like this was the stuff dreams were made of. Besides this man had cost me money – lots of it. I mean, I had shelled out for every CD, every concert, been to see *Rotten to the Core* seven times, bought every poster, T-shirt and every bit of Rocky Cashel memorabilia I could possibly get my hands on. And now that I had my hands on the real thing – man, I was digging on in. *And* I had every intention of making it memorable! The way I saw it, he owed me. Big time!

"Let me up!" His beautiful face, all tanned, manly and dusty, was a study in pleading. They probably didn't even have to airbrush his photos. "Please. Look, I won't even press charges. I'll just get my horse and ride on out of here."

Grinning like a maniac, Sophie held up her hand. "Whoah! Hold it, John Wayne. You can press what you like. Gemma won't object, will you, Gem?"

"This is insane." Desperately he tried to dislodge my arms but, used as I was to restraining Pit Bulls and maddened by lust, it was no contest. "My friends will be back to look for me."

"Oh, no they won't," Debbie snorted. "They'll be too busy tearing some poor little fox to shreds and daubing blood on their faces to worry about you."

"Yeah, some poor little vixen with half a dozen cubs waiting for her to return. Only, she won't! She can't! She never will again." Climbing atop one of her favourite hobby-horses the passion was back in Sophie's voice. Coming closer, she brandished the branch and clocked him one round the head. "Isn't that right, Mr Social Conscience Cashel? Mr Social Conscience Cashel who makes his money singing about the Irish Famine and

83

ripping off Bob Dylan. So, tell me, how do you reconcile your social conscience with tearing a defenceless animal apart?"

"That's a good question." I tried to show my own support for the fox by dint of fixing Rocky with a gimlet eye whilst the other remained in an animated state of suspended lust. The warm feeling circulating in my pelvis intensified with every jiggle of his bottom. I willed him to keep on jiggling and snuck in a pelvic thrust or two on my own account.

"Listen," he tried appealing to our better natures, "I'm anti blood sports, actually. I just made an error of judgement in this particular instance. It was a business deal . . . " He wriggled uncomfortably beneath the concerted glares of my two friends and I gasped with pleasure. Just a little more, I thought. Just a little more and there's gold in them thar hills!

Reverting to the branch she had picked up earlier, Sophie prodded him like he was something that had crawled out from under a stone. "A business deal? Is that what they're calling it now? Not the Blessington Hunt, the Blessington Business Deal?"

"Of course not!" He went brick red. "It just so happens the head of *Slick Discs* is also the Master of the Hunt and it was his idea that we should try and kill two birds with the one stone, as it were."

"Kill one fox with fifty hounds, more like." Grabbing the branch off Sophie, Debbie whacked him hard across the shoulders.

"Hit him again, Debs," I urged, closing my eyes and losing myself, sad cow, in the sensation of his jodhpur-clad buttocks bouncing up and down. "For God's sake, woman! Hit him harder!"

"Ow! Ow! Ow! Please stop!" Defensively wrapping his arms around his head, Rocky cowered above me. "This has all been a horrible mistake. I like animals. Hell, I even like cats and there's very few men who will admit to that."

"Why, what's wrong with cats?" On the look out for offence, Debbie poked him again. He jiggled. I wiggled. It was bliss. If I had to guess I'd say I was at least halfway up the slope.

"Nothing! Isn't that what I'm saying? There's nothing wrong with cats. Like, I'd never drown one!"

"Huh, that's big of you!" Sophie, deprived of the stick, settled for prodding him in the back of the neck. "So, what have you got against poor little foxes?"

"Nothing!" Rocky widened his eyes. They were dark and liquid and I could see my reflection on the point of orgasm in them. I knew I was on the point of orgasm because, apart from the hot 'n fizzy feeling in my pelvic region, my mouth looked kind of slack, my tongue was hanging out and I was dribbling. "As I've already explained, it was an error of judgement on my part." He tried for reasonable. "Look, how about I make a sizeable donation to the Save the Fox fund? Wouldn't that go a long way towards proving my good will?"

"Well," Sophie looked considering, "it would go a

long way towards proving how desperate you are to get away from us. What do you think, Debs?"

"Mm, sounds like a case of money talking to me. Still, I kinda like what it's saying."

Sensing a softening in their attitudes, Rocky wriggled hopefully. It was the last wriggle, the wriggle that broke the camel's back. The summit was nigh. With one last surge of abandonment, I struck out for the peak.

"So, Gemma?" Lost in sensation, I could hardly make out Sophie's voice. "Are we all in agreement, then? Do we take the money and run? Do we let the potato-singer go?"

"Yes!" I yelled, echoes of *When Harry Met Sally*, as somewhere close by an orchestra struck up, waves crashed on the shore and Everest was conquered all over again. "Yes! Yes! Yes!"

CHAPTER 7

"I've a good mind to sack the lot of you." Wielding the Monday-morning newspaper, Guy Evans slanted a look of disdain across the bridge of his narrow nose. "I've a good mind to give you your cards and chuck you all out on the street." Flourishing it in each of our faces in turn, he stabbed wildly at a picture on the front page, firing off a succession of questions and answering them himself. "What's going to happen when our clientele get wind of this? Eh? I'll tell you what. No one will darken this surgery door again, that's what. Why? For fear they'll be knocked to the ground and sexually assaulted, that's why. By who? By three rabid viragos. That's who."

"Oh, poo pants!" Having listened to his potted version of the article, Sophie tossed her head. "All they've got are our first names, hardly uncommon Christian names at that. Now if we were talking Timbuktu, that might be different – but Ireland! There's

Gemmas, Sophies and Debbies around every corner and in every pub."

"That's right," Debbie said, nodding her agreement. "No one knows who we are or where we come from. Besides, he *wasn't* sexually assaulted. Not as such! I mean, it's hardly Gemma's fault if he wiggled about so much."

Dramatically, Guy slapped his forehead. "Not as such, she says! The man's only been raped and not as such, she says!"

"I didn't rape him," I snarled, snatching the newspaper from his grasp in order to have a closer look at the picture of Rocky Cashel and the accompanying banner headlines. IF YOU GO DOWN TO THE WOODS TODAY, BE SURE OF A BIG SURPRISE!' "I just saw an opportunity and grabbed it with both hands, so to speak."

"Hey!" Debbie leaned over my shoulder. "That's not a recent picture. That's at least ten years old. He had more hair there! The vain bastard!"

"Never mind that." Sophie craned over the other one. "What does it say?"

Importantly, I cleared my throat. "It says, '*Rocky Cashel, Ireland's most eligible bachelor, musician extraordinaire and writer of* Rotten to the Core, *was the unfortunate recipient of a big surprise when he went down to the woods at the weekend. Felled by a spud in the course of the Blessington Fox-hunt, Mr Cashel found himself surrounded by a trio of Amazons in the guise of hunt saboteurs, two of whom pinned him down whilst the third, allegedly a close relative of King Kong, proceeded to divest him of his manhood.'"*

Beside me, Debbie drew her breath in on a gasp. "That's a dirty stinking lie. The only thing he was divested of was his riding-hat."

"And a cheque," Sophie reminded her. "Don't forget the cheque."

"And I suppose the King Kong bit is gospel truth?" Viciously, I rattled the paper. "Anyway, listen to this. *'The popular singer, who sustained several broken ribs in the attack, said he was lucky to be alive.'"*

"Broken ribs, my foot!" Sophie interrupted venomously. "Pity we didn't break his damn knees or his neck, come to that."

"Shush!" This time, the admonition came from Debbie. "Carry on, Gem."

"Asked if he would recognise his attackers, Mr Cashel said 'I'll take their faces to the grave with me, especially the one with the squint . . .'

"Squint?" Debbie shrieked. "What squint? He must mean you, Sophie. I've always thought one of your eyes was a bit on the lazy side!"

I held up a restraining hand. "Put a sock in it, Debs. Now, where was I? Ah yes, *'squint, though the one with the halitosis and the flat chest comes a close second'.*"

"Na, na, na, na, na!" Sophie gibed, jabbing a triumphant finger at Debbie before bursting into the 'Hallelujah Chorus' and substituting the hallelujahs

with the word halitosis instead. *"Hal-it-osis, ha-lit-osis, halitosis, halitosis, h-al-ley-ey-tooh-sis!"*

"Shut it," Debbie snarled. "Is that it, Gem?"

"Almost," I nodded. *"Police are on the look out for the trio, believed to be named Gemma, Sophie and Debbie. Due to their common accents, the women are believed to originate from Dublin and to have travelled down for the day. Members of the public are advised that they are extremely dangerous and should be approached with caution especially by the sexually inexperienced. More stories from the Blessington Hunt on page three'."*

Almost tearing the paper in our haste to turn over we discovered that pride of place had been given to an enormous picture of Eco-man triumphantly handcuffed to the thoroughly miserable-looking Camilla Parker-Bowles huntswoman, whilst Earth, Wind and Fire stood around smiling organically and giving back-to-front victory signs. 'OUTFOXED' shrieked the caption. 'OUTSMARTED!' 'OUT OF IT?'

"Outtasight!" Sophie bellowed as Debbie and I dissolved with laughter.

Guy, who appeared to be having some sort of epileptic fit all through my narrative, shook his head and rolled his eyes causing Debbie to look anxiously about for a teaspoon with which to hold his tongue down should such prove necessary. Personally, I'd have been quite happy to let him choke on it.

"Well, I'm glad you're deriving such amusement from it all. That's all I can say. It doesn't take a cartload of brains to figure out that if I recognised your description from the newspaper article, so will others. Knowing you lot, you probably broadcast your movements to the four corners of the earth before even going down there. I mean, I've never known a woman yet who could keep her gob shut about anything."

"Is that a fact?" Debbie fixed him with a withering and accusatory eye. "You've never met *any* woman yet who could keep her gob shut about *anything*?" The words leg-over-on-the-side and wife-in-blissful-ignorance hung between them like a suppurating sore.

Realisation dawning that he'd shot himself not so much in the foot as in the groin, Guy danced about some more. "Oh, well, of course there's always the exception." His knee jerked upwards in a bad parody of Michael Flatley doing the Riverdance. "But it's the exception that proves the rule. In any case, you're bound to come a cropper sooner or later. I mean, it doesn't seem to have occurred to any of you that your victim isn't exactly living a million miles from here. Not even half a mile, as it happens! I mean, does the name *Gothdere* push any buttons with you?"

"Crikey!" Debbie's face was a study in incredulity. "How could we have forgotten that? Gemma! How could *you* have forgotten that? Let me tell you if Cindy Crawford had moved in next door to Sophie, there's no way on earth *she* would have forgotten."

With characteristic lechery, Sophie salivated. "Too buggering right! Not even for five seconds!"

I shrugged defensively. "I don't bloody know. It just slipped my mind, that's all. Actually, I'm not sure that I ever *really* believed it. It's not as if any of us ever saw him coming or going or anything."

"Not like *he* saw *you* coming!" Debbie winked, earning herself a sharp kick on the shin from me.

Suddenly dismissive, Sophie chewed at a ragged cuticle. "Gothdere is probably just one of a million homes he's got, anyway. It's probably just for investment, just part of his property portfolio. All of those millionaire types have property portfolios. Besides, just look at all the free publicity we've generated for him. If he were in England he'd probably have to hire that Max Clifford guy to drum up half the amount and that would cost him a lot more than his dignity." She flinched as her teeth chewed through the cuticle and exposed the sore skin below. "When you come to think of it he should be eternally grateful to us and, personally, I think a whacking great invoice is in order."

Drawing himself up to his full five-foot-seven, Guy tried hard for Machiavellian, finding, alas, only Ronnie Corbett. "Well, personally, I think you should keep your *heads* well down."

"Bet that's what he says to Debbie," Sophie mouthed behind his back causing me to burst out laughing so that he added the jig, the reel and the hornpipe to his dancing repertoire.

"Laugh," he snarled. "Go on, laugh, but we'll see who has the last laugh. And the loudest!"

Coming into the surgery, Martin screeched to a Fred Flintstone halt. "Well, tickle my testicles with a test tube! Talk about feet of flames." Grinning broadly, he honed in on Guy's legs.

Unamused, Guy forced himself to be still, although the occasional spasmodic jerk of his knee betrayed what an effort that was. "Ha ha, everyone's a comedian but you mightn't think it's so funny when you hear what this lot got up to at the weekend."

Martin chuckled heartily. "What? Raping that singer fella, do you mean? Fair play to you, girls! I knew the minute I read the paper it was you lot. It was the common Dublin accent bit that gave it away. Oh, and your names were a pretty good clue, of course." He turned to me. "By the way, Gemma, you'd be doing me a big favour if you could phone the wife and give her a blow-by-blow account from the horse's mouth, so to speak."

Hoisting a sanctimonious look on his face, Guy, the dirty hypocrite, gave each of us the benefit in turn. "I ask you, is there no decency left in the world? Have we thrown our morals out with the bath water? When and where will it all end, that's what I'd like to know?"

"In about nine months, that's when," Sophie muttered *sotto voce*. "As for where – probably in your home, Buster, when your wife finds out about Debbie's baby and takes a meat cleaver to your ging-gangs."

Debbie nudged her warningly. As yet, Guy knew nothing of her pregnancy and, although she knew he'd be as thrilled as she, she wanted to choose her moment. If I knew Debbie, it would be a romantic setting, a candlelit table in a posh restaurant maybe, or a moonlit walk by the river with the stars reflecting in her eyes. If I knew Guy, she'd be wise to keep the table between them, Table Mountain preferably, or if it was the river scenario, make sure they were on opposite banks!

"Open up! Open up before we're all frozen alive out here!" A sudden rapping on the surgery door brought all immediate discussion to an abrupt end and, marching over to the door, Guy threw it open only to be catapulted backwards as a sea of people rushed in bearing with them every conceivable type of animal – large, small, borrowed, begged or stolen – more than one already verging on the corpse-like state. Ninety-nine per cent just an excuse to come and dish the dirt.

Mrs Birch, surprise, surprise had appointed herself General of the Vanguard with poor constipated Kilroy as her Second in Command.

"So what's all this I hear, young Gemma? You and your friends raped that Rocky Cashel fella?" Tapping her nose, she did a quick recce around the surgery. "Oh, don't look so surprised. We're not so green as we're cabbage-looking. It didn't take much to put two and two together and came up with an even number. It was your –"

"Common Dublin accents that gave us away?" I hazarded a guess.

Mrs Birch looked perplexed. "No! Your names!" I'd

forgotten, *her* accent was the same as ours. "It was your *names* that gave it away. That and the fact that you told me the last time I was in that you were going down to Blessington for the fox-hunt. So, coupling that information together with your names and the fact that you've remarked more than once that that Rocky Cashel is a right ride, it didn't take Miss Marple to figure it all out." She tapped her nose again. It occurred to me that she might be one of those Freemasons and that this might be some class of a Freemason's code. For all I knew she could have had a rolled-up trouser leg under her mac. I toyed with the idea of dropping my pen, getting down on all fours and peeking beneath her hemline but, before I could carry out my plan, my attention was seized by an old boy of around eighty accompanied by a dog best described as long departed. All the seats having been taken, he calmly sat himself down on the floor, at great risk as I suspected he'd never be able to get up again, opened a thermos of chicken soup and a packet of sandwiches and sociably offered them round.

"So?" His voice was croaky but audible, nonetheless, for seven counties. "Would ye cut to de chase, Gemma Moorphy, and give's the low-down on yer man. What I want te know is, if *he* wasn't willing – how were *you* able?"

* * *

"I don't get it. How do you rape a man?" Shaking a

bottle of nail varnish like a single maraca, Orla sent me a look that was not so much curious as agog. She'd already applied one coat of Sunset Boulevard in *Vicious Red* to her toenails and this second bottle contained a clear varnish in which little gold and silver suns, moons and stars floated. "I mean, I've always thought either a man was up for it, or he wasn't – up being the operative word."

Sighing wearily, I watched as she screwed the top off and, having ensured the first coat of lacquer was dry, applied a coating of planets to her big toenail. "How many times do I have to tell everyone – I didn't *rape* him. I simply availed myself of his proximity."

Orla giggled. "Is that what they're calling it now?" Fluttering her lashes she adopted a Southern Belle accent. "My, oh my, Rhett, what a big proximity you've got!"

"Oh, shut up!" Leaning my chin on my hands, I wondered how my only sister could sit there so calmly, titivating herself while my life was falling apart. It didn't seem to matter that I loathed her. I was after the sympathy vote and I wasn't too particular about the source. Even Furbee seemed to have deserted me lately and had taken, for some incomprehensible reason, to trailing my Aunty Kay around like a lovesick puppy whenever she called which was far too often for comfort. This defection hurt almost more than anything else. Furbee was not only my dog, but also my faithful and supposedly loyal companion, my canine confidant and soul mate at least on the Chinese Horoscope. He was also the runt of the litter and should have shown a bit more bloody gratitude. Everyone thought he was called after that little Gremlin-type thingy that was flavour of the month a few Christmases ago. It was cute and hairy with big googly eyes and when you spoke to it, it spoke gobbledegook back to you which the manufacturers tried to kid you was English. I got *my* Furbee from Mrs Hunter-Gunn, the nearest thing to aristocracy we had near the surgery and a well-known dog-breeder to boot. Barbara *Walkies* Woodhouse had nothing on her. When Mrs H-G shouted, even grown men rolled over and played dead.

"How, now my deah," she said, coming into the surgery one morning and thrusting a basket into my arms. "See if you can't offload this little chappy, heah."

"Oh, but he's gorgeous," I oohed, as Furbee blinked up out of the basket with a look-mate-if-a-frog-can-turn-into-a-prince-think-of-the-possibilities-for-a-runt look on his face. "Why, don't you want him?"

Mrs H-G bridled. Up till then I'd never been quite sure what that meant exactly but when I saw it in action there was no mistaking it for anything else. "Good Lord, gal. Don't be so fatuous." Bridle, bridle. "Can't you see he's a runt? He's *fur below* our usual standards. Not what we grace our kennels with, at all, at all!"

And so Furbee, bless him, had started life as Furbelow with his present name being no more than an abbreviation.

"Wasn't there some Christian Scientist or Mormon woman prosecuted a few years back for raping a man?" Orla, still harping on about the imaginary rape, cut into my thoughts.

"I vaguely remember something like that, all right." Hypnotically my eyes followed the movements of the brush sliding backwards and forwards over each glossy toenail, each one perfectly cut and squared off at the corners to prevent ingrown toenails. I never cut my toenails, much less varnish them. It's not that I've anything against it as such. It's just that in the grand scheme of things it comes pretty low down on the list, no pun intended. Also, and perhaps more importantly, my stomach tends to get in the way so that it's a bit like trying to clip your toenails over a hedge.

Orla finished one foot and stuck it out beneath my nose. "Here, blow on that for me, will you. I can't reach it myself."

Obligingly I filled my lungs which just goes to show how low I'd sunk. Give me another week and I'd put the limbo dancers of Bonga-Bonga Land to shame. Only a week or so ago I'd have blown her head off. Now, of course, the tables had turned. The balance of power had shifted and Orla had something over *me*. That something was, of course, Rocky Cashel. Neither my mother nor my aunt had figured out yet that *I* was 'the Gemma' splashed all over the newspapers – and that despite spending a large part of the week tut-tutting over 'girls today', 'the state of the world' and 'that poor

98

young man, I hope he wasn't a virgin'. I was only thankful we lived a fair old way from the surgery. Orla, despite having only one brain cell and that dormant, wasn't quite so slow on the uptake.

"Well, you big hoor!" she greeted me, as worn out from fending off a non-stop parade of clients in search of gossip, scandal and salacious detail, I fell through the door the previous Monday evening. *"You're* her!" She stabbed me in the chest with two-inch acrylic fingernails. I was grateful she didn't sever my aorta. *"You're* Gemma! You raped Rocky Cashel. *You're* lucky! What was it like?"

Of course I'd denied it, lied in fact till my nose was as long as the Naas Dual Carriageway but Orla had the bit between her teeth and she wasn't the kind to let it go. Unless, of course, it was a bit of breakfast, a bit of lunch or a bit of dinner! Music, to Orla's ears, was the harmonious sound of toilets flushing. Now, of course, knowing that I was completely powerless to stop her from puking herself into the grave, she could flush with impunity. Mind you, I suppose I could always have come clean with my mother and Aunty Kay but the way I saw it, that wasn't an option. Hell! Orla's life wasn't worth that much!

Satisfied that she'd done a good job on the first foot and that I had fulfilled my designated role and blown her toenails dry, she moved on to the other one. "So, Gemma, you've never really told me the gory details – did the earth move?"

"It did, but only because Rocky Cashel measured his length on it. *And* it was my potato that brought him down." Justifiably proud, I sketched a chalking-one-up-to-me gesture in the air. "*And* it was a bona fide overarm swing – none of your girly underarm rubbish for me."

"Never mind all that." Grabbing a cotton ball, Orla dabbed at the side of her toe where an over-enthusiastic moon had slid onto the skin. "Get to the sex bit. I mean, was he any good? Had he got it going on? How was he hung?"

I gave her one of those I'm-furrowing-my-brow-because-I'm-amazed-at-your-stupidity kind of looks. "Oh, behave! I've already told you there *was* no sex although, and I hold my hand up, a certain amount of carnal knowledge did take place."

"Yeah, right! No sex, only carnal knowledge. Well, dress it up in fancy clothes if you must but, in my book, a bonk is a screw is a shag! Now, sister dearest, don't spare my delicate sensibilities. Give it to me hardcore!"

I drew in a deep breath. "Right! You want it? You got it! This is how it went. He fell, I sat on him, he sat on me, he jiggled, I wiggled and lo and behold there was the clashing of cymbals, waves crashing on the shore and Catherine-wheels farting about in the sky above. Satisfied?"

"Huh! Well, not that easily. It takes a bit more than jiggling and wiggling to get my rocks off. I find it helps if I see a bit of skin and, man, I'm halfway there if I actually get to touch it."

"Yes, well some of us are thankful for small mercies. Look how thankful I was for Tony the Shite Artist."

Orla wasn't making such a good job of her second foot. She'd splodged several nails and had to break out the nail-varnish remover pads and start all over again. "Talking about Tony —"

"Tony the Shite Artist," I corrected her.

"Okay, Tony the Shite Artist. Did I ever tell you how he tried it on with me last Christmas?"

"No!" Shocked, I jogged her arm and an entire nail-varnish solar system landed on the carpet.

"Mm, he did, when you were conked out upstairs pissed as a gnat from drinking too much mulled wine."

God, I remembered that. I'd woken the next day with a head the size of Howth and a headache that would have made Iron Mike Tyson cry. "So, what happened, exactly?"

"Oh, he tried to grope my boobs and slip me the old tongue sandwich."

I narrowed my eyes. "And was he successful?"

"On both counts," Orla confirmed, without a trace of guilt. Conscience, to my sister, was like the *Reader's Digest*, something to which only boring people subscribed.

Cynically I let my eyes play over her boobs which were more concave than flat. She could have made a fortune from renting them out to potholers. "Well now, you do surprise me."

Orla flushed. I'd caught her on the raw. Her breasts or the lack of them were the bane of her life and I knew for a fact she was saving up for plastic surgery. Paradise for her would come the day she was a 34CC. Personally I thought that was a bit ambitious and that the weight would be sure to topple her flat on her face – all in all a pretty good reason not to discourage her in her aspirations.

"Actually, I snogged *all* of your boyfriends." Her counter-attack was vicious. "As a matter of fact, more than one told me they were only going out with you to get close to me!"

Patting the air in front of my face, I mimed a yawn. "Yeah, yeah, play it again, Sam!" To be honest, I wasn't too surprised. She'd always helped herself to whatever was mine, be it my Cindy Doll or my one and only pair of Janet Reger silk knickers. So, why should my boyfriends be sacrosanct? A sudden thought struck me. "You didn't get Rocky Cashel," I grinned hugely. "And *he* was the only one worth getting!"

"Well, neither did you. Or not properly, anyway."

I stuck out my tongue. "Well, I got more of him than you'll ever manage to get *and* he's famous!"

She was gutted. I could tell she was gutted by the way her rosebud lips pursed themselves into a cod's arse. Orla was into the fame-game. She'd lay a hundred-year-old corpse if it had appeared on the telly. Or, to put it another way, she wasn't so much a social climber as an antisocial climber. Honest to God, she'd ride roughshod over you to get to where she wanted. In a past life she was probably first off the *Titanic*. So, the thoughts of me, her big plain-Jane sister, getting within so much as an ass's roar of a celebrity, must have been about as pleasant as farting flames.

"Oh, you'll be smirking on the other side of your face when you find yourself banged up." Always subject to tantrums of the magenta-faced, gob-like-the-Grand-Canyon variety, she gave up on her second foot and sent the bottle of nail varnish crashing against the wall.

Deliberately misunderstanding, I made a great show of being grateful for her concern. "Oh, don't worry about that. His jodhpurs and my jeans were protection enough. My God, it would take a Duncan Goodhew of the sperm world to swim through that little lot." Gazing pensively off into the distance, I gave what I hoped was a wistful, maternal smile. "Not saying, mind you, that it wouldn't have been nice to have had a little Rocky or Rockette to dandle on my knee . . ."

It appeared, however, that I'd gone too far as with a roar that would have felled the Walls of Jericho had someone else not got there first, she pushed me off the bed, launched herself on top of me and with teeth bared and fingernails primed made straight for my jugular. Big mistake! The law of averages was against her and if her one brain cell hadn't been dormant, she might have worked out for herself that if a featherweight enters the ring with a heavyweight, chances are the featherweight's gonna die.

"You make me want to puke," she croaked, flailing about as with a deft twist I body-slammed her against the floor and then, just in case she was still unclear about who was boss, leaned casually against her windpipe all but cutting off her air supply. "You make me want to chuck up!"

Fascinated, I watched almost in a detached manner as her eyes began to bulge like two red-veined ping-pong balls and her face take on that nice maroon colour that contrasts so nicely against a pale cream carpet.

"Tut, tut, tut!" I said, exerting just a teensy bit more pressure. "What a creature of habits you are!"

CHAPTER 8

It was lunchtime and we'd popped down the Fox's Retreat for a quick drop of lubrication. The landlord, with uncharacteristic generosity, stood us the first round because, since word had got round that Rocky Cashel's attackers frequented the joint, trade had rocketed through the roof. And, to a certain extent, I suppose we came to enjoy the notoriety although it wore a bit thin when the five-hundredth yob of the week asked for a 'hands-on' demonstration (in private) of what *really* happened. Through telling and retelling, the story had grown out of all proportion and now Rocky Cashel was reputed not only to have been raped, but to have been gang-banged by all three of us. There had been the odd dark muttering concerning the horse too, but, thankfully, that was so far-fetched as to have died an almost instantaneous death.

"I think we should make a clean breast of it," Sophie said, attempting to draw a shamrock in the head of her pint of Guinness with the aid of a broken matchstick.

"And I think you need your bloody head examined!" Plonking her glass of Ballygowan mineral water onto the counter, Debbie glared. "My child is not, I repeat *not*, going to be born in prison."

"Well, I think Sophie has a point." I shrank away as Debbie turned her sights on me. "I mean, I'm fed up ducking and diving and waiting to feel the long arm of the law tapping me on the shoulder." I clutched my own glass tightly as if I was James Bond and any moment an arch-villain might catapult through the window and try to wrest it from my grasp. "*And* when you really think about it, it's only his word against ours. After all, there were no other witnesses."

"Yeah, his very high-profile, very famous word against ours." Dryly, Debbie stuck her finger in an empty metal ashtray and embarked upon the annoying process of whirling it noisily round and round the wooden counter till it spun so fast the HARP logo became blurred and illegible. "Besides, what about the cheque? That could be viewed as extortion, couldn't it?"

"Not really," Sophie shook her head. "I mean, we didn't stand to gain anything personally by that. It was made out to the Save the Fox fund, remember? *And* we never even paid it in, in case it could be traced back to us."

"Christ Almighty," Debbie went green around the

gills, "that's evidence. What did you do with it? If they find that, we're well and truly stuffed."

"Tore it up!" Sophie grinned. "Don't worry! That's long gone down the sewerage system. There's no way we can be linked to that."

"Listen, Debs," I touched her reassuringly on the arm. "I'm as nervous about this as you. More so, considering the part I played in things. I mean, you only whacked him about a bit with a branch. I knocked him off his horse, for Heaven's sake, *and* had my wicked way with him."

"Gemma's right," Sophie nodded. "She was the main player in the proceedings. To a large extent you and I were only bystanders."

Unreasonably upset because she was, after all, only corroborating what I myself had already said, I shot her a look that would have shelled eggs. "Yeah, like the lions were only bystanders in the Colosseum!"

Sophie ignored me. "The way I see it is this. At the moment the public are colluding with us. They see us as some kind of latter-day Robin Hood figures screwing the rich . . ."

"And giving to the poor," I grinned, thinking of the cheque.

Sophie raised a disparaging eyebrow. "No, just screwing the rich. And, let's face it, that's what everyone wants to do. Now whilst the tide of public opinion is with us, everything is fine and dandy. People will go to great lengths to throw the filth off our trail. The problem is – tides turn!" She took a sip of Guinness, wiping the froth away from her lips with the back of her hand. It was a curiously masculine gesture. Had there been a spittoon on the floor I've no doubt she would have proved every bit as adept in the spitting department as any man.

"So, you think we should just turn ourselves in at the nearest police station and hope we can talk our way out of it. Is that right?" Debbie looked like she relished the idea about as much as she relished the idea of being hung naked by her thumbs and prodded by starving cannibals.

"That's about the size of it." Sophie finished her pint and looked hopefully at the landlord who, far from taking the hint, immediately found himself indispensable at the far end of the counter.

"Well, okay." Suddenly capitulating, Debbie gave the ashtray one last frantic twirl that sent it clattering onto the floor. "But I vote we go for the direct approach – that's to say, we beard the lion in his den."

Sophie threw me a glance chock-full of meaning. "It's the pregnancy! All those hormones floating about the place. They've made her brain soft."

Hormones or no hormones, Debbie intended to have her say. "No, hear me out! Surely it's better to try and reason with the man on a face-to-face basis rather than with some jumped-up little policeman with superintendent's stripes in his eyes? It doesn't take Einstein to figure out that the police aren't going to be interested in hearing the real story, not when they can fast-track their way to promotion on the strength of nabbing Ireland's most wanted!"

"Not that we're interested in *telling* them the real story or anything," Sophie pointed out. "I mean everything in the papers was true bar the personal descriptions and some of those are debatable. We *did* beat him up. Gemma *did* derive a certain amount of sexual gratification. We *did* extort a cheque from him."

"You know, the more I think about it," I said, "the more I'm beginning to think Debbie has a point. I mean, if we were to turn up at his door mob-handed, maybe we could frighten him into a full retraction."

Sophie was disgusted. "Jesus, what are you like? Do you want to get us even deeper in the shit? No, if we go for the direct approach we'd better be prepared to eat humble-pie. Loads of it!"

"That's it," Debbie agreed. "We'll have to kowtow like he's the Dalai Lama, back away facing him and all that crap. Hell, if necessary, even get down and kiss his unwashed feet!"

"And do you think it will work?" Anxiously, I scanned their faces. I had an awful feeling that whilst he might be prepared to forgive the odd whack around the skull with a tree-branch, he might not look so kindly on yours truly.

"It's got to be worth a try," Debbie said. "Besides, with all this hanging over my head I just don't feel I can tell Guy about the baby right now. You know Guy –

there's no way on earth he's going to want the mother of his child to be a jailbird."

I suspected there was no way on earth he was going to want the mother of this particular child, period! Of course I didn't say that. Instead, I confessed a major concern of my own. "Actually, I'm pretty worried myself. Orla's been puking herself into a shadow lately knowing full well that I won't tell my mother in case she spills the beans about me and Rocky. Honestly, if she doesn't get a grip soon, I'm really worried that she'll die." I drew a deep breath. "Okay, okay. Before you say it, I know we're always at each other's throats but she's still my sister."

"And blood is thicker than water." Sophie put an arm around me and for once I accepted the gesture for what it was and forgot to look for ulterior lesbian-type motives. "Poor Gemma!"

"So we're agreed," Debbie said, sounding, I suspected, a lot more confident than she felt. "It's once more unto the breach and all that."

"Yeah, do or die!" Sophie waved a victory fist, then hooked her little finger round mine and then Debbie's, sealing the pact with a gesture left over from childhood. "Right, girls, all we've got to do now is figure out the logistics of getting an audience with the little bastard. After that it's in the lap of the gods."

I checked my watch. "And our jobs will be in the lap of the gods too if we don't get a move on."

"Jeepers!" Debbie checked her own watch. "Is that the time? Guy will slaughter me if I'm late back. He's got some exotic spider coming in this afternoon and he's been boning up on the treatment all morning."

"Huh, I'm thrilled for him!" Sophie said sarcastically, sliding off her bar stool and leading the general exodus out of the pub. "This is his crowning moment, is it? The spider he's been waiting for all his life."

A little defensively, Debbie drew abreast. "Well, it is a bit special, Soph, although from the pictures I've seen, it's a bit on the nondescript side. To be honest, you'd have to be an expert to tell it apart from your common or garden house-spider. Still, apparently, it's from a rare endangered colony only found in the rainforests of Guatemala or somewhere."

"So, what's it doing in Dublin?" I asked, not that I gave a shit or anything. I hate spiders. It's all those legs, all churning together in an I'm-comin'-to-get-you kind of way and you don't need a zoom lens to know that their mouths are wide open and salivating. I don't care what anyone says: *nothing* should need eight legs.

"Actually, it belongs to Dublin Zoo," Debbie explained. "The entomologist who specialises in that particular field has gone down with a bug, no pun intended, and as Guy is regarded of something of an expert on arachnids, they've decided to bring it over to *Vetz 4 Petz* for a bit of a health check."

"Very illuminating." Sophie all but yawned. "Shame I won't get to see it but Rob and I are going out this afternoon to check on some ewes that are just about to lamb."

"Well, let's hope none of them come out looking like *him*," I said, pushing open the surgery doors.

"Perish the thought!" Sophie chuckled but there was real affection in the laugh because despite Rob, allegedly, being a tail-lifter, the pair of them got on together like roast lamb and mint sauce.

* * *

"So, where have *you* been?" Martin Shanahan greeted me with a face that could skin a corpse. "That Birch woman is due any minute with that filthy animal of hers, then there's half a dozen spayings, a couple of despatchings to canine heaven and a randy ferret who needs his knob nipped." Making a gate of his hands, he peered through the gaps in his fingers. "And, as if all that isn't enough for one man to contend with, the wife's mother is coming to stay this evening. For a week, would you believe? Jesus, but I must have been a right character in a past life! I must have been flamin' Hitler 'cause I'm paying the price for it now."

I shrugged. "Oh, well, as the man says, it's just another day for you and me in paradise."

Martin gazed at me suspiciously. "Now listen here, don't you start coming over all religious and quoting chapter and verse at me. I get enough of that at home."

I quirked an eyebrow. "I was quoting Phil Collins, actually."

112

"Well, don't," Martin looked like a sulky child. "I never liked her. All that 'send in the clowns' business. What a load of old crap that was."

"That," I said scathingly, "was Judy Collins."

"Do I look like I give a shit?" Like a hunted man Martin gazed out the window through which, horror of horrors, Mrs Birch could be seen wending her way towards the surgery. He ducked back. "Oh Jesus, stall her for me, would you? Tell her I'm dealing with an emergency. Tell her anything you like, only give me a chance to nip out the back to the Fox's Retreat for a quick shot of the old Dutch."

"What's it worth?" I asked.

"You get to keep your job!"

"Well, you can stuff that," I began, but Martin had already legged it.

"Hello, young Gemma." The draught from the back door was still eddying around my ankles when Mrs Birch arrived through the front. "Shagged any good rock stars recently?"

Completely unruffled, since this had become her standard greeting, I took a leaf out of her Freemasons' book and tapped my nose. "Ah, a chance like that only comes round once in a lifetime, Mrs B. Anyway, how's Kilroy?"

"Packed!" Imploring the heavens, Mrs Birch rolled her eyes in an agonised way. "Packed as an Elizabethan's codpiece."

My heart sank. "Been at the Curly-Wurlys again, has

he? Oh well, I suppose you'd better take a seat. Martin won't be long. He's —"

"Just nipped out the back for a pint of courage?" Mrs Birch laughed at the look on my face. "Ah, don't worry, love. I've known Martin Shanahan for years. Mind you, he'll need all the courage he can get when he sees what Kilroy has in store for him."

And for me, I thought bitterly. And for me!

"Bloody hell!" Martin stage-whispered, peering round the surgery door fifteen minutes or so later. "It's like a bloody zoo out there. Why didn't I listen to my mother and do something respectable like accountancy or law?"

I flinched away from the whiskey fumes on his breath, which, with minimum effort, could anaesthetise a horse. "Well, it's a bit late for that now. Anyway, shall I take Kilroy through before he bursts wide open and destroys the decor?"

"Yeah, no point in putting off the evil moment any longer, I suppose. Lob him in the treatment room. I'll be in in just a minute."

"Righty ho!" Clicking my tongue, I stuck my head round the waiting-room door. "Yo, Kilroy! Time to go, boy. Literally!" The dog looked anxious, as well he might at the thoughts of having a three-foot rubber tube fed up his rear end.

"Ah, you'll be fine." Seeing his hesitation, Mrs Birch patted him on the head. "Off you go with Gemma and tonight if you're a good boy, I'll give you a nice . . ." she caught the warning in my eye, "bit of steak!"

114

"Ah, you'll be fine," I repeated a moment later as he stood shivering and whimpering in the treatment room. "And better out than in, isn't that what they say? Eh?" Leaning down, I patted him on the neck, which is when I felt the tumour. I say tumour although it was unlike any tumour I'd ever felt before. Firstly it moved – of its own volition – scurrying up and down beneath the hair on his neck like a mole on speed. Secondly, it began to excise itself, bit by bit, till out it popped on the surface, a writhing mass of black ugliness that made me want to heave. Lastly, and worst of all, it had legs – lots and lots and lots of legs! With a rapid series of rather coarse Anglo-Saxon expletives, I jumped back, grabbed a notebook off a nearby table and whacked it to the floor. Then, before it could make a bolt for it, I jumped on it. Again and again and again! I was busy examining the sole of my boot when Martin came into the room.

"Holy God! It's like World War III out there. That exotic spider-thing that Guy was treating has done a runner. Everyone, including the clients, are busy searching for it."

"Really?" The connection hit my brain at the same time as my foot hit the floor. Trying hard not to look like a thief who's been caught with her hand in the till, I attempted nonchalance. "Was it a black exotic spider-thing? With lots of legs?"

Martin nodded. "That's right! Have you seen it?"

"Nah!" I lied through my teeth, although I swear I could feel the bloody insect burning into the sole of my boot like a mortal sin into my soul. "Just a lucky guess, that's all!"

"Oh." Martin, never a MENSA candidate, immediately lost interest and switched instead into fooling-Kilroy mode. Patting his thighs, he tried to look encouraging – well, as encouraging as someone can look whose face has been described more than once as about as attractive as a fart in a closet. "Come on, you hairy bastard, you!" he wheedled in a voice so sweet that two of my fillings came loose and the enamel stripped from my teeth in layers. "Let's get this tubey-woobey up your arsey-warsey. Eh? Eh?"

"*Grr, snarl, gnash,*" said Kilroy and neither of us was in any doubt that what he was actually saying was the canine equivalent of, "Stick it up your own arse, wanker!"

CHAPTER 9

"Gemma!"

I was upstairs squeezing a premenstrual spot when my mother called me from the foot of the stairs. Damn! A little more prodding and it would have just about given up its dead.

"Gemma! Come down, would you? You've got a visitor."

My eyebrows rose in the mirror. Visitor? I wasn't expecting any visitors. I wasn't the sort of person who had visitors. *Orla* had visitors! No, I tell a lie! Orla had *guests!* Hurriedly, I searched my memory for invitations issued in the drunken heat of a moment to men who under the influence looked like Brad Pitt but who in reality were simply the pits, but drew a blank. A glorious thought struck me! Maybe it was Tony! Full of remorse and come round to do the old breast-beating and sackcloth-and-ashes penitent number. Glorious, because I was going to spit in his eye and strangle him with his own tongue. "Gemma! I've put him in the living-room." A third roar disabused me rapidly of this notion. My mother would *never* put Tony in the living-room. The living-room in our house was a bit like the banqueting hall in Buckingham Palace: reserved for visiting royalty and state occasions and only rarely open to the public. So, whoever it was, it definitely wasn't Tony but, as she'd definitely referred to a 'him,' it *was* male. A male visitor! And me with a big red spot on my forehead with a big yellow middle! Hurriedly I trowelled on some slap, piling it on top of the eruption as though I could bury the damn thing six-foot under. But it was no good! Again and again it rose to the surface pulsating like a malevolent pus-filled third eye. I wondered if maybe I shouldn't have one last go, exert pressure from all sides as it were, till with nowhere else to go there was no alternative but for it to explode with a satisfying splat against the mirror.

"Ge-mm-aaah!" A note of impatience had entered my mother's voice. I could hear her foot on the first rung of the stairs.

"All right! All right!" I bellowed back, shelving the idea until later. "Keep your HRT patch on!"

"Well, you're a dark horse, lady," she whispered, tapping the side of her nose as I drew abreast of her and I couldn't help but wonder if everyone on the planet had gone stark raving bollocking mad and joined the Masons. Maybe there was a secret Masonic plot to take over the world and the only one not in the know was me. Maybe *I* was a Masonic undesirable, unfit to wear an apron, roll my trouser-leg or partake in secret handshakes, nipple kisses and dubious oaths of allegiance to somebody or other. "You kept *him* to yourself, didn't you? Not that I blame you! God knows, if I were twenty years younger myself, I'd rip his boxers off with my bare teeth."

"Mammy!" I was scandalised. "That's disgusting!" No wonder she was reduced to wearing a full set of dentures these days. Upper *and* lower!

"Huh! Disgusting is as disgusting does!" she said cryptically, manoeuvring me over to the living-room door.

"But, *who's* in there?" I mouthed frantically, hanging back a bit. *"Who? Who? Who?"*

"Oh, you know," her fingers closed over the doorknob, "Blarney! Blarney Stone! No, I tell a lie! Not Blarney Stone!" Her hand twisted. Like in a gothic-horror movie the door creaked slowly open. "Rocky! That's it! Rocky Cashel!" As my world began to spin and the carpet flew up and landed on the ceiling, I felt her push lightly against the small of my back. "In you go now, Gemma! I'll bring some tea and cake through in a minute and then I'll leave you alone with your young man." She winked and in my weakened state I still found the energy to be appalled. Could this lasciviously winking creature possibly be my mother – the same woman who had banned us from watching Benny Hill on TV and who thought sex was what the Mormons are. "Orla's out on the tiles tonight and your Aunty Kay and I are going to the bingo so you'll have the house to yourselves." Her message was clear, embarrassingly clear, even to me caught as I was in the throes of an imminent faint. 'Go on, kids,' she was saying, 'shag yourselves rigid. The house is on me!'

When I came to, Rocky Cashel was blowing on my face. His breath, pleasantly scented with fluoride toothpaste, was cool and reminded me of Furbee. Foggily I wondered if it was the same brand, the one with the red stripe and if that was the reason he too was frothing at the mouth.

"Well, well, well, lookee here!" For a moment I thought I'd confused him with Clint Eastwood. He'd certainly taken to talking like he was a bit player in a bad Western and not at all like Ireland's most eligible bachelor, musician extraordinaire and writer of *Rotten to the Core*. "Doggone if it ain't the Blessington rapist!"

I struggled to sit up but he had me pinned down – by the arms. Obviously he was taking no chances on sitting on me again. "How did you find me?" My voice was weak. That was good. I could work with weak. With a fragile flutter of the eyelashes, I injected a large dose of 'poor little feminine helpless me' intonation into it, hoping it might stir some deeply hidden chivalrous instinct beneath his Meatloaf sweatshirt and send him rushing off on a dragon-slaying spree. "W-who grassed me up?" Flutter, flutter, threatened swoon! Sadly the ruse failed and if anything stirred anywhere it was simply more echoes of Billy the Kid.

"Well, shucks, pardner, ah won't pretend you didn't lead ol Rocky-boy heah a merry dance. But in de end, I always git me mah mayn – or wo-mayn as the case maht be!" Although he kept tight hold of my arms, I could see, by his eyes, he was twirling an imaginary Colt 45.

Bugger the feminine wiles. I struggled to sit up again. "Look, stop pratting about and let me up. John Wayne must be turning in his grave. I haven't heard such a sad attempt at an accent since Nicole Kidman tried to play an Irish colleen in *Far and Away*."

"Christ! That was awful!" he agreed, but seemingly this true meeting of minds was not enough to persuade him to release his grip. "And Tom Cruise wasn't much better – all that touching the cap and 'yes sorr' and 'no sorr-ing' all over the place. It must have set the tourist industry back about fifty thousand years."

"If they'd wanted to see how real Irish people should be portrayed, they should have watched *Rotten to the Core*," I said, nodding agreement from my prone position and I strenuously deny it was an attempt simply to flatter and curry favour.

"You're not just saying that in a strenuous attempt simply to flatter and curry favour?" he asked.

"Absolutely not! Go up to my bedroom," I instructed, "first on the right, off the landing, and see for yourself. There's wall to wall posters of both you and *Rotten to the Core* up there. Look in my wardrobe – *Rotten to the Core* T-shirts! Look on my dressing-table –

Rotten to the Core pens, pencils, erasers, coasters and badges everywhere." I paused for a deeply offended breath. "I resent your currying-favour implication greatly, although, if it *were* to have a favourable knock-on effect . . ."

Rocky shuffled a bit closer on his knees but didn't relax his grip. "Some critics thought the lyrics were very weak, especially the theme song, 'Hunger'. Accused me of ripping off Bob Dylan, if you don't mind. Something about the chorus!"

"Piddle!" I said. "The critics are arthritic!" He laughed. I laughed. I've no idea why we both laughed because quite frankly I've heard funnier one-liners while following a hearse.

"No, seriously," he said, releasing one of my hands in order to wipe his streaming eyes (dust-mite allergy, I found out later and not hysteria) and I realised that here was my opportunity to free myself but somehow the moment passed and it dawned on me that there were worse things in life than being pinned to the carpet by a gorgeous pop idol. Accordingly, I just lay there worshipping at the shrine of his chiselled chin, gazing up into the promising dark depths of his nostrils and wondering if, maybe, I wouldn't score Brownie points by suggesting a nostril-hair clipper as yet another interesting promo tool.

"Seriously," I said, "I love 'Hunger'. I'm always singing it." I refrained from telling him that whenever I did people dived for cover and many were the dark and dire mutterings concerning the proximity of the end of the world. One of two people had even confused me with Nostradamus.

"Sing it to me," he said, exerting a little more pressure on my wrists. "You – owe – me!"

"B – but I can't sing," I warned him, my eyes travelling in a direct line from his nostrils, up along the bridge of his nose to where his eyes gazed back at me, two Guinness pools of black velvet without the head. "I couldn't carry a note to save myself!"

"Sing!" he commanded and, fearful of incurring further damage to my windpipe and as evidence of my good intentions, I did, in a voice both shaky and tone-deaf. By the time I'd finished I wasn't surprised to see tears on his cheeks. Outside on the street people were probably waiting for the trumpets to sound at the four corners of the earth and for bodies to start disinterring themselves all over the place as a prelude to being reunited with their souls.

Wonderingly, Rocky shook his head. "Profound, man! My lyrics are profound. ABBA has nothing on me. Did you get the subtext?"

"Oh, I did," I lied, wondering what the hell a subtext was but fortunately Rocky, like Guy, was one of those people who often asked a question, then answered it himself, in this case going into huge detail about irony and symbolism and iambic pentameters, whatever they were – words which, at school, bored the crap out of me but which, when uttered from between his oh-so-masterful lips, took on a quality that enthralled, though not necessarily enlightened.

"Oh," I said, limply as he finally ran out of breath. "Cool!" Actually what I really wanted to say was, 'What the bloody hell are you on about and do you think you might consider sitting on me again?'

The answer, as he got to his feet, bent down and hauled me to mine was obviously, disappointingly no! "You know, you're not half bad for a King Kong look-alike."

Reminded, I shot him a look so filthy it should have been handled with rubber gloves and disposed of in a sealed container marked 'Hazardous'. "Like, I don't know how you could have said that. That was really below the belt."

"Huh! As if you can talk! Below the belt is exactly what caused all this trouble in the first place."

I was pleased to find I still had the grace to blush. "I – er – wondered when we were going to get onto that particular subject."

"Well, shucks, honey, wait no longer." It was back to the cowboy-speak again.

"Look," I said, "before we go any further, what's all this howdee-pardner-and-mine's-a-hoss-and-saddle stuff in aid of?"

"Oh?" Rocky looked surprised. "Didn't I tell you I'm getting in character for my new musical, *Young Guns*?"

"*Young Guns*?" Bewildered, I shook my head. "But

surely that's been done before with all those Hollywood brat-pack actors?"

Rocky tapped his nose. Mason alert! Mason alert! Exterminate! "Ah, but this is *Young* Irish *Guns*!" Excitedly he pushed me into a nearby armchair. "When do you think it's set?"

"During the Irish famine?" I hazarded a guess, not because I thought he was predictable or anything but to date everything he'd done had centred around that particular period in Irish history.

"Good guess! But this time it's not set in Ireland."

"Oh, I see. The Irish famine, not set in Ireland but featuring guns."

"Exactly!" Rocky grinned "Actually, it's about the young Irishmen who escaped to America on the coffin ships and went off and became cowboys. I've just written the theme song. It's called 'The Green Green Tumbleweed'."

Thinking of a certain Welsh singer with a big voice, a nose job and a face like an elderly ram, it was on the tip of my tongue to say, 'I can feel a big lawsuit coming on here', but seemingly, he could read my mind.

"And before you mention Tom Jones, my 'Green Green Tumbleweed' is nothing like his 'Green Green Grass'."

"Thank God for that!" I said, not that I've anything against Tom Jones or anything but I wouldn't throw my knickers at him. Mind you, after a few drinks it's not unknown for me to have a go at belting out 'Delilah'.

No, the relief was more because my faith in Rocky was justified and there really was a whole goldmine of untapped originality there. *Real* Irish cowboys – well, it made a refreshing change from Irish cowboy builders which, to date, were the only type I was familiar with.

A tentative tap at the door brought all conversation to a temporary end as, a moment later, my mother oozed herself around it, a tray laid with her best willow-pattern china balanced on her hip.

"I hope you like Battenberg, Blarney." Placing the tray on a nearby coffee table, she shot him a flirtatious look and I was amazed and annoyed to find that even women of her age were obviously not immune to his charm. Whatever I expected, it was certainly not competition from my own mother.

"It's Rocky," both Rocky and I said together, although my voice, several degrees colder than his, had come straight off a shelf in the mortuary. "Rocky Cashel!"

"Well, all right, if I didn't knock it down, I staggered it." Unblushingly, she cut a large chunk of the yellow and pink-squared cake and placed it on a side plate. "I knew you were called after a famous Irish landmark anyway, though why your mother couldn't have called you Malachy is beyond me. You would have made a lovely Malachy."

Rocky grinned and took the plate she passed across. "Oh, I think it might have had something to do with where I was conceived."

"Really?" I asked, feeling a bit foolish because a) as his Numero Uno fan and b) having read every bit of trivia going and then some, I thought I knew everything there was to know about him. "I thought that was just a stage name and your real name was something more banal like Reggie Dwight."

Rocky shook his head. "No, Elton already bagsed that one."

My mother's antennae went up. "Stage name? Do you know, I thought I'd seen you before." She clicked her fingers. "Give me a minute, it'll come to me." And then, to my mortification and also, it must be said, to my relief because I thought she was going to twig he was the guy splashed all over the newspapers, "You're not one of those crotch-grabbers, are you? One of those young chaps that appeared on the *Late Late* one night and made an awful show of themselves?"

"That was Boyzone!" I cut in indignantly. "And, no, he bloody well is not!"

She chuckled indulgently. "Silly me! Of course, you're not. They're all gay, aren't they? You wouldn't be here courting my Gemma if you were gay." Conveniently forgetting about her feelings towards Sophie, she clapped a declamatory hand across her heart. "Oh, not that I'm claustrophobic or anything. Live and let live, that's my motto."

"I think the word you're looking for is homophobic," I muttered and then more loudly, "and he's *not* courting me. He . . . he's . . ." Struggling, I looked to him for help which was pretty foolish when you considered he probably had the house surrounded by marksmen with high-powered rifles trained at every window and door. For all I knew, there might even be a red dot hovering somewhere in the centre of my temple like a Hindu woman's *bindi*.

However, he apparently was just as tongue-tied which is understandable, really. I mean, how do you go about telling someone's mother – someone's mother, mind you, who has just made you tea and given you Battenberg cake on her best china plate – that her daughter is a rapist who spends her weekends molesting men in lonely places and that you are her latest victim. Also, that her house is surrounded by marksmen with high-powered, telescopic rifles trained at every window and door and that by this time tomorrow all the neighbours will be in the know and pointing the finger at her for being a bad mother. Because it's always the mother who gets the blame. Every amateur psychologist knows that. Heck, even Cracker knows that and he's an alcoholic as well as being Scottish!

"I . . . er . . .um!" Honestly, I would have felt quite sorry for him were it not for the fact that he held the power of life and death over me. "Well . . . um . . . aar . . . nyeh!"

My mother laughed, a light girlish sound that went about as well with her crow's-feet and baggy jowls as tassels on a nun's nipples. "Ah, you want to keep a low profile about it, the pair of you. Is that it? Well, I don't blame you. I suppose it's early days yet and publicising it might well be the kiss of death. Look what happened to that Randy Andy and Koo Stark. All over each other like chocolate round a kiddie's mouth they were but the minute the big Q got the wind of it, Koo's goose was kooked." A knowing look in her eyes, she wagged her head wisely. "And, of course, you're going to want to keep Orla out of the equation, at least until things are established."

I scowled, furious at the implication that Orla had only to snap her manicured fingers and my boyfriends would come running, and was just about to let rip with a well-earned piece of my mind when Rocky got there first.

"Poodles!" he spluttered in a way that made it sound like bollocks! "Poodles!"

'P-poodles?" In the manner of someone who suspects she's been got at but who's not exactly sure how, Mammy exchanged a look of bafflement with me. "He did say poodles, didn't he, Gem? I mean, I know my hearing's not up to scratch these days – it's the wax, you see – you could make a Paschal candle out of it, and Dr Farrelly can't fit me in until next week – but, I'm sure he said poodles." Considering, she bent her head to one side, as if the echo might still be lingering in the room and she could tune in for an action replay. "Although, I can't swear to that. I mean, he could have said noodles. Or doodles." She knit her lips tightly. "Although, where

129

would be the sense in that? No. It was definitely poodles! *Why*?" she demanded, swinging from me back to Rocky who, finding himself impaled on the end of a basilisk stare, found it improved his powers of rhetoric not at all.

"Er – em – um – because, I have one. A poodle, I mean," he finished in a rush. "And it's got er – em – um pink-eye, yes, pink-eye – that's what the poor beast's got. Nasty thing – pink-eye! And I hear your daughter, er, Gemma here, is regarded as, um, something of an expert on – on – pink-eye in poodles." His confidence increased with every lie. "Isn't that right, Gemma?"

Honestly, I could have nailed his ass to the Cross were it not for the fact that Mammy, overcome by Saint Jude finally answering her prayers and apparently turning me into a model citizen, was looking as though she might collapse at any minute.

"Really, Gem?" Despite her devotion to the Patron Saint of Lost Causes, her eyes were alive with a mixture of disbelief and fear – disbelief that it really was me Rocky was talking about and fear that she would wake up any moment and find that I, her first born, was still the unacceptable face of young Irish womanhood.

Anxious to keep that look of unaccustomed pride on her face a bit longer, I reluctantly put Rocky's crucifixion on the back burner and went along with the charade. "Oh, I am!" I lied. "A real expert! There's nothing I don't know about pink-eye. Go on, ask me anything." I quickly backtracked at this juncture as her mouth made like a fish and she looked as though she might be about to take me up on the invitation. "Not that I'd want to bore you or anything. Or, worse still, turn your stomach. All that blood and gore! It's not pretty – pink-eye! Is it, er, Rocky?"

"Devil the pretty!" Like a pantomime villain, Rocky slapped his thigh. "I wouldn't wish it on my worst enemy – but I'll tell you what. Why don't I call round to the surgery tomorrow and fill you in on the whole story?"

"Oh, good idea," I said, sending up a quick prayer of thanks to whatever deity might just happen to be loafing about in the ether. "Why don't you do that?"

"Why didn't he do that in the first place?" Mammy sniffed, after I had practically frogmarched him out of the house and banged the door behind him. St Jude or not, her maternal antennae were on red alert. "I'm telling you, Gemma, there's something fishy about this whole business. Something's rotten in the state of Denmark!"

Never mind Denmark. Personally, I blamed St Jude. He obviously hadn't done his job properly! Returning upstairs, I hastily removed my make-up and began a full frontal assault on the spot on my forehead. Mammy was right though! There was something fishy about the whole thing. If Rocky had wanted to expose me, why hadn't he? Why hadn't he come right out and said 'Mrs Murphy, I hate to tell you this, but your daughter is a sexual predator and I, Rocky Cashel, Ireland's most eligible bachelor, musician extraordinaire and writer of *Rotten to the Core,* am her prey.' Why the elaborate cover-up, the far-fetched story about some poodle that presumably existed only in his fevered imagination? I caught my breath and held fire on the spot for a moment. Unless, of course, he felt we had unfinished business. In which case, I'd be only too happy to finish what I'd started that day at the Blessington Fox-hunt. And with a bit of luck, this time, he might just take a more active role.

CHAPTER 10

"He didn't!"

"He did!"

"He didn't!"

"He bloody did!"

"But poodles?" Like the revolting kid in the Ready Brek advert, Debbie made circular sweeps across her stomach. It was a very annoying habit she'd developed since finding out she was pregnant. "Whatever possessed him?"

"I don't know but my mother's face was a picture. I'm sure she thought he was taking the piss. I mean, there she was in full flow pratting on like we were Romeo and Juliet and what does he come out with: poodles! I ask you!"

"And then what?" Agog, Debbie paused with the kettle suspended over my mug.

"Oh, he went off into some big spiel about owning a rare albino poodle and how he'd heard I was something of an expert on that particular breed and that's why he'd turned up at our house like a bad smell in a mortuary."

"Albino poodle!" Coming back to life, Debbie tilted the kettle and let the water flow. "Is there such a thing?"

"Damned if I know but, according to Rocky Cashel, I'm the world's number one expert on pink-eye in poodles, whatever that is."

Picking up my pig mug, I added my own milk and a disgusting saccharine tablet which was my sole concession to losing weight and which made me feel really virtuous as well as really sick.

Debbie chuckled. "I bet your mother wasn't half chuffed."

"Chuffed! She only thinks I'm next in line for the bloody Nobel, that's all. As for Orla, she was hopping, not only because she'd missed Rocky but also because, the way she sees it, he's let me off the hook. Nothing less than pillorying by tabloid will do for her. She doesn't so much want to see me brought low as completely flattened and peeled off the road like that coyote in *Roadrunner*. I had to threaten her with immediate quadriplegia to force her to keep her mouth shut."

"And will she?"

I shrugged. "Dunno. She'd better, although with the amount of weight she's losing she won't be around for much longer."

"God!" Debbie looked really distressed. "You are joking, aren't you?"

"No." I shook my head. "She's so thin now that whenever she has a power-shower she has to be careful the force of the water doesn't wash her down the plughole. Talk about incey-wincey spider!"

"Well, what does your mother say? Surely she can see something is not right?"

"No!" I took a sip of my coffee. "Orla's managed to convince her she's normal-size for a model or 'muddle' as she calls it when she's trying to be posh and, although Mammy would prefer her to put on a bit of weight, she thinks Orla can do no wrong."

"Well, what about your Aunty Kay? She doesn't strike me as a woman who could be easily taken in. Can't she do something?"

"No. She's as besotted as my mother and any time I open my mouth I'm accused of being jealous of my sister." I gave an unladylike snort. "As if!"

Debbie grinned. "But you are!"

"Well, only of her blonde hair, baby-blues and way of getting whatever she wants," I admitted. "Still, I'm happy enough the way I am."

"You big filthy liar!" Debbie threw a teaspoon at me. "That's why you're always wittering on about your fat thighs, hairy back and your moley bottom."

I threw a warning look over to where an elderly gent, eighty if he was a day and accompanied by his equally ancient African parrot, was all that remained of the day's clients. "Shush! You might get Mr Keyes all excited and he has a dicky ticker."

"There's nothing wrong with my hearing, though." With a sly grin, the old man leered across at us. "And there's nothing wrong with my dicky either if either of yis fancy a test drive. Or yis could ride tandem if ye like."

Debbie pretended to be shocked. "Behave yourself, Mr Keyes! Is that any way to talk to a couple of innocent convent-educated girls?"

"Innocent bedamned!" Mr Keyes shoved his false teeth out on the end of his tongue then sucked them back in again, a bad move if he wanted to have women hurling themselves butt-naked and gagging for it at his feet. "Ye want te try tellin that to that beatnik fella ye raped down in Blessington."

"Try telling him yourself," Debbie said with a sudden quaver in her voice, her eyes darting to the surgery door where Rocky Cashel had suddenly materialised and on which, regardless of the closed sign, he had begun pounding for admittance.

"Bloody hell!" Alarmed, I dived behind the reception desk. "What does he want now? Do you think maybe he's brought reinforcements with him? Like any moment now, we could have some cop on a megaphone inviting us to come out with our hands up. Quick, get down, Debs. Maybe he'll go away if he thinks there's no one here."

"Oh, behave!" Debbie said, but I couldn't help noticing her own knees had buckled to the extent where her eyes were barely above counter level.

"Well, are yis goin to let the fella in or what?" Mr Keyes roared out as the banging on the door increased. "Or do yis want me to set Gorby on him?"

"Oh, would you?" I begged, knowing from past experience that Mr Keyes's parrot, ancient or not, could drill straight through a rhino's hide and all the way into the bone beyond.

"No, don't!" Debbie said just as quickly and with a filthy look at me. "Have you gone completely mental? Supposing it pecks his eyes out?"

"Well, it wouldn't necessarily mean an end to life as he knows it," I said callously. "Look at what's his face – that 'I Just Called To Say I Love You' guy – he's blind. If anything it might give him a certain amount of cachet, boost his image, bag him the bleeding-heart chart sales."

"You *are* mad!" Pulling herself back up from behind the counter, Debbie, taking a lifetime's worth of courage in her hands, strode over to the door and threw it open.

"About bloody time too! Didn't you hear me knocking?" Trailing, much to my amazement (because I had thought the beast purely imaginary), a particularly hideous-looking toy poodle, tie-dyed in Cartland shades of pink, Rocky barged past and made straight for where he could see one of my feet poking out from behind the counter. "Why is it," he asked, looking over the counter, "that whenever I meet you, sooner or later, you always end up on the floor?"

I gave a feeble oh-I'm-just-down-here-because-I'm-conscientiously-picking-up-dropped-paper-clips-and-rubber-bands grin. "Er . . . I suppose you could say I'm prone to it. *Prone* to it! Geddit?"

"If you say so. Anyway, get up – I have a proposition to put to you. To be honest, it's what I called around for last night, but your mother put me off. Man, she is one scary woman! Those teeth! That Battenberg!"

Well, I couldn't argue with any of that. Mammy's false teeth really were a sight to behold. Cautiously I got to my feet, not altogether convinced as to the purity of his motives and squinting over his shoulder for any sign of navy uniforms and peaked caps. "So this . . . er . . . proposition – what is it?"

"I want you to come and work for me." Without further ado, he went into Jesse James mode. "Y'all know, dahn on the ranch."

"Hang on," I said, body tensed, ready to dive out of the way in case he should get any ideas and whip out his trusty Smith & Wesson. "Like, I don't get this. Why on earth would you want to offer *me* a job? Especially after . . . " I paused and cleared my throat at this point, hoping he'd join the dots himself.

"Precisely," he said. "Pree-cise-ly! And now it's time to pay the piper."

"Eh?" I sent a look of appeal towards Debbie only to find she'd suddenly developed a profound interest in ornithology and had taken to studying Mr Keyes's parrot with an intensity guaranteed to set light to its feathers.

Seeing my dilemma, Rocky nodded astutely. "It's quite simple, really. Call it recompense if you like – recompense to me, that is. You work for me – you clear the debt. A kind of community service, if you will."

"B – but what about here?" I gave an anxious look around trying to pretend like I gave a toss when really I just wanted to rip off my uniform and conga out the doorway, never to set foot in the place again. Still, I wanted him to think I was a half-decent human being who spent only a small proportion of her time molesting strangers in woods.

"Oh, you wouldn't have to leave here. I'm talking weekends only."

My chin hit the floor. "But what about when you go on tour? Wouldn't you want me to come with you?"

His chin hit the floor. "Perish the thought! I can't think of anything worse. No, I want you to stay and look after Gretchen here."

I raised an eyebrow, or the sliver of an eyebrow to be exact as a result of having run amok one night recently with the tweezers whilst in an alcoholic stupor. In the morning I'd tried without too much success to persuade myself and everybody else that the look was *à la Garbo* and not *à la blotto*.

"Gr-et-ch-en?" Starting as a baritone I worked my way up through the ranks of tenor, contralto then alto before finally ending up as Charlotte Church.

Rocky nodded towards the dog who was busily engaged in giving me a fine view of her bared teeth, liberally coated with drool. "Yes, Gretchen, my girlfriend's poodle."

Well, how sad am I? I mean, I only go and lash out all that money on every flippin' fanzine going and *nowhere*, but nowhere, do any of them mention anything about a girlfriend, much less a poodle-owning girlfriend. I might as well have taken my cue from Orla and flushed my money straight down the bog. Like, come on, of course he had a girlfriend but big dork me had to go believing the publicity spewed out by his agent, swallowing the 'young, free and unattached' tag, hook, line and sinker. It's a psychology thing and they know that! I mean, it's far easier to imagine you're in with a chance if there's no sign of a wife and septuplets vying for your idol's attention. Besides which, imagining your wild-spirit up to his oxters in pooey nappies and with reflux stains all down the shoulder of his leather jacket does rather spoil the illusion.

"Hang on a mo. Let me get this straight." I fixed him with a piercing though puzzled eye. "*You*," I jabbed him sharply in the chest, "want *me* to give up *my* precious weekends," I hammered my own chest like a silverback gorilla, "to look after *that – that* thing?"

"Yup! That's about the size of it." Thoughtfully, Rocky chawed on an imaginary bit of baccy before spitting it into an equally imaginary spittoon located somewhere off to the left of him.

I waved a clenched fist beneath his chin. "Yeah, well, how about *this* for size?"

"You-owe-me!" The man obviously thought I had the attention span of a gnat – hence his propensity for reminding me every two seconds. "Besides, you're the world's number one expert on pink-eye in poodles!"

"What?" The remains of my eyebrows semaphored outrage. "That's piddle! You know very well you just made that up as a ruse to fool my mother."

"Maybe I did, maybe I didn't," he said, cool as a breeze, which was completely ridiculous as this was one issue on which there could be no argument. "Anyway, I'm not quite sure what your beef is. Like, I thought you'd jump at the chance to come and work for me. Millions of girls would give their right nipple for a chance like this."

Well, to be honest, put like that I didn't quite know what my beef was either. Okay, so there was a girlfriend involved and a poodle but girlfriends don't necessarily progress all the way up the career ladder into wives. Sometimes they meet a glass ceiling. Heck! You've only got to look at Tony the Shite Artist and me to prove that. And poodles have a limited lifespan, especially if they just happen to pick up a piece of steak liberally laced with paraquat. Besides, it's far easier to work your wiles on someone if you actually happen to be around them occasionally and not have to rely on charms, spells and incantations *in absentia*. Mind you, it was Rocky's last argument that clinched the deal.

"Of course," he said, beating a reflective tattoo upon his chin, dimpled, naturally, "you might prefer hanging out with the boys in blue. I hear they give great B & B and you get a free bar thrown in. Several of them, in fact!"

"No!" My voice skidded into the high octaves. "I'll do it." I swallowed the massive lie forming in my throat. "I mean, it's not as if I don't like poodles."

Rocky shrugged. "What's not to like?"

Everything, I thought. Everything, from the tips of their stupid-looking bobbly tails to their vicious sharp little yapping snouts. If you ask me, poodles are the Skoda of the canine world – more trouble than they're damn-well worth! Mind you, if Rocky liked them, then, as his future squeeze, it behoved me to develop a taste for the ugly little bastards too. I mean, as *Cosmo*, *Marie Claire* and the other glossy bibles would say, 'whilst opposites may attract, common interests forge the bond'. So, in an attempt to do some bonding and forging as well as garner some Brownie points en route, I stuck out my hand only to have Gretchen latch on to it like Jaws on a severed leg.

"Jesus Christ!" Jumping back, I wrenched what was left out of her mouth leaving the tips of two fingers and a Claddagh ring behind. "What is she, half bleedin pit bull?"

Rocky grinned. "Well, I dare say she may have had pit bull in her at some time or other. She's had most other breeds. Cause you're a bit of an old tart, aren't you, Gretchy-wetchy?" Fondly, he reached across and tickled her behind the ears and the nasty bitch, like every other female on earth, slobbered adoringly back at him begging him with her eyes to do things to her that would have landed him up in court on charges of breaching the beast.

"Gemma!" Debbie, who up till now had been keeping a low profile behind Mr Keyes's African grey, scooted over, her conscience no doubt pricked by the tidal wave of blood spreading across the floor. "You've been bitten!" Well, ten out of ten for observation! Someone give that girl a diploma and a mortarboard to chuck in the air! "When was the last time you had a tetanus jab?"

About as long ago as the last time I had a screw, I thought, but that, of course, was privileged information and not for the edification of the great unwashed. "I don't know!" I shrugged and the sudden movement coupled with the loss of blood made my head reel, so much so that my body quite independently and with no prompting, prepared itself to swoon straight into Rocky Cashel's masterful arms.

"Well, we'd better get you to the hospital quick, so!" Grabbing hold of my elbow, Miss bloody super-efficient Debbie Dunn scuppered my plan in its infancy. "You could get lockjaw!"

"And you could get broken-jaw," I hissed sotto voce, as she dragged me towards the surgery doors all the time keeping up a harangue about the stupidity of working in a veterinary surgery without getting regular tetanus jabs. And, fair enough, she had a point but you know, a time for everything . . .

"I'll see you Saturday, yeah?" Rocky waved a desultory hand, but the warning in his eyes was unmistakable. 'Let me down,' they said, 'and you'll wake up on Sunday morning to find an entire SWAT team camped on your doorstep.'

"Yeah," I confirmed in a voice made gratifyingly breathy and feminine by weakness. Had I Orla's baby blues I would have batted them. Had I a swan-like neck, it would have wilted. Unfortunately, my eyes were your common or garden washed-out denim-blue and my neck far from being swan-like could quite easily have been mistaken for the Eiffel Tower. Still, the voice was a bonus and I made up my mind to get bitten more often.

Outside, by happy coincidence, Rob, after a hard day's sheep-shagging, was just dropping Sophie off to pick up her own car.

"Yo, Soph!" Debbie dragged me across. "Gemma's just had half her hand amputated by a crazed poodle *and* she hasn't had a tetanus shot since Moses was a basket case! Any chance of a lift to the hospital?"

"Shit!" Sophie, looking none too pleased, shot me a look that would castrate a Spanish bull. "I was just looking forward to wrapping my lips round a nice cool Bud or two. Still, I suppose I can't just leave you to bleed to death, much and all as I'd like to. Hang on a mo till I fetch my keys from inside."

"We should have warned her," I told Debbie, as a few minutes later a slightly green-around-the-gills

Sophie re-emerged from the surgery, a bunch of car keys dangling limply from her hand.

"Y- you know who's in there?"

"Yup!" Putting on her Sergeant Major's cap, Debbie commandeered the keys and led the way to where Wanda, all steamed up with condensation, stood squatly on the drive. "We would have told you but as usual, before we had a chance to say Rocky Cashel, you were off and running like a sprung hare."

Sophie looked bewildered, as well she might, not even protesting when Debbie took it upon herself to be chauffeur. "But what . . ."

"It's a long story," I told her, as Debbie folded me into the car, pushing my head down like I was under arrest. "Get in and I'll give you the low-down."

"But, why just you?" Sophie asked as I came to the end of my narrative. "Like, Debs and I were your partners in crime, so to speak. It seems a mite unfair that we should get off scot-free."

I nodded, waving my bloody stump about like an escapee from the *Texas Chainsaw Massacre*. "I know, I've been thinking about that and all I can come up with is the humiliation factor." I struggled to explain. "I mean, you and Debs just thrashed him about a bit and, who knows, maybe he's one of those men who enjoys a damn good thrashing and who shells out wads of cash to women in patent leather catsuits on a regular basis. With me, though, there was that extra element, wasn't there? The stolen thrill? I mean, if he had been the instigator, there wouldn't be an issue. But, in the heel of the hunt, to use a very apt phrase, he was an unwilling participant in an act that made me very very happy but which just humiliated him. And now, I guess, it's payback time!" I flinched, as my stump throbbed painfully. "On the other hand, maybe he fancies the knickers off me and just wants me around for an action replay."

Debbie and Sophie laughed heartily at that, which I thought was a tad unnecessary. They were, after all, supposed to be my best friends, supportive, encouraging and gung-ho!

When we got to the hospital, Debbie dumped me with Sophie and headed off for the maternity unit.

"Just to see what I'm in for," she said, with a big stupid smile draped all over her face. When she came back, just after I'd had my rump punctured by a doctor whose favourite party game was probably pin the tail on the donkey, the smile had been replaced by a white sheet.

"Jesus!" Sophie, who'd been lolling in a most unladylike fashion on a nearby chair jumped to her feet. "You look like you've seen a ghost. Here, come and sit down!" Gently, she guided Debbie into her own vacated seat. "Now, tell us what's wrong!" But Debbie, it appeared, couldn't speak and I wondered if it was possible to catch lockjaw by proxy.

"Debs?" Gingerly, I touched her shoulder. Then, as that appeared to be having no effect and guessing that she was in shock, I walloped her so hard across the face her head rocked back and forth like Zebedee from *The Magic Roundabout*. "For goodness sake, Debs! Talk to us!"

"Yeah!" Sophie chipped in, shaking her until her teeth rattled. "Talk to us! Whatever's happened?"

Gradually, the white sheet crumpled. "I-it . . . it's Guy," Debbie hiccuped, tears coursing down her face like a waterfall down a hillside.

"Guy?" Sophie coaxed. "Well, what about him? Has he been in an accident or something?"

"He's not . . . dead, is he?" This, from me. Well, what other reason could there be for Debbie behaving like Mary at the foot of the Cross?

Debbie shook her head. "No, but he'll bloody wish he was when I get my hands on him!" The last vestiges of the white sheet completely disappeared to be immediately replaced by a mask of such hatred, such intense loathing, such evil intent that Sophie and I exchanged *really* worried glances. I mean, Debbie was normally the most peaceable of creatures. There wasn't a violent bone in the whole of her body (if you leave out the hunt-saboteur episode) yet here she was transformed all of a sudden into a cross between the Ayatollah and Idi Amin, all ready to cannibalise Guy.

"Look," Sophie suggested, waving a verbal flag of peace, "why don't you start at the very beginning?"

I nodded my agreement. "That's a very good place to start!"

"All right," Debbie sniffed, "but I warn you, I don't want to hear any 'I told you so's'!"

"Do you mind!" Sophie looked stricken that anyone might think she was capable of such a thing. I didn't! I knew I was not only capable but adept and a qualified practitioner. Hell, I had letters after my name and a brass plaque on the wall.

Debbie sniffed again, a long violent sniffle and I shuddered at the sound of all that catarrh being drawn back down her throat and sent up a silent prayer of gratitude that I didn't have to kiss her. "Well, you know I went off to visit the maternity wing?" We nodded, a nice Olympic gold-medal synchronisation of both our heads. "And it was great!" For some reason, Debbie looked defiant as if we were going to argue the toss with her. "A nurse took me round and showed me the ultra-sound scanner. That's the scan you have every so often to make sure all is progressing as it should and where they confuse the baby's finger with something else so that you go out and buy boy Pampers when you should be buying girl. Then she showed me the delivery suite, and all the monitors and things, and there was even a birthing chair if gravity was your bag and also a birthing pool."

"Wow!" Sophie tried for impressed, but just looked sick. I knew how she felt. It was the birthing-chair business. Oooh! Just the thought!

"Yeah, it was really cool." Debbie mistook our expressions for enthusiasm. "And then, as a kind of finale, she suggested I visit the nursery and see all the new-born babies . . ." Her voice not so much faltered as fell over, struck its head on the pavement and ended up in intensive care. "And that's when I saw Guy!"

"What? In the nursery!" Sophie looked outraged. "Don't tell me he's one of those pervs who likes dressing up in nappies and Babygros and things?"

Debbie bowed her head. There was defeat in the gesture. "No. No, it was worse than that, from my point of view anyway. He was visiting his wife." Her gaze rose, transfixed us both. "His wife and new-born twin sons, to be exact."

"Bastard!" Sophie and I said together, when we recovered from the shock, which, such was our faith in Guy Evans, took us all of about five seconds.

"Filthy rotten pervy wankering bastard!" That was Sophie.

"Moronic height-restricted vegetative-brained bollocksing bastard!" Me, again.

"Fucker!" Debbie, more succinct, twice as as effective, proving that sometimes less is definitely more.

"Did he see you?" I asked. "Did she?"

Sadly, Debbie shook her head. "No, they were too busy cooing over the two latest additions to their happy little Walton-family unit."

"You should have gone over and punched his lights out!" Sophie's face lit up. "Tell you what, point me in the right direction and I'll do it for you."

Debbie gave a wan little Mona Lisa smile. "And what good would that do? OK, so I might derive a certain amount of pleasure from watching him have his brains splattered all over the walls but, at the end of the day –"

"It's night!" I interjected from pure habit, only to receive a sharp kick on the shins from Sophie.

"At the end of the day," Debbie continued, with a steely look, "he'll go back to his wife and kids and I'll be left with nothing but Cloetus the Foetus and my dreams in tatters."

Cloetus the Foetus? Sophie and I exchanged glances and despite the pathos of the situation I could have sworn I saw a twinkle in her eye and felt an answering gleam in my own. Worse still, I could feel myself building up to a big 'I told you so' but, once again, an intuitive glance from Sophie stopped me in my tracks and probably saved my life. Slipping her arm around Debbie's shoulders, she gave a light comforting squeeze.

"Come on, kid," she said. "It's been a long day. Let's go home!"

CHAPTER 11

I was gutted for Debbie. I mean, Debbie was truly nice and I don't mean that in an insipid way. No, she was genuinely nice in the nicest possible sense, which made the fact that she always seemed to attract bad lots even more incomprehensible. Not, mind you, that I didn't attract my own share of bad lots – take Tony the Shite Artist, for example. Still, I didn't seem to have the same amount of bad luck as Debs. Now, the way I see it, there could be a couple of reasons for this: as in 1) I didn't excite the same amount of male attention and 2) – well, to be truthful, there is no 2). I wouldn't go so far as to say I'm no oil painting because more than one drunken oaf has remarked on my uncanny resemblance to *Whistler's Mother*. Debbie, though, is truly beautiful with the kind of Nicole Kidman Irish colleen looks that make it onto chocolate boxes and postcards with spinning wheels and shamrocks and shillelaghs. You know the type, all wavy auburn hair, buttermilk skin and eyes that put the 'ooh' in blue. Petite, without being a dwarf, you could put a sack on Debbie and she'd still look like a fashion plate. By the same token, you could put a million dollars on me and I'd still look like a dinner plate.

Now, Sophie, on the other hand is striking in a completely different way. Now, I wouldn't say she's horsey but you can't look at her without the words withers, flanks and hocks springing to mind. When it comes to height, you tend to think of her in hands as opposed to feet and inches and, following on with the equine theme, her hair is a mane of chestnut and her teeth, whilst narrowly escaping buck, aren't exactly backward at coming forward. Horse-dealers love her and tend to talk of her in terms of being a 'fine filly', an 'ideal foaler' or a 'great class of a mare'. At school, her nickname was Dessie, after Desert Orchid. I rest my case!

Me? Unremarkable is the first and only adjective that comes to mind. Dark brown hair without so much as a hint of red to burnish it, faded-blue-denim eyes, a mouth that the more generous amongst my acquaintances have described as Julia Robertesque but which the more honest have simply labelled big. I am saved by my legs, though, which are long and well-shaped although the effect is somewhat marred by the overhang of my backside which on a premenstrual day can play tag with the back of my knees. Ditto, my stomach. All seven of them!

I digress. To get back to Debbie, I was really gutted for her although the commonsense aspect of me felt she'd had a close shave and should be thanking her lucky stars. Another part of me, the illogical though not to be ignored part, the 'if-only' part, felt more than a teensy-weensy bit guilty. If *only* Rocky Cashel hadn't come to the surgery. If *only* Gretchen hadn't relieved me of half my hand. If *only* Debbie wasn't such a caring, nurturing friend that she had to accompany me to the hospital. If *only* she hadn't taken it into her head to visit the maternity ward. If *only* Guy Evans hadn't impregnated his wife with twin sons. You get the picture? If *only* Guy Evans hadn't impregnated Debbie! If *only* the bastard had kept it in his trousers/worn a condom/was sterile/was a eunuch/was a million miles away!

* * *

"What am I going to do?"

Debbie hadn't shown up for work the next day and so I'd gone round later, dragged her out for a walk and from underneath the solicitous gaze of her family who thought she was labouring under a heavy cold – hence the red eyes and serial sniffing episodes. "Well, Gem? Got any bright ideas?"

"Apart from strangling Guy Evans with his own penis, assuming it would stretch that far? None!"

"I still love him." Debbie shot me a mutinous look from the corner of a bloodshot eye. "You can't just stop loving somebody. Not just like that! Not even when they've ripped your heart out and kicked it about like an old football."

"Oh," I said. Just 'oh' because as far as I was concerned that was a load of cobblers. Like, I loved Tony once. No, I'll brook no arguments. I did! I really did! Man, I thought he had it going on. I thought he was the spider's gonads but as soon as I caught him with Primrose the Prossie, it was a case of gonad, gonad, gone! Love was a four-letter word beginning with F. And if I did have the odd hanker in the early days, then it was only through force of habit and as everyone knows the best way of curing one habit is to develop another. Which is why I now make a point of picking and flicking several times a day.

"I thought he loved me too," Debbie said, a little catch in her voice. "He said he did."

"Yeah, and Clinton said he was innocent and we all know what a great fat porky that was."

Irritated, Debbie pucked me hard in the soft part of the arm. "For Chrissakes, Gemma! Can we leave Clinton out of this and concentrate on matters closer to home? I mean, you're supposed to be my best friend, my comfort in the storm, my sounding board and uncritical-at-all-times ally." She pucked me again, a mean look coming into her eyes. "Mind you, you never liked Guy, did you? You and Sophie? You thought he was a tosser." The last was said on a note of such incredulity that anyone would have thought he was the

Child of Prague instead of a no-good adulterous bastard who had strung her along for months on end with empty promises and a tissue of lies. *And* put her in the club!

"No," I agreed, moving out of pucking range. "You're right. I can't stand him and I can't pretend I'm surprised that he's running true to form. You've heard of senile dementia? Well, Guy Evans has penile dementia and next year there'll be another Debbie bawling her eyes out and the year after there'll be another and then another and so on and so forth till such time as the only stiffy he gets will be via rigor mortis. And who knows, even then he'll probably put in the odd spirited performance."

"Could be she tricked him into it?" On the Richter scale of gullibility Debbie was clearly going up for maximum points.

"Mm, and I'm the Blessed Virgin!"

"Well, it's not unheard of."

Swinging round, I grabbed her by both her shoulders. "Read my lips, Debs. She did not trick him into anything. You saw how they were carrying on in the hospital. According to you, the Holy Family in the stable couldn't have been more into Jesus than those two into their twins. If there was any trickery afoot then it was Guy, tricking you."

She dashed a tear away. I could see it glinting in the moonlight, the residue leaving a silver snail-trail upon her cheek. "What am I going to do?" Her hand reached down, caressed her stomach. "This wasn't how it was meant to be. I've never been an advocate of single parenthood. All that stiff upper-lipping it and brave-little-woman trash leaves me cold. Coping twenty-four-seven on your own, eating fish-finger leftovers, getting fat, bloated and depressed with the moral majority only too ready to jump on the bandwagon and blame you for all society's ills." Angrily, she brushed another tear away. "God! It doesn't bear thinking about."

I refrained from reminding her that had she been successful in her attempt to lure Guy away, that's exactly the fate to which she would have been condemning his wife, Brigitte.

"How far along are you?" I asked.

Debbie did a quick tot up on her fingers. "Between four and five weeks, I reckon. Why?"

"Because, these days you have options."

Debbie regarded me suspiciously. "Oh, yeah and just exactly what options did you have in mind?"

Stalling for time, I found myself developing a sudden, hitherto totally unknown, interest in the constellations of the night sky. "Isn't that the Great Bear?" I said, pointing vaguely in the general direction of the moon. "Isn't that the Milky Way?" More vague pointing. "Isn't that Uranus?" I pointed to Debbie's rear end.

"Ge-mm-ah!" Debbie came to a sudden stop. "Cut the bullshit! I said, just exactly what options did you have in mind?"

"Oh, you know . . ." I made vacuuming motions with my hand which, admittedly, was in extremely bad taste as were the suction noises I followed up with.

"Jesus!" Debbie sprang to life and clocked me one round the side of the head. "Abortion! You want me to have an abortion! Really, Gemma, how could you be so bloody heartless?"

"Whoah!" Holding up my forearm, I deflected her next wallop. "I never said I wanted you to have an abortion – I was merely pointing it out as one of the options. You said you weren't interested in single parenthood – ergo, abortion is an option. Of course, so is adoption an option. And, if push comes to shove, there's always the option of setting up home with Sophie."

"Sophie! What the bloody hell has she got to do with anything?"

I shrugged. "Nothing if you don't want her to. Everything, if you do! Like she'd make a wonderful father." Then, as Debbie looked completely blank, "Oh, catch up, Debs! Don't say you haven't noticed she's completely potty about you?"

"Me? Sophie? Potty about me? Oh, don't be so daft! Soph is a friend – your friend, my friend – but that's all." She giggled a little, half-hysterically, I thought. "Sophie and me? Like that? I don't think so."

"Well, I must admit I prefer the opposite sex myself," I said. "Still, if I had to choose a woman, I'd definitely give Sophie due care and consideration."

"Well, I wouldn't." Debbie knitted her lips in disapproval. "Women don't do anything for me in that department. Never did! Never will! And that goes ditto for Sophie!"

"Fair enough! But your options are getting fewer by the minute."

"There's one you haven't thought of . . ."

"Oh, yes!" I jumped in. "You could always abandon the poor little mite on the steps of the local hospital or church or such like and hope it doesn't freeze to death before a good Samaritan happens along."

"No! I could always tell Guy!" She narrowed her eyes. "After all, we've condemned him without a hearing. For all we know he could very well prove himself the fine gallant and come rushing to my side bearing economy-size tubs of Cow & Gate and staggering under the weight of large maintenance cheques."

"You *cannot* be serious!" Violently I shook my head. "No way, Debbie. The only thing that would accomplish would be to screw up the lives of another innocent woman and her *five* children." I held up my hand, fingers splayed. "*Five*, Debbie!"

Debbie jerked her shoulder away as though I were suffering from the plague and dying to pass it on. "God, you're so sodding sanctimonious. Who died and made you keeper of the nation's morals, that's what I'd like to know? What about *my* life being screwed up? Eh? You're not so bothered about that, are you?"

"Of course I am," I blustered. "It's just that Brigitte's babies are, like, already here whilst yours is . . . yours is . . ."

"Still incubating?"

"No, still just a bundle of cells. You know, it's barely past the egg stage. There's probably bits of the shell still sticking to it. It's not quite human yet. It hasn't got a soul." All right, so I was a bit short on the old tact but, hey, I meant it for the best.

Debbie, though, didn't see it quite that way. "You know what you can do, Gemma? You can go screw yourself, that's what you can do. You can piss off with yourself!" Stabbing herself vigorously in the chest with her forefinger, her head kept time like a metronome. "I don't need your advice. This is *my* problem and I'll sort it out for myself. Savvy?"

"I'm sorry," I said, because she was right. What right had I got to take the moral high ground with anybody? Me, the Blessington rapist? "You know I'll support you in whatever you decide to do."

"Will you, Gemma?" The knife of hostility was immediately sheathed, the blade wiped down and put away for a future day. "Will you really? No matter what I decide?" Debbie looked suddenly very much younger than her twenty-six years, vulnerable as the unborn baby who had suddenly taken on all the characteristics of an unwanted squatter about to be served with eviction papers.

I linked my arm through hers. "Sure thing, kiddo," I

said, hoping to God I could follow through on my promise. "Sure thing!"

* * *

Saturday came round with the speed of a junkie for his next bottle of methadone. I was nervous. I was excited. I was bloody shitting myself. The first problem, I decided, rummaging in my wardrobe, was what to wear. Definitely not the wet-look rubber catsuit I'd liberated from a Soho sex shop one very drunken weekend away in London and which Tony said made me look like an escapee from a remould tyre factory. Strange, but I'd never managed to feel quite the same about it after that. Like, when I bought it, I'd had vague images of Uma Thurman and Cat Woman. I'd seen myself as sleek, sensuous, kick-ass gorgeous, number one on every red-blooded male's wish list and nowhere, but nowhere, had Dunlop featured! Still, I couldn't quite bring myself to offload it to the local charity shop quite just yet either. I mean, you know what the women are like in those places! Talk about the speed of light – before you know it they'd have me pegged as Ireland's answer to Madam Sin and Miss Whiplash all rolled into one and try explaining that to your mother!

Next to come under my scrutiny was a remnant from my Laura Ashley period, a puff-sleeved, full-skirted floral number which I'd somehow managed to kid myself would make me look dainty. It didn't! It just made me look like Bo-Peep on steroids. Not so much

160

diabolical as anabolical, if you get my drift. Eventually I decided to play it safe and settled on a white cotton shirt and denim jeans that matched my eyes. Like you can't be too rich, too thin or have too many white cotton shirts. *Cosmo* does whole features on white cotton shirts. You know the type of thing. *Our fashion editor took a white cotton shirt from twelve leading manufacturers and gave them marks out of ten for style, wearability and economy blah de blah de blah* . . . And I read them all and then go out and buy the winner, even if I've already got enough white cotton shirts to clothe a whole troupe of Mormons. Cuban-heeled, black tooled-leather cowboy boots completed the outfit, a nice touch, I thought, considering Rocky's mind-frame at the moment. Maybe he'd be so bowled over by my Annie Oakley look that he might even cast me as the love interest in *Young Guns. His* lurve interest! A slick of lipstick (Nearly Nude as, with my wide mouth, anything brighter makes me look like a prime candidate for a slasher move) and a touch of mascara and I was ready for the off, my hair swinging *au naturel* around my shoulders to hide my sticky-out ears. I swear, if ever I win the lottery the first thing I'll do is have my ears pinned back so I can wear my hair up without everybody thinking I'm a plane coming in to land. Then, I might think about having a mouth reduction, liposuction on my stomach, buttocks and thighs, upper arms and neck and, if there's anything left, have laser treatment for that tattoo on my left breast that seemed like such a good idea last summer. Because I'd wanted to make a statement! Do you get me? I mean, I couldn't just open my gob and make a statement like everybody else. No way! Too simple! No, *I* had to have it tattooed in a circle round my nipple. *Tony Forever!* Tony forever, my ass! *And* it had hurt like hell!

"Can I come?" Orla, wearing not much more than a pout, was waiting for me at the foot of the stairs.

"No," I snapped, annoyed because next to her I suddenly felt like Baloo from *The Jungle Book,* all big bum and shambling walk. I swear I could feel my jeans expand by sixteen sizes and the cellulite start to pop out all over my skin like an eruption of boils.

"Why?" The pout turned down at the corners and I was reminded of that horrible kid from *Just William.* *'I'll thweam and I'll thweam and I'll thweam!'*

"Because," I said which, admittedly, was hardly a satisfactory answer.

"Because what?"

"Because you're not invited."

Orla shrugged dismissively. "Oh, that doesn't matter." She twitched the hem of her micro-mini so that it flew up and revealed a butt-cheek no bigger than a sparrow's and with a lot less meat. "He's not likely to stand on ceremony as soon as he sees *me!*"

"That reminds me," my eyebrows semaphored cynicism, "I forgot to feed Furbee."

Desperation forced her to ignore the insult. "Well, *can* I come?"

"That," I quipped, "is a matter for your gynaecologist. Your sex-life isn't of the remotest interest to me."

"Ha, bleedin ha! Goldie Hawn you ain't." Orla's patience, like the rest of her, was wearing thin.

So was mine! "Yeah, and Father bleedin Christmas I ain't either, so piss off and sling yer 'ook!"

"Pig!" Orla reverted to kind. "Look at the state of those boots. What are you going to do, line-dance him to death?"

Swatting her aside, I made for the front door. "No," I said coolly, "I'm going to shag him to death. Shame you can't join us but, well, two's company and all that!"

"Bitch!" Orla expended several thousand calories jumping up and down with rage (so you see, it's an ill wind that blows nobody any good!). "I hope you choke to death on a condom!"

"I can think of worse ways to go," I told her, slamming the door behind me and almost amputating her size-three foot in the process. "Like puking yourself to death, for instance!"

* * *

Rocky's girlfriend, Laura, was no great shakes which surprised, delighted and heartened me, making me feel that all things were possible in this great big wide world of ours, including luring him away from her clutches. When she opened the door to me I thought she must be the maid. Don't ask me why. It's not as if I've ever met a real live maid before, no one round our way ever having had need of one and to tell the truth I thought, as a species, the Dyson had put an end to them.

"Hi," I said, trying to establish an impression of pleasant but not too familiar. I knew from a recent rerun of *Upstairs Downstairs* that it didn't do to hobnob with them-below-stairs too much as it only confused them about their place in the pecking order and made them reluctant to empty your chamberpot. "You must be the maid. I'm Gemma."

"Hi, yourself." She stepped back to allow me entry. "I'm Laura, Rocky's girlfriend."

"Oh, God," I began, scarlet to the tips of my ears – my bat ears, "I'm really sorry."

Laura shrugged. "Don't worry. I'm used to it. I mean, it's not as if I fit the rock-chick stereotype – all peroxide, Ray-Bans and spike heels, is it? Still, that's what makes Rocky so special. He loves me for who I am and doesn't fall for all that music business hype. No, Rocky is very much his own man. No one can tell him how to think. He's got his own ideas and marches to the beat of his own drum." She smiled, a gesture which lent her the fleeting semblance of prettiness. So fleeting, blink and you'd miss it! "In other words, he doesn't give a four-x what anybody thinks of him."

"Oh," I said. "Glad to hear it." Actually I *was* glad to hear it. *Very* glad! If he was that unconventional he might yet come round to thinking yours truly was the best thing since 98% fat-free chocolate, give *her* the push and move me in.

But Laura, though plain as the proverbial pikestaff, was no fool, immediately divining what was on my mind and not so subtly letting me know as much. "I can't tell you how tiring it is to have women constantly chucking themselves at his head. Honestly, they seem to think that because I'm not Cynthia Crawford and a size ten that gives them carte blanche to elbow me out of the way. As if I'm nothing! As if my feelings don't count! I wouldn't mind but Rocky and I go all the way back as far as kindergarten." She made a little moue. "Anyway, what about you? Do you have a boyfriend?"

I shook my head. "Did have, but then Primrose cowface Barry came along and the writing was on the Kama Sutra."

Laura patted my arm. "You see," she commiserated. "Other women are a woman's worst enemy. I'm sure that little bitch never gave a thought to your feelings, did she?"

"Big bitch! Big *fat* bitch! And no, I don't suppose she did."

"And I'm sure, knowing how you yourself felt, you'd never do the dirty on another woman, would you?"

The cute hoor! Too late I saw where she was going. She was making an ally of me and let's face it, it's hard to stab someone in the back when you're round the front shaking their bloody hand. Following her into what I supposed to be the living-room I gave a noncommittal grunt, very glad that I did when my eyes lit on Rocky who was lolling on a massive settee, naked torso'ed and leather-trousered. Well, come on, you'd have to be out of your tiny mind not to want to take a pop at him. That Laura had her work cut out for her. Man, talk about a leaky gusset! I swear I'd Niagara Falls in my knickers!

"Ah, lookee here!" Lazily his eyes drifted over me, starting a little, I thought, when they reached my cowboy boots and I knew I'd been right to wear them. "Hey y'all, say howdee to Gemma, the world's number one expert on pink-eye in poodles." Y'all was a motley collection of what were presumably band members and hangers-on, more than half of whom appeared to be on another planet as evidenced by the large pile of coke they were busy despatching up their nostrils. Members of the Inner Septum, one and all!

"Chill!" a James Dean look-alike, only with dark hair, instructed, patting the empty space beside him on a chaise longue. "Come and tell me all about pink-eye in poodles. Is it similar to scrapie in sheep?"

Rocky grinned. "Gemma, meet Tyrell O'Neill. Tyrell's into sheep in a big way. So much so, his greatest ambition in life is to become a sheep farmer off in the wilds of Donegal or somewhere."

"Well, it's not such a *baa'd* life." Tyrell ran a hand through his James Dean quiff. "Better than all this anyway." From the accompanying shake of his head it was unclear as to whether he meant the people or the room, which, let the truth be told, was a nightmare mixture of mock-Gothic and contemporary. Laurence Llewellyn-Bowen of *Changing Rooms* fame would have had a fit. Either that or tried to wear the curtains!

"Yeah, well, give me the bright lights every time." Rocky pulled a passing Laura down onto his lap and kissed her soundly on the lips. "There's no way you'd find me reclusing it up in the back of beyond."

"Nor me!" I jumped in straight away anxious to demonstrate our compatibility and hoping the raw envy wasn't too obvious on my face. "Let there be lights is my motto, and plenty of 'em."

"Oh, I don't know so much about that." Beneath the perm from hell, Laura showed she had a mind of her own. She shot Rocky a coy look and somehow the cast in her left eye didn't seem to matter. "It depends on who you're reclusing it up with." Bitch! Why couldn't I have said that! Why couldn't I have been the one to make the front of his trousers rise up like a Mexican Wave?

Anxiously the Tyrell guy leaned across as if my answer really mattered to him, as if I had it in my power to make or break his day. Maybe even his life! "So, what do *you* think of scrapie then, Gemma?"

"I like it," I quipped, "but I couldn't eat a whole one!" Everyone laughed, although Laura's laughter didn't quite reach her eyes and a moment later she swiftly put paid to any delusions I might have had about being Miss Edinburgh Festival Comic 2000.

"So, Gemma, do you think you'll cope with

Gretchen? Only she doesn't take to everyone, you know. Personally, I like to think it's because she's a good judge of character. The canine persuasion usually are, aren't they?" I didn't miss the way her eyes slid slyly towards my bandaged fingers. "I mean, they sense things about people."

I shrugged. "Maybe, but on the other hand, could be they're just bitchy!" More laughter, but only from the men.

Laura cast a disparaging cast over me. "You do *like* poodles, I take it, Gemma?"

"Love 'em but –"

"She couldn't eat a whole one!" This, in tandem, from both Rocky and Tyrell who immediately set about slapping their thighs and each other's backs, a physical manifestation presumably, of delight in their own wit.

"Shut up, you two!" Laura turned a mottled shade of red bordering on puce, which clashed horribly with the ginger freckles adorning every square inch of her face. (Listen, when I said she was no great shakes, I was understating the case!) "This is important! Gretchen is like my own child. I'm not going to leave her with just anyone, you know. Which reminds me, Gemma, what references have you got? I hope you don't subscribe to the paraquat school of discipline? I mean, you hear such dreadful stories."

"The parawhat?" I asked innocently as if, only hours before, I hadn't been plotting Gretchen's demise by that very method. A nice big steak, I'd thought, liberally laced with paraquat!

"Oh, don't be ridiculous!" To my amazement, Rocky, whose memory seemed suddenly to have short-circuited, came to my defence. "Gemma's one of the good guys. Her business is saving life. Now, are we going or what?"

"Going?" I asked, aware that my mouth had dropped to a level where I could quite easily have kicked my tonsils into goal. "You're going somewhere? Like, today?"

"Well, why not? There's no reason for us to stay in, is there?" Laura managed to convey an amazement akin to Neil Armstrong discovering the WI already in residence on the moon and swapping recipes for quiche lorraine. "I mean, now that we've got you to take care of Gretchen."

"N – no," I stammered. "Of course not. It's just that I thought there might be a kind of hand-over period?"

"Why? You're the veterinary expert. We wouldn't dream of telling you how to do your job." Laura looked sly or it might simply have been the effect of that damned cast. "Besides, you won't be entirely alone. Tyrell will keep you company, won't you, Tyrell?"

"Yeah, sure." The aspiring sheep-farmer nodded enthusiastically. "I'm just getting over a bad bout of flu, so I'm giving the next few gigs a miss." An eager light in his eye, he drew closer on the settee. "Now, Gemma, tell me this and tell me no more, what are your thoughts on green scour, scurvy and liver fluke?"

CHAPTER 12

"Jesus! You look like a woman who could use a drink."
Sophie was already in residence at the Fox's Retreat
when, wild of hair and wilder of eye, I reeled in late on
Sunday evening after a hectic weekend spent sparring
with Gretchen.

"Understatement of the year," I moaned. "Just set up
a drip, my girl, and keep it coming."

"That bad?" Obligingly Sophie signalled for a bottle
of Bud and then another, as ripping the first out of her
hand, I poured it in one fluid movement down my throat.

"Ah! That's better." Wiping the back of my hand
across my mouth, I shot her a grin that was more like a
rictus. "It were 'orrible, Soph. Truly 'orrible. Not only
did I spend the entire weekend chasing after the bitch-
poodle-from-hell but I found myself at the mercy of a
James Dean look-alike with scrapie on the brain."

"Good God!" Sophie pretended shock. "That can be
very nasty. Has he seen a doctor?"

"It's not a doctor he needs," I muttered. "It's a

bloody shrink!" Bitterly, I let my gaze roam around the bar, galloping swiftly on as it happened upon on an elderly gent intent on digging the wax from his ear by dint of a cocktail stick that had lately played host to an olive. I hoped to God he'd dispose of it in the bin and not leave it lying around where some poor drunk might easily mistake it for a piece of cheese.

"But, James Dean?" Sophie mused. "You used to have a poster of him on your wall once, didn't you? The rebel without a cause."

"Yeah, but I replaced it with Rocky."

"Oh, yeah," Sophie grinned. "The singer without a note! Anyway, I gather you couldn't do that quite so easily this weekend?"

"You gather right!" I said, peering down the neck of my bottle of lager, for no other reason than that I could. "There wasn't much chance of that with the lovely Laura around."

"What?" Sophie's face lit up as it always did at the mention of an attractive woman. "So, she's a babe, is she? How is she in the chest department?"

"Chest awful," I punned. "Seriously though, next to her, I felt like Sharon Stone."

"I always feel like Sharon Stone," Sophie mused. "Do you remember that film she was in with Michael Douglas when –"

"She uncrossed her legs and she wasn't wearing any knickers. Yes, I do," I groaned, "but unlike you, it didn't leave *me* with any basic instincts."

Sophie took an appreciative sip of her own Bud. "Well, it did me and it's become one of *my* favourite fantasies – although occasionally I substitute it for one or two from *My Secret Garden*."

"God, do you remember that?" I could feel the weariness of twenty-something-hood slip from me like a shroud, felt once more the pre-teen horniness of the twelve-year-old desperate to get her hands on a copy of Nancy Friday's much-coveted book of women's secret sexual fantasies. Other missives I'd been desperate to get my hands on included *The Story of O* (never did get it, still want it so if you see it, let me know), *Lady Chatterley's Lover* (much hyped and nowhere near as much nookie as expected) and *Oranges Are Not The Only Fruit* (what the hell was all that about?) – anything in fact that held the merest hint of sexual activity. In the movie department I'd yearned to see *Last Tango in Paris* and *Emanuelle,* numbers 1,2,3,4,5,6 and on to infinity. Not that I understood the half of what was going on, of course, not to mention all those big Latin words – heck, look how I cocked up Horatio with fellatio in the school play. There was also a joke doing the rounds at the time – fly Cunnilingus, the Irish Airline – I was twenty before I understood that one. Still, once I got over the fact that he wore pale-blue Farrah slacks with a permanent crease down the front, Tony went a long way towards improving that side of my education. Mind you, I soon got him out of those and into skin-tight denim jeans. In fact, at one time, I virtually made a career out of getting him in and out of his trousers.

"It's amazing how many women have lesbian fantasies." Sophie broke in on my thoughts.

"Not me!" I asserted roundly, just in case desperation forced her to try and shift me. "I'm 100% hetero. Like I can't even bear to look at myself down *there*, let alone another woman."

"What?" Sophie looked scandalised. "You mean you've never got out the mirror and had a good old poke around!"

"No!" I could feel myself colouring up to the roots of my bat ears, because I *had* and shock, horror, found Rolf Harris staring back at me which was enough to put me off for life and make me suspect every male lover I'd ever had of harbouring homosexual tendencies. Okay, so admittedly I'd been a bit drunk at the time and it was just after I'd watched a documentary about all these women who sat around stark naked gazing at their own and each other's private parts. Because, apparently, you weren't a *real* woman unless you could face your vulva with aplomb and shake hands with your clitoris and sundry other clitorises or clitorii or whatever the plural is. Mind you, the after-effects lived with me for a very long time and it was years before I could listen to 'Tie Me Kangaroo Down' without a quick recce to make sure the sound wasn't coming from my knickers. Honest to God, that Rolf Harris gets everywhere. Every time you turn on the box, he's there! Every time you look at your box, he's there! And I, in my innocence, thought that whenever people spoke of him coming

173

from 'down under', they meant Australia. I know better now and if ever there was a conclusive argument for Philishave – he's it!

"I call mine Gertie," Sophie said, demonstrating that she and the mirror technique were old friends. "Dirty Gertie!"

"Really?" I said dryly. "Well, thank you for sharing that with me, Soph. Like that bit of information has really enriched my life and filled in the gaps in my knowledge!"

Sophie sniffed. "Oh don't be so anally retentive, Gemma. Loosen your stays, girl, and get with the programme!"

"Do you mind if I don't?" I said. "Only I want to wallow in my misery a bit longer. I reckon I deserve at least that much."

"Why?" Sophie went into belligerent mode. "Just because you can't pull some cruddy rock star whose songs are at the best puerile and at the worst downright crap."

"His songs are *not* crap," I protested vehemently. "They've got . . ." What the bloody hell was that word Rocky used? Oh yeah, subtext! "They've got, like, subtext."

"Subtext, my ass!" Sophie hooted crudely. "It's the Emperor's New Clothes, Gemma, can't you see that? There's nothing there really, no substance, only hype put out by a very clever marketing team determined to part you and every other feeble-minded female from her pounds, shillings and pence."

"Just because I don't like kd. lang!" I huffed.

"Just because you're homophobic!" Sophie huffed harder.

"I am not! If I was, what the hell would I be doing sitting here with you?"

"Well, misery loves company!" Sophie made a sweeping motion towards the barman signalling our urgent need for a couple more bottles of Bud.

I gazed at her suspiciously. "Why? What have you got to be miserable about?" As if being a) a lesbian and b) an Irish lesbian wasn't bad enough.

Running a manly hand through her hair, Sophie shifted uncomfortably about on the hard bar stool. "Oh, nothing! Everything! Debbie, if you must know!"

"Debbie?"

"Yes, Debbie!" Sophie spread her hands and half the pub thought there was a power cut. "Look, Gem, I'll come clean. I really fancy her. No, fancy is not the right word. I really *love* her!" Keeping her face averted, she waited for my reaction. I was aware that she had stopped breathing so it was imperative not to keep her waiting too long for a response.

"I know," I said with just the right amount of significant pause and trying hard not to sound smug that I had already sussed long ago in which direction that particular wind was blowing.

"You do?" She started to breathe again, but only just. "So, you're not disgusted then?"

"Not in the least!" I was proud of myself for

sounding all liberal and hedonistic. "I think you'd make a great couple – much better than her and Guy the Sly, anyway. Only thing is, Debbie's hasn't got a gay bone in her entire body!"

"And yet she wears the collar of her shirt turned up sometimes which is, you know, kind of like a signal."

I looked at Sophie as though she'd suddenly grown long brown ears and a tail. "Signal? What signal?"

"Oh, you know, it's a lesbian thing. Gay guys wear bunches of keys hanging out of the left-hand loop of their jeans pocket, ditto handkerchiefs and pink triangles. Lesbians aren't just about shaved heads and Doc Martens, you know. They often wear the collar of their shirt turned up."

"Noooh!" I was appalled, principally because I, myself, had on occasion been known to turn up the collar on my shirt but as a fashion statement and totally innocent of *that* particular subtext. "That's just a load of old cobblers. Debbie's as straight as a die and man-mad even when she was at nursery school. There was one little chap, in particular, whose life was made a misery by her wanting to play doctors and nurses every playtime. In the end his parents came into the school and complained that if he grew up to be a Nancy-boy it would be all her fault for putting him off women at such an early age."

Sophie giggled but wasn't to be deterred. "Despite what you think, lesbianism isn't necessarily genetic, Gemma. Oh, I know it is in *my* case. I mean look at the size of my hands – talk about the bucket on a crane – I mean, I couldn't be anything else! But some women choose it as a lifestyle."

"Well, I've got big hands," I said defensively. "American men always get excited when they see me because, at first sight, it looks as though I'm wearing a baseball mitt."

Sophie shook her head. "No, your hands are long and slender and very definitely feminine. You'd see what I mean if only you'd let your nails grow a bit and stop snacking on them."

"Well, they're low calorie and fill a gap," I said, spreading my digits before me and examining them like they were a rare find that had suddenly turned up on the *Antiques Road Show*. "Hey, you really think they're feminine?"

"Mmm," Sophie confirmed but, to my chagrin, seemed reluctant to waste any more time massaging my ego. "But to get back to Debbie, on a scale of one to ten, how would you rate my chances?"

"Why don't you ask her yourself?" I said, catching sight of Debbie's reflection in the *Chivas Regal Whisky* mirror behind the bar, as she stood there casting about the place, presumably for us.

Sophie's eyes followed mine. "Shush!" She dug me hard in the ribs. "Not a word, all right?"

"Have it your own way." I turned and waved a beckoning hand till Debbie caught sight of it and started pushing her way through the throng of hardened drinkers, parting them with an expert elbow like the waves of the Red Sea. "But what do you think she is, psychic?"

"All in good time," Sophie muttered urgently, as Debbie neared her goal, "all in good time."

And what if there's never a good time I wanted to ask her. What if you're just setting yourself up for rejection? Because *I* know how that feels. I know how it feels to be rejected for a woman who wears dresses so tight her gynae can perform an internal without her taking off a stitch. I know how it feels to have your heart turned into a colander by the well-aimed trampling of a high-heeled shoe. I didn't, of course, because not only had Debbie successfully negotiated her way to the bar but I wasn't so sure Sophie wanted to hear it anyway.

"Here, Debs," Sophie slipped off her seat. "Never let it be said I wouldn't give up my seat for a pregnant woman."

"Thanks." Debbie made quite a performance of climbing up on the stool which I thought might be due to a number of things. One – the bar stool was high and she was short. Two – she was getting in a bit of practice for when she turned into a hippo. Three – she was looking for the jilted-girlfriend-up-the-duff sympathy vote.

"Are you all right?" Well, surprise, surprise, Sophie opted for number three and went straight into concerned expectant father mode like she was born to

the role. "Sure?" she asked as Debbie made brave little
I'll-cope-with-whatever-life-chucks-at-me noises, like
morning sickness, stretch-marks and leaky breasts, as
well as becoming a pariah amongst society in general.

"What would you like to drink, Debs?" I asked,
reaching out a steadying hand as she looked as though
she was about to topple off again.

"I'd *like* a double Bacardi and coke," Debbie said
pointedly, hooking her feet around the wooden
crossbar of the bar stool for stability, "but I'll *have* a
glass of Ballygowan mineral water, please." A halo
pulsated brightly around her head.

"One BeeGee coming up," I said, resisting the urge
to genuflect. "Now wait till I tell you about the weekend
from hell."

"Couldn't have been any worse than mine." Debbie
wrinkled her nose and prepared for a spot of one-
upmanship. "Vomit? You could float a small boat on
what I threw up this morning. Honest to God, the house
was awash – bed, carpets, toilet-pan. It was all I could
do to stop my mother from calling out every emergency
service including the AA and the Red Berets."

"Really?" Sophie looked fascinated and it struck me
how right that old adage was about love being blind,
though I don't recall anything anywhere about losing
your sense of smell. "I thought that was supposed to
ease off after a couple of weeks or so."

"Yeah, right!" Debbie looked pleased at Sophie's
ignorance, no doubt because it gave her a chance to

expound further on the trials and tribulations of impending motherhood. "No, it's usually around the three-month mark and, believe me, Cloetus ain't half making his presence felt in the meantime."

"Poor you!" Sophie sympathised and I could tell she was itching to envelop Debbie in an all-encompassing there-there-it'll-be-all-right bear hug.

I sent her a warning eye. *Snare* not *scare* was the watchword! "So, what did you tell your mother? Surely she must have guessed by now?"

Debbie shrugged. "No! She was convinced I was back on the old anorexic/bulimic trail. I felt really bad about misleading her because she went through hell with all that before but well, let's face it, no matter which way I turn, I'm buggered."

"Look," I said, "I don't mean to seem like I'm on your case all the time but you're going to have to make some hard and fast decisions pretty soon. I mean, you do realise, don't you, that the longer Cloetus is *in situ* the fewer your options become."

Banging down her glass, Debbie sent me a cyanide glare. "Bloody hell, would you believe it? She's back on the abortion ticket again. Talk about a one-track mind! Someone should inform the Pope, have her excommunicated or something!"

"That's not fair!" I gritted my teeth. "I know telling it like it is isn't going to win me any popularity votes but I care about you, Debbie. I *really* care!"

"Like I don't!" Sophie looked aggrieved.

"I didn't say that!" I said. "But the time has come for some straight talking. Pussy-footing around the issue isn't going to get us anywhere. So, Debs, what are you going to do?"

"I don't sodding well know what I'm going to do!" Debbie's voice rose causing heads to swivel in our direction and eyes to light up at the prospect of some free entertainment being thrown in along with the chicken-in-a-basket. "Sometimes I think I'm going off my bloody head. One minute, I want it, want it so desperately I've already put down its name for Trinity College and chosen its career as a rocket scientist. The next, I want to take a tip off Jack the Ripper, dive into my abdomen and rip it out with my bare hands."

"And what about Guy?" I asked, wading in where angels feared to tread and mentally covering my head with my arms as a defence against the inevitable fall-out. To my surprise it never came.

"What about Guy?" Debbie's face looked set, a little pale but surprisingly composed. "Actually, there *is* no Guy any more. I finished with him last night."

Sophie and I exchanged glances.

"What, the gutless bastard let you down, you mean?" Outrage draped itself across Sophie's face like a flag across Guy's coffin – the one she was seeing in her mind's eye, heavy oak with a zinc lining, imaginatively finished off with chains and a very large, very complicated padlock.

Debbie shook her head. "No. No, I didn't tell him."

Her eyes met mine. "Gemma's right. I'd never be happy on the back of someone else's misery and let's face it, Brigitte and the children are the innocents in all this – even if I did try to kid myself that she's a nasty cow who doesn't deserve him." She sighed, the long despairing sigh of a woman who has faced the truth and found it left her not stronger but with a very bad taste in her mouth and an even stronger desire to go back to being an ostrich. "Not that there's any guarantee he'd leave her for me. You two never thought so anyway, did you?"

Put on the spot, both Sophie and I maintained a diplomatic silence for a moment or two before, with a slight nervous clearing of her throat, Sophie jumped back into the fray.

"So, what now? Like, he's bound to notice you getting bigger and bigger, put two and two together and not come up with a helium balloon."

"Well, I'll just have to get another job then, won't I? Not that many employers will take me on when they discover I'm up the spout and that they're going to have to shell out for maternity leave before the ink is dry on my contract of employment. God, the scales are already tipped against you if you're female – make that female *and* of childbearing age and you're practically unemployable."

Sophie snorted. "Yes, well, the scales have always been tipped against women. That's why, in my own small way, I'm trying to redress the balance."

"But you're sure about this?" I asked, talking over Sophie's Pankhurstian protestations on behalf of womankind. Give her another few minutes and she'd have padlocked herself to the bar and produced a big placard out of thin air! "Not telling Guy, I mean? What happens a few years down the road when Cloetus wants to know who his daddy is?"

"I won't tell him. Or I'll make up some story or other about him being the result of a one-night stand, or the contents of a turkey baster, maybe."

"But that's foul!" I was horrified. "A child has the right to know who its parents are!"

"Oh, come on," Sophie looked aghast. "No one, but no one, would want to know Guy Evans is their father. In this case ignorance is definitely bliss."

"I don't agree," I said, taking the moral high ground. The cheek of me, playing devil's advocate! "Besides, there are other more practical issues such as maintenance. If Debbie can't work she's going to need every penny she can get and then some!"

"Gemma!" Debbie elbowed me sharply in the ribs. "You're jumping the gun a bit, aren't you? You both are! I've told you I don't know what I'm going to do yet and who knows, maybe I *will* have a termination."

"No, you can't!" There was a sudden glimmer of tears in Sophie's eyes and I knew the happy dreams she'd spun about family togetherness with Debbie and the baby were flying away on wings. "You wouldn't!" Poor Sophie, she really had homely, domestic visions of pushing

Junior on a swing while indoors Debbie, delightfully arrayed in a gingham pinny and with a smudge of flour on her nose, played at Doris Day.

"I may have to," Debbie said simply. "To be honest, at this point in time, I really don't think I could cope with a baby. For God's sake, look at the mess I've made of my own life! How can I inflict my ineptitude on somebody else?"

"But we'd support you!" Sophie was vehement. "Wouldn't we, Gemma? And what about your family? I thought they were fairly liberal. I mean, they wouldn't drum you out of the clan, would they? Like, 1950s Ireland is dead and gone, thank God. Single mothers are no longer shunned and shipped off to mother-and-baby homes."

"I know all that," Debbie said, and there was the answering sparkle of tears in her own eyes. "And do you not think I've been over each and every scenario in my own mind, time and time again?" She snapped her fingers. "Let's go through the options again. Firstly, I keep it – only, as I've just said, I don't think I could cope with the responsibility for another human being right now. Or secondly, I have it adopted and do my best to forget it ever happened." Her face was a study in misery. "Only, I don't think I could do that either and imagine if it turned up on the doorstep eighteen years later full of angst and resentment and destroying whatever life I'd managed to salvage for myself. Think of the guilt! The accusations on the faces of my husband

and family when they find out I'm not the person they thought I was, that for years I'd harboured a deep, dark shameful secret – that I'd given up my child, my very own flesh and blood to be raised by perfect strangers. Assuming they *are* perfect and not a cross between Cruella De Vil and the Boston Strangler." She shook her head furiously. "No, I don't think I could hack that." She took a sip of her Ballygowan and was quiet for a moment. "And ultimately – there's abortion! Final, drastic and, depending on which side of the fence you're on, downright murder!"

"Look," I said, growing angry though I wasn't quite sure why. "That's just emotive talk. As I've pointed out on more than one occasion, what you're carrying at this point in time is no more than a bundle of cells. It's not a person. Not yet! The nervous system hasn't developed – too early – so it can't feel pain. The brain hasn't developed yet so there's no understanding. There's no soul there, Debbie. So how can it be murder?"

"And how can you be so bloody sure?" It was Sophie's turn to get angry. "You're not God, Gemma. You're not even a frigging scientist so how dare you play fast and loose with Debbie's baby? Besides there are risks to the mother as well."

"Shut up, the both of you!" Sliding off the bar stool Debbie sent us a bitter look. "See, the bloody thing isn't even born yet and look at the dissension it's causing already. I wish to God I'd never set eyes on Guy Evans, much less got involved with him."

"Yes, well, if wishes were horses . . ." Sophie muttered sadly, staring after Debbie's retreating back.

"Beggars would ride," I finished the proverb, hoping if ever *my* wish came true and I got to saddle up Rocky, I too, wouldn't end up blistered and saddle-sore.

CHAPTER 13

I arrived home to the heart-stopping sight of an ambulance parked up outside the front door, a sight hardly guaranteed to lift my spirits which had already dropped so low they were checking into a clinic in Sydney. Putting on a spurt, I covered the last fifty yards in record time, reaching the doorstep just as the paramedics climbed into the cab of the vehicle and drove away, sirens roaring.

"Aunty Kay! Aunty Kay!" I yelled, screeching to a halt beside her as she stood there gazing after it, a look on her face totally unlike the World War II Field Marshal's one usually in evidence. "What is it? Is it Mammy? Is she all right? Is she dead?"

"No, Gemma. It's not your mother. It's poor little Orla, God help her!"

"Orla!" I parroted my voice so high the globe on a nearby lamppost flickered nervously. "Orla?" I don't know why I should have been so surprised. I mean, it's

187

not as if I wasn't expecting it. Like, these days her legs were so thin you could use them to lace your trainers. "W-what happened?"

"Collapsed! That's what happened." Aunty Kay sent me a look that could blister metal. "Collapsed like a house of cards while you and your misfit mates were out drinking up in the bushes, when you should have been at home keeping an eye on your baby sister!"

"Oh, for God's sake, Aunty Kay," I protested, leading the way back indoors and out of earshot of the neighbours who were already gathering for a post-mortem and failing that, a bloody good row. "We weren't drinking up in the bushes – we were drinking in the Fox's Retreat and I'm *not* Orla's keeper. She *is* twenty-two, you know, hardly a baby! And I'll tell you something else, she wouldn't thank me for keeping tabs on her."

My aunt, though, the unreasonable old bag, wasn't to be appeased. "Still, you must have known something was wrong. Even the paramedics were shocked. She can't weigh more than six stone. And you *live* with her!"

"Well," I said in my defence, and albeit somewhat virtuously, "I wasn't the one encouraging her in her ridiculous supermodel aspirations but every time I opened my mouth I was told to shut up, that *I* was only jealous!"

"Well, you *are* jealous of her. You were *always* jealous of her." Unrepentant, Aunty Kay headed for the telephone, presumably to call a cab to take us to the hospital. "Even as a child you had a vicious streak in you. Sure, didn't I find you myself, taking chunks out of her with your teeth when you were only four and she was a babe still in the pram!"

Somewhere, deep in the dim recesses of my mind a memory stirred, a memory of having my arse severely thrashed, a lot of adult arms waving about, a lot of shouting, a baby crying and overlying the lot, a faint metallic taste in my mouth, satisfyingly bloody! It was the first and last time I could identify with Dracula – you know, sympathise with where he was coming from. "All kids bite and pinch," I said. "It's part of the job description."

Aunty Kay gave an Elvis curl of the lip. "That's you all over, isn't it? Mistress of the smart mouth! I wonder will you be so smart standing at your sister's grave, knowing she was worth ten of you!"

"Oh, for goodness sake!" I snapped. "Are you going to phone for a cab or not? At the rate you're going we'll all be cashing in our dinner-pails and St Peter'll have tennis elbow from opening and closing the pearly gates."

Suppressing her ire for a moment, she dialled Babs Cabs, a minicab company where all the drivers were women. Aunty Kay laboured under the misapprehension that all male drivers were either illegal aliens more used to driving camels, or sex maniacs out to relieve her of her virginity. Thankfully, Babs despatched a cab to us at once and, within ten minutes, an uneasy truce having been achieved, we were on our way to St Vincent's Hospital.

* * *

Sitting beside Orla's bed, my mother looked pale and strained, a kind of latter-day Lady of Shalott.

"How is she?" I asked, walking over and staring down to where Orla's thin form scarcely disturbed the smoothness of the hospital covers.

"Not good!" Mammy's hand fluttered up nervously and anchored itself on her collar, pulling it away as though it was choking her. "She weighs less than six stone." Her voice became a wail. "Less than six stone, can you believe it? What sort of a mother am I at all? How could I not have noticed she was fading away before my very eyes? That she wasn't eating?"

Guiltily, I patted her hand. "She *was* eating. The problem is, as quick as she wolfed it down she chucked it back up again. It was all that modelling business, see? No matter how much weight she lost, she still felt she was too fat."

"And you knew about it?" My aunt's voice rose so that a coma victim on the far side of the room staged a miraculous recovery, struggled to sit up, took one look at her face and relapsed with gratitude for a further six months. No doubt she thought she'd died and gone to hell. "You little bitch, you! Why didn't you tell your mother?"

"Yes." Mammy looked hurt, accusing. A sword of

sorrow had pierced her heart. "Why didn't you tell me, Gemma?"

"Because she wouldn't let me!"

"She wouldn't let you! She wouldn't *let* you, my arse in parsley!" Her strident tones rampaging around the ward like an out-of-control mental patient, Aunty Kay stabbed me viciously again. "Since when has poor Orla had any control over the likes of you, you guttersnipe, you!"

'Since she found out I molested Rocky Cashel,' I said, but only in my own mind because there was no way in this life I was going to give the old bitch any more ammunition to fire at me. Eco-man, I thought gloomily, where are you now when I need you?

Thankfully, a fat nurse with a kind face and thick ankles came over and attempted to pour oil on troubled waters. "Look, folks, I don't think we should be apportioning blame at this point in time. People with eating disorders can be very devious, you know. Oh, we've seen it all in here – anorexics smuggling their dinner out to patients on the obese ward – bulimics chucking up into their slippers, hiding them beneath the bed, then forgetting and putting their feet in them." She chuckled comfortably. "I could write a book, so I could, if I'd the time, the inclination and the grammar! But right now, I've got to set up a drip and get some nourishment into this poor girl". (She pronounced it *gerrul* making it clear that her roots were somewhere bog-deep in the West of Ireland.)

"I'll go and get us a cuppa, shall I?" I asked, desperate to make amends if only in some small way.

191

"Yes, you do that!" Mammy's voice was little more than a whisper. Aunty Kay only scowled.

'How would you like it? Milk? Sugar? Arsenic?' I asked her but, again, only in my own mind because I reckoned Mammy had enough on her plate without us belting the bejaysus out of one another and ending up in the hospital next to Orla.

"And don't be too long while you're about it." As usual, she had to have the last word. "Don't go getting sidetracked into any pubs."

Gawd Almighty, as if I was a flippin' piss-head or something! Turning smartly on my heel I headed off in search of the nearest Klix dispenser, my mind in a whirl what with first, Debbie and now, Orla. A moment later, my mood plummeted still further when I realised the bloody machine only took twenties while, as Sod's Law would have it, I had every other conceivable denomination of coin going, bar the one needed.

"Bloody typical," I snarled aloud, giving it a good kick and following up with a flurry of thumps. "Wouldn't you just bloody know it!"

"It's Gemma, isn't it? I thought it was you!"

"Tyrell!" There was not so much surprise as shock in my own voice as, leaving off vandalising the machine, I whirled around and recognised Rocky Cashel's scrapie-on-the-brain band-mate. "What on earth are you doing here? Not been bitten by a mad sheep or anything, have you?"

Pushing the quiff of dark hair back from his

192

forehead, he sent me a lazy smile, which had a most uncanny loosening effect on my stomach and bowels. If I didn't know any better I'd have thought I fancied him. As it was, I put it down to a combination of stress and Aunty Kay – the latter, in particular, always making me want to shit myself.

"No, nothing like that," he assured me. "Actually, I was just visiting Laura."

"Laura? Rocky's Laura? The one with the squint?"

"The very same but it's not a squint – it's a cast. Mind you, it could be worse. It could be a cast of thousands!" He chuckled at his own joke then gestured vaguely somewhere to the right of him. "She's in a private room up on the next floor." He lowered his voice, a habit presumably acquired as a result of frequently ducking and diving from tabloid journalists. "She almost lost the baby."

I could feel myself getting light-headed. "Baby?" I asked. "What baby?"

Reaching out, he pulled me out of the way of a gurney being pushed along at top speed by a bevy of doctors and nurses all shouting out 'Crash! Crash! Crash!' and 'Resuss! Resuss! Resuss!' no doubt in the vain hopes that the director of *Casualty* might just happen to be passing.

"Oh, didn't you know? Laura's nearly three months pregnant. Both she and Rocky are over the moon but it was a close-run thing this evening, I can tell you."

The cow jumped over the moon! Appropriate, or

what? "Really," I said because there's not a lot else you can say when your heart has been eviscerated and carted off for autopsy, right before your very eyes. Sensitive man that he was, Tyrell didn't seem to find anything amiss or perhaps he thought pale and spotty was my complexion of choice.

"So what about you? What are you doing here? I thought animals were your territory or do you moonlight doing a bit of human nursing here and there?"

"No," I said, frantically trying to compose myself as well as being suddenly recalled to exactly what I was doing there. "My sister collapsed earlier on. She's bulimic and before you ask, no, it's nothing like scrapie."

"I'm not that insensitive!" Despite looking offended, Tyrell proceeded to demonstrate that, actually, he was. "Isn't that the disease where you puke yourself senseless so that you're constantly walking round with a mop, a bucket and a bottle of bleach?"

"It's an eating *disorder*," I told him, "and let me tell you Orla would never be caught dead with anything that remotely resembled a household-cleaning implement." I changed the subject, aware that time was fleet-of-footing it. "Anyway, you don't happen to have a couple of twenty p's, do you?"

"Yeah, sure." Digging in his pocket he produced a handful of loose change and a lone condom still in its wrapping. It was a strawberry-flavoured one, I noticed, my favourite although as a rule I'm allergic to soft fruit.

I rolled my eyes. "Just in case you get lucky?" I asked, in the kind of tone a Reverend Mother might use, which was a bit rich coming from one who had been so summarily evicted from a confessional and considering his sex life was nothing whatsoever to do with me. Nor, let me hasten to add, of any interest!

"Something like that, all right," he said, blushing, which intrigued me somewhat as it's not really what you expect from a hard man of rock.

"Well, kind of you to offer, but I'll settle for the coins. To tell the truth, I don't have much use for one of those myself."

"Really? I find that difficult to believe, Gemma. You're so attractive."

"Listen," I said quellingly, and holding out my hand for the money. "I wasn't fishing for compliments, just stating a fact, that's all. Now, I don't mean to be rude or anything but I really must get back to my sister." Further impetus was given to my mission by the awful thought that at any moment my Aunty Kay might come bearing down upon us and denounce me publicly as a whore of Babylon for *'consorting in the hospital corridor while your poor sister is lying ill, possibly even dying!'*.

"Okay, but shall I tell Laura that you'll pop up to see her later?"

"No! Yes! Will Rocky be there?"

Tyrell frowned. "I expect so. Why, is that a problem?"

I shook my head. No, you stupid jerk! I wanted to say. It's essential! I didn't though. Instead I said, "Not at all, only sometimes two's company and three is a disaster."

"Four, actually!" For some reason, Tyrell looked absurdly pleased with himself. "I'm sticking around. Catch you later, yeah?"

"I suppose so," I said gloomily, shoving a couple of coins into the vending machine and punching the 'white' and 'sugar' buttons, then repeating the performance twice more using various other combinations – white with sugar, black with sugar – white, no sugar.

"Well, you took your sweet time." Back on the ward, Aunty Kay was still gunning for me. "Been to Sri Lanka, have you? Picking the leaves, were you? Drying them? Packaging them? Exporting them?"

Ignoring her, I placed the white-with-sugar into my mother's hands. "Here, Mam. How is she?"

"No change." Taking a tentative sip of her tea, Mammy nodded slowly. "Mind you, I suppose no news is good news." Leaning across, she smoothed a wayward lock of Orla's blonde hair off her forehead. "Look at her. She's only a baby, really. Sure twenty-two is no age at all."

"Indeed it isn't." Aunty Kay relieved me of the black with sugar, her own gaze resting sorrowfully on the bone-white face of my sister. "Still, it's always the good who die young, though you'd think by now Jesus would have collected more than enough sunbeams for

196

his solarium. I suppose that's what they mean when they talk about the light of God."

"Stop that, Kay!" Fearfully, my mother turned to me. "She's not going to die, is she, Gemma? Tell me she's not going to die."

Shooting my aunt a glare topped with barbed wire, broken bottle-ends and all sorts of illegal defence weaponry, I squeezed my mother's hand. "Of course she's not! They'll feed her up a bit in here, lecture her on the evils of slimming and before you know it she'll be back home again and we won't get a moment's peace with the phone ringing off the hook as all her boyfriends ring up for the latest health bulletin."

"Sensible girl." Fat Ankles came back, faffed about with the drip a bit, patted Orla's inert foot where it was sticking out from beneath the covers and bustled off again.

Disgusted, Aunty Kay glared after the nurse's retreating acres-of-cotton-covered buttocks. "Ah, sure what would that big Mary Hick know about anything. That one probably can't even spell her name with ignorance."

"Now, now, Kay," Mammy remonstrated. "You've got to pass some pretty tough exams these days to be a nurse, especially in Vincent's. I'm sure she knows her oats from her onions."

"Course she does," I said staunchly. "And you know, I could swear there's a bit of colour coming back into Orla's face."

"You're right!" Mammy said excitedly, examining Orla's cheekbones intently. "Orla, love," she shook her gently, "it's Mammy. Wake up!"

"Yes, come on now, wake up, Orla." Incapable of coaxing, Aunty Kay hectored instead. "Stop all this nonsense now and put your poor mother out of her misery."

"Mammy?" Her voice barely above the mew of a kitten, Orla surfaced slowly, opening her eyes by degrees, gradually taking in her surroundings, the ward and the three of us, a trio of guardian angels, ranged around the bed. Correction, two angels – Mammy and me-and one big, ugly devil! "What happened?"

"You collapsed is what happened!" Not content with getting the last word, Aunty Kay had to have the first one too. "Like an empty paper bag, so you did, and put the heart crosswise in your mother and myself. It's a wonder we're not dead with shock, the pair of us. Aye, stiff as planks up in the mortuary beyond!" By complete contrast with my mother, she not so much sipped her tea as called it up to her in slurps.

"Collapsed?" Orla looked first confused and then to my mother for confirmation. "Did I?"

"Yes, love, you did. But don't try to talk now. Save your strength, eh?"

"I'm all right." Orla struggled to sit up. "A bit weak, but okay."

"You're on a drip," I pointed out unnecessarily, as

though any one could fail to notice they were attached to a massive stand by dint of a three-inch needle through the back of their hand and six feet of plastic tubing.

"I am *not* a drip!" Orla looked aggrieved, her one brain-cell still, apparently, dormant and not improved by her recent collapse.

"I said you're *on* a drip – not you *are* a drip!"

"Oh, *am* I?"

What was that I was saying about no one failing to notice . . .?

"Ah, it's just a bit of glucose to get your levels up." Fat Ankles reappeared and paused by the bed for a moment, an empty bedpan clutched in her rubber-gloved hands. At least, I hoped it was empty. "We'll take it down again in a few hours when you're feeling a bit more human."

"But I want to go home," Orla pouted and seeing that had no effect pussed instead. "I've got an audition tomorrow for one of the big catalogues. There's no way I'm letting that Karen Rogers wagon pip me to the post this time!"

Unmoved, the nurse freed up one hand, grabbed a glass thermometer out of a little container thingy hanging on the wall behind Orla and stuffed it in her mouth. "Yes, well, want will be your master then, because there's no way you're getting out of here until you've put on at least half a stone." Wonderingly, she shook her head. "Honest to God, I've seen more meat on an anatomical skeleton! Now, keep that in your gob till I come back! There's a good gerrul."

"Mitch!" Orla swore after her, the thermometer clamped firmly between her lips. "Mig mat mitch!"

"Now, Orla," Mammy remonstrated, "there's no call for language like that. The nurse is only doing her job. There'll be plenty of time for modelling when you're up and about again."

"That's right!" Aunty Kay nodded her agreement. "No point in modelling the latest line in knotty-pine in the cemetery, eh?"

"Listen, Mam," I suggested, knowing by the thunderous look on Orla's face that an almighty storm was brewing. "Why don't you and Aunty Kay take a bit of a break. Go powder your noses or something. I'll stay here with Orla." I slipped Orla a wink, signifying that I had some momentous news to impart.

"Would you mind, love?" Mammy looked anxious, as if leaving her daughter for a couple of minutes might give other people the right to name and shame her right up there alongside paedophiles, murderers and society's other misfits and undesirables. "I *could* do with stretching my legs. The old varicose veins aren't half giving me gyp and I don't want to end up with one of those deep-vein trombone thingummyjigs. I won't be long. Promise."

Orla waved a desultory hand, presumably because, with her mouth full, it was too difficult to say, 'Well, piss off then if you're going.'

The moment they were out of sight, I leaned across and whipped the thermometer out of her mouth, shook it as I'd seen Fat Ankles do earlier, read it and replaced it in the little container.

"Well?" Orla regarded me cynically. "Am I alive or what?"

"Or what," I said mildly. "Anyway, shut up and listen. Who do you think's upstairs?"

"God?" Orla hazarded a guess.

"No, not that far upstairs – next floor up, I mean!"

"How the bloody hell do I know?" Orla looked pissed. "It's not as if I've managed to get in a lot of sightseeing in the last few hours."

"Rocky," I said excitedly. "Rocky Cashel!"

"Oh, I thought you meant Rocky the Rooster from *Chicken Run*. Not! So, what's he doing here – fell off the stage or what?" A thought struck her. "*You* didn't have anything to do with it, did you? Not been availing yourself of his proximity again?"

Batting her foot out of the way, I plonked myself down on the bed. "No, but he's been availing himself of the lovely Laura's proximity and managed to get so close, he's only gone and knocked her up."

"No!" Orla's mouth formed a round 'o' of shocked delight. "So that rules you well and truly out of the equation, then."

"Not necessarily," I sniffed. "Like she's here because she almost lost it." Now, I know that was an unworthy thought and really I wouldn't wish a miscarriage on anyone – it's just that the smug look on Orla's face got right up my oesophagus.

"Face it, Gemma. You're beat!"

I clung to hope. "Not necessarily," I said again. "I mean, he must feel something for me. Otherwise, why on earth would he want me round every weekend? I mean, looking after Gretchen seems like an awful piddling excuse." I nodded shrewdly. Inspector Morse had nothing on me. "Besides if it was just a baby-sitter for the damn dog he wanted, he could equally well have chosen Sophie or Debs."

Orla was prevented from making any reply as Fat Ankles came back to retrieve the thermometer.

"It's all right," I forestalled any complaint. "I've already read it – thirty-seven!"

"Thirty-seven?" FA looked pleased. "Normal, then. That's grand but don't get any ideas in your head about going home early." She wagged a beefy finger twice the size of Orla's thigh. "We've got to fatten you up a bit, loveen."

"Just like the wicked witch in *Hansel and Gretel*," Orla complained, as having marked up the medical chart, the nurse bustled off again. "Got any chicken bones I could stick through the bars of my cage?"

I grinned. "If it's bones you want, you're spoiled for choice. But to get back to Rocky, what do you think he's playing at?"

Orla sighed. "Look, Gemma, I'd love to go along with you and say there's some great big convoluted plot but I honestly don't think there is. The way I see it, he's crazy about Laura, she's crazy about that damn poodle and he'll pull out all the stops to make her happy including roping you in as an accessary after the fact." She spread her palms, flinching as the needle in the back of her hand reminded her of its presence. "Let me put it another way. With you looking after Gretchen, Laura has peace of mind and Rocky gets to spend more time with her. In the heel of the hunt, to use a pretty apt expression, you were just a happy accident."

"Yeah?" My lower lip trembled because I didn't like what I was hearing. "Well, he wasn't too happy at the time, as I recall."

"Exactly! And he's making you pay for it now *and* killing two birds with one stone, as it were." Pushing back the hair from her forehead, she suddenly sat up a bit straighter and forming her lips into her favourite Pamela Anderson pout gazed off left of field to somewhere over my shoulder.

I sighed, experience alerting me to the fact that a man was in the offing and that he was unlikely to be an octogenarian with an irritable prostate. Following the direction of her gaze I turned, fully expecting to see if not George Clooney then at least Dr Hilary Jones but instead, found myself yet again face to face with Tyrell.

"Hi! So this is your skin and blister, is it?" His smile reached out, encompassed us both like a big warm comfort-blanket and again, strangely enough, my bowels went into overdrive. I wondered if I might be suffering from reflected-glory syndrome as in, Tyrell moved in Rocky's orbit and therefore some of Rocky's vibes were bound to have rubbed off on him.

"Hi yourself, and if by that you mean my sister, yes, this is Orla." I waved a vague introductory hand. "Orla, this is Tyrell . . .?"

"O'Neill," he supplied obligingly.

"Yeah, Tyrell O'Neill, a fellow band-member of Rocky Cashel's," I said.

"*And* aspiring Donegal sheep-farmer," he reminded me as if it were something to be proud of, something to have etched on your gravestone for posterity's edification.

"Really?" Orla oohed in a voice so breathy and fascinated you'd think he'd just announced he was the Second Coming. "I just love sheep. They're sooo intelligent. And Donegal is, like, really wild!"

"Wild, my ass!" I said rudely. "The place is positively antediluvian. What's that joke? Oh, yeah, the best thing to come out of it is the Dublin Road." I rolled my eyes. "And as for you loving sheep, Christ's sakes, Orla, you're even allergic to lanolin."

"No, I'm not! Well, yes I am." Orla shot me a just-wait-till-he's-gone-and-I'll-scratch-your-bloody-eyes-out-bitch look. "But that's just because I'm sensitive." She batted her long eyelashes and a gale-force wind eddied round the room.

Tyrell chuckled. "Well, there'd be no place for you in Bundoran, then. A strong stomach and an even stronger back is what's required there!" He shot me what I think was supposed to be an admiring look. "Now, Gemma, on the other hand, looks like a woman who could chew boulders and spit out bricks."

Ruffling up like an angry pea-hen, Orla tossed her long, blonde hair and I must admit I did a bit of ruffling up on my own account. "Well, *I'm* a muddle!" she said.

"That," said Tyrell, nodding shrewdly, "will be the collapse. Ten to one you've got concussion!" He leaned forward confidingly. "It happened to me once too, you know – fell off the stage at a gig and knocked myself out. Talk about muddled – for a week, I didn't know if I was coming or going and to add insult to injury the fella who sold me the gear told me it was real hot shit."

Orla sighed wearily. "No, I mean, I'm a *mudd-elle*! You know, a muddle!"

"Clothes!" I gave him a hint. "Linda Evangelista? Claudia Schiffer?" It was clear a diagram was required. In fact, so slow was he that it occurred to me briefly that he might be a distant relation of that priest who chucked me out of the confessional a few years previous.

"Oh." Light dawned at long last with the same speed as a very fat camel going through the eye of a very small needle. "That kind of a muddle!"

"Yes," Orla simpered. "You may have seen me on that toothpaste ad on the telly. I play the part of a damsel in distress who gets rescued by the dashing Sir Fangsalot."

"'Fraid not!" Tyrell shook his head. "I never watch

the box – too much to do, you see. Places to go, people to see, sheep to shear – well maybe not sheep to shear right now but, hopefully, in the not too distant future. When I get my farm all fixed up."

Orla batted her eyelashes again and I couldn't help wishing I'd worn something warmer. "Lucky sheep. I imagine it must be *sheer* heaven from start to finish." She tittered at her own witticism – silly cow!

Honestly, the girl was shameless! *And* unbelievable. Like, there she was, weighing less than six stone, one step away from death's door and she was still making, well, sheep's eyes. A few seconds later the same eyes went into overdrive though not, as it turned out, for Tyrell's benefit.

"Ah, there you are, Tyrell, I guessed this is where you'd be lurking. Hi, Gemma! Tyrell said you were here. How's it going?"

"Rr-rr-Rocky?" I stuttered, his name becoming a fishbone stuck in my throat though why I should experience such incredulity was anyone's guess. I mean to say, I had prior knowledge that he wasn't exactly thousands of miles away playing at nomads in the Gobi desert.

"In the flesh!" he confirmed, looking absurdly pleased that this was the case. "And you, lovely lady, are?" His head, like generations of male heads before him, swivelled automatically towards the rip on the drip.

"Orla." Staging a comeback even Lulu would be

proud of, Orla struggled up further in the bed affording him a tantalising glimpse of her non-existent cleavage and holding out a hand, bony and delicate as a piece of skate.

"Ah, Orla – Orla the golden one. Did you know that's what your name means in Irish? And, in your case, the rose certainly befits its name." Suddenly Sir Galahad, Rocky, the bastard, pressed the skate to his lips and I found myself hard put not to follow up with my fist. Like what sort of crap was that? Honestly! *The rose befits its name!* Talk about last orders in Pukeville!

"And, how's Laura?" I asked coldly and pointedly – not that I was jealous or anything. I mean, it's not PC to be jealous of your dying sister, is it? Not when she's lying there with a face like a bleached bone and nipples so inverted they're nudging her vertebrae. Bitch!

"She's fine. Well, as fine as can be expected but the main thing is, Junior's hanging on in there still." Rocky swaggered a bit, proud presumably of Junior's tenacity and, no doubt, aiming to give the impression that it was a trait inherited from his old rock star dad. I wondered if he'd be quite so proud if Junior went on to inherit Laura's cast, freckles and hump. (Okay, fair is fair. She didn't exactly have a hump – just a mild case of scoliosis.) "Mind you, she's worried over Gretchen so I'm really pleased *you've* pitched up here."

Well, that was nice. He was really pleased I'd *pitched up*. What did he think I was – a flipping tent? Oh, there was no rose-befitting-its-name stuff for me. Perish the thought! No, my value lay in my mutt-sitting abilities. Just wait till I got my maulers on an economy-size bottle of paraquat and Gretchen's ass was grass – or weeds, rather – dead ones!

Rocky put on one of those helpless-male-appealing-for-help-from-the-opposite-sex faces which normally have women running from the four corners of the earth to answer the call. I, let it be said, was no exception. Had I been legless and turned back to front in a motorised wheelchair with a flat battery, I'd *still* have managed to answer the call. Had I been stranded halfway up the Alps half-in, half-out of a chasm with severe frostbite of the crampons, I'd still have taken gold at the Olympics.

"I know our agreement was that you'd work only at the weekends but I'd be ever so grateful." A mildly anxious look on his face, he reeled me in like a spawning salmon. "They're keeping Laura in for observation for a few more days so it would mean you'd have to sleep over at Gothdere. Would that be a major problem?"

No, that would be a golden opportunity! Oh, the hardship of it all! Imagine being obliged to spend my nights sleeping under the same roof, only yards away from the man of my dreams! Breathing in the same atmosphere! Being on hand should he need anything during the night! *Anything* at all! Still, it didn't do to look too eager as my Aunty Kay was forever pointing out whenever I had a new man in my sights.

"Oh, there you go again!" At this point her eyes would roll up as she brought God in on the conversation. "All dressed up like a box of chocolates with your soft centres on display. It doesn't do'to be too eager, Gemma. Be a toffee, girl. Give him something to chew on. Make him work for you!"

That, I guess, was her own personal take on the *Forest Gump* chocolate-box school of philosophy. Nonetheless, to hedge my bets, I tried for difficult.

"But what about work?" I asked artlessly, when, in actual fact, I was already composing a stuff-your-poxy-job-where-the-sun-don't-shine-never-shone-and-ain't-likely-to-shine-unless-your-arse-is-suddenly-split-wide-open-by-Halley's-Comet letter.

"Oh, your work needn't suffer." Unwittingly, Rocky fired a volley of gut-wrenching disappointment across my bows. "There are always people about during the day. It's just the nights that are a bit of a problem and I know Laura could relax if she knew Gretchen was safe in your capable hands."

Yeah, I thought cynically. But would she relax if she knew *you* were anything *but* safe in my capable hands? I hoped nothing of my thoughts showed on my face as I went into my Florence Nightingale all-sweetness-and-light routine.

"Well, okay." I tried to keep my voice even and refrain from jumping up and down. "I suppose I can manage to help you out – for a while, anyway." I felt pleased with the way I managed to inject just the right amount of reluctance into the last bit. Still, if I'd expected heartfelt gratitude and Gemma-you've-saved-my-life protestations from Rocky, I'd have been on a hiding to nowhere because, taking my capitulation for granted, he'd already turned his attentions back to Orla.

"So?" His voice was throaty, catarrhal, mind-blowingly sexy. "When you're not lying around playing at Sleeping Beauty, what do *you* do with yourself?"

"*Qui, moi?*" she asked modestly, using her minuscule knowledge of schoolgirl French, a tactic she fondly but mistakenly imagined gave her an air of sophistication, and batting those infernal eyelashes so hard I felt the first stirrings of pleurisy start up in my lungs. "I'm nothing special – just a muddle."

Excitement draped itself across Rocky's face, an exact replica of the expression on the faces of a gaggle of nurses who having gotten wind of his presence were now queuing six-deep just inside the door of the ward and sod Mrs O'Hara, the stroke patient, who had been on the commode for something approaching an hour. "Hey, is that right? You know, I'm planning a rerun of *Rotten to the Core* and I'm sure I could find a part for you."

"Really?" Clasping her hands together like a Victorian heroine, Orla looked like she was already auditioning for the starring role. "Weally and twuly?"

Rocky nodded decisively. "Why not! You can never have too many convincing-looking famine victims."

Talk about a punch in the solar ego. I felt sorry for Orla, really I did, especially when she turned that old familiar shade of magenta and started to choke like the Queen Mother on a herring-bone.

"There, there," I encouraged, thumping her on the back as she all but turned her larynx inside out. "Puke it all up. There's a good girl!"

"So kind," Tyrell muttered appreciatively. "Such a firm hand!"

"And don't I know it!" Rocky quipped, a wry look of recollection on his face. His gorgeous face! His gorgeous, masculine, crotch-moisteningly perfect face!

Look out, Laura, I thought, as suddenly the umbrage stuck in Orla's craw came loose and spewed up all over the bed. Pregnant or not, it's poodles at dawn, my girl. Choose your canine!

CHAPTER 14

Personally, I blame Sophie. Like, it was she who put the idea into my head in the first place. I mean, up till then, I'd never given my hands a second thought other than in the way you might size up the potential of a garden implement. You know, a hoe or a spade – there to do a job. End of story! Now, though, thanks to her pointing out the potential, I'd only gone and subjected myself to the rigours of having false fingernails fitted and rendered myself totally helpless in the process. A descendant of Vlad the Impaler with the Grand Inquisitor also featuring large in her family tree, the nail technician first of all ritually humiliated me over the state of my bitten nails, which was a bit rich when you consider if it wasn't for nail-biters like me, *she'd* be signing on at her local Social. Then, mission successfully accomplished and having reduced me to the size of a squashed ant, she produced from her armoury of torture implements a set of peculiar-looking plastic talon things, which she attached to my nails and began painting on layer after layer of acrylic mixed with glue. Now, as a rule, I've never been into glue-sniffing but the fumes wafting up my nostrils were doing me a power of good and, before long, I found myself drifting off into a kind of nebulous trance that came to an abrupt end as, looking down, I caught sight of a massive, shapeless splodge of white at the end of each finger.

"Bleedin hell!" I waggled them experimentally. "Where did *you* do your training? Madame Tussauds, was it? Mixing up the death masks?"

Arching a pencilled-in semicircle masquerading as an eyebrow, the nail technician (oh, pulleese!) whipped out her trusty nail-file and shot me a look that could have shattered a cannonball mid-air. For a moment I thought she was going to stab me. Well, stranger things have happened. Remember Sweeney Todd? And I didn't reckon much on my . chances of defending myself, not with the massive blobs at the end of my fingers.

"Don't be stewpid!" Her accent was broad Dublin. "I have to foil dem dowan. How long do you want dem?"

"For as long as possible," I said, knowing that hell's fire would splutter and die out before ever I'd be persuaded to set foot inside *Tanya's Talons* again.

"Jesus, Mary and Joseph! I mean length!" Consulting with the heavens, her eyeballs retreated so far up her sockets there was only the whites left. "How long do you want dem and do you want rowand or square tips? What finish do you want? French manicure, nail polish or nail art?"

"Hmm," I said, not expecting to be presented with quite such an extensive menu. "I think, I'll settle for the salad Niçoise and a nice crisp bottle of Chardonnay." I laughed ingratiatingly because there was something about her upturned eyeballs that brought out the coward in me. Bad move! The woman wasn't amused. I doubt if anything, even Jesus Christ coming down off the cross and doing the hokey cokey in the shroud of Turin, would amuse her.

"*C-ah-ahr-mel!*" Washing her hands of me, and in a voice that would grate rivets, she beckoned over her second-in-command, a peroxide blonde with pneumatic Wonderbra-enhanced boobs that gave the impression that she had somehow managed to secrete both Tyson and Naseem down the front of her shirt and that they were engaged in a vigorous round of sparring. "Will you finish off this *lady?* I've got to go and make a phone call!" For 'lady' read 'piece of shit' and I suspect 'finish off' was what she'd have liked to do to me, literally!

Carmel, she of the prize-fighting boobs, bounced obediently over and lifting my hands, inspected them like something yeasty from a baker's oven. "Oh, they're coming along nicely. You've got lovely long, slender fingers, so you have, and I think you should keep the length – say an inch – to really show them off to their best advantage."

214

"Sounds good to me," I said, basking in the compliment as sculptress-like she deftly began to shape and file the shapeless splodges till all that remained were ten perfect pointed talons at the end of my fingers. Dear God, I prayed, just give me the chance to rake them up and down Rocky's spine.

"So?" Big Boobs tilted her head so far to one side she was in danger of overbalancing. "What kind of finish would you like? Personally, I'd vamp it up – you know, do the whole scarlet woman bit. Men are suckers for red nails. Anything red in fact! Red shoes, red underwear, red Ferraris. What's the betting Eve's apple wasn't a Granny Smith?"

"You're probably right," I said, thinking that whilst her philosophy might be a bit on the hare-brained side, I needed all the help I could get. Besides, Rocky did like red as evidenced by the multitude of freckles on Laura's face. Coming to a decision I rubbed my hands together like a Corporation workman getting ready to dig a big hole. "Right!" I said. "Let's go with the red. In for a penny, in for a pound!"

Big Boobs smiled approvingly as though we were kindred spirits, as though I had just been initiated into some exclusive sisterhood way beyond the purses of the general hoi polloi. "A very wise choice, if I may say so! Now what's it to be; *Crushed Crimson*, *Savage Scarlet* or *Revolutionary Red*?"

"*Revolutionary Red!*" I decided, hoping I wouldn't come out looking like Che Guevara. I didn't. Indeed my fingernails were a sight to behold. Long, pointed and decidedly scarlet, they made me feel powerful and Joan Collinsy and filled me with a strange and childish desire to stick them beneath the noses of passing strangers and enlist their admiration.

The rot set in however when, bladder bursting, I got home and tried to pull my knickers down – you know the ones: elasticated with a 'secret' built-in tummy panel and 'bottom lift'. A bitch to get on or off at the best of times, let me tell you it's damn near impossible with a full set of scalpels attached to the end of your fingers. How I didn't manage to give myself a radical hysterectomy was more by good luck than management and it wasn't long before I came to the conclusion that women with long nails obviously don't subscribe to the wearing of underwear. Either that, or someone else dresses them! Not, mind you, that I intended to wear anything other than my skimpiest, barely-there underwear when I stayed over at Gothdere later that evening when, hopefully, Rocky would be the one hooking *his* thumbs under the waistband and easing them down over my ample hips. In which case, all my nails had to do was *look* glamorous – *and* rake themselves down along the length of his spine! A worrying thought occurred; what if, in the heat of the moment my nails got carried away and ended up castrating *him*. But nothing, not even the thoughts of gelding my beloved could dampen my anticipation for long and thus it was with a happy heart that I stepped into the shower, dropped the soap and immediately found myself confronted with yet another nail-biting problem i.e. how to pick it up again. Eventually, having skittered about for several minutes in slippery pursuit and having almost brained myself against the tiled wall time and time again, I managed to successfully skewer it on the nails of one hand. My triumph was short-lived though, as in attempting to dislodge it with my free hand, I ended up with the nails of that one just as firmly embedded, leaving me as effectively shackled as a prisoner on a chain-gang.

"Shit!" I yelled, as the full enormity of my situation became clear. "Shit! Shit! Shit!" Like, there I was, trapped beneath the powerful jet of the showerhead, unable to escape the relentless cascade of water owing to the fact that I couldn't turn off the tap and, believe me, I tried – in ever new and increasingly inventive ways which included the use of chin, wrists, elbows and even a hooked knee. But to no avail. That there water just kept on a-coming! *And* a-coming! *And* a-coming! Had we lived in biblical times I've no doubt Noah would have been readying the Ark against the impending deluge whilst Mrs Noah helpfully rounded up the animals two by two. Had I been aboard the *Titanic* I've no doubt the call would have gone up long since to abandon ship. Unable to push back the glass shower-screen with either the tip of my tongue or the tip of my nose, I eventually gave up, slid down the wall and resigned myself to ending up on one of those 'ridiculous death' lists that get posted over the internet every now and again. You know the type of thing: *Wife hoovers herself up with Dyson – Enraged Husband To Sue Firm Over Misrepresentation. "If no bags are required," says Mr Blah, "what the tarnation is my wife doing in there?"* Mine would be just such another ignominious death: *'Woman Drowns In Shower Impaled By Fingernails On Bar of Soap'* – good for a giggle amongst bored office workers, then quickly forgotten as the conversation turned to far more interesting fare such as the size of Leonardo di Caprio's wedding tackle. And I'd lay money on it that nobody would ever remember that I was the world's number one expert on pink-eye in poodles. Or that I'd *almost* had my wicked way with Rocky Cashel!

"Jesus, what are you like!"

I knew I'd died when Orla's face suddenly appeared and hung like Marley's ghost in the steam above. So it was true what they said – death by drowning *was* relatively painless although I felt a bit cheated that I hadn't been given the film-show bit. God or the Devil, whoever was in charge, presumably hadn't thought my paltry little life worth the bother of rerunning which, when I thought about it, annoyed me somewhat. All right, so maybe it wasn't up there alongside Cleopatra's or Madonna's but there *were* one or two memorable moments – well, one, anyway and Rocky Cashel could testify to that as well as against me in a Court of Law.

"I *said*, what are you like?"

Ophelia-like (See! Given the chance, I always knew I could play that part!) I gazed up at Orla through the torrents of water running down my face and couldn't help wishing for a few garlands to complete the image. "So *you're* dead too? Let me guess. It was Rocky's remark that finished you off and now we're both doomed to spend eternity together, roasting in hell." I quirked a wet-look eyebrow. "It *is* hell, isn't it – like, there's no way they'd let a milker like you into heaven?"

"Shut your face!" Orla snapped. "Or I'll shut this bloody shower-screen again and leave you to your own devices. What was all that yelling about anyway? You could be heard clear across the Atlantic and beyond to New York. I swear, the Statue of Liberty was holding her ears and calling for the *Migraleve!*"

Tragically I extended my arms towards her. "Look! I'm stuck. Why didn't somebody warn me about the perils attached to wearing false nails? Not only did I almost circumcise myself taking my knickers off but I was only moments away from drowning in the shower. And never let anyone fool you into thinking it's a gentle death. Like heck it is! It's horrible. I could feel my lungs filling up, struggling to climb up my neck and out my mouth. And then my life flashed past and *you* were in all the bad bits and what's more I *saw* you pinching my Janet Reger knickers, so don't even *dream* of denying it any more." My voice rose hysterically. "I'll never get over it, I tell you. Never!"

As I paused for breath, Orla giggled, a giggle that evolved rapidly into a full-throated roar as she became fully acquainted with the extent of my dilemma.

"Oh, Gemma. You big eejit! Why do you think I always use shower-gel? Using false nails is a skill – you know, like touch-typing or pot-black. Just because you've got the equipment doesn't automatically make you an expert. You've got to learn how to handle your typewriter/your snooker cue/your false nails. You give up using soap and any underwear that involves the use of heavy-duty elastic or boning of any sort. If you get an eyelash in your eye, you leave it there or risk a detached retina and when it comes to that-time-of-the-month it's back to the good old Dr White's." She nodded meditatively. "Having said that, *they've* come a long way from their old, lumpy hammock image. I've seen the adverts, you know – I've even done one – and unless there's a blatant breach of the Trade Descriptions Act, they improve your social life no end as well as your snorkelling, horse-riding, paragliding abilities *and* you can still wear your tight white jeans all month round."

"Yeah, yeah, the joys of being a woman!" I quavered, cold now that she had leaned in and turned off the tap. "But to get back to these blasted fingernails. Surely there must be some advantage to them, otherwise why put myself through all that humiliation in *Tanya's Talons*?" I made a sort of all-encompassing circular gesture with my head. "Not to mention all this!"

Orla furrowed her brow and I could tell her dormant

brain-cell, which for one brief moment in time had come alive and excelled itself, was yet again under considerable pressure. Still, fair dues, she emerged triumphant in the end. "Well, they *look* good. *And* you can reach further round your back when you need to squeeze a spot. Although, that said, you can't so much squeeze it as stab it!" She took time out to look pensive. "Mind you, a friend of mine almost transplanted her lung – so you've got to be anatomically aware and not just lunge willy-nilly."

"I'll take your word for it," I said dryly. "Now give me a hand, would you, seeing as how my own are temporarily out of commission."

"Couldn't you just have yanked them free? I mean, we *are* talking soap here and not quick-dry cement. Besides, the water would have melted the soap sooner or later. I don't know what all the panic was about except that you always were a bit of a drama queen, Gemma Murphy. Anything for an audience!"

She could talk! That one would cut her own throat just to make an entrance! Still, I judged it wiser to curb my tongue until such time as I was free again and could engage her in fist-to-face physical combat.

"That soap is dead hard, actually. I'd have drowned ten times over if I was waiting for it to melt." A thought occurred to me. "Anyway, what are you doing home? I thought they were going to keep you in hospital until you'd put on a bit more weight."

Grabbing hold of my wrists, Orla began to prise them in opposite directions. "I had to get away. The

Ayatollah, AKA Fat Ankles, was making my life unbearable. When she wasn't sticking a thermometer in my mouth she was trying to force-feed me off-cuts from the amputation ward."

"So you *legged* it?" I chuckled, delighted with my pun.

"Yep!" She giggled appreciatively. "Although, Tyrell gave me a *hand*!"

"I suppose you couldn't *face* staying there any longer." I laughed uproariously, then stopped with the suddenness of a skier balking at the edge of a precipice as the full import of what she'd said sank home. "*Tyrell* gave you a hand? Correct me if I'm wrong but we are talking Tyrell O'Neill here, aren't we and not Tyrell . . . er Tyrell . . ." Heck! I couldn't think of anyone else with such an idiotic first name.

"The one and only!" Orla confirmed, triumphantly tossing my hands back into my lap as they suddenly gave up the fight and decided to part company. "And for what it's worth, Gemma, I think you're stone mad. Tyrell O'Neill is worth half a dozen Rocky Cashels."

"You're only saying that because Rocky insulted you." Unnecessarily, I set about jogging her memory. "What was that he said – oh yeah – you'd make a great famine victim, or words to that effect."

Orla, surprisingly, didn't rise to my bait. "Actually, believe it or not, Rocky Cashel was instrumental in curing my bulimia. It's thanks to him that I finally realised how I looked to *normal* people." She bracketed the word 'normal' between inverted commas made from her fingers. "And Tyrell says there's nothing more sensuous in the world than a nicely rounded woman."

"Except a nicely rounded ewe." Even my pores dripped cynicism. "And what about your modelling? Aren't you worried your new-found nonchalance might put you not so much beyond the pale of that particular profession as beyond the scales?"

Orla shrugged. "There are more important things in life. Tyrell opened my eyes to that."

Really! I wondered if his philanthropy extended to opening her thighs as well, a thought I quickly buried – not that it made me uncomfortable or anything. It's just that it was none of my business. I mean, they were both consenting adults!

"Did you screw him?" Well, what can I tell you? Some thoughts *will* rise to the surface however deep the grave.

"Gemma! Are you calling me loose?" Orla looked shocked which was a bit rich, considering how, in real terms, she thinks a hymen is a greeting to the opposite sex and fidelity is a type of oral contraceptive.

"Well," I persisted, "did you?"

"No!" Orla pouted. "Tyrell was the perfect gentleman. The only time he laid a hand on me was to help me down the knotted sheet."

I grinned, pleasantly surprised. If her near-death-experience resulted in her discovering a sense of humour, I couldn't wait to see what the real thing did for her.

"Actually, and I know you'll find this hard to believe but Tyrell wasn't interested in me. Well, not in that way, anyway. As a matter of fact it's *you* he has the hots for. I never knew anyone could wax so lyrical about someone's muscular thighs, as he put it."

"Huh," I snorted, unimpressed. "Probably saw them as an asset when it comes to wrestling recalcitrant sheep to the ground."

Helping me out of the shower cubicle, Orla handed me a towel. "Don't worry. I told him you weren't interested, that you were the last woman on earth who would want to be buried alive out in a thatched cottage in Donegal, herding sheep by day and spinning unbleached yarn by night with a view to knitting your big, handsome, sheep-farmer husband an Aran sweater."

Actually, put like that it sounded quite romantic. I could just picture the scene: me, humming over my spinning-wheel by the light of a tallow candle; three adorable tousle-headed children asleep up in the loft; and opposite, Tyrell in a rocking-chair, the chiselled planes of his face highlighted by the turf fire, intent on some article or other in the *Farmers' Journal*. And carried across on the still, peaty air would come the soulful sound of a fiddle, the muted thud of jolly Irishmen and women kicking up their heels at the local crossroads and fornicating under hedges and high-bodied, four-wheel-drive vehicles.

"Why?" I demanded, wrapping the towel around

me, crossing over to the sink and embarking on the lengthy process of digging the remaining chunks of soap out from under my nails. "*Why* did you tell him I wasn't interested?"

"Because you're not and *I* am!" Now, there was a turn-up for the books – Orla, interested in *my* rejects! A red-letter day or what! Hang out the bunting! Uncork the champers! Still, always a proponent of Japanese torture methods, I thought I'd let her dandle a bit. Give her the water treatment, drip, drip, drip!

"Maybe I've switched my allegiance. You know, the more I think of it, the more I'm coming to fancy the idea of a little cottage with roses round the door, a backdrop of rolling hills and the gentle lowing of sheep in the background."

Totally unfazed, Orla grinned. "You know, Gemma, for someone who works in a veterinary surgery you're remarkably untutored in the sounds of Mother Nature. You of all people should know cattle low and sheep baa."

"Just testing!" I bluffed. "Anyway, you can't have him. I'm keeping him in reserve."

"So you're not that confident about getting your hooks into Rocky after all, then?"

"Oh, yes I am and phase one begins this very night." Rinsing the last of the soap from my hands, I turned and manoeuvred her towards the door. "So, if you don't mind, I need to get the preparations underway."

Orla checked her watch. "But you've hours to go yet. Still, Rome wasn't built in a day, I suppose."

"Ha, ha, very funny!" I made a face at her retreating back. Her one brain-cell had woken up, it appeared, and making up for lost time was busy going forth and multiplying. Funny, I thought, breaking out a jar of Clarins moisturiser and smoothing it all over my face and neck, I liked her far better when in a persistent vegetative state.

* * *

"Oh, no! What are *you* doing here?" I didn't care how rude I sounded as Tyrell O'Neill opened the door to Gothdere. Honestly, the man was like a scabby leg. There was no running away from him. How on earth was I ever going to get close to Rocky with him always turning up playing spectre at the feast? For a moment I wondered if he might actually be in Laura's pay – there to keep us asunder. Either that or he was secretly gay and harbouring designs on Rocky's person, in which case he'd better think again.

"Nice to see you too, Gemma." With a somewhat disarming smile he stepped back from the door and allowed me entry. "Actually, I'm only here at Rocky's behest to show you what room has been prepared for you and where to find everything. Added to which, I'm trying to finish arranging one of the songs for Rocky's new show, *Young Guns*. So don't worry that I'm here to put a spoke in your wheel and spoil the party."

Guilty conscience making me paranoid, I narrowed my eyes suspiciously. "Party? And just what party might that be? Like, who said anything about any flaming party?"

"Whoa!" Cowering, Tyrell backed off. "Call off your dogs. It's just an expression. No need to burst your implants!"

"There's every need!" I exploded. "And for your information, I don't have implants. I'm a firm believer in growing my own, be it vegetables, bean sprouts or breasts!" Hands on hips, I went into attitude mode. Eliza Doolittle with attitude! *Oi'm a good girl, Oi am!* "Anyway, just what gives you the right to go around casting aspersions? I'll have you know there's *nothing* going on between me and Rocky Cashel. Nothing at all! Party my foot! You call looking after some flea-bitten mutt with delusions of Doberman a party?" My head not so much rocked as rotated three hundred and sixty degrees. It was a trick I'd learned from watching the more aggressive participants on *Jerry Springer*. "Uh-huh, I don't think so. Besides I *have* been here before. There's no need for a reception committee."

Tyrell's expression took the lift fifteen floors and got off at the level marked 'genuinely bewildered'. "Jesus, where did that come from? I *know* there's nothing going on between you two. Rocky is true blue to Laura. He's never looked at another woman although, in our business, there's no lack of offers. You wouldn't believe the lengths some women will go to just to shag a rock star."

Actually, I could well imagine, not to mention write

227

a thesis on the subject. I had, after all, gone all the way to Wicklow myself and, with some justification, now considered myself something of an expert on that very topic. I hoped Tyrell wouldn't notice the rosy glow creeping up my neck and face, the telltale blush of remembrance, the burning brand half-shame, half-lust that ignited my cheeks as, once more, I felt the delicious judder of Rocky's butt-cheeks bouncing up and down on my pelvis. But no, luck was with me. Desperate to extricate himself from my bad books, Tyrell was busy giving me chapter and verse re the righteousness of Cashel for Laura and vice versa.

"Honestly, if ever there was a match made in heaven, those two are it. I mean, they go together like jelly and custard, manna and honey, fish and chips . . ."

"Scrapie and sheep?" I suggested sarkily, not liking what I was hearing one little bit and wanting to throw acid at it and scar it for life.

"Exactly!" Tyrell beamed. "Although, I'd sooner it didn't go with *my* sheep, when I have them, that is. Which reminds me! Did I tell you about the lovely merino I saw at the Agricultural Fair at the other day? I mean, this sheep was to die for. Talk about the Golden Fleece –"

"Yeah? Well, don't spin me a yarn!" Brutally, I cut him off at the ebullience. "Now, if you don't mind, I'm here to poodle-sit, not listen to you spouting mythology, codology and apology. So . . ." I left a significant pause, "if you don't mind."

"Oh, sure."

Apparently un-insultable, Tyrell gave me a quick tour of the parts of the house to which I hadn't yet been, together with a running, not always flattering, commentary. Greedily, my eyes took in all the details. This was, after all, where the object of my desire resided and I wanted to know everything there was to know about him, all the minutiae of his life, from his preference in toilet paper, quilted or double-velvet, to his favourite brand of coffee.

"And this," turning left at the top of a flight of Gone-With-the-Wind stairs, Tyrell, with a flourish, threw open a pair of double doors, "is your abode, for the night anyway. Note the four-poster bed, the king-size mattress, easily big enough to accommodate a Greek orgy although, personally speaking, I'm a one-on-one man myself. So, if you should get lonely or scared –"

"I won't," I said hurriedly, searching hopefully for signs in the lavishly furnished boudoir of an interconnecting door that would, hopefully, lead through into Rocky's room and from thence, under his duvet. Unfortunately there wasn't one, just a pair of floor-to-ceiling French windows covered in swathes and swags of fine, white muslin. "I'll be grand. I like my own company and I don't scare easy."

"Well, that's a relief." Pulling out a handkerchief, Tyrell mopped some imaginary perspiration from his brow. "Only you *do* know Gothdere backs out onto the woods, don't you? And you *do* know Ireland's most-wanted, vicious criminal and serial rapist, Get-em-off

229

O'Brien, has gone on the run and that there have been purported sightings of him in this area?"

"Oh, balls!" I snorted disbelievingly.

"Word is, he brings his own." Tyrell nodded ghoulishly. "*And* a twelve-inch carving knife! Of course, if you're scared, I could always be persuaded to stay here – for a small consideration." Tellingly, his eyes strayed towards the bed.

"I'm sure I'll survive until Rocky comes back." My voice dripping ice, I turned and led the way back downstairs again, past the faux William Morris wallpaper that covered the walls, past an ancient suit of armour rustily guarding the foot of the stairs, past the glass tank containing one of Damien Hirst's infamous works of art – this one, plaited pig's entrails suspended in rhino's urine – the whole collectively demonstrating Rocky as a man of eclectic, if not impeccable, tastes. Never mind, I thought. There would be plenty of time to convert him to MFI. Going in, I threw myself into a comfortable overstuffed armchair. "So, where's the Beast of Bodmin?"

"If you mean Gretchen, she's tied up outside. About half a mile outside in the woods, actually." Unrepentant, he shrugged. "What can I tell you? I couldn't hear myself think, let alone concentrate on music with the racket she was making. Nothing for it then but a long walk, a rope and a big tree."

I gazed at him with new eyes. Admiring eyes. One might safely say awestruck! "What? You mean you hung her?"

"No." Tyrell grinned. "Not that I wasn't tempted."

"What happens if Get-em-off-O'Brien stumbles across her?"

"Then I feel sorry for the poor old bastard. His days of raping and pillaging will be over and that's for sure." Tyrell grinned, a wide, white, toothpaste-ad-man's dream of a grin that showed he didn't hold back on the baking-soda. "Still, I suppose I'd better go and bring her back – just in case Rocky happens to come home a bit early."

He really was most attractive, I decided. Shame I didn't fancy him. But then it's Sod's Law that you always want what you can't have. And I wanted Rocky! Tyrell, much to my astonishment appeared to want me. Orla wanted Tyrell. Debbie wanted Guy. Sophie wanted Debbie. The only people who, seemingly, had got what they'd wanted in their Christmas stockings were Rocky and Laura. High time then for Santa to get stuck in the chimney!

"Why?" I asked, hoping I already knew the reason, hoping, in fact, that I *was* the reason. "Why would he come home early?"

Brutally, Tyrell quenched the little candle of hope that had begun to fan in my heart. "Because we need to run through that little piece I was working on earlier. Time is getting on, as they say, and not a child in the house washed. If *Young Guns* is ever to hit the stage, then we're going to have to pull our fingers out and do some serious work. At the moment it's a complete shambles, especially the theme song." A one-hundred-watt light bulb popped above his head. "Hey! I couldn't run it past you, could I, Gemma? It's always useful to have an outsider's opinion."

Outsider? Well, I didn't much like the sound of that. Still, if I wanted to become an insider, I supposed I'd better show willing.

"Oh, go on then. I expect Gretchen can wait a while longer."

"Right!" Positioning himself at the Steinway in the corner of the room, Tyrell flexed his fingers, then ran them up and down the keys of the piano with all the skill of a latter-day Liberace. I must say, I was impressed, though less so with the song that followed which despite Rocky's previous protestations, sounded both in words and melody remarkably like a Tom Jones song, especially the line at the end of the chorus that went 'it's good to touch the tumbleweed of home'.

"Well?" With a flourish of musical notes and a crashing crescendo, Tyrell drew to a close. "What do you think?"

"I think," I told him without making the slightest dent in my limited store of diplomacy, "that you'd better hire a damn good lawyer."

Tyrell sighed. "Too 'Green Green Grass of Home'?"

I nodded. "Just a smidgin."

Standing up, Tyrell banged the lid shut. "See? I told Rocky that but, well, he just doesn't listen. I mean, it's a miracle how he got away with 'Hunger' and, okay, I wouldn't go so far as to say it was a complete rip-off of one of Bob Dylan's better-known ballads, but it was a bit too near the knuckle for comfort."

"Well, they're both musical geniuses," I said, comfortingly. "They're bound to have something in common."

"Yeah, but not Siamese twins!" Tyrell snorted, collapsing down beside me into the armchair and carrying the distinctly masculine whiff of good old soap and water about his person. Mmm, I had a sudden urge to lick behind his ear. "God! The sooner I'm out of this the better. A sheep! A sheep! My kingdom for a sheep!" Rhythmically he began banging his head backwards and forwards against the upholstery.

"But wouldn't you miss it all?" I asked curiously. "You know, the fame-game, the paparazzi, the designer labels, the first-class travel, the girls chanting your name and trampling all over one another's skulls in an effort to reach the stage – *'Gerr ourra me way, Britnee! I seen him furst!'*"

Tyrell shook his head. "Not a bit! With me the music-business is just a means to an end. Not that I don't like music. I do, but *real* music. You know, the classics, Mozart, Chopin, the Beatles, Janis Joplin, the Wombles. What we put out is just candy-floss and other people's thinly-veiled candy-floss at that!" Swivelling round, he grasped both of my hands and pulled them tightly to his chest. "Run away with me, Gemma, 'and be my love and we shall all the pleasures prove'!"

I shrieked delightedly. He was quoting Shakespeare or someone at me. No one had ever quoted anything at me before, barring the Riot Act. Now, if only Rocky had been here to play at Poet Laureate instead, everything would have been just peachy. Reluctantly, I pulled away. Reluctant because, even if he wasn't the right man, it was still very pleasant to be on the receiving end of flattery from a member of the opposite sex and especially one as good-looking as Tyrell O'Neill. But, let's be honest here, another part of me didn't want to take any chances on Rocky coming in, getting hold of the wrong end of stick and, gentleman that he was, backing off and leaving the field clear for Tyrell.

"Don't you think you'd better go and fetch Gretchen?" I reminded him, glancing at my watch. "Rocky could be here any minute and how are we going to explain abandoning her in the woods with a knife-wielding maniac on the loose?"

Sighing, Tyrell extricated himself from the armchair. "I'd sooner pluck out my right eyeball! But you're right. There's no putting off the evil moment any longer. Fancy coming for a roam in the gloam?"

I shook my head. "No, I'll leave you to do the honours. Besides, I want to savour my last few minutes of mutt-free freedom."

"I can understand that," Tyrell nodded. "But are you sure you don't want me to stop over tonight, keep you company? Sing to you, even? I mean, Gretchen isn't exactly renowned for her conversational abilities."

I shook my head. "No, it's all right. Besides, Rocky will be here."

A shadow crossed over his face, fleeting, but visible nonetheless. "Rocky! Yeah, of course. Silly of me to ask! All the nice girls like a rock to cling to."

"It isn't like that . . ." I began, but it was and we both knew it.

CHAPTER 15

"Gemma Murphy!" Lunch-time at *Vetz 4 Petz* and Debbie stuck me to the floor with a steely look. "And where exactly do you think you're going?"

"Just out for a walk," I said, trying hard to sound casual, trying hard to sound like a seasoned rambler whose greatest pleasure in life is to trek, booted and rucksacked, over the roughest terrain and in the vilest of weather conditions imaginable. I reckoned without Debbie's intimate knowledge of my character though.

"Oh yeah, because you like to go a-wandering." Her facial features arranged themselves in sneer mode. "Like fun you do!" With a most undignified, one might almost say school-marmish click of her fingers she ordered me back. "Come on, Murphy. Give! Or do I have to wring it out of you? What happened last night? When you *Goth-dere* was the cupboard bare? Or, did you have your wicked whey-hey-hey?"

Sulkily, I turned and retraced my steps. "What do

236

you think?" I stuck my chin out. "Does this face look like the face of a woman triumphant? Does this face look like the face of a woman who's seen paradise at first hand and partaken of its forbidden fruits?"

Debbie shrugged. "No, it looks like the face of an Antichrist not to mention a lazy slut who's forgotten to put her make-up on and swallowed a bucket-load of prunes into the bargain."

I shook my head. "Not forgotten – just didn't bother. Like, why should I? What's it all about, Alfie? It's not as if tarting myself up *gets* me anywhere. I'll bet that Rocky Cashel wouldn't notice if he fell over me stark naked with a shag-me-rigid sign slung around my neck."

Opening a packet of sandwiches Debbie tried to foist one on me, which by dint of spitting to one side and making gagging gestures, I ungraciously declined. Since falling pregnant, her predilection for weird foods had expanded to include such epicurean delicacies as sandwiches with a marshmallow, cheddar cheese, and strawberry-jam filling. Any day now, I expected to find her down on her hands and knees in the street outside, scrabbling in the dirt and shovelling it wholesale into her mouth with all the consummate pleasure of Michael Winner shovelling in the beluga.

"Oh, dear!" she commiserated, her voice totally at odds with the expression on her face that said, 'Oh joy! Out with the dirty laundry. Go forth and gather the public! It's washday!'

"Not so much oh dear!" I said. "As, oh dear, oh dear, oh bugger!"

"Or not, as the case may be." Half a chocolate-covered gherkin hanging out of her lips, Debbie regarded me avidly. "So, what exactly happened last night? Give it to me in glorious Technicolor. Or do you want me to drag it out of you by dint of a large pair of pliers, a kerosene blowtorch and an epilator?"

Crossing one first finger over the other, I backed away Hammer House fashion. "No! No! Anything but the epilator! The first and only time I used one of those it ripped off not only the hair on my legs but three layers of skin and a varicose vein as well. Anyway, what's to tell? Suffice it to say nothing happened – a big fat zilch! Heap big zero!"

"Ah!" Slurping in the tail-end of the pickle and helping herself to another, Debbie held up a forestalling hand. "Don't go and spoil the ending. Give me details. The gorier, the better! Take the A-roads. Remember, no one goes from departure to arrival without a few twists and turns along the way. It's called the scenic route. Although, to be honest, I'd prefer something more along the lines of the obscenic route, myself."

"Yeah, you and me both, mate!" I said feelingly. "But, unless you count Gretchen, the most obscene thing that happened to me was I grilled my finger-nails."

"Did what?"

"Oh, I'll come to it! After all you're the one insisting on the cross-country trek. So, all in good time!"

* * *

Huh, famous last words! That's how Rocky had greeted me when eventually he arrived home some time around midnight by which stage, it must be said, I was doing a good impression of *Woman on the Edge of a Nervous Breakdown*. Seemingly I was not as impervious to Get-em-off-O'Brien as I'd thought and the woods behind the house, although undoubtedly dark and deep, were anything but lovely.

"So, Gemma, having a good time, are you?" Erupting into the living-room, he'd myopically failed to notice anything amiss, including my stance which, like Eros, was poised for flight, or the fact that I was wielding a massive Ming vase with a view to indulging in a bit of skull-crushing should his credentials prove to be the least bit suspect.

Trembling, I replaced the vase atop a piece of furniture that bore all the hallmarks of an Egyptian sarcophagus. Probably another one of Damien Hirst's works of art containing the petrified remains of his maternal grandmother or something. "Oh, yeah! It's been a laugh a minute! That Gretchen had me in stitches all night. Did she ever tell you that gag about the forensic scientist? As in, what's a forensic scientist's favourite melody? No?" Without waiting for a response, I delivered the punch line. "Pubic 'air on a G-string! As for Tyrell, well, talk about let me entertain you! Robbie Williams was only trotting after him!"

Unamused either by my sparkling repartee or acerbic tongue, Rocky did a swift recce round the room. "Speaking of the sheep-farmer, where *is* Tyrell?" His glance wandered over me in a suspicious kind of looking-for-bloodstains way as though, maybe, I'd cut him up into tiny pieces and dissolved him in a bath of acid or, like Angie-Baby in that Helen Reddy song, secreted him in a nearby radio with a view to ravishing him on a regular and ongoing basis. "He was supposed to be working on 'The Green Green Tumbleweed'."

"Oh, really? Well, from what I could hear it seems like Tom Jones has already done all the work." Okay, maybe it wasn't exactly the most tactful thing to say to someone with whose genitals you wish to form a more intimate acquaintance but, it had to be said – for his own good. He didn't see it like that, though. To say he was annoyed would be a bit like saying Mount Etna in full eruption is a bit smoky. And, if I needed further evidence of his annoyance, he gave it to me in the deliberate and idiot-proof way he asked me to read his lips.

"Read-my-lips, Gemma. Tom Jones's 'Green Green Grass' is nothing like my 'Green Green Tumbleweed'. The only similarity is in the title. Remember there's forty shades of green in Ireland. No two are the same!"

Borrowing from my Aunty Kay's repertoire of sarcastic gestures, I rolled my eyes in different directions – a trick it had taken me years to perfect. On a good day, I could also waggle my ears. When I did both together it brought the traffic to a standstill and was a great way of breaking the ice at parties. Though not literally! "Oh, go and tell it on the mountain! It's pure plagiarism, Rocky. You'll be had up!"

"Rubbish!" He frowned, plunging his forehead into little grooves that, far from rendering him unattractive, gave him a slight air of danger, an aura of piratical magnetism deadly attractive to a certain calibre of woman. Like me, for instance. "Besides, what would *you* know? *You're* just a kennel-maid."

"As well as being a CD-buying member of the public and your number one fan!" I reminded him huffily and then with a last-ditch attempt to make him see sense. "For God's sake! Tom Jones's song and yours are identical twins. I'll go further, they're clones." And then I said something *really* stupid, something I knew even as I was saying it should *never* be said. "Even Tyrell thinks it's crap!"

"Does he, by Jove!" Rocky must have dredged that one up from his days of reading PG Wodehouse. "Well, to be honest that doesn't come as too much of a surprise considering I've never credited him with much taste. Take you, for example!" The furrows in his brow knitted themselves into such a complicated pattern that I could just about make out the promising beginnings of a woolly jumper. In cable-stitch!

"That's not very nice!" I wasn't so much cut to the

bone as dismembered. I had an awful feeling that this conversation was leading nowhere near the direction in which I wanted it to lead i.e. towards the bedroom although, at a push, the carpet was deep pile and an acceptable substitute. And, if terra-not-so-firma wasn't an option, at least one of the settees in the room could easily accommodate two.

"Nice?" Rocky took a threatening step towards me. "I don't *do* nice! I *do* music! I do *original!* I leave *nice* to the Tyrell O'Neills of this world, the going-nowhere-quick kind of people, except to the wilds of Donegal!"

"There are worse ambitions in life!" Oh God, what on earth was I doing defending Tyrell when I should have been down on my knees kowtowing to and salaaming the man of my dreams, assuring him I'd made a terrible mistake, assuring him that 'The Green Green Tumbleweed' was pure genius, the best thing I'd ever heard and, undoubtedly, destined for chart success. Still, someone, somewhere must have overdosed on the old perversity gene when programming my embryonic DNA and now it was determined to kick in and destroy me. "Better a sheep-farmer than a plagiariser! At least it's an honest occupation."

The woolly jumper unravelled and reassembled itself into a hair shirt I had an awful suspicion was meant for me. "Oh, so honesty is a trait you admire, is it?"

Tentatively, I nodded.

"Well, in that case, why the bloody hell are you

going around purporting to be an expert on pink-eye in poodles when you and I know full well you're just a fraud?"

I stamped my foot in frustration. Honestly, the man was insufferable and infuriating as well as being gusset-wringingly gorgeous. It was all I could do to stop myself from hurtling over, bowling him to the floor and shagging, as opposed to gagging, him into silence.

"Oh, you're not going to start that again, are you? You know very well you were the instigator of all that nonsense and it was just a convenient ruse to confound my mother and get Laura to allow me to Gretchen-sit."

"Stop right there!" A traffic cop, Rocky ordered me to pull over, switch off my ignition and produce my ID. "It wasn't *my* idea that you should Gretchen-sit. That was all down to your good buddy, Tyrell. And, hey, who was I to put a spanner in love's young works? Besides, I had a hankering to play Cupid. It's that loincloth of his, those wings, those cherubic lips, that deadly accurate aim with a bow and arrow. It's a power thing."

Confused, I sought enlightenment. "What exactly are you telling me? Like, I didn't even know Tyrell till the first time I came here and you introduced us."

"Ah-ha!" Obviously another initiate into the Masonic School of Secretive Nose Tappers, Rocky tapped his right nostril. "That's not to say *he* didn't *know you*."

"Rubbish! I'd never clapped eyes on him before in

my life!" I was confident of that. There was no need to ask the audience or phone a friend. In my part of the world, attractive men were about as rare as vestal virgins, so there was no way I wouldn't have remembered if a tasty, male morsel like Tyrell O'Neill had crossed my path.

"Okay," Rocky conceded. "Maybe you didn't exactly meet him, *per se*. Let's just say he saw you and was smitten by your . . . er . . . smitten by your . . . er . . ."

I curled my lip. Rocky was obviously having difficulty in finishing the sentence in the usual way. "Beauty!" I told him. "Beauty is the word you're looking for."

He was unconvinced. "Oh, am I? Yes, well anyway, the story goes like this. Tyrell has an uncle who's a vet in that *Vetz 4 Petz* place where you work. Rob, I think he said his name was. Yeah, that's it. Rob something or other."

"Not Rob Kilbride?" I screeched, in a voice so filled with helium it was all I could do to prevent it from floating up, up and away in a beautiful balloon.

Rocky snapped his fingers. "Kilbride! That's it! Anyway, apparently he often meets his uncle after work – they have a love of sheep in common – and that's how he spotted you." Rocky grinned. "The poor, sad bastard just sits in his car outside gazing at you through the windows like you were the Mona Lisa in the Loo."

"In the Louvre!" I corrected him, but in a half-hearted fashion because I couldn't quite get my head around what he was telling me.

"Whatever! Anyway, Tyrell was with me when the police showed up with some likely mug-shots of my assailants in Blessington and Tyrell got all excited when he recognised you as the wet part of his dreams."

All feeling suddenly leaving my legs, I groped about for a nearby chair. "The police showed up? God, I'd no idea they were so hot on our trail." I could feel myself breaking out into a cold sweat. Imagine it! The ignominy! Being carted off in a tumbril, handcuffed like a common criminal, Aunty Kay bringing her knitting to the guillotine, bagsing a seat in the front row and that Scarlet Pimpernel bastard nowhere in sight.

"*See!*" Vindicated, she'd work those needles till sparks came off them. Click! Click! Click! "*I always said she was a basket case! She didn't get that from our side of the family. Oh oh, no! Mind you, her father was always a limp short of a wooden leg, so what can you expect? The pins of the father and all that!*"

Rocky nodded with the kind of satisfied nod Dracula must have given upon encountering a particularly juicy and pulsating jugular vein. "Oh, they were hot on your heels all right, so hot I'm surprised they didn't raise blisters. And, be in no doubt, I was of a mind to prosecute. I wanted to nail your ass to the wall. I mean, nobody, but *nobody*, takes advantage of Rocky Cashel without buying a ticket at full price so you can thank your lucky stars, or rather, Tyrell O'Neill, that I didn't."

I was beginning to feel very sick as well as very stupid. Orla was right. There was no big, convoluted Rocky plot. There was *never* any big, convoluted Rocky plot –. I wasn't here because Rocky secretly fancied me and hankered after an action reply of my pelvic thrusts. Apparently, I wasn't even here for Gretchen's benefit. Instead, I was here at the behest of an aspiring sheep-farmer, a man whose veterinarian uncle had to be chaperoned in the presence of under-age sheep. And to think I had gone to all that trouble of having my nails done!

"So, now you know!" Rocky said in a tone that showed just how much pleasure he'd taken in nuking my illusions. "I just want to make it plain that, had the ball been in my court, you would have been its co-defendant in the dock."

"Message received and understood." Miserable as sin, I hung my head. Gemma Murphy over, down and out!

"Anyway," Rocky, either oblivious to or completely uncaring of my misery, stretched himself, arching his arms high over his head, "now that you *are* here, do you think maybe you could make yourself useful and make me something to eat? I can't stomach hospital food. Even in the canteen it's all boiled cabbage, steamed cod and anaemic rice pudding. It's no wonder half the patients end up in the morgue."

Like, would you believe it? Having pushed me headfirst into an abyss, he'd only gone and flung me down a rope-ladder a moment later. Of course! Mentally, I snapped my fingers as hope did, indeed, spring eternal. What was that old saying about the way to a man's stomach being via his oesophagus and then, by a circuitous route, onward to his heart? Here was my chance to recover lost ground. So, Rocky didn't fancy me? Not now, maybe. But he *would!* Yes, suh! Again, mentally, because if I did it for real I'd end up being incarcerated in the secure wing of the nearest mental hospital, I clicked my heels and gave a smart salute! As for Tyrell O'Neill – well, I suppose I should thank him, really. He had, after all, saved my bacon *and* gained me admittance to Rocky's lair, so to speak. Were it not for his misguided machinations, I might well be cooling those same heels behind bars and dodging the advances of desperate lesbian convicts and twisted screws. Listen, I've seen *Bad Girls!* I *know* what happens. Talking about desperate lesbians – Sophie and Debbie had a lot to thank me for too. I mean, but for the intervention of Saint Tyrell, they might also have been bumping up the overcrowding statistics in the cells next to me. Although, come to think of it, Sophie might have had a slightly different take on matters, by which I mean, the words lesbian, women's prison and sweetie shop do give rise to certain connotations.

"Sure!" Reprieved, I endeavoured to look like a

female Marco Pierre White. Competent, creative and with a sound working knowledge of electric whisks and bain-maries. "I'm sure I can find my way around the kitchen and rustle up something to suit sir's discerning palate. So, what exactly did you have in mind?" Too late I realised the folly of that particular question coming from someone who once tried to boil an egg in an empty kettle with pretty explosive, not to mention stinking, consequences.

"Oh, osso bucco, crown of roast lamb, moussaka. Any old thing at all really." Rocky roared as he caught sight of the mounting horror on my face because to be honest, I wouldn't know a moussaka if it jumped up and bit me on the arse. As for Osso Bucco – I could have sworn he was one of the Italian racing contingent, sponsored by Ferrari or someone. "Relax, Gemma, I'm only joking. A cheesy toastie will do just fine." Rocky grinned modestly. "I know it's difficult to believe but, actually, I'm a man of rather simple tastes."

Well, that's where he was wrong. It wasn't all that difficult to believe at all, at least, not when you brought Laura into the equation! Like, they didn't come much simpler than her! Careful to mask my thoughts, I opted for cheerful, promising and forgiving. Sexy would come later. "One cheesy toastie coming right up! Worcester sauce on top?" That was a little tip I'd picked up from an advert on the telly.

"The bizz!" Rocky rubbed his hands together in anticipation and my spirits rose another notch, which would have been pretty gratifying were it not for the fact that the only notches I was interested in really were the ones I intended to carve on my bedpost in the, hopefully, not too distant future. Or, on his bedpost! I had no moral dilemma about screwing Laura's fella in Laura's bed. Hell, I would have screwed him in a bed of nettles and relished each and every sting! And on this happy note I made my way into the kitchen, deliberately humming 'Green Green Tumbleweed' as further evidence of my complete capitulation. In retrospect, he was dead right! It wasn't a bit like Tom Jones's 'Green Green Grass'. Perish the thought! And perish Tyrell O'Neill! If he hadn't mentioned it in the first place, the thought would never have entered my head and I would have seen Rocky's song for what it clearly was, a masterpiece of originality and musical genius. 'Ah, but it would have entered your head!' a little voice chided me. 'Nay, *did* in fact and before ever you met Tyrell O'Neill what's more!' But that was the voice of my conscience and taking a leaf out of Orla's book I treated it to a deaf ear before immersing myself in the makings of the best cheesy toastie to be found this side of Christendom.

"As I stepped down from the coach!" I sang. There! No similarity whatsoever. What on earth was I thinking of? Cheesy toastie assembled (I used Double Gloucester with chives to give it extra zing – I was really getting into this Delia Smith cookery lark!), I placed it on the eye-level grill pan and lit the gas. Correction! I

attempted to light the gas. My egg-in-a-dry-kettle experience having imbued me with the greatest of respect when it comes to anything with explosive properties I was, to put it mildly, somewhat perplexed when, after a false start or two, it gave a faint *phut* and went straight out again. Turning my back for a moment I searched the kitchen for inspiration, finding it in the shape of a small spider that was valiantly attempting to Tarzan-swing from the curtain-pole onto the windowpane but missing by about a mile. Undaunted, it simply clambered back up its web and lined up for a further attempt or six. Now why did that little tableau set the bells to ringing? Of course! Robert de Bruce – holed up in a cave somewhere and giving up all hopes of escape till a little spider made him buck up his ideas and move towards the light. Picking up the box of matches, I bucked up my own ideas too and moved towards the light – in this case the pilot light. Try, try, try again, Gemma, I told myself, running the lit match up and down alongside the little gas jets. You'll succeed at last and, hopefully, refrain from blowing yourself up in the process and, if you don't, well, they say being blown to smithereens is quick and relatively painless!

"And did you?"

I started. God, I'd forgotten entirely about Debbie! "Yep! I succeeded all right. Better than I could ever have imagined. Like, one moment, I was lighting the grill, the next my fingernails went up like an inferno and I spent the next ten minutes howling and hopping up and down like a demented banshee."

Grabbing my right hand, Debbie scrutinised the charred and blackened remains of what, for a short period of time, had been my pride and joy. The pinnacle of my femininity!

"Jesus, Gemma!" she hooted, almost choking on a mouthful of chocolate-covered gherkin, the unsympathetic cow. "What are you like?"

Huh! So well she could laugh but it might well have been a different story had she been the one on the receiving end of Rocky's wrath. God, even the memory was enough to bring me out in a cold sweat, which in the light of recent experiences wasn't altogether without its brighter side!

An ancient mace, wrested from the suit of armour at the foot of the stairs, whirling about his head, and under the impression that we were being invaded by aliens, zombies or worse, Saxons, Rocky came rushing into the kitchen, wild-eyed, wild-haired and apparently ready for battle. "What? What? What? What the hell is going on, Gemma?"

Like, I should have thought that was obvious unless, of course, sex-god, that he was, he was completely inured to hot women.

"What the bloody hell do you think is going on?" I shrieked, scooting round and round the kitchen like a whirling dervish. "Like, I'm on fire, man! Do something, can't you? Well, don't just stand there!" I panicked as he proceeded to do just that with the mace spinning in ever-decreasing circles around his head. *"Put me out!"*

Realisation slowly dawning that we were not under attack, nor was I playing at Thor lobbing thunderbolts and lightning as a prelude to grilling his cheesy toastie, Rocky was galvanised into action. Hurriedly exchanging the mace for a mini-fire-extinguisher off the kitchen wall, he took aim and thirty seconds later found me doing an impressive impression of the abominable snowman. All, except my fingernails, which, like the Olympic torch, were still merrily ablaze and with every intention of staying so until the next Games four years down the line. With an aim that bad, it was, presumably, more by good luck than management that he'd managed to impregnate the fair Laura. It took a further two attempts before the blaze was finally extinguished and we could survey the damage.

"Women!" Rocky snorted, picking up my smouldering wrist and gazing in amazement at the curled and blackened stumps adorning the tips of my fingers. "Why? Why do you do it to yourselves? All this artifice! False nails! False tits! Liposuction! Tummy tucks! Why can't you be happy with yourselves the way you are? The way God made you? Take Laura, for instance, a one hundred per cent natural *femme fatale*, whose only concession to vanity is a bar of Pears soap and a pumice stone."

And boy, did it show! It was all I could do to stop my eyes from rolling crazily around in their sockets.

Well, sod it! I might have known all lectures would eventually lead to the fair Laura. *Femme fatale*, my butt! If I were her I'd be queuing up for the works, false nails, false tits, liposuction and as much collagen and silicone as it's humanly possible to squeeze into one human body. Then, maybe I'd think about having a double corneal transplant and, if funds stretched to it, dermabrasion on any part of my body that showed so much as a hint of ginger freckle.

Meekly allowing myself to be led over to the kitchen sink, I flinched as he dunked my hand unceremoniously beneath the cold tap. This kind of bodily contact was not exactly what I'd had in mind when I signed up for this trip. Still, it was as good an opportunity as any to sneak in a bit of moaning and groaning and to lean helplessly back against his masterful chest, hopefully sending his protective male instincts into overdrive.

"Stand up straight, would you," he snapped, cottoning onto my little plan right away. "Or you'll have us both on the floor. Then again, maybe that's been your intention all along."

Annoyed at being rumbled, I made a great play of indignation. "Oh, really? So you think having my fingernails fried to a crisp is my idea of foreplay? You think having my fingers fused from the knuckles upward turns me on, do you? You think the smell of burning flesh has aphrodisiacal qualities, like oysters and chocolate and Spanish fly? You think ruining my best, my *only* Karen Millen dress with a badly aimed fire-extinguisher moistens the parts soft words, sonnets and champagne don't reach?" Twisting round in his arms, I addressed his collarbone, which as collarbones go was pretty much in a class of its own, being nicely tanned and not overly bony.

"Okay, okay, spare me the sermon! I suppose we should get you to the hospital just in case you need a bit of your backside grafted onto the burns or something." Like a spinning-top, Rocky whirled me back round again, which is when I became pleasantly aware of the sensation of his rock-hard abdominals pressing against my butt as I leaned over the sink. Talk about being between a Rocky and a hard place. And loving it!

"No!" I said hastily. "There's no real damage done – well, apart from my nails that is. I mean the tips of my fingers are only a big singed. I've had worse from toasting marshmallows." Yeah, right! Like Irish people go around making a habit of toasting marshmallows. Like, it's not just something you read about in books like ginger beer and macaroons and other jolly Enid Blyton stuff. Next, I'd be telling him my favourite pastime was listening to excerpts from the Bible whilst cross-stitching *'The Devil Makes Work For Idle Hands'* or some such other improving proverb on a sampler. Still, my head would have needed to be hanging on by a single sinew, my limbs scattered to the four corners of the earth and my tongue ripped out at the roots before

I'd relinquish my one, my only chance to spend a night under the same roof as Rocky Cashel. Alone . . . together!

Rocky coughed dubiously as the acrid stink of third-degree burns rose up and caught at his throat. "You're sure? I mean, I could always call you a cab to take you to the hospital."

"What?" My face registered shock. "You mean you wouldn't drive me?" Was that callous or was that callous?

Rocky shook his head. "Nah, I'm dead beat. There's no way I'm going back out there. Not for anything! Besides, I've got a heavy schedule of rehearsals ahead of me tomorrow and a guy needs his beauty sleep, you know." He ran distracted fingers through his hair. "Plus, if you want to know, it's been a bitch of a day and not one I'd ever want to go through again!"

Did I say callous? Callous my foot! He needed his beauty sleep! Of course he did! I would provide the beauty and the sleep would come later. Deliberately I avoided asking for a blow-by-blow account of his day from hell. The way I saw it, my job was to lift his spirits, not send him spiralling down into a clinical depression for which the only answer was a straitjacket complemented by a long course of Prozac. Call me an optimist but I began to feel quite hopeful again. A dab of calamine and I'd be back in the pink – literally!

"Look," I said brightly, in an effort to prove just how absolutely un-needy of hospital care I was. "Just point me in the direction of your first-aid kit and I'll be back in a jiffy and then, if you're still hungry, I'll make you a sandwich or something." I crossed my heart. "*And* I promise to stay away from all things combustible."

Rocky yawned hugely, giving the impression that if the rest of him was half as well hung as his tonsils, I was in for the night of my life. "Don't bother. I'll just grab an apple from the fruit bowl and turn in. It's been an exhausting day. Don't forget to feed Gretchen, though. There's a nice piece of fillet steak in the fridge."

Turn in? He couldn't just turn in! I wasn't finished with him yet. Hell, come to that, I hadn't even started with him! Frantically, I looked about for a delaying tactic, finding one, fortunately, without too much trouble and hoping it didn't sound like too much of an afterthought.

"Er . . . hang on a sec, Rocky! You never said how Laura's coming along. And Junior? How's Junior? Still hanging in there, eh? Still got his womb reservation? Managed to swing a later departure time, did he?" I grinned, as evidence of my big-hearted attitude towards his progeny – a case of love him, love his sprog. Though not his dog! "Well, who can blame him? I mean, like he's got a nine-month fully inclusive holiday there on the Costa del Placento; maid service, private, heated swimming-pool, food and drink ready chewed, while the best most of us can manage is a ten-day, package-deal in a two-star Spanish hotel with dodgy gas flues and non-existent fire escapes."

A strangled sound from Rocky showed me that, yet again, I'd put my foot so far down my neck my toes were eroding my cervix. Crumpling like an empty paper bag, he dropped into a kitchen chair and covering his head with his hands began to rock to and fro, a wailing issuing from between his lips that, whatever it was, was most definitely not 'The Green Green Tumbleweed'! Putting two and two together I came up with a guess. Oh, Lord! She'd lost the baby! Laura'd gone and lost the baby! "Oh, Lord, Rocky!" I said, sinking to my knees beside him and wrapping my foam-covered arms about his shaking shoulders without, and I swear it, the least hint of lasciviousness in my actions. "She's lost the baby, hasn't she? Laura's gone and lost the baby! Why didn't you *tell* me? You should have *told* me. I should have *noticed*! Oh, God!" His head came up. His eyes were bleary. His breath was beery. Funny, that was the first time I noticed he'd been drinking! No wonder he hadn't noticed the state of me when he'd first come in. No wonder he hadn't wanted to get the car out to drive me to the hospital. No wonder his aim had been so off with the fire extinguisher. Imagine! The light of my life and I hadn't noticed he'd been breaking his heart, hadn't noticed he'd been drinking. Well, that said a lot for my sensitivity, didn't it? If we were truly to be soul mates, it seemed I had an awful lot of swotting up to do.

"What?" I asked, putting my ear close to his mouth as the wailing turned into an even more unintelligible noise that consisted of a grunt, a syllable, another couple of grunts and a sibilant hiss. I don't know what Carol Vorderman would have made of it on *Countdown*. Not so much, give me a consonant or a vowel, Carol, as give me a grunt, a hiss and a snarl! "Wh-ha-aa-t? " I said again, strapping the word on a rack and drawing it out to all four extremities. "What are you trying to say?"

"Snot mine!" Either he'd lost the ability to speak English or the grief had driven him mad. "Snot mine!" he said again, only louder as if to increase volume was to increase understanding. "The fucking baby! Snot mine!"

Like Paul having his epiphany on the Road to Damascus, I had mine on the kitchen floor. "Oh?" I said, as light, like freshly ground coffee, slowly percolated through. "You mean, the baby's not yours?" Hmm! Interesting! So Ms Rocky-and-I-go-all-the-way-back-to-kindergarten went even further with someone else. "So, if you're not the father, who is?"

Rocky dropped his head again. "The milkman!"

I shrugged. "Okay! Okay! I deserved that. It was insensitive of me to ask."

Rocky pinioned me with dead eyes. "No, really! The milkman!"

"No! You mean *really* the milkman?" Aghast, it was all I could do to stop my chin from cracking the tiles on the floor. "What on earth does he have that you haven't?"

"Hell, I don't know!" Rocky laughed hollowly. "Maybe he creams her knickers in a way I never could."

"But are you sure it's the milkman's?" I pressed, scarcely noticing the vulgarity, so intent was I on getting to the root of matters. "You didn't have a row or anything, did you? Maybe it was just something she said in the heat of the moment, something designed to waft up your kilt and expose your Achilles' heel, amongst other things!"

"No!" Brokenly, Rocky examined his fingernails. "There was no row. She was as cold and clinical as a surgeon's knife; said she couldn't go on pretending; said I had a right to know because, fundamentally, I was a decent guy but she was in love with the milkman and well, you can't help your heart, can you?" Slamming a closed fist on the table in a series of thumps, Rocky engaged me in eye-to-eye contact. "*Fundamentally!* Jesus! *Fun-da-ment-ally* I'm a nice guy! I spend the best part of my life in love with her, planning our future together, kids, pensions, his and hers funerals, a fluffy cloud made for two so we can carry on our love affair in the hereafter but, while I've been living in a fool's paradise, she's been seeing me as no more than a nice guy! Fundamentally, a nice guy!"

"I can't believe it!" Wonderingly, I shook my head. "I mean, she seemed so into you. God, the first time I met her, she practically put a gun to my head warning me off."

"Really?" Unimpressed, Rocky delved in his pocket, withdrew a tissue and honked for Ireland. "Sounds like she was trying to convince herself. The truth is I was the one who made *all* the running, *all* the time. As for Laura – well, she just went along with it until, I guess, she met Mr Gold Top and found out there was more to life than fortune and fame."

Did I mention Laura was ugly? Well, make that ugly *and* thick! "If you ask me," I said, staunchly, "she wants her head examined."

"Nice of you to say so, but it's not actually true. Laura is one of the sanest people I know. That's one of the things I love about her. She's grounded. She's not impressed with the material things in life – hence, her willingness to trade in a fleet of Mercs for an electric milk-float and follow her heart." He caught my eye and I detected the slick shine of tears in his own. "I would have given it all up tomorrow, you know, if it made her happy. I would have gladly settled down and played Mr Average in a suburban semi, content to potter about in the garden at weekends, kicking a football with Junior and taking him for piggy-back rides. But she never gave me the opportunity. Instead she found someone else to father her child. Seems like I was aiming for the sun but firing blanks and it took a milkman to hit the target." Rocky sighed, a tortured sound that dragged itself all the way up from his shoes before exiting through his mouth on a waft of Guinness. "I wouldn't mind only I was really looking forward to being a father, exploring the paternal side of my nature, oohing over milk teeth, first words and the poetry of baby motions."

I pulled myself onto a chair opposite as echoes of a conversation came back to me. Rocky, talking about his love of the city life, all things bright and beautiful.

"Yeah, well, give me the bright lights every time. There's no way you'd find me reclusing it up in the back of beyond."

Laura: *"It depends on who you were reclusing it up with."*

And I had thought she'd meant Rocky but now, in the light of recent revelations, I couldn't help wondering if she'd actually meant the milkman. God, I'd been so jealous, especially when Rocky had pulled her down onto his lap and kissed her, and jealous, let's face it, of how right they looked together, how much of a *couple* they were. But, like a magician sawing through his assistant's torso on stage, it was apparently all just an illusion. Just an act! Talk about a bitch in the manger! What right had she got to go warning me off Rocky when she plainly didn't want him herself? Leaning across, I patted his knee consolingly.

"Look, you're young. You're pant-wettingly gorgeous. You're a rock star. There'll be no shortage of women falling over themselves in an effort to incubate the fruit of your loins." The words 'and I'll be at the forefront' went unspoken.

"But *not* Laura!" Resignedly, Rocky stood up and gave himself a little shake. "Anyway, sufficient unto the day are the evils thereof. I'm off to bed. Don't forget to feed Gretchen and, by the way, she'll probably want to sleep on your bed."

"Wait!" I got to my own feet and, feeling like Joan of Arc, prepared to sacrifice myself for the greater good. "I'll come with you. You really shouldn't be alone tonight."

Rocky shot me the rictus of a grin. "What? Offering to give me a sympathy shag, are you? Thanks, Gemma, but I think I'll pass. Not that I'm not tempted, mind. An ego boost is just what I need right now and I must say you don't half clean up well."

Blushing furiously, I protested my virtue. "Don't be stupid. I didn't mean *that*! I just meant I'd stay with you – you know, keep you company, keep the gremlins away and the things that go bump in the night."

But Rocky wasn't fooled. He knew exactly what was on my agenda. Sadly, it wasn't on his. "It's not the things that go bump in the night I'm worried about, more like the things that go *hump* in the night!" He swept me a courtly bow, which just went to prove he was more pissed than I'd thought. "And so, fair Gemma, I bid you goodnight."

It was difficult getting to sleep – not least because every sense was on red alert, every pore achingly conscious of Rocky sleeping just across the hallway but also on account of Gretchen not only insisting on sleeping across my feet, but attacking them whenever I had the audacity to try and shift into a more comfortable position. Ears straining, I listened for the slightest indication that Rocky was awake, willing him to provide me with the slightest excuse to go in and offer my . . . er . . . services. But there was nothing, not a breath, not a sigh, not a snore. Rocky, it appeared, was either dead to the world or, like me, lying quietly awake and staring at the elaborate frescoes adorning the ceiling in which case there was no reason I could think of why we couldn't get all fresco together. Losing myself in happy fantasies of mutual ceiling-gazing it was some time before I became aware that Gretchen had started to growl, a guttural sound that started deep in her throat and which worked its way steadily up the staves to a steady thrum.

"Oh, shut up, you!" I snarled, showing my own prowess at the sport and lashing out with my feet. "Unless you want to end up with your pathetic, pink powder-puff tail shoved wholesale down your neck!" Ignoring me, Gretchen continued to growl and as I struggled up in bed the better to perfect my aim, I noticed her whole body was tense, her ears pricked, her head pointed towards the window. And that's when I remembered the woods onto which my bedroom backed and, following hot on the heels of that thought, Get-'em-off O'Brien. A moment later my worst fears were realised as a dark shape materialised at the French windows and after a bit of ludicrously easy fiddling about with the catch, simply opened them up and stepped through. Like the scream that froze in my own throat, Gretchen's snarl froze halfway between a growl and a yelp, both of us turned suddenly to stone. Happily, though, her paralysis was of the temporary variety and a moment later saw her launch herself like a guided missile towards the intruder's ankles. Scrambling out of bed on legs that whilst shaking were rather hard to stir, I groped about for the light switch praying that, as in all the best fairytales, once the light went on the bogeyman would disappear. He didn't though. Instead he leapt about just inside the window, bleeding heavily from any number of puncture wounds, lashing out at Gretchen and swearing blue murder. As might be expected, all this commotion woke Rocky if, indeed, he had ever been asleep and a moment later found him erupting into the room with the mace, once more his weapon of choice, whirling about his head.

"What the hell is going on here?" I could tell by his face that he wasn't past thinking it was some kind of a set-up, that I'd deliberately engineered this mad axe-man situation to get him into the same bedroom as me and from thence into the same bed.

"I-it's Get-'em-off O'Brien." I shrieked, my voice making a kind of Kate-Bush-in-Wuthering-Heights-mode shriek and pointing a tremulous finger towards the dressed-all-in-black-and-wearing-a-ski-mask-like-all-the-best-intruders-do figure who was being dragged slowly, inevitably to his knees by a poodle made vicious with bloodlust.

"For God's sake, Rocky! Call her off!"

At the sound of the intruder's voice, Rocky and I exchanged glances, suspicious on my part, amazed on his, or apparently so. Like, why on earth should Ireland's premier rock star be on first-name terms with Get-'em-off O'Brien, Ireland's premier rapist and absconder from the law?

"Gemma! Help me! Pleeeze!"

Jesus! My body jerked like a marionette whose strings have got all tangled up together. Not only did he appear to know Rocky but, horror of horrors, he appeared to know *me*! The bastard knew *me*! *How* did the bastard know me? A moment later I found out.

"For feck's sake, you pair of shites! It's me, Tyrell! Now call her off, would you, before I lose the very little that remains of my dignity and my blood."

"Tyrell?" Rocky and I queried in tandem, which is possibly the only time we ever had or ever would achieve perfect unity.

"Tyrell? Tyrell O'Neill?" Striding over, Rocky, dredging up all the strength of his well-toned biceps, commenced prising Gretchen off the intruder's trouser-front, a procedure which called for much delicate micro-surgery if his fellow band-member was not to end his days as a frond-waving eunuch. "Just what the hell do you think you're playing at?" Mission accomplished, he passed a sated but worn-out

Gretchen to me. "This isn't some kinky game of yours and Gemma's, is it?"

"Certainly not!" Affronted, I tossed the poodle onto the bed where after a short episode of victorious barking and circle-turning, she lay down and went promptly to sleep, the red of Tyrell's blood drying about her mouth and clashing horribly with her pink-dyed fur.

Ripping off his ski mask, Tyrell proved that it was indeed he and not Get-'em-off O'Brien unless, of course, Get-'em-off was an alias which, let's face it, was looking more and more likely by the minute. "No! It's got nothing to do with Gemma. Well, actually it has. That's to say, indirectly it has."

"How?" I demanded, my lips pulling themselves into a straight, obdurate line. "How has it got anything to do with me?" A pulsating halo of innocence about my head, I hoped Rocky would see that this time no blame could possibly attach itself to me, that I was shriven of any wrongdoing and as pure as the driven snow. I also hoped he had psychic abilities and could differentiate between my innocence and Tyrell's guilt (manifested by dint of shuffling about, shifting from one foot to the other and generally giving the impression of someone who's been found in the parlour at the same time the Colonel's copped it).

"Well, it's the Milk Tray Man, innit?" he said eventually, his hands half-rising then falling helplessly to his sides again.

"What is?" Agog, Rocky stared at him suspiciously. "Have you been snorting white lines, Tyrell? Been talcing your nostrils, have you? Got a bad batch, did you?"

"No! No, I have not!" Self-consciously, Tyrell kicked at the tasselled fringing of a Chinese rug on the floor. "I wanted to impress Gemma. That's all."

"What?" Outraged, I took a threatening step forward. "By sneaking in through the window and scaring the living daylights out of me? By putting the heart across me? Oh, very impressive, that! Tell me, what do you do for an encore and would you like a curtain call and a standing ovation?"

"Aw shit! This isn't how it was meant to turn out. Not at all!" Not content with kicking the tassels, he next attempted to extinguish all signs of life by grinding them into the floor with his heel. "And if that nasty,. vicious excuse for an animal of the canine persuasion hadn't been here, everything would have turned out fine."

Two swallows on the wing, my eyebrows scaled Mount Everest. "Oh, yeah? If you can call ending up raped, pillaged and strangled *fine!*"

To my annoyance, Rocky started to laugh. Either the man had a very sick sense of humour or there was a joke somewhere I simply didn't get. In fact such was his merriment, I was sure he would bring on a hernia at the very least.

"I get it! The Milk Tray Man! But, of course! You

were sneaking in to leave a card and a box of chocolates on Gemma's bed! Problem is – you reckoned without Gretchen. As far as she was concerned you were in the wrong place at the right time and romantic gestures bedamned!"

A bitter and thwarted man, Tyrell shot the dog a look that said: give me five minutes alone in a locked room with her, armed with a cricket bat and then let's see who emerges the bloodier!

Cynically, I ran my eyes over his black-clothed body, searching for evidence of telltale lumps and bumps secreted about his person. "Yeah, right. The Milk Tray Man! So old hat! So *passeé*." And then on a different, a greedier note. "So, where are they then? These chocolates? An illusion, maybe? A complete and utter fallacy or phallacy should I say, like Get-'em-off O'Brien? A figment of your fevered and psychotic imagination?"

Palms out, Tyrell admitted his guilt. "Okay! Okay! I'll come clean. It's true! There *is* no Get-'em-off O'Brien but the chocolates are real all right. I dropped them out the window when Gretchen attacked me. *And* they were Thornton's best hand-made truffles!" He gestured with his shoulder towards the open window. "You can see for yourself if you don't believe me."

"But why?" I asked, resisting the urge to fling myself through the still open window and begin gathering them up immediately with a view to stuffing them down my neck. If ever there was a better time for gorging on chocolate, I couldn't think of it. "What on earth would possess you to do such a stupid thing? I mean, the Milk Tray Man? Like, get a grip!"

Impatient, Rocky butted in on the inquisition. "Oh, for goodness sakes, Gemma! Can't you see the man's in love with you?" Embittered, his glance bounced from me to Tyrell and back again. "And lurve, as anyone with half a brain cell knows, makes fools of us all.

CHAPTER 16

"Ain't that the truth, though!" Wiping the residue of the chocolate-covered gherkin off her lips, Debbie jerked her chin towards her still flat stomach. "Look what lurve got me, morning sickness, boobs that feel like they've been attacked by a meat tenderiser and the prospect of nine months' hard labour with nothing but a screaming bundle of trouble to show at the end of it all."

"Yep!" I said, nodding agreement. "Life's a bitch all right. There's you up the iceberg without a harpoon and there's poor Rocky gutted because he's not the father of Laura's baby after all. And now he's convinced that he's been firing blanks for years and will never have a teenage daughter to warn off ciggies, alcohol and accepting hollow wooden elephants from strange men while on holiday in Egypt or Morocco!"

Rising from her seat, Debbie walked over and poured herself a cup of water from the water cooler in the corner. "You know, it's true what they say. If you want to make God laugh, just tell him your plans. Like, he must be wetting himself when he looks down and sees Rocky and me – two wrecks surrounded by the flotsam and jetsam of our silly, little human aspirations. He must be bloody hysterical."

Dolefully, I nodded. "Mm. I bet he sits up there on a big, golden cloud pushing us all around like we were chessmen on a board."

Debbie downed her water in one, her throat convulsing like an anaconda swallowing a sumo wrestler. "Yeah, and right now it's checkmate for me. Honestly, Gem, I've painted myself into a corner. No matter which way I turn now, I'm going to put my foot in it and make a helluva mess. So, I guess I'd better follow the path of least resistance."

"Look!" I said staunchly. "You know Sophie and I will always support you."

"Always?" Debbie fixed me with her forget-me-not blue gaze. "Always is a very long time, Gemma. Times change. People move on. Sands shift!" She smiled with her mouth but her eyes were sad. "No, Gemma. I'm grateful to you and Soph. Of course I am but I've made up my mind. I'm not ready for this baby. I'm definitely going ahead with a termination." Sighing, she chucked her empty paper cup in the bin. "It's best all round."

"Oh no, it's not!" So intent had we been on our conversation that neither one of us had noticed Sophie come in and now she stood there, white-faced and

271

shaking, like a child who's queued for hours in Disneyland only to find she doesn't meet the height restriction on the roller-coaster ride. "It's not best for the baby. It's not best for you! You'll regret it, Debbie. You know you will."

White-faced herself, Debbie rounded on her. "Oh, for heaven's sakes shut up, Sophie! Do you think this is a decision I arrived at on the 14A bus? I didn't. Nobody knows how I've agonised over it, the sleepless nights lying awake tossing and turning, searching for a solution and coming up with nothing but a panic attack and a future as bleak as a life without MTV and Johnny Depp."

Plainly upset, Sophie laid a tentative hand on her shoulder. "I'm sorry, Debs. I know it can't have been easy for you. It's just that there must be a better way."

"Believe me, Soph, there isn't." Debbie threw up her hands. "Oh, look, let's put our cards on the table here. I know you have some misguided idea that you can just wave a magic wand and make everything all right for me but really, it would never work. I'm not like you. You, me and baby makes three simply doesn't light my touch-paper. Sad and all as it sounds, I need a *man* to make me complete. Much and all as I value you as a *friend*, that's all it is, friendship! Pure and simple."

Honestly, I felt sick for Sophie, knowing that with every word Debbie was setting fire to her ship of dreams and floating it off down the Ganges. And yet, I could see where Debbie was coming from too. And, when all was said and done, wasn't it kinder really to demolish Sophie's delusions of *Little House on the Prairie* before they got entirely out of hand and she started trying to force Debbie into gingham pinnies and calico bonnets to a rousing rendition of 'Bringing in the Sheaves'?

"Oh God!" Frustrated, Sophie drove a clenched fist into the palm of her open hand. "*Why* wasn't I born a man!"

Desperately trying to inject a bit of levity into an atmosphere that had become barbed with tension I hoisted a seductive leer on my face. "If you were, we'd be queuing six deep and ripping your boxers off with our teeth." Echoes of my mother's depravity! Thanks, Mammy!

Sophie made a little moue but I was relieved to see the hint of a smile about her lips. The merest *soupçon* of a grin! "If only!" she said, her eyes fixed on Debbie like a glutton's eyes on a prime side of beef. "If only!"

"Hey!" Every bit as anxious as me to restore the equilibrium, Debbie reached over, squeezed her hand. "Sorry, Soph. That's just the way the cookie crumbles. No hard feelings, eh?"

Resigned, Sophie shrugged. "More like the way the nookie crumbles! Still, it was a nice daydream while it lasted. And Gemma's right. We'll stick by you like superglue whatever, won't we, Gem?" I nodded wordlessly as Debbie smiled her thanks.

"Oi!" The sisterly bonding experience was brought

to a swift end as Martin, with his usual lack of diplomacy, came storming through to reception. "Do you three witches know what time it is? You might be 'ladies who lunch', you know, but you're also ladies who work, or who are *supposed* to work, so come on, get your collective asses in gear." And then, to me, "Move it, Gemma! Your favourite patient awaits."

I groaned. "Oh no, not Kilroy again!"

"The very same and as for you, Debbie, you'd better make tracks too. I swear since Guy lost that exotic spider thing from Dublin Zoo he's been like a cross between Hitler and that one – what's-her-name that does the *Weakest Link* on TV. That Anne Robinson one."

Yeah, but not only because of the exotic spider, I thought, watching as, at the mention of Guy's name, Debbie's hand stole down almost involuntarily to gently cradle her abdomen. Could she really go through with an abortion? Somehow, I didn't think so. Neither was the gesture lost upon Sophie and as I turned to follow Martin from the room I couldn't help but notice that despite her seeming capitulation, the optimist in her eyes was alive and kicking and living in hope eternal.

* * *

"Any more of that shepherd's pie left, Mammy?" Her knife and fork in an upright position, Orla glanced hopefully over at the cooker. "Only I'm trying to build my strength up before I go away on my travels again."

Jealous, my ears pricked up. "So which of the

fashion capitals are you jetting off to this time? London, Paris, Milan?"

The light of a zealot in her eye, Orla launched into a speech that would have had David Koresh reaching for the box of matches immediately. "None of them. I told you before I'm finished with all that fashion business, left it fairly and squarely in the past. I'm a reformed character and now that the scales have fallen from my eyes and my weight has gone up on the scales, I can see what a shallow world it is: all those women starving themselves, desperately trying to conform to an image attainable only when they're dead and decomposing for a good eighteen months or so." As she shook her head, her blonde hair fanned out about her shoulders like a Timotei advert. All that was missing was the Kingfisher and the hypnotic lapping of a sylvan stream. "Uh huh! From now on it's the good life for me. That's right, folks; the material girl is going organic. In future the only fashion statement I make will be to advocate the wearing of waxed jackets, Aran sweaters, corduroy britches and gumboots in hunter green." Shooting a quick look over to where Mammy was busily engaged in ladling a monster helping of shepherd's pie onto her plate, she screwed up her eyes and stuck her tongue out at me. "Yep! I'm going to learn how to thatch a roof, mend a fence, and whitewash a wall. *And*, in my spare time, I'm going to bonk Tyrell O'Neill till he begs for mercy."

I narrowed my own eyes for no other reason than

that I always narrowed my eyes when talking to Orla. That way, when she pissed me off as invariably she did, I was already in pissed off and squinting mode. "Tyrell O'Neill?" Funny – I *knew* she'd piss me off. "And just what on earth has *he* got to do with anything?"

"Plenty." Orla made smacking and appreciative noises as Mammy placed the steaming seconds of meat and potatoes before her, then toodled off to begin on the washing-up. "You know me, sister dear. I never believe in paddling solo and if I'm going to ruminate off in the arse-hole of Donegal, I'm damn sure there's going to be a fit and handsome male of the species ruminating right alongside of me – Tyrell O'Neill to be exact!"

Pausing only to pick my chin up from where it had banged itself on the edge of the table, I hawked up as much phlegm as I could muster before rounding on her. "Ruminate? What's with this ruminating lark? I thought you were looking forward to going all Felicity Kendal and Charlie Dimmock, growing organic children, slaughtering your own lamb chops and designing water features and garden decking all over the place. Like, what was all that big country-loving spiel you just gave me about?"

Airily, Orla waved a forkful of food about. "Oh that! I was just rehearsing what I was going to tell my agency and the other girls in the business. You see," she explained seriously, "if I was simply to leave without giving an explanation, everyone would say I couldn't hack it, that I just wasn't good enough to make it in the modelling business, that I was second-rate, a catalogue model fit only to model thermal underwear and slipper socks with non-stick Teflon soles." Transferring the contents of her fork to her mouth, she took time out to masticate and swallow before nodding sagely. "On the other hand, if I let it be known that I'm giving up everything for love and going off to bury myself in the wilds of Donegal with the man of my dreams, who just happens to be the sheep-farmer to die for, everyone will sigh at the romance of it all." Happily, she refilled her fork. "And, in years to come, surrounded by the trappings of their success, the Jags, the designer rags, the facelifts and souvenir bottles of liposuction, they'll talk longingly amongst themselves of me, the one who got away. 'Orla could have been bigger than Sophie Dahl,' they'll sigh, as their masseurs squeeze, pummel and rub scented oil into their spoiled, overindulged, plastic-surgery-invaded bodies. 'But she threw it all away to follow her heart – simply upped one day and legged it with her bit of rough and hasn't looked back since.'"

I shook my head in wonder. Jesus, she had it all worked out! That one brain cell of hers must have encompassed the whole of that human genome thing that's been popping up lately in all the newspapers and on the TV. I felt a grudging admiration. I also begrudged her, full stop. Laura and I had obviously more in common than I'd realised. I mean, she begrudged me Rocky when all along *her* heart lay with the milkman (with whom she was lying) and here was I begrudging Orla Tyrell

O'Neill when really *my* heart lay with Rocky Cashel. Nonetheless, I validated my dog-in-the-manger attitude by telling myself that it was a sibling thing and therefore not only natural but righteous, a kind of place-for-everything-and-put-Orla-in-her-place philosophy.

"But it's hardly fair on Tyrell O' Neill, is it? You using him just to save face?" Evangelical, I smote my breast. "Listen, Orla. Just like Martin Luther King had a dream, this sheep farm in Donegal is Tyrell's dream, so watch where you're putting your size three Guccis."

"Oh, don't be such a worry-wart! I intend to see he enjoys being used, just as I intend to enjoy, even – dare I use the word *relish* – using him." Orla grinned and, one appetite at least assuaged, laid aside her knife and fork and, with a not-so-ladylike belch from behind her hand, rose from the table. "That was gorgeous, Mammy. Shepherd's pie is my absolute favourite." There was an emphasis on the word 'shepherd's' totally lost on Mammy who, beaming like a maternal version of the Tusker Lighthouse, bore her daughter's dirty dishes off to the sink.

"That's what I like to see," she said, breaking out the Fairy Liquid with a view not only to cleaning the dishes but also to keeping her hands nice and soft. "A nice, clean plate."

"And a nice clean slate," I murmured sarcastically. "Shame you're going to dirty it so soon."

Orla shrugged. "Well," she said, heading off to sort

out her negligées and cocktail dresses with a view to roughing it in Donegal, "a girl's got to doodle who a girl's got to doodle."

* * *

"But *you* don't like Tyrell O'Neill." Skilfully, Sophie dug her pitchfork into a mound of hay and tossed it over the half-door of one of the loose boxes located at the back of the surgery where, from time to time, various farm animals convalesced. Idly rubbing my bottom up and down against the neighbouring door, rather than offering a helping hand, I shot her a and-your-point-*is* kind of look. "*You* told him to stuff his poxy flowers *and* his apologies when he called around the other day after that Milk Tray Man fiasco. Heck! I felt quite sorry for him. I mean, it takes a real man to debase himself the way he did *and* in front of an audience too. Not to mention Mrs Birch the town crier, and Kilroy."

Dismissive, I snorted. "Huh, if you ask me that was just a calculated move. He believed that old saying about safety in numbers and thought there was no way I'd shoot him down in front of a load of witnesses." I chalked one up to me. "Big mistake! Obviously he's never watched *The Battle of Britain* and who knows, in a past life *I* might even have been Douglas Bader, that World War II ace fighter-pilot guy."

"It's possible," Sophie conceded. "Heaven knows, I've seen you legless often enough. Still, I just don't understand what your problem is. If the truth be told, you should be thrilled for Orla. After all, it's only a little while ago that she was shaking hands with the big D as a prelude to entering the darker realm and now, here she is, winning her battle with bulimia and forging out a new life for herself. More power to her elbow, is what I say."

I tried for reasonable. "Look, I'm all for her forging out a new life for herself, only not with Tyrell O'Neill." Huckleberry Finn style, I bent down, picked up a piece of straw, stuck it between my teeth and embarked on a mutinous round of chewing.

"And why *not* Tyrell O'Neill?" Leaning on her pitchfork, Sophie looked genuinely perplexed as well as John-Boy Waltonesque. Even the denim dungarees complete with bib and shoulder-straps were in keeping. The only thing missing was the gormless look and the hairy mole and at least one of those was debatable. "By your own admission, *you* don't want him. Maybe a fresh start with Tyrell O'Neill well away from the fleshpots of the city is just what the doctor ordered." Looking as if she might burst into a rendition of 'Zippety Doo Dah' at any minute, Sophie waxed lyrical. "Imagine it! All that crisp clean countrified air, blue-tinged in the evening, redolent with the smoke of a hundred and one peat fires *and* in the summer, just to ring the changes, the heady scent of a hundred and one fuchsia bushes perfuming the balmy Atlantic ozone." In the manner of a woman who has watched *Master Chef* once too often for her own good, she kissed her fingers to her lips. "*Mmwah!* What more could one ask for?"

"How about a bit of civilisation?" Disgusted, I ripped the straw from between my lips and flicked it away into the surrounding atmosphere made redolent only by the last equine occupant's own particular brand of manure. "God Almighty, Sophie, you sound like an advert for the Irish Tourist Board. Get real! Like, we're talking Donegal here, *not* the bloody Seychelles."

"Get real yourself!" Suddenly impatient, Sophie embarked upon a mad bout of digging and pitching, tossing the hay into the air with a fury bordering on frenzy. "Why don't you admit it. You can't bear Orla to have Tyrell O'Neill because you *want* him for yourself."

"Bollocks!" I was fast whipping myself into a fury. "Tyrell O'Neill is nothing to me – less than the dust beneath my Doc Martens, in fact. I mean, come on, how could anyone fall for someone so . . . so . . ." At this juncture words failed me.

"So – what?" Sophie impaled me with a three-pronged glance every bit as lethal as her pitchfork. "So good-looking? So decent? So down to earth?"

"No! So – so, well, sheepish!"

"*Tah!*" Sophie spat, a sound somewhere between disgusted and brassed off. "Wake up to yourself, Gemma. Men like Tyrell O'Neill aren't buy one, get one free. Huh, even I know that and I'm a lezzer totally devoid of aspirations in the boxer-shorts department except when it comes to wearing them myself. Calvin

Kleins, I find, are particularly comfortable and hardwearing and don't you just love the way the logo is printed round the waistband?"

"I *know* that," I said mulishly, completely disregarding the bit about waistbands and logos. "And I don't mind being his *friend*. But that's all!"

"Oh yeah?" Viciously Sophie pitched the last of the hay higgledy-piggledy into the air. "Well, Gemma, this might come as a bit of a shock to you but sometimes friendship just ain't enough!"

She was thinking of Debbie, of course. Ashamed, I backed off, hoisting an imaginary white flag of peace above my head. If I'd had a couple of doves I would have stuck an olive branch in their beaks and released them into the wild. "Sorry," I said, which fair enough, wasn't the most effusive apology I've ever made in my life. Nonetheless, it was genuine and from the heart and luckily, Sophie accepted it as such.

"S'all right! It's me, really. I'm a tad sensitive at the moment, a tad ready to find fault with everything and anything." Tossing the pitchfork aside, she hooked a grimy hand through the crook of my arm. "Tell you what, let's finish up here and bunk off for a lunch-time drink at the Fox's Retreat."

Relieved to be back in her good books, I squeezed her arm conspiratorially. "Sounds good to me. Lead on MacDuff!"

* * *

I deliberately hung around on Saturday morning till Tyrell arrived to whisk Orla off to the wilds of Donegal and that despite having promised Rocky I'd be over first thing to take Gretchen for her morning constitutional. Still in hospital for observation, it was becoming more and more unlikely that Laura, in the light of recent disclosures, would return home to Gothdere at all. When I'd gotten over my own surprise it dawned on me that there was a certain inevitability about things in so much as Laura was a cow and her paramour was a milkman. Here's a pencil. Fill in the gaps! In the meantime Rocky, labouring under a massive cloud called umbrage and with a burning desire for revenge, had decided to hold Gretchen hostage on a permanent basis. On the grounds, bullet point one, that he had bought her in the first place and, bullet point two, that Laura had abandoned her.

"But Laura *didn't* abandon her," I'd argued, playing devil's advocate. Not, you understand that I bore the woman any love or misplaced brand of loyalty, but rather because there was no way I wanted Gretchen as a permanent fixture when I intended to become one myself. "She had to go into hospital and the last time I looked they didn't allow pets on the wards, for some piddling reason or other. Or maybe piddling *was* the reason."

"And *why* did she have to go into hospital?" Rocky said, his mouth so hard it wouldn't have surprised me if De Beers had put in an offer for the mining rights.

"What sort of lame excuse is that?" The words issuing from between his teeth in a series of hisses, Rocky nodded venomously. "No way is she having her poodle and leaving it! I'm keeping Gretchen and that's final. Laura can pursue me through every court in the land but there's no way she's getting her back, not unless she's wearing the latest line in taxidermy and a realistic pair of glass eyes."

"Who, Laura?" I giggled and couldn't help reflecting bitchily that, if anything, such alterations could only improve her overall appearance.

"Oh, get lost, Gemma!" Clearly unamused by my sparkling repartee at his ex-fiancée's expense, Rocky stormed off, presumably in search of some new song to plagiarise. Probably 'How Much Is That Doggy In The Window?' or, 'You Ain't Nothing But A Hound Dog' or even, 'Old Shep'.

Speaking of 'Old Shep' or young shep or young aspiring shepherds even, Tyrell O'Neill drove up right on time in a four-wheel-drive Range Rover. Peeping from behind the lace curtains at my bedroom window, in a manner similar to the hundred or so neighbours I suspected were doing likewise, I watched with devilish interest as Orla emerged from the house, just for the fun of seeing her try to negotiate the climb up into the high-bodied vehicle in her six-inch-heeled Jimmy Choo sandals. Just as Cinderella wowed her prince with glass slippers, Orla inevitably wowed her prince of the moment with the £350 pair of designer shoes she smugly informed the world she'd got free on a photo shoot because *nobody* else was a dainty size three.

"Actually," she'd giggle coyly, her Le Grand mascara-enhanced eyelashes batting tirelessly for the Irish cricket team and blowing the ball way off course, "I don't really *have* feet as such – just a tiny bit of my ankle turned up!" And the men, the big eejits would swallow it hook, line and sinker and make tis-no-wonder-Victorian-men-swooned-at-the-sight-of-a-lady's-ankle-if-their-ankles-was-anything-like-as-sexy-as-your-little-feeteen noises! Huh! If any one swooned at the sight of my ankles, what's the betting that the minute they recovered they wouldn't be putting in a call to the National Guard and wittering on about the BFG. Then, before you could say lisle is vile, Quentin Tarantino would be sussing out the movie potential and signing up Vinnie Jones to play the part of my right foot with Daniel Day-Lewis typecast to play the left. I leaned a little further forward to get a better look but Princess Anne got in the way. Well, hold the press! Did I say Princess Anne? That was no Princess – that was my sister, clad head to toe – titter ye not – in padded green anorak, hunter-green wellingtons *and* a headscarf. A headscarf! I swear I wouldn't be seen dead in a headscarf. Headscarves are for the Dot Cottons of this world and other old women long past giving a shit about how they look – female members of the Royal family, for example! Although, to be fair, Orla's headscarf, whilst boasting the obligatory foxhounds, horses' heads and bits of riding-tackle print, was wrapped about her head in a chi-chi way more reminiscent of Brigitte Bardot and the South of France than Albert Square or Balmoral. Trust Orla to get it exactly right but then she always got everything right on the fashion front, infuriatingly, exasperatingly right. Even as a child she'd worn her Wednesday knickers on Wednesday and, with a logic that could not be faulted, her Friday knickers on Friday. The only time I'd seen her stumped was when, suffering from a really bad dose of the collywobbles, she ran out of weekdays well before Monday was even halfway over. Honest to God, I treasure that memory and whenever I find myself tempted to look up the Samaritans' phone number I go to my mental filing cabinet, 'Comedy' section, subsection 'Orla's Misfortunes', look at it, savour it and *know* beyond the shadow of a doubt that there is a God! Into your hands I commend Orla's misfortunes, oh Lord. My saviour!

"So, are we all set?" That was Tyrell, his voice rising on a wave of Aran-jumpered, moss-stitched testosterone and floating in through the bedroom window I'd conveniently forgotten to close.

"I'm ever ready!" Orla tinkled saucily up at him, her lips arranged in a provocative pout. "I'm like that battery off the telly."

Yeah, you just go on and on and on, I thought sourly, feeling the urge to indulge in a bit of assault and battery myself and casting about me for a convenient piano to drop on her head in a nice example of life imitating cartoon violence. Sadly there wasn't any, nobody in the family being of a musical disposition except, perhaps, for Aunty Kay who after a gin-soaked evening could be relied on to engage in a drunken rendition of 'Oh My Darling Clementine' on the harmonica. Via her right nostril and still with a roll-up clamped firmly between her lips.

"So, did you remember to bring your sailing gear?" My ears pricked up at that. Like, I know when it rains it rains in Donegal but hardly enough to warrant commissioning your own ark.

Below, on the pavement, Orla sketched a girly salute, "Aye, aye Cap'n! I've got me the works; sou-wester in a nice shade of sunflower yellow, waterproof cape ditto, a big box of Fisherman's Friends." She tinkled again. "I passed on the flares though, cos flares are like, *so* last season Jean Paul Gaultier!" Oh the wit of it all! I was laughing so hard I could feel the onset of a deep anal fissure.

"Orla? Is that you!" At the sound of Aunty Kay's nicotine-laden, nodule-encrusted vocal cords arriving suddenly on the scene, I couldn't help but inch forward another bit despite increasing the risk of detection. "Sacred Heart, Blessed Mother and Divine Saint Anthony!" her voice made the sign of the cross. "Don't tell me you've gone and joined the army. Don't tell me she's gone and joined the army," she repeated, only this time to Tyrell accompanied by an over-familiar puck on the arm. "Are you her commanding officer? I must say you make a commanding enough figure if it wasn't for that big ignorant class of an Aran sweater you're wearing." She pucked again. I could feel his pain. "Sure nobody wears them nowadays, only American tourists who don't know any better and sheep-farmers in Donegal where there's no fear of anybody seeing them – well, anybody who's not the mentally retarded product of an incestuous relationship, anyway!"

"Aunty Kay!" There was a rage in Orla's voice the likes of which hadn't been equalled since Pinocchio discovered his nose doubled as a lie detector *and* his genitals were still Scots pine. "You can't go around insulting people like that. Tyrell is a respectable rock–and–roller." Uncomfortably, she cleared her throat and lowered her voice a few decibels so that only those neighbours with their hearing-aids on full had any chance of picking it up. "*And* he's an aspiring sheep-farmer."

"Is that a fact?" I could tell that in the face of Tyrell O'Neill's six-packiness, Aunty Kay's views on sheep-farmers were undergoing a swift and radical transition. "Oh, there's nothing unworthy in sheep-farming as such – only the ones in Donegal." Screwing her finger into her temple her voice broke the sound barrier and the neighbours rubbed their hands in glee and put away their ear-trumpets and sundry other hearing apparatus. "Did you know there's more nutters per capita in Donegal than anywhere else in Europe? Honest to God! I hear that when that Jerry Springer fella runs out of hillbillies in the US of A he's going to go to Donegal for a fresh supply." She gave a throaty, pre-cancerous chuckle. "Well, he won't have to look very far, that's all I can say. Anyway, where are you two youngsters off to?"

"Donegal! We're off to join the other inmates at the asylum," Orla said in a voice as flat as her bra size. (Did I mention the fact that if her chest were a life-support machine, life would have been pronounced extinct?)

Back-pedalling at a rate that would have sent her twice round the world backwards, yet still allowed her to finish first in the Tour de France, Aunty Kay waved a dismissive hand. "Oh, you don't want to be listening to what people say. Too much time on their idle hands is the problem, and the devil making work for them! Personally, I've always found Donegal to be a perfectly acceptable county, provided you avoid those Gaeltacht places where they all go around congregating under hedgerows, talking Irish, and hiding priests and things. Never trust a man who's got his education from under a bush. That's what I say, anyway."

"Thanks for the warning. We'll certainly bear that in mind." That was Tyrell, sounding suspiciously like a man who had derived more than his fair share of education from under a bush or two. "Anyway we'd better be making a move. It's a long way to Tipperary and an even longer one to Donegal."

"Especially if you go *via* Tipperary!" That crack came courtesy of Orla, and speaking of cracks, I felt my anal fissure expand to the extent where my large intestine was in danger of making its final descent onto the floor.

"Oh, sure, you two push off with yourselves. Don't let me keep you." All mother-hen affability, Aunty Kay made the kind of shooing motions more often seen on a chicken farm. "And I must say you make a lovely couple. It's a shame our Gemma couldn't find herself a nice fella too. Mind you, I know blood is thicker than water but the truth is that poor girl was behind the door when the looks were given out." She sighed grudgingly. "Although, credit where credit is due, she's got a good brain on her." Behind the curtain I flinched, knowing from experience what was coming next and feeling the humiliation wash over the back of my neck and face like the tide of the Red Sea. Thank God it was Tyrell down there listening to my aunt slagging me off and not Rocky. "Still," she continued blithely, as I'd known she would, her stentorian tones causing havoc with the foghorns miles out at sea, "what fella in his right mind goes into a restaurant and orders a plate of brains when he could treat himself to a nice, tender piece of rump?"

Wasting no time in jumping on the let's-give-Gemma-a-real-bollocking-while-we're-at-it bandwagon, Orla went into mock-teasing-laced-with-caustic-soda mode. "Oh, Tyrell has a soft spot for Gemma, haven't you, Tyrell? Or maybe it's a hard spot. In fact, so taken with her at one time was he, that he practically haunted *Vetz 4 Petz* – well, if *Gemma* is to be believed, anyway." The bitch! Wherever she'd licked that from, it certainly wasn't from me. God, what must Tyrell have thought? That I was going around making fun of him, blowing my own trumpet at his expense? What a sad cow he must have had me pegged for. With the ease of a rock star well versed in denying everything to the press, Tyrell sighed under the weight of yet another apparently false allegation.

"I have an *uncle* who works at *Vetz 4 Petz*, Orla," he said pointedly, *too* pointedly, the implication being, of course, that if he was hanging around, then it was for that reason and for that reason only. "Rob and I have a lot in common, as it happens. Not only do we share a certain amount of DNA but we're both into sheep in a big way."

Below on the pavement, Aunty Kay's ears not so much pricked up as began a lunar ascent. "Rob? That wouldn't be Rob Kilbride by any chance, would it?"

"That's right," Tyrell confirmed. "Do you know him?"

Aunty Kay performed the vocal equivalent of clapping her hands with delight. "Oh, indeed I do and now that I look at you I can see the resemblance, so I can. Same gorgeous black hair. Same gorgeous blue eyes. Same gorgeous tight bum!"

"Aunty Kay!" Orla pretended shock or maybe she wasn't pretending. Like, it's not every day you see your aged, spinster aunt metamorphose into a salivating sex-fiend in front of your astonished eyes. To tell the truth I was shocked myself. What with my mother ripping men's boxer shorts off with her teeth and Aunty Kay passing lewd and lascivious comments on the contents I was beginning to make some sense of my own less-than-ladylike behaviour on the day of the Blessington Hunt. A case of the apple not rolling too far from the tree! Like my fat thighs and sinusitis, lechery was obviously an inheritance. If, through no fault of my own, I was the possessor of a debauched gene, then I could hardly be castigated for any of my less than moral actions. Damn! If I'd known that, I might have taken things even further and insisted upon Rocky removing his jodhpurs that day at the Blessington Fox-hunt.

Totally unrebuked by her niece's apparent disgust, Aunty Kay reached round and pinched Tyrell on the behind. "Just making sure," she said archly as, like a horse who has just discovered its hide to be the main course at a mosquitoes' banquet, Tyrell jumped six feet into the air. "Time can play funny tricks on the memory, you know."

Plainly annoyed at such an unseemly display of skittishness in an older female member of the family, skittishness being her own preserve, Orla successfully propelled herself into the Range Rover. "Hands off, Aunty Kay! Can't you see you're embarrassing him?"

"Embarrassing him? *I'm* not embarrassing him! Am I embarrassing you?" Amazement writ large on her face, Aunty Kay carefully withdrew her hand from where it was sneaking round for a repeat of the experiment. "I'm only saying he's the mirror-image of his uncle, is all. Sure where's the embarrassment in that?"

Choosing to downplay matters, Tyrell quickly followed Orla into the Range Rover, nervously revving up the engine before Aunty Kay could figure out a way of levering her hand between the seat and his bum. "Ah, you're all right!" he said. "I'm flattered really. I mean, it's not every day an attractive young pensioner pinches your butt. Still, time and tide and all that!"

Slipping on a pair of Ray-Bans, which should have looked incongruous with the rest of her outfit but somehow managed to look like the last word in Parisian chic, Orla tossed her Brigitte Bardot head. "Speaking of tides: Tyrell's taking me out on his boat, the *Sea Ewe*." Ah, a piece of the jigsaw slotted into place. Tyrell had a boat, hence the earlier reference to sailing gear. Nothing to do with the Donegal weather at all! My own ears prepared to slip their moorings and lift off as I wondered how come I never knew he had a boat. I thought the only boats he was interested in were those white fluffy ships of the hills. Somehow the knowledge stuck in my gorge which, all things considered, was unreasonable to say the least. So, Tyrell had a boat? Like, so what? It wasn't as if I was jealous or anything. God, I couldn't think of anything worse. Poor Orla! Imagine being lumbered out in the wilds of Donegal with a man who not only idolised sheep but who, in his spare time, played at Long John Silver on the freezing Atlantic. For the first time it struck me that far from simply being a point-scoring exercise over me, Orla must be really serious about him. I mean, up till now she'd never evinced interest in any man who didn't have Rolex as, at least, his second name. Not, mind you, that Tyrell appeared to be short of a few bob. He was, after all, a member of an extremely successful rock group, which with the likes of yours truly splashing out on concert tickets by the new time, not to mention memorabilia in the shape of T-shirts and coasters and things, must have netted him a fair old pension fund. Still, if he were intent on dissipating his fortune amongst the sheep population of Donegal, it wouldn't be long before he'd be singing for his supper all over again.

"Oh, you have a boat?" Aunty Kay echoed my own surprise. Presumably, like me, she was wondering what the hell a sheep-farmer wanted with a boat. "Up in Donegal?"

"Killybegs," Tyrell confirmed, on a note of pride.

Killybegs! My pity for Orla grew. For fecks sake! The only time Killybegs ever got brought to the public consciousness usually involved a co-existing mention of heavy seas and mass loss of life. In other words, we weren't exactly talking the Côte d'Azur on a hot summer's day!

"I can't wait!" Geography never being her strong

294

point, Orla's excitement was palpable. "I've always wanted to go yachting. There's something so romantic about the idea of stretching out on deck, clad only in tiny bikini bottoms, eyes closed, a glass of ice-cold Chablis within easy reach and silence all around but for the gentle, hypnotic tap, tap, tapping of the water against the sides of the boat."

With not so much ice-cold Chablis as ice-cold reality, Tyrell insensitively scuppered all flights of romantic fantasy. "Orla! The *Sea Ewe* is not a yacht. It's a trawler, a fishing boat. And a *working* fishing boat at that."

"Oh," Orla said. Nothing else, just "Oh." But there was a world of disappointment in that one word, not heard since Ireland won the Eurovision song contest for the umpteenth time and consequently, for the umpteenth time, had to fork out to host the bloody thing all over again the following year. It was also a tribute to her courage that she did not immediately, as I would have done, run screaming from the vehicle to bar herself behind several bolts, chains and padlocks of ascending size and weight, till Tyrell had safely taken himself off to Donegal, his sheep and his fishing boat. Alone!

"Oh, a fishing boat, is it? Well, bring me back a nice bit of cod or herring for me tea!" A woman, comfortably at one with the demands of her ever-expanding stomach and equally comfortably oblivious to the modern trend for calorie-counting, Aunty Kay sounded pleased at the prospect of a free meal. "None of that old whiting, though," she warned. "Whiting gives me gas, something terrible." Waving them merrily on their way, she stepped back a bit as the Range Rover accelerated suddenly away from the kerb, a somewhat gutted Orla peering miserably back over her shoulder at a rapidly receding civilisation. Soon, she would be frozen and filleted too. Laugh? I soaked my gusset!

CHAPTER 17

"And just where do you think you've been?" A pugnacious Rocky opened the door before I had time even to ring the doorbell. "Gretchen's had her legs crossed so long she may never walk again."

Scowling on the outside, love-struck on the inside, I followed him into the hallway. "Gretchen," I reminded him darkly, "is *not* my dog. Gretchen is *your* dog. Or, more correctly, Gretchen is *Laura's* dog."

"Either way, she *is* your penance." Rocky nodded triumphantly, choosing for once not to dispute the issue of ownership. "Now take her out for her walk, would you, before there's a flood and we're all drowned."

Making obedient, slave-like noises, I shuffled like something out of *Uncle Tom's Cabin* over to where Gretchen, poor thing, had taken on all the appearance of an over-inflated barrage balloon. "Yes, Bwana. Yessuh, Massa Rocky. I's a goin now! Mm mm, yessuh! I sho is afo' you whups mah sorry black hide." Nodding

297

earnestly, I retrieved Gretchen's leash from its habitual home on the coatstand and clipped it onto her collar. "When ah comes back, ah 'spec, yo gwinna wan' me out in de fields a-pickin' cotton till mah fingers done bleed and mah back done just 'bout break."

"Bloody hell!" Rocky rolled his eyes. "Is she always like this?"

"No. Usually, she's ten times worse." Surprised, I glanced up to find Debbie had materialised in the hallway, a great silly beam covering her face. "Hiya, Gem! About bloody time you showed up. What on earth kept you?"

"Never mind what on earth kept me! What on earth are *you* doing here?" I don't think I could have been more taken aback if the Pope had shown up on a Harley with the Ayatollah, in full leathers, riding pillion.

Debbie shrugged airily. "I wanted to see you about something and, it being a Saturday morning, I knew you'd be here – although if I'd known you were going to keep me hanging about this long, I'd have called at your house instead." She grinned, a bit wickedly, I thought. "Still, Rocky and I have been taking the time to get better acquainted and, would you believe, he's almost forgiven me for clocking him round the head with that tree-branch down in Blessington!"

Rocky twinkled. Bastard! He never twinkled like that for me. "Well, call me a stereotypical male chauvinist but I've always had a weakness for a pretty face."

"You're a stereotypical male chauvinist!" Debbie and I shrieked together but, as usual, I had to go one step further.

"So, how do you explain Laura, then?"

"I don't!" Rocky's reply was terse. "Well, not to you, anyway. Now, git, while Gretchen can still stand – otherwise, you just might have to roll her along like a barrel – and don't forget the pooper-scooper."

"*Sieg heil!*" Sketching a Nazi salute, I jerked my head towards Debbie. "Coming?"

"Yeah, sure." Cheerfully she turned and fluttered her fingers to where Rocky stood watching us go. "Catch you later, Rocky. Sorry again about the branch."

"No worries," he said, suddenly coming over all Crocodile Dundee. "I tell you what. Let's do lunch some time. There's a brilliant little bistro place I know on the seafront in Howth. Lobsters to die for and the best champagne this side of France."

"Sounds great." Debbie, like the promised champagne, almost popped her cork with enthusiasm as Rocky went back inside the house. "Doesn't it, Gem?"

"Yeah, just what the doctor ordered or, in your case, just what the doctor didn't order," I said nastily, wanting to hurt her because I knew by the storm clouds gathering on Rocky's brow and preparing to rain down fire and brimstone, that the invitation didn't include me and resenting her for it.

If she caught the ire in my voice, however, she chose to ignore it, as linking my arm, she fell into step beside me. "Actually, that's what I wanted to talk to you about. I've made up my mind, Gem. I'm *definitely* having a termination and I want you to come to England with me."

"Are you sure?" Almost garotting poor Gretchen with the lead, I jerked to a sudden halt. "I mean, I suppose I never really thought you'd go through with it. Oh, I know you said you would but . . . well, somehow I thought . . ." My voice trailed off as a sudden horrifying thought struck me. "Hey, this *is* your own decision, isn't it? Like, you haven't let me talk you into it or anything, have you?" Guiltily I recalled the vacuuming motions and suction noises I had indulged in on an earlier occasion, the adamant assertions that, as yet, Debbie's baby was nothing more than a bundle of cells, an embryo barely past the egg stage with bits of yolky shell still sticking to it.

Adamant, Debbie shook her head. "No. I reached it all on my lonesome ownsome and while I can't help wishing things were different, they're not and I have to face up to reality." Her eyes fell away from mine, focussed unseeingly on Gretchen who now the possessor of a sore neck as well as a bladder full to bursting and unable to hold out any longer, was gushing like Niagara Falls all down her own leg. "And the reality is and ashamed though I am to admit it, I'm just not cut from the cloth of single motherhood."

"And Guy?" I asked, somewhat tentatively it must be said, for fear she might suddenly dissolve into hysterics, and I would have to get violent to calm her down. "Is he well and truly out of the picture?"

Thankfully she didn't dissolve. Instead she took on that stern-faced look more commonly found amongst the Reverend Mother population. "Yep! Where he's concerned my life is a blank canvas and the funny thing about it is I feel I should care more than I actually do. I mean, sometimes, at work, I look at him and it's like we're no more than a couple of strangers. Like, it's hard to imagine that there was a time when he was the absolute centre of my world, a time when I did practically nothing but pivot about him, a time when I fuelled his fantasies in stockings and suspenders and painted his nipples with milk-chocolate body paint." (NB: Scrap the Reverend Mother allusion.) Grimly, she started walking again, hauling both Gretchen and me along in her wake. "I wouldn't mind only it's loaded with calories and what's the betting it wasn't a contributory factor to the root canal I had a few months ago."

"God!" My mind boggled. "How much of the stuff did you use?"

"Tons!" Debbie shrugged. "And not only on his nipples. *And* it was the good stuff. Lindt. I melted it down myself. Mind you, once I got it wrong and used pistachio instead of plain and he ended up with –"

"More nuts than he bargained for?" I guessed. "Could have been worse, I suppose. Like, it could have been *hole* nuts!"

Debbie gave a lopsided grin. "Anyway, I'm only using that as an example of how far I've moved on since those days, or nights if you want to be pedantic about it. Nowadays, Guy Evans is not so much history as voluntary amnesia. I mean, I'm trying hard to forget him but, let's face it, Cloetus makes that more than a little bit difficult."

I slipped my arm back through hers and squeezed a little. "Well, I said I'd stand by you so just say the word and I'm primed and ready to do whatever needs to be done."

Debbie returned the squeeze with interest. "Thanks. I've already made a booking at one of those Marie Stopes-type clinics in London for next weekend, so if Rocky will let you have the time off, it's all systems go."

"Not a problem," I assured her, sounding far more confident than I actually felt. Still, Rocky Cashel or no Rocky Cashel, there was no way I was going to let my best friend go through something like that on her own. "Speaking of problems or potential problems, have you told Sophie yet?"

"No!" Debbie sighed heavily. "I've been trying to psyche myself up to it but I'd sooner nail my tongue to the rear end of an articulated lorry, than rob poor Sophie of her illusions." In perfect accord, we executed a neat about-turn and headed slowly back towards Gothdere.

"So you're going for a *fait accompli*, then?" I asked, prodding Gretchen in the backside with the toe of my shoe in an effort to discourage her from decoding the multitude of noxious calling cards dropped *en route* by every other passing canine.

Debbie shrugged. "Well, what other option do I have? You know Sophie; she'd probably come barging into the clinic trying to rescue me or something. I know she'll be bulling but, as the saying goes, you can't please all of the Sophies all of the time."

"Oh, I don't know," I said, mock casual. "I've a feeling *you* wouldn't have too much difficulty in that department."

Debbie groaned. "Oh, not that old chestnut again. Gimme a break, would you? If I've said it once, I've said it a thousand times: women just don't float my boat." She made a little moue. "Come to think of it, neither do men these days. I'll tell you what, there's no way any one, and I mean *any one*, man, woman or Russell Crowe, is ever going to sail in the good ship Debbie again. From now on I'm keeping my legs crossed twenty-four seven and if any one displays a modicum of interest in me, it'll simply be because of my resemblance to a giant human plait."

"Or a giant human prat," I giggled, earning a sharp dig in the ribs for my pains.

"Talking about prats . . ." Debbie gave one of those chock-full-of-darker-meaning sighs and I knew, from experience, I wasn't going to like whatever came next. "Don't you think you're making a bit of a prat of yourself over Rocky Cashel?" Stopping dead, she proceeded to wheel me about and, nose to nose, interrogate and insult me by turns. "I mean, it's not as though he's even civil to you, is it? Like he orders you about the place like some poor little minion and you jump to obey his every command."

"No, I don't," I protested and, typically illogical, contradicted myself in the same breath. "And so what if I do, anyway? I mean, what's the alternative? A couple of years' hard labour rotting in some women's prison dodging the advances of every criminally insane, sexually frustrated, lunatic dyke? Let me tell you poodle-sitting is a piece of cake in comparison to that!" Dragging myself free of her grip I stormed onwards, meanly depriving Gretchen of the opportunity of forensically examining a particularly large and still steaming dog turd.

Not to be put off, Debbie caught up with me and not so much linked my arm as yanked it free of its socket. "But what about that little thing called pride?"

"Oh that!" I snorted. "Well, that came before Rocky's fall. Besides, as the Catholic Church will tell you, pride is a sin and I am now, officially, at the shriving stage."

"Balls!" Unimpressed, Debbie struggled heroically to hang on to the crook of my arm as I struggled every bit as hard to disengage her. "Look, face facts, Gemma. Rocky Cashel is not interested in you. At least, not in the way you want him to be. I know you think Laura's fall from grace has left the road clear for you but, not to put too fine a point on it, you're doing a Gretchen on it."

"And what exactly do you mean by that?" Viciously, I attempted to dig my nails into the soft flesh of her arm but, as there were only stumps left, it was a plan that like the Wright Brothers' first attempts at plane building had very little hope of ever getting off the ground.

"I mean, you're barking up the wrong tree. Rocky Cashel isn't interested, Gemma. Wake up and smell the piss-off. This is Tony McCann all over again. If you would just open your eyes for a moment you'd find that once more in the ongoing love annals of Gemma Murphy, you've fallen for a king-size bastard all over again." Giving up the struggle, she liberated her arm, finding better use for it as the fins of a windmill. "Never mind that a perfectly lovely guy like Tyrell O'Neill is head over heels in love with you. Never mind that he's tall, dark, handsome and very likely loaded – possibly in more ways than one. I mean, he *has* got very big feet which, you know, some people say is indicative of largesse in other regions!" Flailing even faster, presumably for dramatic emphasis, she bent a look of complete incomprehension upon me. "Like, what is it with you, Gemma? Low self-esteem or something? Why can't you choose the good guy for a change? Why can't you give the Ronan Keatings of this world a look in and lay off the Liam Gallaghers? Maybe you should try reading a little bit of Louise L Hay. Start with that *You Can Heal Your Life* book or tune into *Oprah* or better still find yourself a therapist or a skull detective and find out why your self-preservation button is jammed on self-destruct!"

"Bleeding hell!" I went into my eye-rolling routine with such verve that, anyone looking on would have found themselves suffering from a severe bout of vertigo. "Talk about the horse with the dirtiest arse cocking up its tail! I mean, come on, you're hardly in a position to preach from the pulpit. Like, I'm not the one cultivating a bun in the oven as a result of playing away with a married man." I jabbed my finger in her chest. "*You* are!"

Debbie jumped quickly back out of poking range. "So, *learn* from my mistakes!"

"Have *you*?" Belligerent, I poked my chin out to its furthest extent. "Have *you* learned from *your* mistakes because, from where I'm standing, it looks like you're getting ready to repeat them all over again."

"Meaning?" Either Debbie was a very good actress or her air of innocence was one hundred per cent entirely genuine. Jealous, I chose to put my money on the former.

"Meaning, that far from looking out for my interests, you're simply looking out for your own." Okay, okay, so I knew I was wading into uncharted territory but, like a lemming jumping to its doom, someone had sabotaged my braking system. "So what's the story? Rocky Cashel look like a good prospect, does he? Especially now that he's discovered he appears to be firing blanks." Spitefully, I thrust the dagger of blind and jealous accusation in up to the hilt and twisted. "But you can provide him with a ready-made family, can't you, Debbie? *You* can still come out smelling of

Mother Teresa. And the devil take the hindermost, including your friends." Debbie blanched but, the bit of envy firmly between my teeth, I ploughed on. "Poor old Sophie. Spinning her homely little fantasies around you." Switching from rolling my eyes, I threw them up to heaven instead, accompanying the gesture by slow but repetitious shakings of the head to underscore my complete and utter disbelief. "Little did she know that whereas she saw you cooking up a storm in the *Brady Bunch* kitchen of her dreams, you, in reality, were cooking up your own dish of the day. Rocky Cashel to go! Hold the friendship!"

"Haven't you forgotten something? I'm having an *abortion*!" There were tears in Debbie's eyes. "Besides, how could you even *think* such a thing? It's *you* I'm thinking of. I just don't want to see you getting hurt all over again, like when Tony McCann dumped you." Turning up the volume, she angrily brushed away a tear that had begun the inevitable downward trek along her cheek. "Just in case your memory has short-circuited, let me remind you of what a mess you were. Honest to God, I've seen laddered tights hold it together better than you! Sophie and I spent yonks picking up the pieces and gluing you back together again." Her eyes shot fire. "*Not* an experience I particularly want to repeat. As for Rocky Cashel – you can put your jealousy back in its holster. Rocky doesn't even *know* I'm pregnant. So there goes yet another one of your famous theories, shot down in flames!"

"Well, bully for you!" I clapped my hands, and tunnel-visioned, honed in on the only part of her conversation that had managed to pierce through the thick membrane surrounding my cerebellum. "Rocky doesn't even know you're pregnant! Smart thinking, Batman! Maybe after a night or two on the horizontals you'll be able to convince him that Cloetus is actually his and when it's born a couple of months early – well, big deal – lots of babies are born premature, aren't they? And never mind that it tips the scales at a good ten to twelve pounds, he'll be only too happy to put that down to his manly prowess."

Debbie stamped her foot. "Hello! Hello! How many languages do I have to say it in before it gets through to your thick skull, Gemma Murphy? *I'm having an abortion!* Cloetus will never see the light of day." Unable to keep them in check any longer, the tears spilled over and white-water rafted all down along Debbie's face.

Oh, God! I pulled myself up short as a ten-thousand-watt volt of guilt shot through me and brought me back to earth with a shock. What in heaven's name had I been thinking of going off the deep end like that, accusing my best friend of all sorts when she was at her most vulnerable? When only moments before she'd bared her soul and asked me to go to England with her for the abortion? Talk about the bitch-friend from hell! Realisation dawning at my appalling and complete lack of sensitivity and fearful of reaching out and being blasted into Kingdom Come, I shrugged an apology.

"Oh shit, I'm sorry, Debs. I don't know what came over me except that it had the pea-green eyes of a little yellow god. There's no excuse for what I said, none at all except that Rocky Cashel seems to bring out the bloodthirsty, hair-pulling, earring-yanking, illogical worst in me." Flapping my hands about in a desperate and futile attempt to explain the inexplicable, I tried hard to coax her onside again. "You know the way some people are hooked on mind-altering Class A substances or alcohol? Well, yours truly is hooked on Rocky Cashel. You might say he's my drug of choice. And believe me, Debbie, he's every bit as detrimental to the health and, never mind having a government health warning slapped on him; he should have, like, a complete and utter government ban. I mean, ideally the man should be quarantined indefinitely."

"Jesus!" Wiping her nose on the back of her hand, Debbie gave a soft disbelieving whistle through her teeth. "You really *have* got him bad. I never realised quite how badly."

"Yep, close contact has made me rabid," I admitted. "A case of once bitten, twice gagging for it. Anyway, for what it's worth, I'm really, *really* sorry." Reaching out, I pulled her into a bear hug. "You're my bestest friend in the whole wide world and I'm sorry I hurt you and, I *swear*, I'll never do it again."

With a sniff, Debbie returned the hug with interest. "Ah, you're all right. Sure it does everyone the world of good now and again to have a bit of a barney. Clears the air, and all that. Balances the yin and the yang. The ding and the dong!"

"Well, if you say so," I said, doubtfully, still shrouded about in a massive mantle of guilt.

"I do!" Firmly, Debbie grasped my elbow. "Now let's get cracking before your drug of choice calls out a search party."

In an attempt to lighten proceedings even further, I clicked my heels smartly together. "Yes, *mein Führer*," I said, attempting to goosestep, an action that brought me crashing to the ground and Debbie along with me. "Not clever, Gretchen," I snarled, as the knowledge slowly filtered through that while Debbie and I had been standing still, Gretchen, like a whirling dervish had been winding her leash round and round our legs. "Bad, bad girl! Not clever at all!"

CHAPTER 18

"Pink curtains, yellow walls," Debbie shuddered, looking nervously around. "Not exactly *Changing Rooms*, is it?"

I shook my head. "Actually, it's very much *Changing Rooms*, as far as I can see. Get a load of those MDF partitions. This place has been furnished on a shoestring and that's for sure and not so much as the sniff of an interior designer."

Debbie sighed heavily. "Oh, well, I don't suppose ambience matters too much in these places. Let's face it, anyone who comes in here has more on their mind than the colour schemes and paint effects." Nervously, she reached out and grabbed my hand, the shake in her fingers transmitting itself to her voice. "Oh, God, Gemma, I wish it was all over. I wish it had never happened. I wish I could wake up and find it was all just a bad dream and everything was back to normal."

"I know you do." Moving a little closer up along the hard, wooden bench in the waiting-room, I squeezed her hand, a small and pretty-much useless attempt at comforting. To tell the truth I was scared rigid myself. I mean, what if something went wrong? Supposing the surgeon cocked up and Debbie bled to death in the operating theatre? Supposing I had to go home and tell her family that the daughter they so fondly imagined as living it up for the weekend was, in fact, lying dead in a chilly London morgue, the victim of a botched abortion. God, it didn't bear thinking about!

On the bench opposite a young girl still in her late teens, and dressed in skin-tight lycra jeans and a crop-top that displayed her pierced navel, leaned forward in a sympathetic manner. "First time, is it, luv?"

Debbie and I exchanged speaking glances. "First and *last* time," Debbie said pointedly. "I mean, it's not exactly a Butlin's holiday camp, is it? It's not as if you'd rush off to the travel agents to rebook the minute you got home."

"You're scared," the girl, observed knowingly. Zoe, according to the garish tattoo adorning her upper arm. "Well, there ain't no need ter be. Ain't nuffin' to it. They just whips yer in, knocks yer aht and before yer can say make mine a Maliboo and Coke, yer home tugging at the old man's Y-fronts, all ready for an action replay." She grinned, displaying teeth that had deprived some dentist somewhere of a very good portion of his pension instalments. "Mind you, this is my fourth time, dozy cow that I am. Keeps getting boozed up, yer see, and fergetting to take me pill." Scratching indelicately at her groin, she seemed utterly oblivious to the fact that she held the rest of the room completely in the palm of her chipped nail-varnished hand. "Anyway, I've already got one little bugger and, let me tell yer, our Brandon is enough fer anyone." Chewing meditatively on her tongue-stud, she filled us in on her financial position. "Besides, I've already managed ter swing meself a nice council flat, two bedrooms in a lovely 'igh-rise aht Battersea way, wiv a garage in a block and a nice patch of grass for the young 'uns to play on. Me Income Support's all sorted *and* I do the odd bit of work on a market stall, cash in 'and, which pays fer me ciggies and booze." Her cup clearly running over, she waved an airy hand. "*And* me old man's on the disability! Nah, I know when I'm well orf, me! There's no way I'm lettin' some snotty-nosed little bleeder go and cock it all up, so there ain't!" Clearly a winner in life's lottery, she lay back against the hard back of the bench, sighed happily and, picking up an old copy of *Take A Break*, started in on the arduous task of filling in all the words of no more than three letters in the crossword grids.

"I don't think I can *do* this, Gemma!" Debbie hissed *sotto voce*, alarm writ large all over her face. "I mean, I'm not like her, am I? Please tell me I'm not like her. Tell me I'm not flippant and materialistic and self-obsessed. A disregarder of human life!"

I dug her in the ribs. "Don't be daft. You won't get many of her to the dozen. That one's subhuman, the result of an unfortunate collision between a deranged sperm and an egg with learning difficulties. Just look around. Every one else here is shit-scared and riddled with doubts. Just like you."

"And that bloody noise certainly doesn't help!" Shakily, Debbie brought a hand up to her mouth and started in on her nails, a nervous habit I hadn't seen her indulge in since we were at both at junior school and in line for a first-class bollocking from the headmistress.

"I know." To tell the truth the background noise, a sort of dull roaring that started and stopped every so often, was having an equally detrimental effect on my own nerves. Unfortunately, in my case, I had no nails left to chew so had to make do with systematically winding strands of hair about my finger as a prelude to yanking them out. At the very least I'd be sporting a Friar Tuck tonsure before Debbie came back from theatre. "Excuse me." Leaning across, I wafted a hand between Zoe's nose and the crossword which, judging from the array of bemused and downright bewildered expressions flitting across her face, she was clearly finding more than a little bit challenging. "Have you any idea what on earth is making that bloody noise?"

Clearly grateful for the interruption, she laid the magazine down across her lap, cocking her head to one side, considering, appreciative, as though listening to a particularly fine rendition of Bach or Eminem. "Oh, that! That's just the incinerator."

"The inciner – whator?" Debbie's voice was faint.

Zoe widened her kohl-rimmed eyes. "The incinerator.

Well, they has to get rid of them somewhere. I mean yer can't just go chuckin' foetuses abaht the place like any old rubbish. Nah, it's against elf 'n' safety, innit?" Sighing, she picked the magazine back up again. "Now, give's an 'and here. What three-letter word beginning with 's' and ending with 'x' is another word for cop – ul – a – tion?"

"Fucked if I know!" I told her, leaping up and legging it after Debbie who upon hearing the words incinerator and foetus together had broken Florence Joyner's Olympic record in her haste to get out of the building. I caught up with her heaving and retching over a litter bin, much to the disgust of the passing, pin-stripe-suited, stiff-upper-lipped brigade of British businessmen going about their unlawful business.

Weakly she wiped the back of her hand across her mouth. "I-I'm sorry, Gemma. I can't go through with it. I just can't! I mean, how could I live with that upon my conscience." A deep shudder ran through her. "God Almighty, what on earth was I thinking of?"

"Shush! It's all right! You don't have to do anything you don't want to." Reaching out, I put my two arms about her as, trembling like a leaf, she fought for control. "Tell you what – there's a Starbucks just across the road. Let's go and get a cup of coffee. That'll help get things more into perspective. Put new life into us."

"New life . . ." Musingly, Debbie's hand went down, cradled her still flat stomach. "And that's just what this is – new life, Gemma. And to think I almost – I almost – God, I'll never eat toast again!"

"Don't!" Shakily I placed a finger across her lips, more than a little amazed at the relief coursing through my own veins. I mean, I'd thought I was so modern, so *laissez-faire*. Up till now abortion, as far as I was concerned, was just another one of the many options open to the emancipated women of today. Except that it wasn't – well, not to us anyway! The products of an Irish Catholic upbringing, we'd had it drummed into us at an early age that all life was sacred, even when that life was barely past the egg stage, a microscopic embryo. God, I could have kicked myself when I thought how cavalier I'd been about this baby. Flippant, even! The problem was I couldn't see past Guy, couldn't see that this child was a person in its own right and might actually enrich not only Debbie's life but the lives of those surrounding her. No! Instead, I'd seen it as a problem, a disturbance of the equilibrium, something to be disposed of as soon as possible. Something to be incinerated!

More than a little guilty and on legs that had turned to jelly-moulds, I steered Debbie across the road and into the coffee shop where I ordered two large glasses of caffè latte and a couple of cinnamon Danish pastries. Sick with nerves, both of us had hardly eaten a thing since the previous day. Even so, Debbie waved her Danish away.

"I couldn't," she said, dipping her head low over her glass but not before I caught the shine of tears again. "Oh, Gemma. I can't believe that was *me* in there. I can't believe I actually thought I could go through with it. *And* I can't believe there are women in the world like that Zoe who use abortion as an alternative to contraception."

"I know. She turned my stomach as well. Still, she's the one who's got to live with her own conscience, so put her out of your mind and let's think about what you intend to do now."

"Do?" Debbie raised her head, the beginnings of a defiant look in her eyes. "As far as I'm concerned, there *is* only one thing to do now: I'm going to have this baby and what's more I'm going to keep it. After that episode back there, any other option is unthinkable."

"Fair enough." I took a sip of coffee, wiping away the resultant frothy moustache with the back of my hand. "But will you tell Guy?"

"Actually, I was meaning to talk to you about that." A little shamefaced, Debbie dropped her eyes, minutely examined the wooden surface of the coffee table like a detective searching for clues – or perhaps it was just a simple tactic to avoid looking at me. "Well, you know how I told you I gave him the big heave-ho?" Her head came up a fraction, dropped again. "Let's just say that wasn't exactly the truth, the whole truth and nothing but the truth. Far from me giving *him* the big E, *he* dumped me."

I could feel my eyebrows embarking on the first rung of a very tall ladder. "But I thought –"

Debbie cut me off. "For Christ's sake, Gemma, I

know it's hard to believe looking at the state of me now, but I *do* have *some* pride, you know. Well, *did* have some pride, anyway." Absentmindedly, she reached out, broke a piece off her Danish pastry and crumbled it between her fingers. "Actually, it was ironic really. Like there I was building up to telling him about Cloetus, hoping – okay, I admit it – that we'd have the fairytale happy ending, that somehow Brigitte and the twins, who incidentally I'd managed to convince myself were the result of a one-off duty shag, would magically disappear and I'd be left with a clear field and a clear conscience." Sighing deeply, she broke off another bit of her pastry and crumbled that too. "It didn't work out like that though. Instead, he beat me to it, hauled me off for dinner in a posh restaurant and came clean about his new-born twins." Sardonic, she quirked an eyebrow. "And me, in my ignorance, thought he was finally going to set a date or two dates rather; a date to divorce Brigitte, a date to marry me! Perish the thought! Not likely! Oh no, instead he'd been boning up on the old psychology lark and planning to dump me on neutral territory where I was less likely to cause a scene in public. You know Guy – he can't bear anyone showing him up!" Self-deprecating, she attempted a little chuckle but it caught in her throat and turned into a sob. Steadying herself, she took a sip of coffee and a couple of deep breaths. "And then, Gemma, he turned in the Oscar performance of a lifetime. Talk about Evangelical! I could have sworn he was John F Kennedy reincarnated, only it wasn't so much a case of 'ask not what your country can do for you' as ask Guy what he could do for Brigitte and the children." Voice heavy with irony, she left off scrutinising the table and scrutinised me, instead. "They *needed* him, you see, and it was only *right* that he have one last crack at his marriage. Now *I*, on the other hand, was still young. A free spirit, with no ties. *I* could start again but Brigitte and the children – well, they were the innocent victims!" Earnestly her eyes sought mine. "Honestly, Gem, by the time he was finished I felt like awarding him the Victoria Cross for valour and self-sacrifice. It was like he regarded saving his marriage and hara-kiri as one and the same thing. I almost expected drum rolls, celestial trumpet calls and bolts of lightning to mark the stupendousness of the occasion." A little helpless, she shrugged. "And, of course, after that, there was no way I could tell him about Cloetus. Well, not without looking like the Bunny Boiler out of *Fatal Attraction*."

"The bastard!" I shook my head in wonder. "It's a mystery how such a stinking little shit always comes up smelling of *Samsara*!"

Debbie brushed the crumbs from her fingers, picked up her coffee, took a quick sip and set it back down again with a decisive thump. "Oh, look, let's be honest about this. I didn't exactly behave like Snow White, myself. Hell, I knew he was off limits and God knows both you and Sophie warned me off often enough." *Mea culpa*, she smote her chest. "But I turned a deaf ear

319

because the *feeling* was too strong. It was *fate*. Kismet! Like Romeo and Juliet we were *meant* to be together. So, when all's said and done, I suppose you could call it poetic justice, the law of karma and all that."

"Law of karma, my ass! He took advantage of you." Annoyed at what I saw to be Debbie's attempts to shoulder all the blame, I attempted to redress the balance and point the finger of blame firmly in the direction to which it belonged. "*You* weren't the one who was married. He was – correction, *is*! *Plus*, he's almost old enough to be your father." Rhythmically I shook my head from side to side in that age-old gesture of puzzlement. "Honestly, Debs, it beats me what you ever saw in him. Like, grey pubes – how on earth could that turn you on?"

Debbie shrugged. "Horses for courses, I suppose! Anyway, it's all over now. Dead in the water! *Finito!* The scales have fallen from my eyes. As far as I'm concerned, Brigitte is welcome to him. I wouldn't have him back now if his dick was dripping with diamonds and his arse was gold-plated."

I giggled at the picture that conjured up. "Well, there's no fear of that. Still, what about Cloetus? Will you tell him about his father, assuming it is a him and not a her?"

Palms up, Debbie made a who-knows motion. "Maybe. Maybe not! Anyway, I'll cross that bridge when I come to it which, hopefully, won't be for another eighteen years or so. Right now, though, I've got enough to do taking care of today. Mystic Meg can take care of tomorrow."

"Well, just so long as you know I'll be there for you today, tomorrow and however long it takes. Still, at the very least, I'll expect to be godmother. Mind you, you'll need to come up with a better name than Cloetus for the poor child."

Debbie smiled, the first real smile of the day. "You betcha – and Sophie can be godfather."

"*The* Godfather." Huskily, I attempted a Marlon-Brando-in-Godfather-mode voice. "Yeah, she'd like that, kiddo. Who better to instil some good moral values than good, old Soph?"

Debbie looked suddenly serious. "Actually, all joking aside. Sophie really *is* a good person. Full of moral fibre. If it wasn't for her penchant for chasing after every female in a thong, I've often thought she'd have made a very good nun."

"What?" I could feel my pupils dilating, readying themselves against that moment when they would throttle into full-on goggle. "Sophie? A nun? Nun of this! Nun of that! Nun of *the other*. Like, I don't think so." I giggled as a vision of Sophie kitted out in robe, wimple and a veiled expression of lust in her eyes, rose up in my mind's eye. "Still, I feel really bad about how we deceived her."

Debbie sighed. "I know. But what could we do? Despite her show of support, you and I both know she was only paying lip-service. The truth is, she would have done everything she could to put a spanner in my works. At the very least she'd probably have ended up wrecking the clinic and beating that Zoe character to a pulp with her bare hands."

"Yes, well she could have borne with beating." Grimly, I thought about the girl who appeared to give about as much thought to aborting a child as to the position of her next piercing or tattoo. Probably less! "Call me naive but I honestly never thought people like that existed."

"I know. It was a bit of an eye-opener, all right. Still, I suppose it takes all types and, hopefully, she's one in a trillion." Squinting up her eyes she gazed after the back of an open-top tour bus, disappearing up the street outside. "Which is more than can be said for your sister. I swear I've just seen her go past on the top of that bus. And if it's not her then it's definitely her clone or doppelgänger or whatever it is they call them."

I followed her gaze but the bus was already disappearing around a corner and in another moment it was lost from sight. "Must be her clone. Orla's off playing at pirates with Tyrell O'Neill."

Mournfully, Debbie gazed back out the window again where, in keeping with her mood, the skies were black with the threat of imminent rain. "Well, I hope it keeps fine for her. If I'm any judge it's going to chuck down stair rods at any minute. And if it's like that here, can you imagine what it must be like in Killybegs?"

"Yep! Twenty-foot rollers, with any luck! God, I hope, for her sake Tyrell likes the windswept look."

Debbie, with her usual sense of fair play, leapt to Orla's defence. "Oh, fair deuce to her! When all's said and done, she's done pretty well, considering how not all that long ago she was laid up in a hospital bed suffering from bulimia. That can kill, you know. All that vomiting can do terrible damage to your internal organs."

"Rubbish!" Dismissive, I finished my coffee, set the glass back on the table with a thump. "Orla never really had bulimia, as such. I know that now. The more I read and hear about the condition, the more I realise it's not something that can be cured overnight. Not at all! With Orla, puking was only ever a means to a skinny end."

Debbie shrugged. "Maybe, but whatever the case, I'm glad she appears to be getting her life together. I only hope mine pans out as well."

"It will," I assured her, with a vague sweep of my hand. "In a couple of weeks we'll have forgotten any of this happened at all. Mind you, if it's all right with you, I wouldn't mind catching the first flight home. I mean, I don't know about you but I'm not really in the mood for socialising."

"God no!" There was relief in Debbie's voice. "That's fine with me. What'll we tell the folks, though?"

"Ah, we'll tell them we were mugged or pickpocketed or something and that's why we've come home early. And what's the betting that after a bit of oohing and aahing and 'isn't it a shocking state the world is in entirely when you can't go out without being assaulted left, right and centre', no one will pay any further attention to it at all."

"At all, at all!" Debbie grinned, regaining a bit of her former spirit.

"At all, at all, at all, at all." As usual, I had to get completely carried away with the story. "And what's even better, Sophie won't even have had time to miss us. Anyway, if you're finished mangling that poor Danish pastry, I think we should make a move."

Debbie stood up. "Okay, let's go straight back to the B&B, pick up our things and . . . where do we need to go from there?"

"Victoria Station." I told her knowledgeably. "There's an express train that runs from there into Gatwick every fifteen minutes or so and I don't suppose we'll have that much difficulty catching a flight home. If the worse comes to the worse, we can always go standby."

"The way I feel right now, I could happily dive into the sea and swim home."

I shuddered dramatically. "Now *there* I draw the line. Orla might be up for a soaking, but not me. If there's one thing I loathe in life, it's getting my feet wet."

Debbie's blue eyes glinted wickedly. "Ah, but in Orla's case the compensation will be well worth it." Half-closing her eyes, she shot me a sultry look. "Imagine it, Gemma, Tyrell O'Neill coming up behind you, enveloping you in a big, warm fluffy towel nicked from some five-star hotel or other, whispering sweet obscenities in your ear. And then, completely oblivious to the Donegal wind whistling round the eaves, snuggling down with a bottle of bubbly in front of a roaring turf-fire as a prelude to getting down to the real business."

"Hmm. Change it to Rocky Cashel and I might go so far as to dip my big toe in."

Linking my arm, Debbie steered me out of the cafe. "You know what? You are completely incorrigible. Have you ever heard that old saying about be careful what you wish for?"

"Mm," I replied smugly. "I'm also familiar with that old saying, never venture, never gain. Also the one about love conquering all."

Beside me, I sensed rather than saw Debbie roll her eyes God-wards and plead with the heavens. The heavens that were growing ever more black with threatening rain. There was no doubt about it, we were in for a belter of storm. "I give up!" she moaned. "I bloody give up!"

"I don't!" I said. "I *won't!* Not so long as there's still breath in this Pamela Anderson body of mine and Rocky Cashel's still got a pulse."

"And a penis." Debbie giggled.

"Yep!" I giggled myself. "That would help!"

CHAPTER 19

"Gretchen missed you."

"She did?" Unaccountably pleased by this disclosure, considering how much I disliked the animal, I searched Rocky's face for some echo of this same sentiment, finding alack, alas, only a scowl as black as the thunderclouds still hovering outside.

"Well, I don't have time to be nursemaiding her while you go off junketing on dirty weekends in London and deserting your post. If you were in the army you could be shot for going AWOL, you know."

Protesting my innocence, I pushed past him. "But I didn't go AWOL. Debbie asked if it was all right if I went away for the weekend with her and *you* said it was." I furrowed my brow. "Actually what you said was 'No problem, Debbie. Of course she can. I'm not an ogre, you know. I don't chain her up and beat her with a big stick. Some people have even called me sensitive. Once or twice'. That's what Debbie said, anyway." Was it my ultra-sensitive imagination or did his face soften at the mention of Debbie's name, did his eyes grow dreamy, did his lips grow slobbery? I decided it was my imagination as a moment later the scowl was not only back pinned firmly in place, but it had recruited a snarl to keep it company.

"Yes, well, sometimes I'm too generous for my own good. With the new production of *Rotten to the Core* due to kick off in London in the next couple of weeks, I need all hands to the helm, right now. On top of that, my record company is pressuring me to put the final touches to 'The Green Green Tumbleweed'." He gave a martyred sigh. "Added to which it doesn't help that Tyrell is off playing at Little Bo-Peep and the Grand Mariner with your stick-insect sister." He jerked his head towards the sky. "Although, if he'd any sense, with the kind of weather we've been having lately and the rotten weather forecast which, incidentally, is for further storms, gales and tempests, you'd think he would have had the foresight to go to the Canaries or Cyprus or somewhere warm."

"Hardly," I said. "The sheep don't speak the same language. Anyway, you could always have given Gretchen back to Laura."

"What! Back to her and Frozen Yoghurts? Like, I don't think so."

"Well, be it on your own head, then," I said callously. "But remember, Gretchen, like herpes, will always be with you and – carrying on with the STD theme –

there'll be embarrassing flare-ups when you least expect them and at the most inconvenient times." Of course, I said that just for effect. The reality was, I had no intention of going anywhere. So long as I was within Rocky's orbit, Gretchen notwithstanding, I was happy. Mind you if he'd seen his way to bonking me, I'd have been a damn sight happier. And the more he bonked me, the happier I'd have been. I know that for a fact, having had a sneak preview down in the woods on the day of the Blessington Fox-hunt.

Waving an imperious hand, Rocky dismissed me like just one more sycophant. "Oh, buzz off, Gemma! Go walk Gretchen. Some of us have important work to do." Like Chicken Licken he glanced at the sky again, no doubt expecting it to fall in. "You'd better be quick, though. That storm's not going to hold off much longer." As an amateur weather-forecaster, he was definitely on the right track. Man, those clouds were doing all sorts of roiling and broiling and tempestuous adjectiving as a prelude to chucking it down in spades. Smiling blissfully at this hitherto unprecedented concern for my wellbeing, I arranged my expression into a mixture of Boadicea, Joan of Arc, and Helen of Troy in fearless and breast-plated battling mode. "Oh, I'll be fine. Don't worry about me."

"I wasn't." Viciously, Rocky overturned my chariot, set fire to my stake and attacked my wooden horse with a hatchet. "It's Gretchen I'm worried about. Dogs hate thunder. Being a veterinary nurse, *you* of all people should know that."

328

Sod being a veterinary nurse, I thought bitterly, leading Gretchen out of the house, up the driveway and off to do her business to the accompaniment of the first smattering of raindrops. Where was the glamour in that? Aunty Kay was right. Shoving hosepipes up assorted animals' recta was no life for a girl. A recta inspecta, if you will. *I* wanted to be a rock star's missus, and not just any old rock star either. *I* wanted to be Rocky's girl. I wanted to be photographed at premieres and press conferences, hanging on his arm, grinning inanely and wearing unsuitable Indian-style outfits, Jemima Khan style. Shalwar Kameezes! Only in my case nothing came easy. Jemima Khan, Gemma can't! I reflected bitterly, as the heavens opened and Thor, with a vengeance, set about the upkeep of his reputation as the God of Thunder. If ever there was a better time to look on the shite side of life . . . well, I couldn't think of it.

* * *

"*G-e-m-m-aaah!*" Drowsily I turned over and went back to kissing Ian Paisley. "Oh, Ian," I moaned softly. "Do that to me one more time." Snuggling closer, I buried my face deep in the folds of his neck, of which there were many. Folds, I mean. Not necks. "I can never get enough . . ."

"*G-e-m-m-aaah!*" Jesus! Why was he shouting at me? And in my *mother's* voice! Talk about a turn-off! "Gemma Murphy, would you get up this minute before I go up there and batter the life out of you!" Patience being a waste of time where my mother was concerned, this stricture was almost immediately followed by the rapid sound of footsteps on the stairs and a moment later found me bolting upright like a mental patient who's been the recipient of a massive overdose of ECT. God Almighty! I thought, as full consciousness dawned. Ian Paisley! *Ian bloody Paisley!* Of all the fantasies in all the world, why oh why . . . well, you know the rest. Like, what on earth did *Ian bloody Paisley* think he was doing sticking his tongue in *my* ear in *my* fantasies! I shuddered as the full force of my night of passion struck me. Chalk another one up to the eejits of this world. Why couldn't I do *anything* right? I mean other women dream about George Clooney or Richard Gere or if they're the shy and retiring type, Mr Darcy from *Pride and Prejudice* complete with sopping shirt. But me! Ian *bloody* Paisley. The sinister minister! The bionic gob!

"Gemma, get up quick!" Breathless from her Linford Christie sprint up the stairs, my mother erupted round the bedroom door, legged it over to the bed and proceeded, without further ceremony, to yank me out of it. For a moment, as I stood quaking and shivering in my beloved paisley-patterned pyjamas (aaargh!), I thought she'd flipped; that the hundred or so plastic spiked rollers she insisted on shoving in her hair every night had finally succeeded in puncturing her brain with the resultant loss of essential grey matter. "Well, for God's sake, don't just stand there," she ordered, looking it must be said, quite terrifying with her Medusa head and a pink, candlewick dressing-gown that had known better days. Principally, the days before she had started experimenting with hair dye in a nice shade of Autumn Russet! Even the gigantic Bugs Bunny slippers, a jokey Christmas present from Orla, but thankfully received on account of their bunion-cushioning properties, only added to rather than dispelled the illusion of lunacy. Well, I knew how to deal with lunatics. I'd seen *One Flew Over the Cuckoo's Nest*. I was fully equipped. First you waited till they were asleep. Then you smothered them with a gigantic pillow. If they weighed about twenty stone, and were of Red Indian extraction, so much the better. "Gemma Murphy!" Gums bared, and totally oblivious to the complicated processes of my mind, Mammy roughly manhandled me into my own seen-better-days dressing-gown. Gums, because at this unearthly hour, which according to my alarm clock was still only something to six, her dentures were still, presumably, merrily fizzing away in the glass of Steradent beside her bed. "Get down that stairs before I swing for you!"

"But why?" Now, I know there's an old saying about how you can't argue with madness but, with a raging storm knocking on my bedroom window and howling for admittance and the cosy spot in my bed still warm and missing me already, heck, I was going to have a damn good try. "For heaven's sakes, woman. It's barely past the witching hour. Go back to bed like a civilised geriatric, can't you? I know you're long past saving but some of us still need our beauty sleep, you know."

With an agility impressive in a woman half her age, she bent down, whipped off one of her slippers and waved it threateningly in the air. "I'll give you beauty sleep! See how beautiful you'll be when I wrap this round your face for you. Now get down that stairs pronto and deal with that Blarney Castle fella. Though what he thinks he's doing coming a-calling at this hour in the morning, I don't know. The dirty little pagan!"

Now I *knew* Bedlam was definitely missing an inmate. "*Rocky Cashel*," I said with the barely suppressed irritation of a daughter faced with a mother in the last stages of senile dementia and already planning her next foray to the shopping centre – stark naked, "is, no doubt, at home even as we speak, dreaming sweet dreams of the Irish Famine and sundry other national disasters. So, go on, be a good maternal role model and go back to bed or I might have to resort to smothering you with a pillow. By the way, did anyone ever remark on your slight resemblance so Sitting Bull? Could it be that we have Red Indian blood in the family?"

Slipper still in hand, she advanced a step closer. Close enough for me to see that her scalp had been pulled upright into little peaks by the force of the rollers which were also dragging her eyes up at the corners and giving the illusion of a decrepit Yoko Ono. Small wonder then that she was like a walking lunatic. The poor woman was clearly in agony. It just goes to show that age is no bar to vanity. "I'm telling you, Gemma, he's downstairs and all red in the face he is too. In a state, I'd say. Definitely in some sort of a state! Maybe it's that poodle of his, again. Maybe it's got red-eye or purple-eye or green-eye or whatever-eye and he wants you to use your expertise. In any case he's downstairs pacing up and down on the living-room carpet like a soul in torment."

I really couldn't understand why a soul in torment would want to pace up and down on our living-room carpet. Nevertheless the picture was finally getting through to me, loud and clear, with no snowy bits or wavy lines and without the necessity of rabbit's ears. Rocky Cashel was in *my* house at six o'clock in the morning with a tempest raging outside. That could only mean one thing. Trouble!

"I can't go down looking like this," I shrieked, my voice going suddenly all Ann Boleyn on her way to the chopping-block. "I mean, just look at these pyjamas. *And* I forgot to clean off my mascara last night and now my eye has slid all down my cheek."

Completely unmoved, my mother gave me a sharp taster of the slipper treatment. "Listen, lady, if I can go down without my teeth and with my hair in rolling-pins, I'm damn sure you can go down in your PLJs."

"Curling pins," I corrected her, taking my hands in my life. "Or rollers. And PLJ is a drink. An aid to slimming, if the blurb is to be believed, but only as part of a calorie-controlled diet –"

"Scat!" Gums gleaming, she brandished the slipper. "Now, before . . ." I didn't wait for any more. If Rocky had a heart attack at the sight of me, well, so be it! As it happened, Rocky scarcely noticed my appearance or maybe it was just that he didn't expect any better of me. Hence, had I turned up with a tricorn hat on my head and scarlet feather up my ass, the likelihood is that he wouldn't have batted an eyelid. As it was, my paisley (aaargh, again!) pyjamas and tatty old dressing-gown elicited no more than a quick blink and then it was straight into snarl mode.

"And what the bloody hell kept you? Haven't you seen the news?"

My mother was right. In a state just about summed him up. "What news?" I shrugged grandiloquently, a gesture meant to convey complete and utter bewilderment, which it did, thus demonstrating that some things do exactly what they say on the box.

Rocky ran a distracted hand through his hair. "A trawler's gone down off the coast of Killybegs. All hands are feared lost."

"Oh well, so long as they've still got their full quota of arms and legs . . ." I joked weakly, the full purport of what he'd just said going straight over my head. My only excuse was, and remains, the fact that it was still the wee small hours of the morning. Too early for my brain to have cranked into gear. Too early even for the early bird to think about early worms.

"Gemma!" A soul in torment (ten out of ten for observation, Mammy), he grabbed me by the shoulders and shook me till my teeth rattled. "Didn't you hear what

I just said?" He made a point of repeating himself, slowly, rounding out each word, shaping each individual letter with his mouth, turning to phonetics as a last resort. "A – trawler – has – gone – down – off – the – coast – of – Killybegs!" And as I continued to look like one whose mental abilities would snap under the strain of moving the beads about on an abacus, he chipped in with a few hand signs. "It's the *Sea Ewe*, Gemma. *Tyrell's* boat! Remember Tyrell O'Neill? The guy your sister went away with? To Donegal?"

"Oh, my God!" My hand flew to my mouth as, at the same time, my eyes flew towards the ceiling. "What will I tell Mammy?"

Rocky shook his head. "I don't know. Anyway, nothing has been confirmed yet. Still, she'll have to be told and, all things considered, it would be better coming from you." He shifted uncomfortably. "Like, I don't really know your mother."

"No!" A note of real hysteria entered my voice. "I couldn't. She thinks I hate Orla and what's the betting that somehow the whole sorry mess will land up at my door." Frantically, I glanced about the room looking for inspiration while unbidden, pictures of Orla's emaciated drowned body rose up and floated before me, her eyes wide open, pale-blue and accusing, bits of seaweed, Neptune's noose, wrapped around her neck.

'It's all your fault,' I heard her say in that drawn-out, spooky tone peculiar to Celine Dion and those who have gone-towards-the-light, her wraith dripping and diaphanous, her finger pointed accusingly as with all the best ghosts. 'If you hadn't threatened to open your big gob to Mammy about my bulimia, I'd never have lost the *Sensuelle* contract to that poxy Karen Rogers and I'd never have ended up on Tyrell O'Neill's poxy boat in poxy Killybegs.' Wail. Wail. 'A pox on you, Gemma Murphy! Prepare to meet thy doooohm!'

"Well, someone's got to tell her, to prepare her, like," Rocky reasoned, happily unaware of the haunting taking place not two yards away from him, the spectre of Orla giving me a right old bollocking! "Haven't you got an aunt or neighbour? Somebody who could come in and sit with her?"

"Of course! Aunty Kay!" I could have kissed Rocky for handing me the solution. I could have done the Martini on him – you know, kissed him any time, any place, anywhere – but that's a different story to be reserved for a happier occasion. "I'll go and phone her now."

"Right, and then go and pack a bag. We're going to Killybegs to see if there's anything we can do." Unsaid, the words 'Besides, somebody's got to identify the bodies' hung, like ectoplasm, in the air between us.

Miserably I walked over to the receiver, picked it up and began to dial. I didn't want to identify Orla's body because, God knows, although I'd wanted her dead more times than I could remember and had whiled away many a pleasant hour dreaming up how best such an objective might be accomplished, now that she was missing, presumably drowned, I wanted her alive again. I wanted to put my arms around her and hug and hug. I wanted to blow the nail varnish on her toes dry. I wanted to give her my Janet Reger knickers. For keeps! She'd shrunk them in the hot wash, anyway. The bitch! My little sister! I wanted her back!

"Don't cry!" Coming up behind me, Rocky enfolded me in his arms but, unfortunately, I was far too distraught to enjoy the experience.

The phone rang for what seemed like an eternity before it was picked up on the other end. "Aunty Kay! Aunty Kay!" I sniffled, when finally she answered on a querulous and utterly confused note. "The *Sea Ewe's* gone down and I need you to come and sit with Mammy."

"See *who*?" Plainly another one whose brain had not yet cranked into gear, she turned the volume up full. "Now, listen here, I don't want to *see* anybody! How many times do I have to tell you lot, I don't *want* double-glazing! Or a conservatory. Or incontinence pads." She broke off for a moment to give vent to a hacking smoker's cough that turned both her lungs and my stomach inside out. "Thank God. I've still got complete control over bladder and bowel. So you can take your double-glazing and shove it where the sun don't shine!"

It must have been hysteria that suddenly made me want to laugh but with a gargantuan effort I brought myself back under control and bawled down the receiver again. "Aunty Kay! It's me Gemma! Would you stop pratting on and just listen for a moment?"

"As for chair-lifts . . ." A woman with a mission, she cut me dead and in the space of a heartbeat was off and running on yet another spiel. "What happens when there's a power cut and you're halfway up the stairs, that's what I'd like to know. And you've no family that live close by. And your nearest neighbour doesn't drop in any more on account of a row over the giant Leylandii bush you planted a couple of years previous and which condemned her to a life of eternal darkness." She gave a disparaging sniff. "So let's face it, in the St Bernard Rescue Dogs calendar, she's going to be a cat, isn't she? I mean, she's not going to give a stuff if you're stuck halfway up Mount Fuji. I mean . . ."

I'd had enough. "Aunty Kay!" I bellowed and continued to bellow her name mantra-like until such time as light filtered through, albeit by degrees. Honest to God, it was like sieving cheddar.

"Gemma?" Gradually the hectoring tone gave way to amazement, followed immediately by her own version of *Twenty Questions*. "Gemma Murphy, is it? My niece, Gemma? What on earth are you doing selling double-glazing? Have you given up the veterinary nursing then? Well, I've always said it was no class of a life for a girl! All that sticking your hand up unmentionable places." She was obviously wide awake now. I had a mental vision of her fastening the chinstrap of her Wehrmacht helmet, fussily adjusting the Nazi armband around the sleeve of her winceyette nighty. "Still – double-glazing? Isn't that just a commission thing? Couldn't you have done any better for yourself? Got a job as an air-hostess or something? A trolley-dolly, isn't that what they call them in the popular press? Mind you, any dog and divil can become an air-hostess, these days. Never mind height and looks, it's all pull – *who* Daddy knows – *who* Mammy screwed! Honest to God, you could be a dyslexic dwarf without an exam to your name but if you've the right connections, you're home and dry." She gave a throaty chuckle. "Or, should that be abroad and high?"

Losing my temper, I hammered the telephone against the side of my head. "Shut up, Aunty Kay!" I screeched, the sound making even the hairs on the back of my own neck stand to attention. "Just shut up and listen, can't you!" I paused to make sure she was following instructions and, reassured by an in-drawn indignant breath, plunged without further ado straight in the deep end. "The *Sea Ewe's* gone down and Orla's drowned!" Admittedly, had I not been so upset myself, I might have tried harder to couch it in more gentle terms, the way I did at the surgery when Tibbles, Mimi or Bentley turned up their toes and the news had to be broken to their distraught owners. As it was I came close to a perforated eardrum as Aunty Kay dissolved on the other end of the phone into a screaming mass of hysteria out of which the only clearly distinguishable phrase to emerge was, "It should have been you, you little hoor, you! Dear God! It should have been you!"

"Don't mind her," Rocky comforted a short while later, as emotionally battered and bruised and made to feel guilty for being alive, when Orla wasn't, I replaced the handset. "She doesn't know what she's saying. It's the shock talking. Shock affects people in all sorts of funny ways. Makes them say things they'd never normally say in a million years."

"I-I know." Making a valiant attempt at stiff-upper-lipping it, I brushed the flat of my hand across my face in an attempt to eliminate all evidence of tears before I went upstairs to throw a few necessities into a bag. I felt bad about not telling my mother, who judging from the soft snores issuing from her room, had gone back for a further snooze. Like, she had a right to know. Orla was her daughter. Her favourite daughter! Still, there was no way I could deal with another bout of histrionics, not when my own nerves were in tatters and stretched as taut as a telephone wire and, all things considered, wasn't it better to leave her in happy ignorance, at least for a while longer? No, I decided, mentally arguing the toss back and forth. Aunty Kay could deal with matters far better than I ever could. Besides, I couldn't bear to look in her eyes and wonder if, like Aunty Kay, she too, was wondering why it couldn't have been me. I'd phone her later. That's what I'd do. In the meantime, I'd scribble a note for Aunty Kay and leave it somewhere she'd be bound to find it.

With no time for a shower, I changed quickly into jeans and sweatshirt, ran a quick comb through my hair and, having grabbed an assortment of clothes and toiletries, threw them into a bag and headed determinedly downstairs. Rocky was right. I would be far better employed doing something active, going up to Killybegs and seeing how things stood at first hand. Besides, I couldn't bear to think of Orla being manhandled by strangers – well-meaning no doubt, but still strangers. Strangers who, when they recovered her body, would find themselves faced with no more than an empty shell; strangers who would never know her for the exasperating, egocentric, maddening, funny, spirited girl who was once my sister.

CHAPTER 20

"Come on." Masterfully, Rocky took charge. "Let's get out of here before the *paparazzi* show up in droves. Because they will," he warned. "Just as soon as the names are released and someone makes the connection between Tyrell and me and finds out your sister was the lurve interest. I'm telling you, Teddy Kennedy and Chappaquiddick will have nothing on it!"

Oh, God! I hadn't thought of that. Still, if any of them had the impudence or imprudence to show up on our doorstep, Aunty Kay would soon put them to rout. It's a shame Princess Diana didn't have her in her retinue or history might have been rewritten.

We were quiet on the long journey up, both of us lost in our thoughts, flicking through our memories; memories grown twice as precious now that both Orla and Tyrell were missing, presumably drowned. It was much the same as with that Van Gogh painter fella. Nobody wanted to buy his paintings when he was alive, thought they were a joke if the truth be told. The work of a crank! But no sooner had he chucked off his mortal coil and floated up to discuss rag-rolling and stencil effects with his Maker, than the *aficionados* were queuing knee-deep in turpentine, desperate to get hold of his *Sunflowers* or canvas with dot, dash and splash.

And I had thought Orla a joke. A crank! A bit of a send-up! A silly ass with nothing holding up her ears but a scaffolding of make-up: the proud possessor of the IQ of a lowly mollusc. Funny, I'd got what I wished for, a world without Orla. A world totally devoid of that distinctive giggle, that peculiar cross between the tinkling of bells and the high notes on a piano which enchanted everyone else but only made me sick to my stomach. Funny, I'd have paid big money to hear it again. Even employed, as it usually was, at my expense, I'd have paid a king's ransom. Guiltily, I shifted about, eyes fixed in front, seeing without registering the long ribbon of winding road that snaked ahead, the patchwork fields on either side, the sheep and cattle gazing out with mournful, empathetic eyes that said without need of words, 'We understand what it's like to lose someone. We've got family in England. Even at this distance, we can smell the smoke.'

Inevitably, my thoughts strayed on to Tyrell. Tyrell O'Neill, the Milk Tray Man, Mr Scrapie-on-the-brain, the aspiring Donegal sheep-farmer! God, I'd been horrible to him too. Positively obnoxious! God knows how many times I'd slapped him down, thrown his compliments back in his face, wished him at the far reaches of Timbuktu or Kingdom Come. In case he'd spoil my chances with Rocky, you understand. I sniffed loudly, felt Rocky's eyes slide across then veer uncomfortably away again. Big joke, that! I never *had* a chance with Rocky Cashel. I simply wasn't his type. Be that a penchant for freckles or squints, it simply wasn't me! But it had taken the deaths of my sister and his best friend to pile-drive that through to me.

"Shit!" Rocky swore, accelerating suddenly and jerking me out of my reverie and back to reality. "Some asshole is right up my rear end."

Now in normal times, there was no way I would have let a comment like that pass without turning it into something of a joke. 'Why, yes, Rocky,' I would have said. 'It's your own, dear. Nothing to get excited about!' Now though, I turned listlessly around, gazed listlessly out the back window and turned listlessly back again.

"It's just Wanda," I said, listlessly. "Sophie and Debbie must have heard the news."

"Oh," Rocky said. Just "Oh!" But sneaking a glance at him I could see that for him, anyway, some of the gloom had dissipated.

* * *

"Are you okay, Gem?" Slipping an arm about my shoulders, Debbie cuddled me close. "I couldn't believe it when Sophie phoned first thing this morning.

Apparently she'd gone out on an emergency call with Rob when the news came over the car radio. We both went straight over to your house but you'd already left with Rocky."

"How was Mammy?" Anxiously, I tore my gaze away from the ocean, where the waves were whipping themselves into a triumphant frenzy, to focus anxiously on her face.

Debbie gave a little shrug. "I honestly don't know. We met your aunt just outside the door and well – let's just say, she looked like someone who hadn't slept for a month."

"I know. She's devastated. We all are. Mind you, she blames me. In fact she thinks it should have been me and not Orla."

"Nonsense!" Debbie brushed a wind-blown tendril of hair out of her eyes. "That was just the shock talking. If it had been you, God forbid, she'd have been just as devastated."

"Maybe!" I said. "Maybe not! Like, maybe she's got a point. I mean Orla would never have gone off with Tyrell if it weren't for me, in the first place. Oh God, I *wish* it was me!"

"Yeah, yeah. And if wishes were riches there'd be no Third World." Firmly, Debbie steered me down to where Sophie, Rocky and a gaggle of other people were standing helplessly about on the pier below. They had that distinct aura of waiting about them, an unmistakable stillness as though waiting for the axe to fall. "Listen, Gemma, there's far too many ifs and buts in this equation for anyone ever to come up with an answer that makes sense. One thing I do know though, none of this is your fault."

"All right, Gem?" Sophie walked a little way to meet us, hesitant, her hand rising slowly as though to touch me, then falling back again, unsure quite what to do. She looked pale, upset, ill at ease – nothing like the old boisterous Sophie I saw every day at the surgery. "How are you bearing up?"

I started a little. How are you bearing up? Wasn't that one of the standard questions people trotted out to the recently bereaved? How are you bearing up? As if you were a table laden to capacity and in danger of imminent collapse or a house of cards, shaky and insubstantial and liable to crumble if someone so much as blew on you. 'I'm sorry for your trouble!' That was another one of them, a trite, pat phrase that tripped off the tongue, words meant to comfort but which somehow left you feeling more and more isolated. More and more helpless! A watcher as opposed to a participant!

"I-I'm okay. Have they found any – thing, yet?"

Sophie shook her head. "Only a bit of wreckage." She fixed me with an honest eye, reluctant to get my hopes up, preparing me for the worst. "But it's definitely the *Sea Ewe*, Gemma. They found the nameplate. And apparently Tyrell was talking about taking her out yesterday."

"Aye, he was that." A young, ruddy-faced fisherman, the maritime equivalent of Benny from old *Crossroads* approached, diffidently kneading his woollen hat between his fingers. "I warned him, mind. Told him it was blowing up a gale . . . there were white horses out there, the likes of which I've rarely seen before." He trailed off, shrugged, twisted his hat into a limp rag. I could almost see the perspiration and dirt drip from it. "He didn't have that much experience on the sea. Sheep were more his thing, like."

"And he wouldn't be told, no doubt." Angrily, Rocky joined us, kicked viciously at a bit of seaweed-covered boulder. "That's half his problem. You can't tell him anything, whether it's to do with music, or sheep-farming or anything else. Tyrell O'Neill is a law unto himself."

"Shut up!" Angry myself, I lashed out at the same boulder, sending a whole colony of insect life scurrying beneath the shingle. "You're just pissed off because he criticised your 'Green Green Tumbleweed'. And, my God, can you blame him? I mean, it's hardly Offenbach, is it? More like Lloyd-Webber."

"Gemma!" Shocked, Debbie laid a restraining hand on my arm. "You're upset. We all are but there's no point in having a go at Rocky. I mean, none of this is his fault."

She was right of course. If there was any spleen to be vented then yours truly was number one suspect in the ID parade. There was no reason for me to take it out on poor Rocky. None at all. "I'm sorry," I shrugged contritely. "I shouldn't have said that."

"It's okay." He waved away the apology, but I could tell by the way he dropped his eyes that the reference to Lloyd-Webber had left him gutted.

"Look!" A shake in her voice, Sophie pointed to where a craft could be seen skimming its way towards the shore. "Isn't that one of the rescue boats?" Alarmed, she turned to Debbie. "Debs, maybe you should wait here with Gemma while Rocky and I find out what's going on."

I shook my head, aware in some detached part of my mind that my legs had dissolved into jelly and that the freezing-cold prickling that suddenly enveloped my entire body had very little to do with actual climatic conditions, inclement though they still were. "No. I'm coming too."

The others exchanged glances but nobody tried to dissuade me. Instead, like a couple of bodyguards, Debbie and Sophie ranked themselves one on either side of me and, protectively taking an elbow each, guided me down to the jetty.

"Nothing!" One of the lifeguards put us out of our misery straight away. "Nothing but flotsam and jetsam. Not a body in sight!"

"Oh, thank God!" Despite the support of both women, I felt my knees give way, felt myself buckle to the ground, felt relief course through my body like a powerful, fast-acting course of antibiotics. "That means they must be all right, mustn't it?" Hopefully, from my prone position, I scanned the lifeguard's face. On another occasion I might have noticed his resemblance to David Hasselhoff, his rugged jawline, his tanned and weatherbeaten skin, his aura of raw sexiness. His Donegal accent, so thick it could plough a field of turnips! Now, though, all I noticed was his resemblance to Jesus Christ, the man who could work miracles. "It must, mustn't it?" I insisted, allowing Sophie to haul me to my feet again. "I mean, if there's no bodies, that must mean they're okay . . ."

The lifeguard cleared his throat, busied himself with some sort of sailing tackle, shifting it first to one side, then to the other, achieving precisely nothing. I suppose there are certain things you never get used to no matter how many times you go through the motions and breaking bad news to grieving relatives must rank high up on that particular list.

"I don't want to give you false hope," he began. "Sometimes, it can take days for a body to surface. It all depends on tides and conditions and a multitude of other factors." He gave an expressive sweep of his head. "I mean, in these kind of conditions it's not uncommon for a body to be swept way out to sea, or even to get snagged on something and get pulled under. Sometimes they can even get washed up miles and miles away, in a completely different direction from where the boat went down. Sometimes, they never surface at all."

I bowed my head. "So what you're telling me is, there's no hope."

Stepping out of the boat he laid a kind, weatherbeaten hand on my arm, gave a reassuring squeeze. "No, that's not what I'm saying. There's always hope. Never give up believing in miracles!"

Sadly, though, that advice had come far too late. I'd stopped believing in miracles the day my very first boyfriend cheated on me with Babs Richardson. I was ten and she was the class bully and already well on her way to a career as a second Joan Rivers and, as far as I was concerned, it had been downhill all the way ever since.

"Where are you going?" Sophie caught my arm as, infused with a sudden determination, I turned away.

"For a walk," I said, gently but firmly shrugging her off. "I just need to be alone for a while. Don't worry! I'm not going to do something stupid like top myself. I just need some quiet time, on my own. Do you understand?"

She nodded and behind her, pale-faced, Debbie nodded too. "Well, when you're ready, you know where we are."

"Thanks," I said and headed off up along the shore, scarcely noticing where I was going, head bent into the wind, face lashed by a mixture of rain and ocean spray, feeling more alone than I had ever felt in my whole life before. Bereft, isn't that what people called it? I was bereft. I remember looking it up in the dictionary once when, as a child, I'd confused it with beret. For a long time, I was the only girl to go to school wearing a blazer, gymslip and bereft. Deprived, that was the definition. I was deprived. Deprived of Orla. Deprived of Tyrell O'Neill. Then a thought struck me. Well, to be honest, it didn't so much strike me as blow me away. I'd forgotten to phone my mother. The poor woman must have been going off her head. For once I wished I carried my mobile but, as I could never remember to charge the damn thing, it usually remained snugly at home, of use to neither man nor beast but costing me an arm and a leg in line rental every month. Of course, there was bound to be a phone in Killybegs itself. I mean, any town in Ireland worth its salt usually had at least a hundred churches, five hundred pubs and a couple of public telephones. And so, turning my back on the sea, I headed off towards the huddle of buildings that made up the fishing port of Killybegs, my feet reluctant pieces of lead, my heart heavy as a stone.

CHAPTER 21

"All aboard! All aboard! Come on now, don't be shy. The natives are friendly and some of them even speak English."

Drenched in gloom, my head jerked up at the sound of the bantering, good-humoured voice distinctly at odds with my own black humour and found myself looking into a pair of twinkling blue eyes.

"What do you say, Miss?" The elderly owner of the eyes pantomimed filling his lungs with cool, clear draughts of fresh air, smacking his lips as though he could taste it. "Leave the smell of fish behind and come with me to the Lake Isle of Innisfree where peace comes dripping slow, as that poet fella said." He gave a pixyish grin. "Actually, I'm not going to Innisfree. I'm going to Bundoran." Proudly he patted the side of an old red double-decker bus that had once done time on the streets of London. Brixton, during the riots, by the look of it! "Chitty-Chitty-Bang-Bang here will have us there in next to no time and, if you don't mind me saying so, you look like a young woman who could do with a bit of cheering up." He tapped the side of his nose. God, those Masons really get around! "And you know what . . . it might never happen!"

It was on the tip of my tongue to say, "Actually, for your information Mr Always-look-on-the-bright-side-of-life, Mr-bloody-Pickwick, it already *has* happened. Even as we speak my only sister and her boyfriend are floating belly-up somewhere in the sea behind us; my mother and aunt are on the verge of a nervous breakdown and I, myself, am most likely riddled with cancer from the stress of it all." I didn't though. Instead, phone call gratefully procrastinatated, I found myself handing over my money and climbing meekly on board. Bundoran! Wasn't that where Tyrell had his farm? He even had a song about it, an old comeallye, 'Beautiful Bundoran' or some such. I remember him crooning it one evening at Gothdere, fingers rippling over the piano keys, teasing a gentle melancholy from the instrument far more used to the heavy demands of rock-'n'-roll. A plaintive keening that had even the most die-hard rockers blubbing for their Irish roots and rehashing the legendary exploits of Finn McCool, Brian Boru and Daniel O'Donnell. With a tear in his eye and a catch in his voice, one waxed particularly patriotic: "You know for such a small, small country, man, we is a great, great nation." His name was Temtitope and he was Nigerian. Only Rocky had taken the piss, which now that I thought about it, was a bit rich coming from a man who stooped not to conquer but to rip off Bob Dylan and Tom Jones. Funny that, not only were the times-a-changing but my feelings also seemed to be in a state of flux. Like, I had thrown my weight behind Rocky then, laughed aloud and berated the rest of the room for being a pack of poor sad bastards obsessed with living in the past.

"Ireland," I'd announced baldly and, shame the devil and speak the truth, a bit drunk, "is only an annexe of England. And England is only an annexe of Europe. And Europe is only an annexe of . . ." At which point Tyrell told me to shut up, sit down and leave the Bacardi Breezers alone.

I had a sudden, overwhelming urge to see him. Tyrell! Not Rocky! An urge to reach up and proprietarily brush back the quiff of dark hair from his forehead. An urge to witness him at work in the landscape of his dreams, herding sheep, mending fences, thatching roofs, a true son of the land. But sadly, it would seem, not of the sea! Reminded, I flinched at the pain of my loss, eyes reluctantly probing through the built-up grime on the window, searching for signs of the little group I had left on the seashore waiting for the sea to give up its dead. My dead! It was almost a relief when the bus with an emphysemic cough spluttered suddenly into life and after a final spirited bout of arguing with its gearbox, turned tail on Killybegs and headed up the coast for Bundoran.

It wasn't difficult to find Tyrell's farm. Everyone, it seemed, knew Tyrell O'Neill. Everyone sang his praises and those who were tone-deaf and couldn't sing, spoke highly of him instead. The cynical side of me couldn't help but wonder if this canonisation was a recent thing that had only come about on account of his death and if, up to that point, they hadn't been badmouthing him. You know, going on and on about rock'n' rollers, and drug addicts and bad elements and people who thought sheep-farming was just a hobby, something you could pick up and put down as the inclination took you and not something other people depended on to make a living. Bad cess to him! But, if such were their true feelings, they kept them well hidden. Instead, everyone went out of their way to be helpful.

"Oh, aye, that'll be Nirvana, you're looking for." And, as I must have looked puzzled, "Nirvana – Tyrell O'Neill's place you're wanting, is it? The sheep-farm? Yerrah, sure that's just a hop, skip and a jump away from the town. A mile and a bit. No more."

A mile and a bit. That would be an *Irish* mile and a bit! In real terms then, we were talking about at least five miles. Nonetheless, as the bus went no further than the town and there appeared to be no taxi service, I struck out on foot aware that the stormy weather was abating somewhat. With a bit more effort the sun might even be persuaded to put in an appearance. Not that I gave a shit really, the miserable weather complemented my mood perfectly.

Nirvana! He'd called the farm after a rock group, appropriately enough. That was something I hadn't known but then again, I realised, there was a lot about Tyrell I didn't know. Hadn't been interested in knowing, if the truth be told and now that I was interested, would never have the opportunity to know. Life, as they say, really is a bad joke!

My feet were aching by the time I finally reached the farm and pushed through the wooden gate that led down a deeply rutted, somewhat overgrown track to the farmhouse. Which wasn't a farmhouse, as such, but a cottage! A traditional, low-slung, whitewashed cottage of the variety that featured on postcards with a thatched roof, a green half-door and, oh my Lord, there really were roses round the door! And fuchsia bushes. And, would you believe it, a rainbow, God's promise, arching high in the sky above. For a moment, I felt as Dorothy must have felt when she first set foot in the Land of Oz. Honest to God, it wouldn't have surprised me if a welcome committee of Munchkins had stepped suddenly out from behind the nearest fuchsia bush with the Lollipop Kids hot on their heels. Only my footwear, the furthest thing from ruby slippers you can imagine gave the game away and brought me back to reality. Sitting down on a sawn-off tree-stump, I gazed slowly around. I might not have been in Oz but I sure as hell *was* in awe. This place was truly a feast for the senses. I could see now why Tyrell was prepared to give up everything to come and live here. This wasn't 'downsizing'; this was 'quality-of-lifing'. And then I knew why he'd really called it Nirvana. Nothing to do with the rock group, of course. This was Tyrell's Nirvana. This was Tyrell's zenith, the culmination of all his desires. I felt crushed by a sudden weight in my heart as the realisation dawned that I too could have been happy here. *Here* in Donegal. *Here* in this cottage. *Here* . . . with Tyrell O'Neill! In the distance the low hypnotic thrum of a distant tractor seemed suddenly to grind to a halt. The sheep grazing on the hillside beyond grew suddenly motionless, their white fleeces reminiscent of giant dog-daisies against the green of the grass, their baa-ing muted in deference to . . . what? To the beauty surrounding them? The tranquillity? Or to my sudden acute, painful perception that *I* was in love with Tyrell O'Neill? Stunned, I repeated the words in my head. Slowly, one by one, as if such action could imbue them with sense. I-was-in-love-with-Tyrell-O'Neill! Truly, madly, deeply . . . in love with Tyrell O'Neill. Only, I wasn't! My head argued with my heart. I couldn't be! I was in love with Rocky Cashel! Wasn't I? Like, that's why I gave up my weekends to mind that ugly mutt, Gretchen. Because, I wanted to be close to Rocky! Because, I wanted to please him. Because, I loved him! Except that I didn't! I knew that now and the knowledge, coming too late as it did, was bitter. Like lemons! Or aloes! Or Al Gore after the American election recount. Oh, I was in love with the *idea* of Rocky, all right. Rocky the rock star! Rocky the VIP! Rocky the unattainable! I was in *love*, though, *real love* with Tyrell O'Neill. The man!

And hot on the heels of that realisation came jealousy. Of Orla! I mean, searing, hateful, spiteful jealousy. Even knowing her lifeless body was probably being tossed about like a rag-doll somewhere out in the Atlantic at that very minute! I was jealous because *she* had come here with him, to Nirvana, when it could have been me! It *should* have been me! Goddammit! It *would* have been me if only I hadn't been such a big, blind, idiotic fool! In the background, I was dimly aware that the tractor had started up again, that the sheep, heads bent, a flock of woolly lawnmowers, were once more moving slowly across the hillside. Because, even for the broken-hearted, life goes on!

Settling myself more comfortably on the tree-stump, I brought my gaze back to the cottage, which gazed prettily though blankly back. If only those walls could talk, I thought, what would they say? Would they tell me about Orla's arrival here, the arrival of the Queen of Sheba, a few days earlier? Would they reminisce sweetly about the contrast of her tinkling laughter musically mixed with his deeper shades of baritone voice as he lifted her up and carried her with ease over the threshold? Ruefully, I reflected that there was no way he could have carried me over the threshold – well, not unless he was prepared to subscribe to a chiropractor for the rest of his life. And later, when daylight had given way to mysterious night and the sprigged muslin curtains had shut them off from the rest of the world, did they make love on a sheepskin rug? Well, in his case it would *have* to be sheepskin, wouldn't it? Like a zebra skin wouldn't do! At first wildly, hungrily and then, first passion spent, slowly, languorously, content to take their time exploring each other's bodies in the flickering light from the open fire! Her soft, slender body! His hard, muscled body! Angrily, I gave myself a little shake. Jesus, what was wrong with me! My mind was turning into a mush of Mills & Boon. I should be happy for the pair of them, not angry and resentful because, heaven knows, their happiness had been short-lived.

Almost absent-mindedly, I rose and walked about the garden, stopping briefly to examine a particularly lovely Canterbury Bell fuchsia bush, the leaves and blossoms still wet from the recent rain, glistening . . . like tears. I wondered if they'd found them yet, Orla and Tyrell. If, even at this moment they were looking for me to tell me the bad news. Worrying about me! Well, let them look a while longer! Let them worry! I was possessed of a curious, selfish contentment here at Nirvana. Content and confused, bewildered and angry and every other emotion under the sun, all at once. In no fit state to deal with anyone else or *their* emotions! Walking over to the front door, I tried the handle, not expecting it to open, surprised when it did. Still, I suppose I shouldn't have been too surprised. Out in the country people were less security-conscious or maybe just more honest. There was no need for spy holes and padlocks and burglar alarms and armed heavies equipped with Armalite rifles, tear gas and rubber bullets. Dark on the inside, it was reflective of the black clouds that had begun once more to mass outside, preparatory to drawing up their agenda for an onslaught of further storms, gales and tempests. Feeling about for the light-switch on the wall just inside the door, I located and turned it on sending a flood of mellow light about the room. Everything was just how I imagined it would be and indeed how, given the choice, I would have furnished it myself. Funny how I felt right at home here amid the utilitarian rusticity of the Shaker-type furniture. Honestly, I could move in bag and baggage and not five minutes later feel as though I'd lived here all my life. As though I *belonged* here. Which, I told myself, Orla most assuredly wouldn't have. No way! Orla was a real *Homes & Gardens* girl, more your gilt, cornice and silk-wallpaper type girl. A graduate of the Jocasta Innes school of stencilling and soft furnishings. Maybe she just had better taste than me but somehow that didn't seem to matter any more. Nothing seemed to matter any more. Cocooned as I was in a strange kind of detachment, I felt apart from other people, as if nothing or no one could ever touch me again. I was in my very own state of Limbo, caught between two worlds, and you know what, there was a lot to be said for it. Walking over to the mantelpiece above the fire (I was right, there was a sheepskin rug on the floor) I picked up a unframed photograph that had been carelessly propped up between a Toby Jug and an empty bottle of Guinness and promptly burst out laughing as Tyrell, his arm draped companionably about Rocky's neck, stared back at me. And beside them stood Laura, Gretchen in her arms, and a cartoon bubble coming out of her mouth that said 'Milkmen deliver every day!' Tyrell had not only added the bubble but also horns and a beard and even Gretchen had a Hitler moustache. The laughter though verged a bit too much on the hysterical and a moment later, I was in bits again, weeping and wailing to beat the band. Unwittingly a picture of my Aunty Kay rose up in mind.

"Aha!" she was wont to say. "Laughter and tears are very close bedfellows and while you might be laughing now, Gemma Murphy, it won't be too long before you're laughing on the other side of your face!"

Much and all as I hate to admit it, she was usually right. Pulling myself together, I set off on my travels again, moving about the room, picking up objects and putting them down again, lightly touching the backs of chairs and running my fingers along the keys of the old upright piano that took up one whole corner of the room. I stopped to examine some sheet music, not that I could read music but simply because I felt compelled to touch everything that Tyrell had touched, everything that was precious to him. 'The Green Green Tumbleweed'! I felt another hysterical giggle rise as the first line caught my eye and I was reminded of how appalling it actually was.

Replacing it, I accidentally dislodged another sheet from the rack behind, knocking it to the floor. Bending to pick it up again, I found myself rocking back on my heels, brought up short as the title jumped out at me. 'Song for Gemma.' Gemma! Surely it was more than just coincidence? Could it be that Tyrell O'Neill had written a song for me? Warily, I scanned the words, seeking confirmation.

> *I'm looking at you, Gemma,*
> *But you're looking right through*
> *To somebody else, Gemma,*
> *Who doesn't see you.*
> *Well, he doesn't love you*
> *But, darling, I do,*
> *He's looking at you, Gemma,*
> *But he's looking right through . . .*
>
> *Here's looking at you, Gemma,*
> *Here's looking at love*
> *Here's looking at hearts 'n' flowers*
> *'N' starlight above.*
> *Well, he doesn't love you*
> *But, darling, I do,*
> *He's looking at you, Gemma*
> *But he's looking right through . . .*

That's all there was and my God, it was truly awful but, in a horrible, mixed-up kind of way, it was also truly wonderful. I mean, not everyone can boast about

having a song written for them – well, apart from Annie
and Rosemary and Donna and Claire in that song by
Gilbert O'Sullivan, and a couple of thousand more or
so. Mind you, having said that, I'm not altogether sure
I'd want to boast about this one. Something about the
metre made me suspect it of having CW leanings which
was okay by me because, although I'd never dare admit
as much to my friends, I really am a closet Garth Brooks
and Trisha Yearwood fan. I even like Dolly Parton and,
before you get your knickers in a twist, just remember
she wrote that 'I Will Always Love You' song that was
such a massive hit for Whitney Houston. Cool or what!
Now Debbie, on the other hand, loathes and detests
CW with a passion surpassed only by her hatred of
South American panpipes and the Spice Girls, especially
Posh, and Sophie supports her dislike one hundred per
cent. That said, Sophie *does* have a bit of a thing about
Shania Twain and that 'Man, I Feel Like A Woman'
song has become something of an anthem for our Soph.
Poor Sophie! Talk about a case of never the Twain shall
meet! Thoughtfully, I went to replace the song-sheet,
then something, I don't know what, made me crumple
it up and jam it in my pocket instead. Maybe I wanted
to feel closer to Tyrell. Maybe I just didn't want anyone
else seeing it and taking the piss when they came to deal
with his effects as, inevitably, they would. Maybe . . .
just maybe . . . it made me feel a bit special. Then a most
unwelcome thought struck me. Maybe he wrote one for
Orla, as well. Maybe he went around all over the place,

the demon songwriter, writing songs for women as a way of gaining entrée, a way of getting his leg over. A kind of singing Don Juan! Like some men bought flowers and chocolates. Like some men wined and dined. Maybe Tyrell O'Neill wrote songs! Not so much sing for your supper as sing and then tup 'er, to use yet another sheep analogy. Suddenly, I didn't feel that special any more, even though a quick check through the rest of the music rack turned up nothing to support my suspicions. Suddenly, I wanted to break something and the Toby Jug on the mantelpiece fitted the bill as well as anything else. Striding across the room I picked it up, took aim, and then the phone rang. Let me tell you there is nothing more eerie than the sound of a telephone ringing in a house that's meant to be empty. A dead man's house! As it happened, I didn't have to throw the Toby Jug. Instead it dropped from my nerveless fingers and shattered along with what was left of my self-composure all over the stripped wooden floor. I don't know how long it rang for but it seemed to go on forever before, finally, the answerphone clicked into place and I found myself clutching for support at the nearest armchair as Tyrell's voice filled the room.

"Hi, this is Tyrell O'Neill. Sorry I can't take your call right now but I'm most likely out on the lash somewhere. Leave me a message and I'll get back to you just as soon as I'm sober."

God, what a shock, hearing his voice like that again! Feebly, I worked my way around to the front of the armchair practically collapsing into it, which is just as well as, a moment later, I was in for an even greater shock.

"Hi, Tyrell. It's me, Orla." Orla? Christ, I could feel the sweat begin to teem down my forehead; the goosebumps break out all over my body. "Listen, I'm really sorry for jumping ship like that." There was a girlish trill of self-conscious laughter. "Well, what can I tell you? Once a muddle, always a muddle! Donegal is not for me. I knew that the minute I saw the first signpost written exclusively in Irish. Anyway, I'm in London now and, would you believe, just to keep the wolf from the door while I'm waiting for my lucky break, I've got a job as a tour-bus guide." She trilled again. "Problem is, I keep mixing up Madame Tussaud's with Buckingham Palace and the zoo with the Houses of Parliament. What am I like!" More trilling, trying for self-deprecating but managing only to sound like she should be on the Queen's Honours List. "Anyway, got a bus to catch. See you later. And Tyrell –" there was a tiny, pregnant pause, "don't give up on Gemma. She's not really in love with Rocky. She only thinks she is!"

As the receiver went down at her end and silence reigned once more, I realised that I was panting, as if I'd run a full twenty-six-mile marathon at full pelt decked out in full Womble regalia and my heart was about to burst. There was a swirl of red mist across my eyes and just for a moment I was an angry bull pawing at the ground, itching to impale Orla upon my horns and then, with a vicious toss, trample her into the dust beneath my hooves. The bitch! Relief mingled with anger mingled with more relief, then more anger till I was struggling under the weight of equal quantities of each. Orla was alive. She hadn't drowned. The rat had made it off the sinking ship. "*Sea Ewe* later," she'd said to Tyrell and promptly long-legged it over to London where the sharp-eyed Debbie had spotted her on the top of that open-top bus. I wanted to kill her! I wanted to hug her! I wanted to batter her senseless. For the anxiety she had caused me *and* my mother *and* my aunt *and* just about everybody else. *And* for shrinking my Janet Reger knickers! Pressing my hand against my heart, I waited for the palpitations to subside. Just imagine! We'd all been running round like headless chickens while *she* was swanning about playing at *On The Buses.* With a deep ragged sigh I rose shakily to my feet. I would have to telephone my mother at once, put her and Aunty Kay out of their misery. There was some consolation in knowing that for them, at least, I would be the bearer of glad tidings even if I didn't feel very glad myself. Well, I did and I didn't. I mean, Orla was only half the picture. Tyrell O'Neill, the man I had only just found out I was in love with was still lost to me. Lost at sea!

CHAPTER 22

"Orla's all right? Well, of course Orla's all right! Sure, Orla's in London."

In disbelief I gazed down the handset of the telephone receiver as if the voice at the other end was speaking in fluent Swahili. "You mean you *knew* Orla was safe in London? All this time while I've been running around wetting myself like a blue-assed fly, you *knew* Orla was all right?"

A disembodied squawk, my mother's voice covered the distance from suburban Dublin to rural Donegal in the space of a nanosecond. Isn't technology a wonderful thing?

"Well, of course I knew. She phoned a few days ago to tell me about her change of plans and do you know it must have completely slipped my mind. Well, what can you expect? I'm not as young as I was, you know, and something has to give. I'm only glad it's not my hair. There's a lot to be said for a full head of hair, you know. Mind you, it's hardly my fault if you took off like a hot snot to Donegal with that Blarney Castle fella."

"Rocky Cashel," I corrected wearily, wondering why on earth I bothered especially as, by this stage, she must have exhausted every possible permutation. Sooner or later she was bound to hit the jackpot! "So Aunty Kay is all right too, then?"

There was something like a whoop from the other end. "All right? She's more than all right. Between you and me this whole drowning business has its own silver lining." The tone changed slightly, became pious. I could almost picture her, eyes upturned towards the heavens, her hand flush against her heart – a bit like that painting of Saint Theresa, the Little Flower, that hung in our local church and which made the poor woman look like she was strung out on dope. "Not but what I don't pray to God and all the saints above that that poor boy will be pulled out alive. Still, it's an ill wind that blows nobody any good and your Aunty Kay has travelled up to Killybegs in the company of Rob Kilbride, no less, to search for Orla and Rob's nephew."

Puzzled, I gave the receiver a slight tap not altogether certain that she hadn't switched to Swahili again. "But, I thought you said she *knows* Orla is all right?"

The piety gave way to a slight note of impatience as she willed the penny to drop. "Yes, she *does* know that and *I* know that and now, *you* know that. But Rob Kilbride doesn't. And neither does anyone else! And what's more likely to draw the pair of them together than comforting one another over their mutual loss. I mean, what could be more natural than that they'd find solace in one another's arms?" There was triumph in the words, a personal sense of achievement. The Little Flower did a quick transition into Cilla Black on *Blind Date*. Any moment now and she'd be sallying forth in search of a big 'at for her big 'air for the impending nuptials. "Honest to God, Gemma! This is a great opportunity for your Aunty Kay."

"It's sick!" I yelled, totally incensed as indeed the penny not so much dropped as turned into an atomic bomb and blew the world up around my ears. "*She's* sick! *You're* sick!" I burst into tears. "What about Tyrell O'Neill? Tyrell's dead and all you can think about is Aunty Kay getting it on with his uncle?"

She had the grace to sound slightly ashamed. "Aye, well, if there really is no hope for him, that's a bit unfortunate all right. Still, like I said, it's an ill wind that blows nobody any good and I'm sure he'd be delighted to see his uncle happily settled with a good woman."

"Unfortunate?" I screeched, my voice flying off the Richter scale and panicking a flock of sparrows out of a hedgerow in the garden outside. "No, Mammy. Losing a bet is un-for-tun-ate. A steep rise in mortgage interest rates is un-for-tun-ate. Putting on three stone before your wedding day is un-for-tun-ate. Losing the love of your life is bloody *tragic!*" There was dead silence on the other end of the phone, the kind of silence that denotes the turning of cogs and wheels and sundry other pieces of reasoning equipment.

"But," she said tentatively, as a fan belt or valve or something clicked into place and the motor in her brain sparked suddenly into life, "I thought Tony McCann was the love of your life."

For a moment, I wasn't quite sure who on earth she was talking about and then, as light dawned, I shook my head in disgust. "Jesus Christ! What stone have you been living under, woman? Tony McCann, like your teeth and your ability to rip men's boxer shorts off with them, is ancient history! *Ancient*, ancient history!"

"Oh." She sounded like she'd been slapped in the face. "Well, why don't you come on home and we can talk about it?"

"There's nothing to talk about," I told her. "Nothing at all. Tyrell is dead and I might as well be. Life as I know it, Jim, is now officially defunct! There's Klingons on the starboard side!" Replacing the receiver, I stood with my hand resting on it for a moment or two debating on whether to ring Sophie or Debbie on their mobiles. Strictly speaking there should have been no room for argument. It should simply have been a matter of explaining that contrary to belief, Orla, far from resting at the bottom of the beautiful briny sea, was in fact living it up in London. Scale down the search! But then, they'd probably want to return the compliment by telling me how Tyrell had, at last, been dragged ashore, his poor drowned eyes pecked out by low-flying seagulls. And I wasn't ready for that. Not yet! Not while I was standing in his home, surrounded by his things and filled with strange empty yearnings for what might have been. How I wished I could turn the clock back, but a quick glance outside to where the billowing storm clouds were slowly eating up the sky assured me, like so many before, that time marches to its own drum and little hopeless voices like mine are simply crying in the wilderness.

God, I could have kicked myself when I thought of all the time I had wasted mooning after Rocky Cashel, making a complete and utter fool out of myself. And look, while I'm doing the old shriving bit here, let's get it all out in the air – dirty linen, open to the public! Like, let's face it, it's not even as if Rocky led me on. Far from it! For God's sake, I practically did a John the Baptist on it and offered my head and the rest of me up to him on a plate, but he never so much as had a nibble! Looking back, I squirmed with embarrassment when I thought of all the times he had insulted me and how I, delighted to be on the receiving end of his attention no matter how negative, continued to aid and abet him in my own debasement. Now that the scales had truly fallen from my eyes you'd think I'd be furious, wouldn't you? With myself! With him! And humiliated? And, to a degree, I suppose I was both, but considering how utterly obsessed I'd been, it was remarkable how little in the grand scheme of things Rocky Cashel actually seemed to matter right now. With the true hindsight of the bolter of the stable door I realised that rock-god though he was, Rocky would never, not in a million years, play the Milk Tray Man for *anyone*. Rocky would never, not in a million years, write a song for any woman unless, of course, it was for Mother Ireland featuring as a famine victim. And so, on to the real bugbear – the reason I suspect Laura *really* left him for Mr Gold Top – the Damien Hirst conceptual sculptures! I mean, talk about the emperor's new clothes! Oh, he could waffle on and on till the cows came home about symbolism, allusions and illusions but, call it a gut feeling, when it comes to plaited pig's entrails suspended in rhino's urine, Rocky Cashel, it must be said, was suffering from delusions! Like, give me the *Crying Boy* any day! *Or* a nice copy of the *Mona Lisa* or Constable's *Hay-Wain*, come to that!

Suddenly I felt very tired, bone-weary, world-weary and in need of a lie-down and where better to lie down than in Tyrell's bed where I could hug his pillow and imagine it was him. Slowly, I made my way out into the corridor, opening doors at random until I found what I knew beyond a shadow of a doubt to be Tyrell's room. Echoing the living-room, the furniture here was simple, Shaker style, the colour scheme a clever mixture of rich burgundies, browns and creams, unmistakably masculine and reassuringly devoid of any female influence. A bookcase on which the classics jostled cheek by jowl with various tomes on sheep-farming, livestock diseases and endearingly, *Harry Potter* took up almost one entire wall. So Tyrell dreamed of being a boy wizard, did he? Well, he'd certainly worked some magic on me. Sadly though, for both of us, the spell had taken effect far too late.

Tyrell was gone to a watery grave but his presence, here in this bedroom at least, was still very strong, his aftershave, a mixture of lemon, honey-flavoured throat lozenges and Palmolive soap, lightly scenting the air. Sighing, I stood for a moment in the doorway, letting my eyes roam about, familiarising themselves with the bed, still rumpled, the duvet half-trailing on the floor, the book he'd been reading opened flat on its face on the bedside cabinet, as if he'd only put it down a moment before. I could see the spine from my post at the doorway. *Mama Tina*, the follow up to Christina Noble's *Bridge Over My Sorrows*, this one telling all about her work with the street children of Vietnam. I myself had finished it not so long ago and found it one of the most awe-inspiring books I had ever read. Something else Tyrell and I had in common, then. Funny, I couldn't imagine Rocky Cashel ever reading a book like that. No way! *Viz* was more his style or, for heavier reading, a biography on say, Kurt Kobain, Michael Hutchence or that complete nutter, Marilyn Manson.

Stepping further into the room, I felt Tyrell's presence enfold me like a pair of welcoming arms. In fact, so strong was the sensation that I wouldn't have been overly surprised if, at any moment, he were to come swinging through from the en suite bathroom, dabbing at his freshly-shaved jaw with a towel, another towel casually knotted about his waist, his hair seal-wet and slicked back, his dark blue eyes made darker by intentions that weren't altogether strictly honourable. I felt myself grow weak at the thought – at the clarity of the thought! With longing! With lust! With sheer, bloody frustration. Why, oh why, didn't I bang him when I had the chance! With an effort I wrenched my thoughts back to reality but, for some reason, imagination had the upper hand.

'Gemma,' he'd say. Nothing else, just, 'Gemma!' But there would be a wealth of meaning in the word, a wealth of seduction and promise and he wouldn't have had to say my name twice before I'd have been there, plucked like a Christmas turkey and all ready for stuffing.

"Gemma!"

I know I said he wouldn't have had to say my name twice but what can I tell you, imagination is a powerful thing.

"Gemma!"

So powerful, I could feel the cold draught of his breath on the back of my neck, which was odd, because if he was coming from the bathroom, he would have had to be round the front of me, not round the back. *And* his breath would have been warm.

"Gemma Murphy, what on earth are you doing here?" His breath became so cold, so tangible, that the hairs stood up on the back of my neck

The daydream was rapidly turning into a nightmare, the welcoming arms turning into a pair of ice-cold hands that slowly, insistently turned me around till I found myself face to face with the dripping wet apparition of Tyrell O'Neill. Which is when I measured my length on the floor.

"Gemma!" The apparition was slapping my face. "Wake up, Gemma!"

"Wh . . .what?" Struggling to open my eyes, I closed them rapidly again, squeezing them tight as the apparition dripped water all over my face.

"Gemma, get up this instant! What on earth are you doing here?"

I opened a baleful eye, tentatively, just a slit, just enough to cop a load of the ghost of Tyrell O'Neill, on its knees beside me. "Shouldn't *I* be the one asking that?" I asked in a trembly voice. "I mean, what on earth are *you* doing here – *earth*, being the operative word. Like, *you're* supposed to have *departed* the earth, gathered up your chains and moved towards the light like any self-respecting ghost. Like, you've got no right to hang about here frightening innocent people." I opened the other eye, a matching slit, in the vain hopes that the first might have been hallucinating, a delayed reaction to the magic mushrooms I had experimented with once when I was only fourteen. It wasn't. The ghost was still there, large as life, and sopping wet. Changing tack, I tried cajoling him. "I'll tell you what, I'll have a Mass said for you. How would that be, eh? To speed your immortal soul on its way." With a quick transition into double-glazing salesman mode, I gave him the hard sell, tried to make the prospect of rowing across the Styx in the company of the skeletal ferryman more attractive: make it sound like a bit of a five-star holiday. "You can send me a postcard. Something nice, a celestial scene maybe, with clouds and harps and angels and things on it." Blimey, I was really getting into the swing of this Judith Chalmers *Wish You Were Here* business. "I know, you can get me God's autograph. Get him to make it out to 'Gemma, with love'. Just think, I could put it in a celebrity auction and make a mint."

Bemused, the ghost shook its head. "Jesus! I think the fall's unhinged her, Paddy."

Paddy? One eye shot open – all the way. Paddy! He was travelling in the company of a ghost called Paddy? A ghost called Paddy who, when it came to agreeing with a fellow spectre, certainly wasn't backward at coming forward.

"Well, she's not the full novena, Mr O'Nayle, and that's for sure. Honest to God, you'd get more sense out of a scalded hen, so you would. D'ye think maybe we should call an ambillance?"

A ghost called Paddy who wanted to call an ambulance? Something wasn't right here. Taking a deep breath, I opened both eyes to their fullest extent and reaching out an exploratory hand touched the wet sleeve of Tyrell's jacket. It felt cold – cold, but substantial. Experimentally, I ran my fingers up along the arm, across the shoulder and all the way up to his wet face. His face felt cold – cold but substantial. Reassuringly human!

"You're not a ghost!" I said wonderingly as logic forced its way through into my brain and put two and two together with the resultant correct sum total. "If you were a ghost, my hand would have gone straight through you. It would! Wouldn't it?"

"A ghost? Me?" Tyrell gave vent to a hearty roar. "Did you hear that, Paddy? She thought I was a ghost!"

Paddy, who I now saw to be a man every bit as substantial as Tyrell, as well as every bit as wet, obediently echoed the laugh. "A ghost, is it? Well, you're the healthiest-looking specimen of a ghost I've ever seen, Mr O'Nayle, and no mistake."

Raising me to my feet, Tyrell guided me over to the bed and gently pushed me down on the side of it. "Whatever put an idea like that in your head?"

I shrugged, initial relief giving way to anger. I mean, this man had put me through hell. Inadvertently, maybe, but still . . . "Oh, nothing really or maybe just the fact that half of Ireland is out trawling the sea, even as we speak, looking for your poor, dead remains. That, and the fact that your name is being bandied about all over the newspapers and television as missing, presumed drowned." Meditatively, I tapped my chin. "Oh, and let's not forget the fact that the *Sea Ewe* is now nothing more than bits of painted driftwood scattered about the Atlantic."

"What?" If Tyrell hadn't been a ghostly shade of pale before, he was certainly hell-bent on making up for it now. "What on earth are you talking about?"

"Just what I said. Everyone is under the impression that you took the *Sea Ewe* out yesterday despite the appalling weather forecast, a theory that was given weight by the maritime equivalent of Benny from *Crossroads*."

Tyrell shook his head in disbelief. "But I *didn't*! Surely nobody could have believed I'd be so stupid as to take the trawler out against all advice?" My silence said it all. Tyrell bent his head in his hands. "Jesus H Christ. They must have me pegged as a right greenhorn! A right arrogant shit!"

Another thought struck me, one that was guaranteed to add fuel to the fire. "Oh yes, and lest we forget! We all thought Orla went out with you so they're searching for *her* body as well."

"No!" Tyrell groaned, his pallor, what I could discern of it, taking on a greenish tinge. If I didn't know better, I'd have said he was seasick. "But she *didn't*! At the first sign of a field of grass, Orla upped and legged it off to London. Let's face it, she's more of an up-town girl than a down-farm girl." His head came up, his eyes seeking mine, meaningfully. "Mind you, it wasn't my suggestion that she came in the first place but your sister can be very persuasive." Now, dear reader, if you will – I wanted to believe him. Really I did, but experience had shown me that where Orla was concerned men, as a rule, never needed much in the line of persuasion. And why should Tyrell O'Neill be any different? Like, he had a dick. The brains of the operation! Need I say more?

Rolling my eyes, I mimed a yawn, and stretching my arms high above my head I adopted one of those look-mate-it-doesn't-matter-a-stuff-to-me-one-way-or-the-other expressions. "Well, anyway, that's the story and anyone who's anyone, including your Uncle Rob, is pulling out all the stops in Killybegs looking for the pair of you."

"But I *told* you, Orla didn't *go* with me."

"I know she didn't but only because I heard a message from her on your answerphone, mind. Up till that point, like everybody else, I thought she was plankton too."

Light broke over his face. "Oh, so you phoned them? As soon as you heard the message, you phoned them and put them in the picture – about Orla, anyway. Didn't you?"

I cleared my throat. "Er . . . not exactly."

"What do you mean not exactly?" I must say, I didn't like the way Tyrell's complexion kept changing colour. Having exhausted the myriad shades of white and green it was now embarking on the crimson palette. "Why didn't you? Why didn't you phone? Surely that's the first thing any sane person would do?"

Maybe. If they *were* sane. I hadn't been sane at the time, though. I'd been *insane*. Off my head with grief. For him! However, I wasn't going to give him the satisfaction of telling him that, not while he was intent on examining me with the same sort of disgust as something Gretchen deposited on her morning walks. Uh huh! No way was I going to tell him that I couldn't bear the thoughts of hearing that his body had been found, his poor eyes plucked out by low-flying seagulls. So I took the easy way out. I lied. Easily. I've had a lot of practice.

"Of course I would have phoned," I tried for aggrieved – misunderstood, even, "but I didn't have my address book with me and I can *never* remember mobile-phone telephone numbers. They're like, so long, *and* they're all the blooming same."

Tyrell let that one pass. "So, as far as everyone is concerned, Orla and I are dead meat!" He slapped his palm against his temple in a gesture of sheer frustration. "God, we'd better phone the Lifeguard Station in Killybegs or the police or something and explain, get them to call off the search. I only hope they don't want to send me the bill." Making for the door, he caught himself up short. "Speaking of explanations, Gemma: would you mind explaining just exactly what *you're* doing *here*!" He gave a sudden start, as if the sheer incredulity of the situation had only just struck him for the first time and with all the ferocity of a sledgehammer in the breadbasket. "*Here!* In *Bundoran!* In *my* house! In *my* bedroom!*"

Paddy, who up till this juncture had more or less stayed quiet, saw fit to throw in his two ha'pence worth. "Yerra, Mr O'Nayle, with all due respect, isn't it obvious? She wanted to be near ye, if only in spirit. Sure it's obvious to a blind statcha – the girl's crazy about ye."

Well, thank you, Paddy, for your eloquent and unwanted contribution, you big, gormless, culchie bastard! If he'd hit him over the head with the same blind statue, Tyrell O'Neill couldn't have looked more knocked for six. I could feel a sweat-soaked SOS breaking out beneath my armpits. Help! Maybe I'd misread the signs yet again. Maybe Tyrell O'Neill wasn't the slightest bit interested in me. Maybe the Milk Tray Man stunt had been just that, a stunt, a kick, a perverted way of getting his rocks off, the way some men dress up in dog-collars and tights or hang themselves from the back of hotel doors with an orange in their mouth. Maybe that song had been inspired by somebody else. Another Gemma! One with firm thighs and a degree in sheep-farming.

"Is that true, Gemma?" Tyrell walked back to the bed, bent over me, beseeching almost. "Is what Paddy says true?" He cleared a frog from his throat. "Are you . . . er . . ."

"Crazy about you?" I prompted. "Well, crazy certainly, but –"

"Not about me!" Self-deprecating, Tyrell snatched the words right out of my mouth and twisted them out of all recognition. "Of course, stupid of me even to ask, when it's plain to all and sundry that you've only got eyes for Rocky." A bitter twist to his mouth, he placed a finger under my chin, tilted it upwards. "But he doesn't love you, Gemma. Rocky Cashel doesn't even see you – not in that way, anyway."

"Don't tell me!" I held up a forestalling hand, hurt and angry now which was pretty unreasonable considering how he was only voicing what I, myself, had already worked out. "I'm looking at him but he's looking right through."

The wind taken out of his sails, Tyrell's hand flapped helplessly about in the shallows. "Oh, you've found the song, I see. I won't ask what you thought of it because that's crystal-clear from the look on your face." He shot me the rictus of a grin. "I'm sorry. I didn't mean to embarrass you. Seems like we were both barking up the wrong tree, eh? Story of my life, that is."

The shuffling of a pair of size twelve wellington-clad feet reminded us of the large, looming and very much out-of-his-depth presence of big, gormless, culchie Paddy. "Er . . .well, I think I'll be off then, Mr O'Nayle." Pointedly, he headed for the door. "Ye don't want me hanging around at a time like this. Much obliged for your help, out on the mountain. I'm sorry it landed you in such hot water."

Tyrell got to his feet. "Ah, you're all right, Paddy. None of this is your fault and I only hope Maisie gets back to full strength." He went and held the door wide for the other man. "And, Paddy, for Christ's sake, man, stop calling me Mr O'Neill. It makes me feel about a hundred. I'm Tyrell to my friends."

Paddy tipped his cap and another moment found us alone with each other.

"He didn't," I pointed out. "He called you 'Mr O'Nayle' and what did he mean about the mountain and who's Maisie?" My jealousy antennae had gone into full twitch and were signalling competition.

Good humour restored for a moment, Tyrell grinned. "A ewe. A prize ewe, to be exact, and Paddy's pride and joy. She got stranded up on the mountain overnight and so did Paddy and I when we went to the rescue. Hence, the reason I was incommunicado and had no idea a red alert was out for me in Killybegs." A bewildered look replaced the grin. "Honest to God, are they thick or what? I mean, once I heard the weather forecast was for gales and the like, I simply did an about-turn and came straight home. The *Sea Ewe* must have come adrift in the heavy seas."

"Well, the forecast didn't stop you from going up on the mountain," I pointed out. "So, maybe *you're* the one who's thick."

"Could be, I suppose. Still, we didn't expect the weather to turn quite so quickly but once the clouds came down and the rain started, I swear, Gemma, you couldn't see your hand in front of your face." He gave a Harrison Ford tough-man shrug. Blasé, almost, giving the impression that if anyone could snatch the *Jewel of the Nile* in near impossible weather conditions, he could. "So, we sheltered as best we could under an outcrop of rock and judged it best to wait until morning. Mind you, as you can see, it took us the best part of a day to get back down again."

"Well, all's well that ends well, I suppose," I said, not liking to think of him stranded up the mountain, freezing cold and in danger of being crushed by a glacier only to be found a million years hence, perfectly preserved like one of those big hairy mammoths. All ready for exhibiting in some space-age museum or other! Still, it was marginally better than imagining him lying at the bottom of the sea with the little fishes playing tag in and out of his empty eye sockets and the piranhas stripping the flesh from his bones. Never mind that piranhas don't, as a rule, frequent the seas around Ireland.

Tyrell gave himself a little shake. "Yes, I suppose you're right. All's well that ends well, on which note I'd better go and phone the authorities, tell them the dead have risen and appeared to Gemma. Then, I must get out of these wet, stinking clothes and have a nice warm shower and something to eat."

Must you? I wanted to say. Only, can't we stay here a little longer, just you and me and, like, start over again? The first one to mention Rocky Cashel gets a wallop. Oh, and you can still get out of those wet stinking things. Hell, I'll even *help* you to get out of those wet stinking things. In fact, I've just had a stonker of an idea. How about if I actually get into the shower with you? You know, wash your back, get into all those hard to reach places, all those nooks and crannies: play

Charm the Water Snake? I didn't, of course. I couldn't, because, unlike Orla, I've never been that forward – because, unlike Orla, I've always been frightened of rejection and with good reason. Take Tony the Shite Artist, for instance, *and* Rocky Cashel *and* all those one-night-stands down through the years who had woken up, sobered up, taken one look at me in the bed next to them, made their excuses and left never to return – not even my phone calls!

"Yes," I said. "I suppose you'd better. Rob will be over the moon, unlike my Aunty Kay who given the chance would probably hold your head under the water as soon as look at you."

Tyrell registered puzzlement. "Why? Why such violence? What have I ever done to her? I mean, the last time I saw her she was all over me like a rash on account of my being related to Uncle Rob. Even pinched my ass, if you can believe it. I swear, I thought women of her age were long past that kind of thing. It gave me quite a turn, I can tell you."

Briefly I came clean about the phone call home, explained about Aunty Kay and my mother's machinations. "So you see, the plan is to offer him succour whilst landing the poor sucker at one and the same time."

Tyrell gave a disbelieving whistle. "Well, I wish her luck so, because many and better women have boldly gone there before only to come back with their tails between their legs." He looked considering. "Still, it would be nice to see old Rob settle down in the arms of a good woman. Do you know, sometimes I think he's too much into his sheep for his own good – a dyed-in-the-wool bachelor, if you will."

I coughed delicately and taking a leaf out of my mother's book, glanced all around checking for Cold War spies or hidden tabloid journalists. "And *is* he? Into his sheep? I mean *really* into his sheep?" Another quick glance from left to right to denote the covert exchanging of state secrets. All I needed was the Pink Panther mac and a big spyglass. "You know, is he, to use common parlance, a sheep-shagger?"

"What?" Unfamiliar with the rules of espionage, Tyrell's voice rose to a level where whole flocks of birds in Africa rose from their nests in panic, herds of elephants stampeded and crocodiles slipped warily beneath sundry and assorted swamps with only a surface eye to warn of their presence. "A sheep-shagger? My Uncle Rob? Not bloody likely! What on earth would give you that idea?"

"Oh, something and nothing," I said, dismissively, sorry now for opening my big gob. "Still, I'm very glad to hear it. I mean it's bad enough that my Aunty Kay is going to find herself kicked into touch but to be kicked into touch in favour of a *sheep*. Like, even she doesn't deserve that."

Tyrell snorted. "Huh! I'm not so sure about that. I'm beginning to think all the women in your family are a bit – how can I put this delicately – nuts! Take Orla for instance. There she was banging on and on about how it's always been her dream to live in the country, how she's just a simple girl at heart despite her success in the cut-throat world of modelling." Suddenly embarrassed he cleared his throat, embarked on a bit of a soft-shoe shuffle. "How she knew I was soft on you and how you made fun out of the fact to all your friends." Meditatively he tapped his chin. "Now, what was that she said they called me? Oh yes, 'Gemma's little stalker'. Never mind that I'm over six feet tall and the only stalking I've ever done is to stalk sheep on a hillside."

"What?" Outraged, I shot up off the bed. "That's a dirty stinking lie! I never made fun of you." I could feel my face beginning to flame. "I know I wasn't always very nice to you but that was because I was simply misguided by my hormones. Hormones do that to you sometimes and not just once a month, either. It's a woman thing. It's all to do with oestrogen and ovulation and eggs and things. You wouldn't understand!" I sent him a challenging glare but, much to my disappointment, he refused to rise to my bait. Disappointment because it's usually been my experience that passionate arguing and passionate lovemaking are kissing cousins on the emotional spectrum and one can very easily lead to another especially if there happens to be an empty, king-size bed handy. Which, in this case, there was! Sadly, it seemed destined to remain empty.

"Anyway," Tyrell said pointedly – pointedly but

mildly, "to get back to Orla, she only goes and twists my arm up my back to take her away to Donegal and then at the first sign of nature in the raw, the first realisation that meat actually originates from real live animals and not from neat vacuum-packed portions on a supermarket shelf, she does a bunk off to London leaving me high and dry." Ruefully he glanced down at his wet clothing. "Or, rather, high and wet!"

"Serves you right for being so gullible." I jabbed him in the chest. "Forget Madonna! I could have told you Orla is the original *Material Girl*. Even as a baby it was all Mothercare designer this and that. My old wicker cradle wasn't good enough for our Orla. No way, hers had to be all pine and frills and canopies and hand-painted Beatrix Potter characters. Even her nappies were lace-trimmed and her dummy was by Cartier." Aggrieved I stamped my foot, dimly aware that an unhinged note had entered my voice. "Is it any wonder I bit her? I should have given her the *One Flew Over The Cuckoo's Nest* treatment when I had the chance; you know, smothered her with her designer, lace-trimmed pillow. No one would ever have been any the wiser. Cot death, they would have said and my life would have been one long party."

"I wouldn't mind," Tyrell continued, as though I hadn't spoken, a bit bewildered, a bit confused like an American tourist in Dublin who instead of shamrocks, shillelaghs and leprechauns finds himself confronted by a metropolis buzzing with high-tech Japanese gadgetry and wall to wall gridlocked traffic. Oh, and a property ladder so steep not even his oil well in Texas could secure him a foothold. "I wouldn't mind," Tyrell reiterated, "but I don't even fancy your sister. She's, you know, too *nouvelle cuisine* for me – pretty to look at but not much substance." He fixed me with a beady eye, his voice changing, becoming less mild, developing, if anything, a note of danger. "Then, there's your Aunty Kay and your mother. Dear, oh dear, oh dear! What's the best thing that can be said about those two scheming old biddies? Nothing! Or nothing that wouldn't land me up in court, anyway, charged with involuntary euthanasia. Involuntary on their part! I mean, the whole thing is a bit sick, isn't it; carrying on the pretence that Orla is missing, your Aunty Kay crying crocodile tears all over poor Rob's shoulder in order to have her wicked way with him. I mean, that brings desperation to a whole new level, don't you think?"

Well, I couldn't disagree with that. I couldn't agree with it either, well, not out loud anyway, haemoglobin being thicker than the clear stuff, even if I could gladly have sent Aunty Kay to the firing squad, myself. And my mother, along with her! And denied them a last request! So, I said nothing, just hung my head in shame and waited for him to start in on me, which he obligingly lost no time in doing.

"Which adjective brings us neatly on to you, Gemma. Talk about desperate! Whenever you were around Rocky, you wore your desperation like a banner for all the world to see. Honestly, all he had to do was say 'jump' and instead of telling him to piss off and wake up to himself like anybody else would, rock star or no bloody rock star, you said –" at this juncture he screwed up his mouth and adopted a prissy voice that made me cringe with recognition, "'No problem, Rocky, just point me towards the nearest precipice.' Like, have you got no pride, Gemma? Can't you see, where Rocky Cashel's concerned, you're just another one of the many sycophants he surrounds himself with?" He paused for breath. "Actually, strictly speaking, that's not quite true. Rocky's involvement with you would have come to a speedy end once he'd laid charges against you for assault and battery. It was only my intervention that got you off the hook. That, and your dubious skills as a veterinary nurse which I pointed out could well be canvassed on Gretchen's behalf."

"I know that!" I snapped, unable to listen to any more, and feeling the hateful pricking of tears building up behind my eyes. "Rocky already told me, made a point of telling me, actually. So what do you want, Shylock? A medal? A pound of flesh? God knows I've got plenty of that to spare!"

Tyrell shook his head. "No, Gemma, but a bit of gratitude would be nice." He paused, thought about it. "Actually, you can stuff your gratitude. What I want – correction, wanted past tense – was you! But, like I said before, it seems like I was barking up the wrong tree."

Suddenly he started to laugh, but there was a hollow sound to it and his eyes were as humourless as Prince Philip in the midst of a crowd of Chinese students. "God, the irony of it all! That's what we're all doing, isn't it? Barking up the wrong tree? Rocky and Laura. Your aunt and my uncle. Me and you! Talk about a comedy of errors!"

"Except, it isn't funny!" I said, but he was right. We were all barking up the wrong tree, Sophie and Debbie included. But what was saddest of all was that my right tree had been there all along but, never one to embrace all that tree-lore stuff, I'd done a Gretchen, raised my leg, pissed all over it and taken off to Stonehenge – home of big rockies!

CHAPTER 23

"Well, don't smile or you might crack your face, will you?"

"Sorry, Mrs Birch. I was miles away." Quellingly, because I wasn't in the mood for Mrs Birch or for anybody else come to that, I bent my head and continued furiously scribbling on Kilroy's appointment card. But Mrs Birch, being made of stern stuff, the stuff that had seen off two husbands and every close member of her family barring Kilroy, was not to be so easily deterred.

"Would that be miles away up in Donegal, like? With that gorgeous Tyrell O'Neill fellow who did a Reggie Perrin on it up in Killybegs recently and disappeared off into the water?"

"How do you know about that?" I snapped and could immediately have shot my foot off.

Mrs Birch grinned, displaying a row of ill-fitting dentures, and threw in a nose-tap for extra insurance. "Ah, you know. People talk. Word gets round."

"Well, *people* obviously don't have enough to keep them busy. *People* should mind their own bloody business." I practically threw the appointment card across the counter at her. "And so should you, you nasty old bag!"

"Gemma!" Sophie, wafting manure from a recent farm visit all over the place, marched up to the counter, a concerned expression on her face. "Is everything all right here?"

"No, it most certainly is not!" Aggrieved, Mrs Birch threw in her tuppence worth. "I must say the world has come to a pretty pass when a body can't pop into the vets without encountering a barrage of abuse. Time was when custom was a welcome commodity. Time was when you could expect to exchange a few pleasantries without fear of getting blasted to Kingdom Come." She struggled to hold on to her teeth, which were threatening to leave their moorings and launch themselves onto the market as a new range of tombstones. "Well, vets are two a penny, so they are, and I'll take my custom elsewhere, so I will. I expect Kilroy could do with a change of scenery, in any case." Teeth safely anchored, she gave a catarrhal sniff. "I know *I* certainly could."

"Kilroy," I told her, my own teeth bared and notwithstanding Sophie trying to gag me by dint of placing her hand over my mouth, "could do with a change of owner! And correct me if I'm wrong, but you've been thrown out of every other veterinary surgery for miles around for persistently going against expert advice and feeding Kilroy Curly-Wurlys when you know *bloody well* they upset his digestive system!" Poor Mrs Birch! Unwittingly she'd released all the pent-up fury and frustration that had been building in me since my little contretemps with Tyrell a couple of weeks earlier in Donegal. Jabbing her in the chest with the biro, I could feel my face contort out of all recognition, the features being pulled into the kind of distorted grimaces of the kind more frequently seen in a fairground mirror. "Maybe, if you were the one who had to let him crap all over you, you'd think twice before filling him up with chocolate bars and all kinds of muck."

"Gemma!" Alerted by the yelling, Debbie appeared from a nearby treatment room and joined in the fray. "Come on out the back and I'll make you a nice cup of tea. You're not yourself at the moment. She's not herself at the moment," she explained with a conspiratorial look at Mrs Birch. "Things have been getting on top of her a bit lately."

"Really?" Mrs Birch pretended sympathy. "I suppose you're referring to that Tyrell O'Neill although, from where I'm standing, it looks like the problem might be that he *hasn't* been getting on top of her, if you get my drift. Mind you, I always thought it was the other one she'd set her cap at. You know, that fella that sings about the rotten potatoes. That Rocky Cashel fella, the one she raped down in Blessington." Trying to look like the Virgin Mary, she rolled her eyes. "Girls today, eh?

Tramps and trollops every one. I've always said you can tell the moral decline of a country by the size of its underwear and these days it's so small it wouldn't cover a gnat's backside. Soon it'll be a case of the Emperor's New Clothes – all in the imagination!"

"That's enough, Mrs Birch!" Sophie snapped, fighting to restrain me as, lunging across the counter, fingers clutching convulsively, I made throttling motions towards the old woman's neck. "That kind of talk certainly isn't helping matters. Now take Kilroy home, would you, and lay off the blasted Curly-Wurlys!"

"Fair enough!" A woman scorned, Mrs Birch grabbed Kilroy's lead and stalked over to the exit. "Far be it from me to outstay my welcome. Maggie Birch knows when she's not wanted." With a superior sniff, she sent one, last disparaging glance sweeping around the room. "Come on, boy, let's go home. Sure, this place is like a den of iniquity anyway, with hoors and harlots and sexual deviants lurking around every corner! Someone should write to the bishop! Have the place closed down!"

"Are you all right, Gem?" Debbie asked, laying a gentle hand on my shoulder when the door had closed behind Mrs Birch with a slam and as Sophie, her sexual deviant's brow corrugated into a worried frown, looked on.

"Yeah. I'm okay." I attempted a wry grin. "There's nothing wrong with me that a truckload of Heineken wouldn't put right. Or a night on the horizontals with George Clooney!"

"Good!" Debbie's touch turned into a series of little pats, as though she was already getting in a bit of practice against the day Cloetus would emerge full of windies and in need of burping. "The clinic is almost empty, anyway. Tell you what. Why don't you go out the back and get a bit of air. Sophie can take care of Martin's last few clients for you, can't you, Soph?"

Sophie nodded obligingly. "Yeah, sure. Rob and I have just come back with some sheep that need treatment on site, so we won't be going out again. Debbie's right, Gem. You go and get a bit of air and then we'll all go over to the pub and have a major Bud transfusion." A significant glance passed between herself and Sophie. "Besides, there's a lot we've got to talk about."

The look wasn't lost on me but I was just too dispirited to care. "All right," I said. "I'll see you in a bit but be warned, Soph, Bilious Bella has swallowed the family car or something, so watch out for the splatter factor. Wear your wellies."

"Don't worry about that." Sophie manoeuvred me out the door. "Everything is under control here. Just go for a walk, or pop in and have a look at the sheep and little lambs Rob and I brought back. They're absolutely gorgeous. Tyrell O'Neill would give his right arm for them." Her hand flew to her mouth as if she could call back the words already at large on the air and already causing havoc with my emotions. "I-I'm sorry, Gemma. I didn't think."

"No, you bloody didn't!" Furious, Debbie pucked her on the soft part of the arm. "You never bloody think!"

"It's all right, Debbie." I came to Sophie's defence. "You *can* say his name, you know. I'm not going to die just from hearing the sound of it. Besides I've got to build up a kind of immunity to him and the only way I can do that is to hear his name spoken over and over again. You know, it's a bit like allergy testing. You lay off a certain food or something for a while. Then, gradually, it's introduced back into your diet in small doses till eventually it has no effect on you whatsoever and your stomach doesn't bloat any more. The diarrhoea stops. " And your heart doesn't break.

"Fair enough!" Debbie said, but there was still a murderous glint in her eye for Sophie. "See you in a bit, then."

Outside, although spring had long since sprung, there was still a distinct nip in the air and my breath sent up Red Indian SOS signals of despair. God, how could I have got things so terribly, terribly wrong? Funny I'd never have compared myself to that Scarlett O'Hara woman in *Gone With The Wind* in a thousand years but, thinking about it, we had a lot in common. I mean, she'd gone hell for leather chucking herself at that wimp Ashley, when, all along, Rhett, that symbol of firm-thighed, cheroot-smoking, Southern manhood, had been desperate to gain entry into her lace-trimmed pantaloons. Then, by the time it dawned on her that

397

Ashley and that mealy-mouthed wimp, Melanie, were well suited and she was ready to loosen the drawstrings for him, old Rhett no longer gave a fiddler's fart. Or it might have been a damn! Either way she was left high and dry. Just like me! For Ashley, read Rocky. For Rhett, read Tyrell. Honestly, I could have swooned from the injustice of it all. Miserably, I walked around the yard, head down, idly kicking at the dusty ground, scarcely aware of my surroundings, when a sudden noise from the stables brought me rocketing back to full alert. There was somebody in with the sheep Sophie and Rob had brought back earlier. Well, okay, that wasn't unusual in itself. What was unusual though were the moans and groans and well, to be blunt about it, panting and threshing noises that accompanied those selfsame moans and groans. Holy Saint Anthony! I clapped a disbelieving hand across my eyes. So it *was* true, after all. Rob Kilbride, Tyrell's uncle, was officially a sheep-shagger. Now, I'm not voyeuristic by nature, but it would have taken a saint just to turn around and walk away again and, as you'll know by previous actions, specifically those pertaining to Blessington, there's no mention of *my* name on the papal canonisation list. Hence, I felt perfectly justified in tiptoeing closer and attempting to peer over the half-door. Unfortunately, between the dark, dusty interior and the bales of hay piled six foot high, it was impossible to make out anything. Oh well, I might not be able to see anything. But I could still hear, couldn't I, and my imagination would just have to fill in the gaps.

"Oooh, you little lamb, you! You beauty, you! Where have you been all my life?"

I was right! It was Rob. I could hear him plainly and I must say I wasn't impressed by his chat-up lines. Neither was the sheep apparently, as it continued to maintain a discreet silence.

"By Jaysus but I must say you're a right animal! I'd never have guessed you'd have it in you. Mind you, they always say it's the quiet ones you have to watch."

The poor, bloody sheep. I bet it never guessed it would have *it* in it, either! More moans, pants and groans. Then Rob again, persuading, ordering, coaxing, in turn.

"Come on, darling! Get those hips moving! Harder! Faster! Rotate! Ooooh! Attagirl! Almost there, now. Keep on truckin! Ooh, my God! Ooh, you little devil! Ooh! Ooh! Ooh!" And then one final, triumphant scream! From Rob! Not the sheep! "*G-o-a-l!*"

I'll tell you what, by the time things drew to their natural conclusion, the sweat was rolling off me. I could see it dripping off the end of my nose, feel the damp patches under my arms and in the small of my back, spreading like an oil slick under my clothes. Poor Tyrell! I was rooted to the spot in horror. I mean, you hear about these kinds of things but you never *really* believe them. They're just something to be rude about, something to snigger about over a few beers with your mates. You know the sort of thing, loads of *double entendres*, lewd winking and Benny Hill asides. Especially if there happens to be an Australian present when someone will invariably, in a very loud and very Wild West accent go 'Australia, where men are men and sheep are scared', at the very real risk of ending up with a glass bottle embedded in the side of their face. Mind you, I don't know why it should be a Wild West accent, just that it always is. Anyway, as I said, I stood there like Lot's wife with the blood rushing round and round in my head when the unmistakable sound of flies being zipped back up relieved me of my temporary paralysis and sent me scooting round the nearest corner. And not a moment too soon, as it happened, because peering gingerly around I saw the stable door open and Rob, brushing hay out of his hair emerge, followed closely by a . . . yes, you've guessed it . . . a sheep! Well, I'd be have been sorely disappointed if I'd been expecting Jennifer Lopez!

"Oh ho, no, you don't!" Turning, he pushed her back into the stable and I thought how bloody typical of a man. Like, a minute ago he was all over her like a rash – now, he couldn't wait to see the back of her. Actually, let me rephrase the last part of that sentence. Now that he'd had his jollies, he wanted rid of her as quickly as possible. He'd no respect for her any more. She was just another tarty sheep, an easy lay. Not the kind of sheep you'd bring home to meet your mother! "Go on, back inside now," casually, he pushed at her with his booted foot, "before I make mutton stew out of you." The cheek of him! I squinted my eyes. Bastard! Not five minutes before when he was having his wicked way with her, she was a 'little lamb'. Now he was making out that she was mutton dressed as lamb! Talk about giving a sheep a complex! "So, are you coming or what?" I did a double-take as he opened the door to its fullest extent. Jesus! Talk about a man of mercurial moods. No wonder the sheep looked stupefied. *And* the coaxing tone of earlier was back in his voice. "Do you fancy a drink? I know I do. All that passion has worked up a terrible thirst. We could nip round to the Fox's Retreat, if you like. They do a good pint there!" Man, this was getting too surreal for words! I could just imagine everyone's face when Rob Kilbride came in with a sheep hanging on his arm.

"By God!" they'd say with many shakings of the head and wry looks. "All these years we thought he was normal, a regular bloke, a Chelsea supporter, into five-a-side and women but all this time he's been pulling the wool over our eyes! Talk about a wolf into taking sheep's clothing off!" Poor Tyrell, he'd never live it down! A happy thought struck me. Maybe, just maybe, he'd need a bit of comforting and maybe, just maybe, yours truly could provide the comfort blanket. And the warm drinks! And the hot sex!

"I'd love a drink, Rob." Bleeding hell, the sheep was talking! My eyes raked Rob Kilbride, searching for latent signs of Doctor Doolittle. "But not a pint! Ladies

– real ladies, that is – don't drink pints." As the sheep spoke again, I realised that I'd heard it before. Many times in fact and usually when it was engaged in the act of giving me a good tongue-lashing! No, there was no mistaking that nasal, catarrhal, pre-cancerous, noduled-encrusted tone. That was no sheep. That was my Aunty Kay! "So, I'll have a port, if you don't mind!"

Well, beam me up, Scottie! Talk about any old port in a storm! It *was* my Aunty Kay, still adjusting her skirt as she emerged from the stable. A bit more rumpled than usual and bearing a striking resemblance to Scarecrow from the *Wizard of Oz* on account of the amount of hay protruding from her hair, her clothes and every visible orifice. *And* wearing a look of satisfaction on her face not seen since she'd last had the pleasure of seeing me get dumped. Well, life's a bitch! And so's my Aunty Kay! No surprises there! Still I must admit to feeling gutted. The little ruse she and my mother had cooked up had obviously worked. By fair means or foul, Aunty Kay had got her man. In a way, she'd robbed Rob! Robbed him of the truth. Allowed him to comfort her in her time of pretended trouble. More than ever I was convinced there was a debauched gene at large in our family DNA. To be honest, though, Rob looked far from unhappy, as slipping an arm behind her, he pinched her substantial rear end.

"Ladylike, is it?" Jovially, he jerked his head towards the stable door. "There was nothing ladylike about your shenanigans in the stable, Kathleen Healy. I wonder what the Three Wise Men would have made of it all!"

Aunty Kay blushed! Get this, she actually blushed! For a moment she looked quite pretty in an OAP kind of way. I mean, let's face it, there was no getting past those sags and bags and truckload of double chins. "Get away with you, Rob Kilbride. There's a fair bit of buckshot left in your own old blunderbuss yet. Honest to God, I feel like I'm nineteen again." Huh, I thought sourly, looking at this unseemly display of geriatric flirting, I bet it didn't feel that way to Rob. I bet it felt like she was ninety with the skin of a Tyrannosaurus Rex. Having said that, he was obviously into Natural History in a big way, because grabbing her again, he kissed her soundly on the lips. And when I say soundly, I mean soundly. Like, it could be heard echoing all round the surgery yard.

"So?" he said, when finally he managed to disentangle his dentures from hers. "Are we going for that drink?"

"Yes." Aunty Kay nodded with enthusiasm, fornication being thirsty work. "Only don't let's go to the Fox's Retreat. That's where Gemma and her mates drink and, honest to God, the sight of that one always brings me out in rare bad humour." She tried to soften her vitriol with a sheepish look. Ha! So that was the attraction! "Although, I know I shouldn't speak like that about my niece. Still, you know what they say, you can choose your friends but not your family!"

"Ah, Gemma's all right." I'd like to say Rob leapt to my defence but it was more like a nice, slow amble. "Our Tyrell had a bit of a thing about her, you know." He chucked Aunty Kay under her most predominant chin, thereby setting a rippling effect in motion and somewhere on the other side of the world there was felt the first stirrings of a tidal wave. "Seems the women in your family have an irresistible draw on the men in ours."

Aunty Kay sniffed and threaded her arm through Rob's, preparatory to moving off. "Well, if you ask me, young Tyrell's had a very lucky escape. That niece of mine has rocked around the block a fair old time or two. Oh, she can get the men, all right, but she can't keep them. But then it's always been my experience that the male of the species can't resist a bargain, present company excepted of course, and Lady Gemma's nothing if not cheap!" She sniffed again, presumably at my perceived wantoness. "Oh, they get the value out of her all right!"

"Well, that may be so," Rob argued as they began to walk, and I could have blessed him for his sense of fair play, "but I always speak as I find, and as far as I'm concerned Gemma is a decent, hardworking kid. No better and no worse than any other! And, if Tyrell were to set his cap at her again, he'd find no objection from me. Now come on, woman, before the tongue dries up in my head."

"Ah, maybe you're right." Amazingly, Aunty Kay

did a three-hundred-and-sixty-degree about-turn never yet equalled in the long history of the Monaco Grand Prix, which just goes to prove that love can work miracles. "I suppose when all is said and done, Gemma is not the worst. To tell the truth, she sometimes reminds me of myself when I was young. All that gobbiness! All that enthusiasm for life! All that misplaced trust in men who use you, abuse you, and then throw you away like you're nothing but a piece of snotty tissue." A surprised look stole across her face, slowly, by degrees, the way a lunar eclipse steals slowly across the moon. The look of someone who can't believe the evidence of their eyes, someone who makes a momentous discovery like the entrance to King Tut's tomb, or how to open a carton of milk without it splatting all over the place, especially when you're wearing black. Did you ever notice that? It always seems to happen when you're wearing bloody black? "Do you know what, Rob? I do believe, I actually love her! Now isn't that a turn-up for the books!"

It certainly was and I don't mind telling you I had mixed feelings about the whole thing. I mean, it's a bit disconcerting to grow up hiding under the bed and fearing the bogeyman only to find out he's really Barbara Cartland in drag.

"Of course you love her." Hugging her to his manly chest, Rob epitomised affability. "You, my darling, haven't got a bad bone in your body. Now hurry up

405

before I take you back into the stable for an action replay."

"Oooh, you are awful, Rob Kilbride," Aunty Kay sniggered like an aged schoolgirl. "So you are! So you are! So you are!"

CHAPTER 24

"So your Aunty Kay finally got her man!" Sophie raised her bottle of Bud high in the air, toasting the victory. "Well, fair play to her!"

"Yeah, fair play to her," I agreed. "Only you must admit her methods were a bit dubious to say the least."

"Well, you know what they say, Gemma," Debbie raised her own glass of mineral water and clinked it against Sophie's bottle, "All's fair in love and war."

"I suppose so." I didn't raise my own glass. To tell the truth, I still had mixed feelings about the whole thing although, on closer examination of my conscience, I found I was if not ecstatically happy for Aunty Kay then, at least, moderately pleased. I mean it did give me a slight feeling of warmth in the pit of my stomach, or that may simply have been the effects of the Jack Daniels whiskey I was downing like there was no tomorrow.

"Speaking of which." There was a distinct tremble in Debbie's voice. "All being fair in love and war, I mean.

I have something to tell you, Gemma." She broke off, sighed deeply and eyed my glass of whiskey with more covetousness than a shopaholic eyeing a Gold American Express card. For its Dutch courage properties, I presume. "And I warn you, you're not going to like it."

"Oh?" I hoisted an eyebrow into enquiring mode. "Why's that then?"

"Be – cause," Debbie drew the word out, then finished in an almighty rush, "it concerns Rocky Cashel." She cleared her throat. "Rocky Cashel and me, to be precise."

Sophie banged her empty bottle down on the bar, signalled with a jerk of her head for another, and by dint of making a little circular, twiddling movement of her hand indicated that all three of us were in the market for a top-up. "What she's trying to tell you and making a complete hash of it is, the pair of them have got it together. Yes folks, it's happy family time down at the old OK Corral. You might even say, Debbie *Gothdere!*"

"Shut up, Sophie." Tears suddenly standing in her eyes, Debbie shot her a killer glare. "Don't be so crass. It's not like that. It wasn't planned. I'm sorry, Gem! You know I wouldn't hurt you for the world." Helpless, she gave a little shrug. "It's just . . . I can't help how I feel. I really love him, Gemma. He makes me feel – oh, I don't know, wanted, cherished, like the only woman in the world, special even – all the things that Guy didn't."

Well, it wasn't the most shocking news I've ever

had. Neither was it altogether unexpected. I mean, you'd need to be blind, deaf and dumb not to notice the way Rocky looked at her, or the way his voice softened whenever he changed from addressing me to addressing her. The difference between granite and satin!

"It's all right!" Reaching across, I gave her a reassuring pat on the back of the hand. "You haven't hurt me. What I felt for Rocky wasn't really love, just a fantasy really. I know that now." I knew that now, because what I felt for Rocky could never compare with what I felt for Tyrell O'Neill. Rocky only hurt my pride. Tyrell broke my heart. "I'm really pleased for you, Debbie. Actually, I think you'll be really good together. To tell the truth, subconsciously I must have recognised that fact ages ago – hence, the reason I practically attacked you with a machete that day you came to Gothdere and we took Gretchen out for a walk." A thought struck me. "What about Cloetus, though? Is Rocky okay about the baby?"

Debbie nodded happily, her impending motherhood lending her peachy skin even more of a glow than usual. "More than okay. He's going to be a great dad, Gemma!"

"And Laura? Is she well and truly out the picture? I mean, she's not likely to become lactose-intolerant, is she, and come storming back demanding her rightful place in Rocky's bed as well as parental responsibility for Gretchen."

"No way!" There was a certainty about Debbie's

voice, the certainty of a woman in love and who knows she is loved in return. "Rocky wouldn't have her back, anyway. Not even if she turned into Catherine Zeta Jones overnight!"

I giggled, thinking of Laura's cast and freckles. "Well, that's about as likely to happen as *me* turning into Catherine Zeta Jones! Actually, I think I'm probably in with more of a chance."

"As for Gretchen," Debbie answered my second question. "Well, we talked about it and in view of the fact that there'll be a new baby in the house, Rocky decided to hand her back to Laura on account of her vicious and jealous nature."

"Well, he was with her long enough," I pointed out, deliberately obtuse. "No disrespect, Debs, but he even wanted to marry her once."

Debbie sighed. "Not funny, Gemma! You know very well I was referring to Gretchen! Hey, you don't fancy taking her on, do you, and before you start coming over all thick again, I mean *Gretchen*."

"I thought you said you were handing her back to Laura."

Debbie shook her head. "No. Laura's had a change of heart. Well, she's having a baby too, so I suppose it's understandable. Anyway, suddenly poor Gretchen is canine *non grata*! Hence, we're on the look-out for a suitable home." She tipped her head to one side, coaxingly. "So, what do you say? Could you find it in your heart to give poor little Gretchy Wetchy a homee womey?"

Immune to her wiles, I shook my head, though surprisingly it cost me a pang. I mean, Gretchen and I had unwittingly developed one of those kidnapper/kidnappee relationships where a degree of affection builds up between the parties based on mutual disrespect. "No! No, I couldn't. I've already got Furbee and he'd take one look at her and have her for breakfast."

Debbie made a little moue. "Oh, well, it was worth a try. And I suppose there's no point in asking you, Soph?"

"Correct!" Sophie shot that clay pigeon straight out of the air. "You know I don't consider poodles to be proper dogs. Give me a Great Dane or a German Shepherd, but a poodle! Like, no way José!"

There was a slight lull in the conversation as the barman, with a sneaky look down Debbie's cleavage, slid our drinks across the counter. I shot him a filthy look which he obviously misinterpreted as jealousy because, in the spirit of fairness, he then attempted to do the same to me, but balked at the sight of Sophie.

"Anyway," I said, when he had moved away to ogle elsewhere. "Leaving Gretchen to one side for the moment, what about Guy the Sly? Where does he come in?"

"He doesn't." Clearing her throat with a sound more commonly heard amongst the rutting rhinos of Rhodesia, Sophie shifted uncomfortably on her chair. "He . . . er . . . goes out! Out of Debbie's life! And out of Brigitte's life also, as it happens."

"What?" I could feel my eyebrows paying out fourteen million quid for the privilege of tagging along on the next Russian space expedition. The one leaving, like, yesterday! "He's left Brigitte?" God, where had I been for the last few weeks? In the advance Russian party? One thing for sure, I'd completely tuned out of everything that was happening around me on earth. The Tyrell O'Neill episode must really have fried my brain. "Good grief, he must have been gutted when he found you no longer wanted him, Debbie. Talk about burning all your Brigittes!"

Sophie cleared her throat yet again and shuffled about some more. "Well, that wasn't quite how it happened, actually." Clearly she had designated herself chief raconteur of this particular soap opera, though why that should be I had no idea. I mean, correct me if I'm wrong but I kind of thought Debbie and Guy were the main players. I *was* wrong. A substitute had come off the bench and scored a goal in Guy's penalty area. "Brigitte kicked Guy out!"

"Really?" Carrying on with the lunar theme, I felt my eyes shape themselves into flying saucers. "Why? Did she find out about the pair of you?" This question was directed towards Debbie but, once more, Sophie took it upon herself to fill in the blanks.

"No! It was nothing to do with Guy and Debbie. What she found out about, if you like, was herself." And as I plainly looked as unenlightened as a blind man being tutored in the intricacies of the offside rule,

Sophie took a deep breath and plunged in the deep end. "To put it bluntly she found out she's wearing my team's colours. Or, to put it in laywoman's terms, she's gay!"

"No!" Shocked, I almost bit a chunk out of my glass. "But she can't be! She's got five children, for heaven's sakes! *And* she's a married woman."

"Neither of which factors preclude her from being gay," Sophie told me sternly. "She was just a bit late in finding out but when her mates took her out to a gay club a couple of weeks ago, just for a bit of a giggle, she realised something was missing from her life."

"And that something," Debbie butted in, eyes alight with loving mischief, "or *someone*, rather, was none other than our very own Sophie!"

"No!" This time I did bite through the glass and suffered a cut lip for my pains as well as a filthy look from the landlord. I just knew the old bastard would charge me for it later. Either that, or water down my drink for the next six months or so! Either way he'd get his money's worth. Sadly, it seemed, our brush with infamy had long worn off together with the extra custom it generated. Nowadays we were just three more punters, ripe for ripping off. "You must be joking," I laughed through shredded lips. "Sophie and Guy's wife? Brigitte Evans? The supermodel? Oh, get real!"

Rummaging about in her handbag, Debbie produced a tissue, which she pressed into my hand. "There, use that, you silly cow! Honestly, we can't take you anywhere! If you're not busy losing half your fingers, you're biting through drinking glasses. *And*, I can assure you, Gemma, this is as real as Coca-Cola! Sophie and Brigitte are officially a couple and I, for one, wish them every happiness in the world."

"Oh, well, so do I," I spluttered, still not totally convinced that they weren't taking the mick. "Yeah, of course, I do. It's just that . . . it's just that . . ."

"I know it's hard to believe, Gemma," Sophie fixed me with a pleading eye, begging for understanding, "but it's true and I'm really happy. I mean, that's what I've always wanted, a wife of my own, a family of my own." Fervent, she whacked her fist down on the table. "I swear, I'm going to be the best husband and the best daddy ever!" With a wink, she paid homage to Debbie who flushed rosily. "Rocky excepted, of course! I'll tell you, those kids will want for nothing, whether it's a garden swing or a swimming-pool." She flexed her muscles. "Even if I have to dig it with my teeth!" Eyes shining, she reached across and squeezed Debbie's hand. Co-conspirators in domestic bliss, Debbie returned the squeeze, the pink of her small hand whitening beneath the pressure and suddenly I knew what it was like to feel excluded in the playground. To be the loner, the wallflower standing in the corner, the one with the bottle-end spectacles and braces on her teeth; to be on the outside looking in with your nose pressed against the windowpane – Tiny Tim, in *A*

Christmas Carol, with a gammy leg to add insult to injury! Thankfully though, Debbie and Sophie were true friends, and no sooner had the first stab of self-pity struck me than they were reaching over to include me in their hugs and pats and squeezes.

"All we need now, Gem," Debbie sighed, "is for you to find somebody and everything will be perfect!"

"I already found someone," I reminded her. Then, trying for flippant, I opened my arms to their fullest extent. "You should have seen him. He was this big but he got away."

"Maybe he'll come back," Debbie, ever the eternal optimist, said hopefully. "I mean, he was really into you, Gem. Remember that Milk Tray business."

I gave a reluctant grin. "How could I forget it? Believe me, the memory of Gretchen gnawing on his shinbone will live with me for a very long time."

"And he wrote that song for you," Sophie chipped in brightly.

"True, but I *told* you, it had Country Western leanings."

"So?" Debbie frowned, as if to denigrate Tammy Wynett would never occur to her. "It doesn't matter if it had Tower of Pisa leanings – the point is he wrote it for you. For *you*, Gemma! Not for anyone else!"

"Yes, well, I'm sure Rocky will eventually get around to writing one for you, too. That Richie Valens song, 'Donna', would lend itself quite well to plagiarism, don't you think? All he'd have to do is substitute the names." Okay, I know that was a bit below the belt, a bit bitchy but hell, like I said, I'm not a saint! I was pleased for Debbie and Sophie, of course I was, but there *are* limits. I suppose, if I'm being truthful, I wanted to quietly slink away and lick my wounds in private. I wanted to take myself off to the elephants' graveyard, lie down and die. What I didn't want to do was sit around like a death's head casting a pall over my two best friends' happiness. Still, I couldn't help but think it was a mite unfair that everything seemed to be panning out for everyone else, all the odd socks forming themselves nicely into matching pairs; Debbie and Rocky, Sophie and Brigitte, Aunty Kay and Rob Kilbride. According to her frequent emails, even Orla had, apparently, met her Romeo over in London. His name wasn't Romeo, though. It was Maurice and he was a minor royal. A Maurice Minor! Her modelling career had taken off too and now, in a parody of that famous Wonderbra poster, Orla, striking a blow for the less well-endowed, mammary-challenged female of the species, was plastered on billboards all over the place. Only, instead of reading *Hello, Boys*, the caption below read *Hello, Toys!*.

So, doing the maths bit, it looked like Guy and myself were the only spare parts still knocking around and no, don't even go there, sister. I never even thought about it. I'd sooner give birth to twin Sumo wrestlers via my left nostril, than hitch my wagon to his. As for Tyrell, well, wherever he'd got to, I'm sure he wasn't alone and the next woman that got her hooks into him would, no doubt, be a damn sight quicker to reel him in and land him than I had been. Dusting my hands together in a gesture of finality, I stood up to go.

"Anyway, all that stuff between me and Tyrell O'Neill is ancient history. Like, he made it quite plain that he thinks my entire family is straitjacket material. Nutters! Escapees from Bedlam! So that's that! The only thing for me to do now is to move onwards and, hopefully, upwards."

"Well, you'll get no arguments from us on that score, will she, Debs?" Gung-ho, Sophie enlisted Debbie in the let's-cheer-Gemma-up-from-her-clinically-depressed-and-verging-on-the-suicidal frame of mind.

"No, no objections at all." As expected, Debbie threw the full force of her featherweight (pregnancy notwithstanding) behind Sophie. "Onwards and upwards! I'm all for the power of positive thinking." She pushed the boat out at the risk of killing me with kindness. "Anyway, knowing your track record, it won't be long before you've a string of new men dancing to your tune."

I gave a tight smile. I knew it was tight because even my anus contracted. "Yep, that's me all right! Good old good-time girl, Gemma! Party-animal, Gemma! Left-on-the-flamin'-shelf-again, Gemma!"

As Sophie and Debbie flinched as though they'd been struck, I wrinkled my nose apologetically, sorry for that vitriol of that last remark, even if it *was* true. "I'm sorry, guys. Don't mind me. I'll be fine. Really, I will. Let's face it. It's not the first time I've been dumped. I'm getting to be quite an old hand at it, a bit of a phoenix really, rising again and again from the assholes."

"Of course you'll be fine!" With a quick transition back into hearty mood, Debbie saluted me with her glass. "Tell you what, though. Maybe you could do with a change of scene. Go and visit Orla in London, or something."

"Yeah!" Once again, Sophie underwrote her. "That's a great idea. Or you could go on one of those 18–30 holidays."

Shit! What is it about people who, just because they've finally managed to partake of the rarefied air of coupledom, suddenly come over all Claire Rayner and start dishing out the advice left, right and centre to their single friends. I was just about to pose this question through lips that had now become so taut I was in danger of being forced to imbibe my evening meal via a straw, when I realised that, actually, it wasn't such a bad idea. God knows, Orla was always banging on at me to come over, principally so she could crow over her *je-suis-arriveé* town house in fashionable Kensington, her equally fashionable Vivienne Westwood and Anna Sui-clad friends and, of course, her very own mini-royal, Maurice.

"You know, that's not a bad idea." I sat back down again and rapped for another JD and a fresh round for the girls. Water for Debbie, of course! "Maybe I'll come back with a new perspective."

Sophie giggled. "Yeah, or a dose of the clap." She widened her eyes. "Or engaged to Prince Charles. Well, anything is possible and technically, he *is* a free agent. Besides, you've already got royal connections to pave the way or, at least, Orla has."

"I'd sooner have the clap," I giggled, beginning to brighten up a bit. "At least there's a cure for that!"

"Right! That's settled then." Debbie got straight down to business. "When will you go? You've got some holiday due, haven't you?"

I nodded. "Yep! I've hardly used up any of my holiday quota, as it happens. I think I'll email Orla tonight and, all being well, I'll go at the weekend." The last bit of starch went out of my lips. "Hey – thanks, guys! And I'm sorry for being such a miserable bitch."

"Don't worry about it!" The soul of understanding, Sophie nodded thoughtfully. "You know what they say. Old habits die hard!"

CHAPTER 25

"So, what do you think?" Proud as Punch, Orla gestured round her living-room. "It's being featured in next month's *Homes & Gardens* and I'm shitting a brick."

"Well there's no need to. It's absolutely gorgeous," I assured her, glancing about and taking in the huge cream leather three-piece suite, the floor-to-ceiling windows, draped and flounced to within an inch of their lives in Liberty prints, the artfully placed urns of fresh flowers placed at strategic points about the room.

"Protea," she told me gleefully, "specially imported from South Africa. No scent but *fabulous* to look at and called after the African God, Proteus, who could change himself into all sorts of shapes!"

To be honest, it was information overload. I'm the kind of person that plants take one look at, throw up their hands in horror and promptly keel over and die. Still, they *were* lovely, the muted pinks and creams obviously having been selected with an eye to reflecting the impeccable colour scheme of walls and ceiling. If there was a jarring note at all, then it had to be the massive goldfish tank that occupied practically one whole corner. Something to do with Feng Shui, I found out later though, such was my ignorance, at first I thought she was referring to the oriental-looking maid who flitted noiselessly, unobtrusively about, providing us with coffee and *petits fours* – fancy buns, to you and me. Yes, folks, I had finally got to meet a real live maid and she was nothing like Laura! Orla had certainly arrived!

"Good woman, yourself, Feng," I said, as she arrived just as noiselessly to whisk away the empty cups. "That was lovely, a real treat. Did you bake the cakes yourself?"

"Jesus Christ, Gemma!" The pseudo-British accent Orla had adopted disappeared in the same instant her bottom leapt six foot off the settee. "That's Lilly, for Christ's sake! My Malaysian maid! Feng Shui is the Chinese art of something or other – enriching your life and improving your fortune, I think. As well as balancing your clackers, or something!"

"Clackers?" I asked suspiciously. "Surely not! Aren't they those little plastic, conker-ball-type things poor technology-deprived kids used to play with back in the 70s? A kind of consolation prize for anyone who couldn't afford a Space Hopper or a Raleigh Chopper?"

Orla frowned. "You're right! No, not clackers!" She snapped her fingers in a eureka kind of way. "Chakras – that's it." Clearly wrong-footed, she went on the attack again. "Anyway, don't you know anything? Hasn't Feng Shui reached Ireland yet?"

"What?" Scraping her down off the ceiling, I pretended amazement. "Arrived? I'll have you know, not only did Feng Shui arrive in Ireland, but it arrived with the Vikings and left with the Normans and it was all so long ago we've forgotten all about it. Don't tell me England is only catching on to it now?" To give Orla her due, she giggled. "Now, shut your mouth, you pretentious cow," I instructed, "and while you're about it, drop the accent. Like where does this superfluous 'r' you keep tacking onto the end of words that should end with 'a' come from? I mean, *arear* and *Annar* and *dramar* and *panoramar* etc! Get the picture? Could it be you're trying to impress Maurice with your *refeenment*? Is he, by any chance, an 'r'se hole?" Making a big production out of it, I looked all around, lifted the cover of a glossy coffee-table book of Cézanne, designed not for reading but to impress, and peered underneath, lifted a cushion and checked behind it. "By the way, where is the chinless wonder? Not disposed of him yet, have you? Not relieved him of his fortune and buried the body in convenient bite-size pieces? No suspicious bloodstains in your bathroom, eh?"

Orla giggled again. "Do you know what, Gem, you do me good. All this keeping up appearances lark can get very tiring. Honest to God, I've really had to clean up my act. I can't swear because it's *'not ladylike'*. I can't fart because it's *'not ladylike'*. I can't drink pints because it's *'not ladylike'*." Clearly frustrated, she reached out and karate-chopped the head off one of her prize Protea. "I can't even scratch because –"

"It's not ladylike?" I saved her the bother of finishing. "Well, I hope this Maurice is L'Oréal although looking around I'd say he is!"

"Oh, he is!" Orla agreed, her eyes lighting up. "Well worth it. He's also absolutely loaded and in more ways than one, which is a real bonus." She closed one eye in a lewd wink and made an even lewder gesture with her hand.

"I'll bet he is," I said as we both broke into crude laughter that was anything but ladylike. "But do you love him, Orla?"

"Well, I love his money . . ." Orla began, then went off into another peal of laughter, that horrible cross between the tinkling of bells and the high notes on a piano which enchanted everybody else but struck such a discordant note with me.

Except that it didn't! Not any more! My younger sister, Orla, the bane of my life had suddenly grown up and come of age. I was even beginning to feel something rather like the first stirrings of affection for her. Scary stuff!

"I'm only joking, Gem. Of course I love him and he's not a chinless wonder – quite handsome really and not at all horsey despite his royal connections." She considered for a moment. "Well, maybe only a little bit – around the teeth!"

I settled myself more comfortably back against the settee, enjoying the luxury of my surroundings. It was a far cry from our 1930s semi in suburban Dublin, I can tell you. I mean, we thought we were posh when we got a parquet floor in the hallway. Well, it wasn't *real* parquet – more like that cheap, interlocking veneer stuff – poor man's parquet, really. "Well, I can't wait to meet this paragon of money. Where is he anyway?"

"Oh, messing about with his advertising company," Orla said airily, as if messing about with a company was the norm and not sweating blood and tears trying to turn a profit. "Well, he's got to be *seen* to be doing something and not just sitting back and waiting for his old man to die and leave him his millions. Besides which, the Big Q is cutting back on the Civil List and minor royals aren't getting much of a look in any more. Personally, I blame that Princess Pushy woman with her me, me, me, me philosophy. It's made it pretty hard on the likes of poor Mo, I can tell you."

"What? You mean he's getting no Mo?"

Orla gave one of those bored, funny-ha-ha-type laughs, picked up the Cézanne art book (I suspect it was the first and only time she'd ever picked it up) and whacked me over the knee with it. "Anyway, let's leave Maurice aside for the moment. You'll meet him soon enough. I'm only sorry you didn't get it together with Tyrell O'Neill." Replacing the book, she held up her hands, palm outwards in a kind of don't-want-no-trouble-mister, backing-off fashion. "Listen, I know I messed about there a bit but nothing happened between me and him. That's the truth. Tyrell never saw me as anything other than a social butterfly and, let's face it, a social butterfly is of no use whatsoever to someone only interested in cabbage-moths."

"Actually he didn't," I interrupted, not much relishing being implicated either as a cabbage or a moth. "He saw you as *nouvelle cuisine* – pretty to look at, but not much substance."

"Did he, indeed?" Orla looked miffed, then grinned good-humouredly. "Actually, he's not wrong really. I suppose I am a bit of an airhead. Luckily, Maurice doesn't seem to notice or maybe, having grown up amongst the aristocracy that's what he's come to expect. Either way, it suits me."

"Well, something certainly suits you," I agreed, admiring her. I must say she wore Maurice's credit card well. Her hitherto waist-length mane of blonde hair was now tamed and shaped into a sleek and sophisticated geometrical bob, long on both sides, short at the back. Her make-up, always that bit too bright, that touch too Kylie Minogue, was toned down to a subtle blend of beiges and browns with just a hint of cerise about her bee-stung lips. Still unnaturally slender, though in a healthy, toned, celery-stick kind of way, she was dressed head to toe in a Karen Millen tracksuit which must have cost the equivalent of six months' worth of my salary.

"Thank you," she accepted the compliment gracefully.

"I don't make myself sick any more, you know, Gem. Well, I don't need to. I have a personal trainer now, who makes sure I'm eating the right things and doing the right exercises. And what do you think of my *Hello, Toys!* advertising campaign?"

"Great!" I told her honestly. "Just great! But what happened to your dream of great big bazookas?"

Orla smiled, a woman clearly content with her lot – or in this case, not a lot. "Maurice happened. He's into all things organic which, when you consider that he's a distant relation of Prince Charles, is kind of fitting. He's pretty clean-living really. No passing the Duchy on the left-hand side, for him!" She giggled at her own joke, which, admittedly, brought a smile to my own lips. Money definitely improved Orla. "Must be something in the blue blood. Anyway, he likes the natural touch and, besides, my androgynous front is getting me loads of modelling work. I've even been asked to stand in for David Bowie." Jokingly she curled her palm and blew all along the fingernails (long as ever, beautifully manicured and not a singe-mark in sight). "These days, I don't get out of bed for less than five quid! Naomi Campbell *et al* are pea-green."

I laughed again. Really, the improvement in her was enormous and I was just about to tell her so when she went and spoilt things by harking back to Tyrell O'Neill again. Like, I was here to *forget* him, wasn't I? I was here to shop till I dropped, take in a couple of West End shows, trip the light fantastic in Stringfellows or the

426

Hippodrome and, if time permitted, traipse around a boring art gallery or two, just to be able to claim when I got home that I actually did something vaguely cultural.

"It's such a shame!" Orla had that same expression on her face as Debbie and Sophie, that so-sorry-you're-excluded-from-the-inner-sanctum-of-sacred-coupledom look that patronised even as it sympathised. "I mean, you were so suited. Everyone could see that except you. You were only interested in getting your Rockies off!"

My look of dawning benevolence was rapidly replaced by a sarcastic sneer. I took it all back. She was still a bitch. "Well, if you thought we were so suited, why did you pull that little stunt in Donegal?"

Orla did her backing-off number again. Somehow I got the impression that she wasn't on for a sisterly mill on the Axminster carpet which, incidentally, was so deep that the first time I set foot on it I was in over my head in seconds and struggling for air. Do you believe me when I tell you I had to practically swim over to the sofa?

"Look, I've apologised for that. The best I can say is that I was all at sea at the time –"

"Oh, no you weren't!" Quick as a flash, I was in there clubbing her over the head with the big stick of accusation. "At sea is precisely what you weren't and what a to-do that caused."

"Yes, well, how was I to know everyone would go off the deep end like that. Besides, I did phone Mammy, you know, so if anyone's to blame she is." Running a complacent hand through her hair, she closed one eye in a mischievous wink. "In any case, Aunty Kay did pretty well out of it. So you see some good came out of the whole fiasco." Well, to be fair, I couldn't really argue with that. Aunty Kay and Rob had come out about their romance and I don't mean just out of the stable. No, they were officially an *item*, as Aunty Kay put it, trying hard to formulate her hirsute upper lip into something approaching coy. Honestly, it was enough to turn your stomach. Now, I wouldn't call myself ageist but, really, people of their age should be banned from performing lewd acts. I mean, there's no need for sex at their age. It's not as if they need it for the purposes of procreation and, if it's recreation they're after, then why not pop along to the nearest DIY centre and invest in a garden hoe or a nice pair of secateurs? Then, of course, there's always the bingo and if, due to fortuitous and regular pension plan instalments, they find themselves, in old age, with a fair old wodge in the bank, they can always go on one of those SAGA holidays, complete with complimentary incontinence pads. No need for incontinence on the continent! "Shame," Orla continued, on a somewhat mournful note, "the only one who hasn't managed to cop off with anyone is you!"

"Oh, give it a rest!" I snapped. "Haven't you ever heard of *que serà, serà*? Whatever will be, will be?"

"Mm," Orla nodded judiciously, "but I also believe in serendipity and whatever you *want* to *serà* can *serà* – if you give it a little nudge in the right direction."

"Is that right, Plato? O Wise and All-Seeing Oz?" I sneered, overdoing it on the sarcasm. "Tell me, what do you do in your spare time? Help out at the Samaritans? Dish out advice to lost and hopeless causes – like me!" I drew in a deep indignant breath. "Well, you know where you can shove your advice, don't you? Right up your designer thong!"

Orla, refusing to get rattled, bent on me a look that was positively verging on the Virgin-Mary-in-beatific-mode. "Now, now, put your bristles away, Gem. All I'm saying is it's a pity things didn't work out for you. That's all! It wasn't a criticism. It just seemed like Tyrell O'Neill was completely bats over you. To be perfectly honest, that's another reason I did a runner from Donegal. Like, he never stopped banging on about you." She fixed me with an honest and somewhat self-deprecating eye. "It was a whole new experience for me, I can tell you – me, that's used to being the centre of attention!" She dusted her hands together. "Still, you know what they say? For every old boot there's an old sock and Mo, bless his little aristocratic heart, is my old sock. And, who knows Gem, maybe you've yet to meet *your* 'sole' mate."

"Oh, enough! Can't we just drop the subject and talk about something else?" I said wearily, knowing full well I *had* met my soul mate and that there was unlikely to be another old boot knocking about this planet that would support my fallen arches quite so well. Far better to resign myself now to a life spent hobbling along on flat and blistered feet than to spend the rest of it baying futilely for the moon. Failing that, I could always reconsider my career options, inquire at the nearest convent regarding vacancies or, at a push, go over to the other side and join the Sophies of this world. I mean, everybody knows lesbians aren't fussy and don't ask for your CV. Mind you, at some point in my life I must have envisaged having children because suddenly the prospect of a childless old age seemed to rise up and engulf me in tidal waves of pain. To tell the truth the prospect made me want to burst out crying, made me want to scream and shout and go 'Wah, wah, it's not fair! It's not bloody fair!' with my mouth wide open and tonsils clearly on display. On display and *vibrating* like those cartoon characters you see in the *Beano* or on *South Park*! Well, can you blame me? I mean, what's left in life at the age of seventy-odd but the enjoyment to be derived from publicly embarrassing your children and grandchildren with grandiloquent displays of senility?

Mind you, to be completely cold-blooded about it, these days the absence of a love life was no barrier to getting pregnant. I mean, an obliging male friend and a turkey baster could do the job just as well.

Orla stood up decisively. "Fair enough, Gemma! If you want me to drop the subject, I will." Dramatically, she made washing motions with her hands. "From now on Tyrell O'Neill's name is a dirty word in this house and anyone caught using it will incur severe penalties. Satisfied!"

I nodded. "Fine. But you're not to try pawning me off on your single male friends either – you know, carrying along a spare man like a spare wheel everywhere we go, just to perpetuate the myth that I'm not alone and a twenty-six-year-old failure."

"I won't. Promise!" Orla grinned. "Besides, the only single men I know round here are all Hooray Henrys with the emphasis on the *hoor*! Not your type, I can assure you."

"Yes, well, I daresay I'm not their type, either. Not slim enough, blonde enough, young enough, blue-blooded enough or rich enough!"

"God, you're determined to wallow, aren't you?" Yanking me to my feet, which was some accomplishment, considering she was half my size, Orla steered me towards my bedroom. "Now, you must be tired after your plane journey and all that messing around at the airport. I know it's only a short hop, skip and jump from Dublin, but it would wear you out all the same. So, I'll tell you what. Why don't you catch a bit of shut-eye and then, later on, have a nice shower and put your glad rags on because, baby, are we going to hit the town tonight! I swear, London ain't gonna see anything like it since the Blitz!"

"Really?" I perked up a bit. "Why, what have you got in mind?"

Orla tapped her nose, conclusive proof that once those Freemasons have you in their grip, they never let go. "It's a surprise but – you know how you always fancied Ricky Martin . . ." Her voice trailed off, tantalisingly.

"*Yes!*" Tired or not tired, my right hand of its own volition clenched itself into a fist and launched itself into the air in a series of victorious punches that tore holes in the ozone layer. "*Yes! Yes! Yes!*" Tonight I was going to see Ricky Martin. Tonight, I, Gemma Murphy, lowly recta inspecta from suburban Dublin, was going to be living it up! Living *la vide loca!* Eat your heart out, Tyrell O'Neill! Long live Latin men! Long live Latin men, in tight, tight trousers!

As I drifted happily off to sleep in Orla's spare bedroom, Laura Ashley themed, with tastefully matching bed linen, wallpaper and Austrian blinds and lulled by the muted sound of the London traffic through the double glazing, I imagined Ricky singing to me and everybody else fading completely out of the picture. "*A little bit of Gemma in my life . . .*"

* * *

"So? How do I look?" Emerging from the bedroom, I attempted a twirl on the living-room carpet, forgot how deep the pile was, and went flying as my spindle heel got caught, managing only to save myself by dint of grabbing on to the hair of a man who was sitting on a nearby armchair, and promptly relieving him of the same.

As helplessly I stood there, like Running Wolf or Big Black Cloud or some other Indian brave during the

American Civil War, hoisting aloft the scalp of some poor, hapless Yankee drummer boy, Orla dissolved into a fit of hysterics. " Maurice, meet my big sister, Gemma. Gemma, as you can't fail to have noticed, likes to make a bit of an entrance."

So this was Orla's Mr Right, Maurice, the minor royal, the Maurice Minor, this balding vision of English aristocracy who with typical British reserve seemed to be completely unfazed by my somewhat unorthodox method of introducing myself.

"Er . . . hi . . . Maurice," I stammered, horribly embarrassed and unsure of the correct etiquette of the situation. Like, should I play it cool like him, pretend nothing had happened, pretend that the big hank of black hair growing out of my hand was a result of a thyroid deficiency? Hirsuitism, I think they call it. Or, should I pass it back to him without comment, cool as a cucumber, making like it was an everyday occurrence to find yourself in possession of a complete stranger's wig. Toupee or not toupee, that was the question. Helplessly, I looked to Orla for clues but the bitch was doubled over clutching her sides and I realised in a flash that her transition from total airhead to normal decent human being was still a long way from being complete.

Luckily for me though, Maurice took charge of the situation, rising to his feet and sweeping me a courtly, old-fashioned bow. "Pleased to meet you, Gemma. I've heard a lot about you and now, can I have my hair back, please? It gets so cold without it, don't you know. But then, the thing is so horribly itchy and . . . well, Orla *will* insist. Says without it I look like that chappie – what's his name – yaw, right, Crackerjack! No, not Crackerjack! Some pesky Greek or Rusky name or something. Kojak – yes, by Jove, that's it! Kojak! Bald fellow, big nose, likes lollipops! No accounting for tastes? What?"

By golly, he was right there. Bewildered, I sought Orla's eye only to find that she had cashed in her hysterics for a look of pure dogged devotion, which she was busy levelling at her beloved.

"Oh . . . er . . . of course," I stammered, reverently replacing the wig on the bald head he inclined towards me and helpfully tugging it this way and that in an effort to make it seem less like a dead crow.

"Jolly good!" Straightening up, Maurice added his own brand of patting and pulling but there was no getting away from it. The creature was undoubtedly road-kill!

"Ooh, Gemma!" Orla gave a not-altogether-convincing penitent squeak. "I meant to warn you, really I did but, well, Maurice's wig is so much part of him, I simply forgot. Mind you, nobody, not even Jesus Christ, could have predicted you'd whip it off him before ever I had a chance to introduce you." Closing one eye, she winked lewdly in Maurice's direction. He, with all the panache of a dignitary at a Court function, was now happily playing at mein host with a bottle of Courvoisier and three Waterford crystal tumblers. "She always was a fast worker, you know, Mo. Oh, the tales I could tell! They'd turn your wig white!"

Did I actually say I was beginning to like her? That she had grown up and come of age? Jesus wept! I must have been doting. I must have been just one drool short of full-blown senility. "Shut up, Orla!" I hissed out of one side of my mouth, trying simultaneously to arrange the other into a polite smile of thanks as Maurice pressed a glass into my hand.

"Thanks very much, Maurice," I said and I'm sorry about the . . . er . . . the um . . ." At a loss for words, I made vague fluttering motions in the general direction of his head.

Ever the gent, Maurice raised his glass in a toast. "Perfectly all right, dear girl. Chin! Chin!"

"Yeah, sure, whatever!" I clinked my glass against his. God, this was surreal. It wouldn't have surprised me if at any moment Jeremy Beadle were to leap out of a nearby closet with an inane grin on his face. *"Gemma Murphy, you've been framed!"* Only he didn't. This was real, all right. I must say I was more than a bit surprised at Orla's choice of paramour considering how she had always had an eye to the pretty boy sector. Pretty rich too, it must be said, but Maurice, although he more than adequately fitted the last part of the bill, could never, not in a million years be accused of entering into the kingdom of hunkdom. *And* while I wouldn't exactly go so far as to say he was like the back of a bus, if he had 155 and Brixton Station tattooed on his forehead, people would have tried to board him. Still, to give Orla her due, she appeared to be genuinely smitten. I mean, wig notwithstanding, she'd described him as quite handsome really. I rest my case! I also made a note to check with her when she'd last paid a visit to her friendly, local optician.

"So, what's the plan of campaign? We're going to the Oxo Tower, yaw?" Maurice glanced from me to Orla and, following his cue because I hadn't the foggiest notion what he was on about, I looked to her for guidance too.

"Yaw!" Orla confirmed, going into pseudo-British mode again. "You're going to love it, Gem. It's a restaurant way up at the top of the Oxo Tower building overlooking the Thames. Honestly, it's absolutely gorgeous! You can see for miles all down along the river over to Westminster, Big Ben and the Millennium Wheel and in the opposite direction to Tower Bridge and all across London. It's breathtaking, like Fairyland. Oh, and the food's pretty good too!"

"Hmm, sounds good to me!" I licked my lips in anticipation. Never mind the sightseeing, I was that hungry I could eat a baby's butt through a wicker chair.

"And then we're going to see that singer chappie fellow Gemma's so keen on, shake a tail-feather, yaw?"

"Yaw!" Orla confirmed again, demonstrating quite clearly that in this particular house, the yaws had it! "And I must say, Gem, you look absolutely fantastic. Have you lost weight?" I nodded happily. Losing weight was the upside of a broken heart, the silver lining in my own particular cloudburst. "And that dress," Orla, her forget-me-not blue eyes narrowed, raked me from head to foot, "that's by Gaultier, isn't it? I'm sure I saw that on the catwalk during London Fashion week. Didn't I see that on the catwalk, Mo? That model, what's her name, Linda Evangelista was wearing it."

Mo nodded dryly. "Quite possibly. You certainly saw everything else and bought most of it with my credit cards, if I remember correctly. That Christian Dior fellow, in particular, is laughing all the way to the *banque*."

Actually, Orla was wrong. My dress was by a little-known Irish designer and what I paid for it wouldn't have paid for the sleeve of a Jean Paul Gaultier number. Still, it *was* gorgeous, a soft lavender voile that brought out the blue in my own eyes and that clung in all the right places. It also finished some six inches above the knee thereby revealing my best feature, my long, shapely legs, encased in high-gloss tights and spike-heeled strappy sandals, totally unlike my usual Doc Marten footwear. And do you know what? For once in my life, I felt beautiful, beautiful and feminine and not at all ungainly or out of place beside my fine-boned glamorous sister, kitted out head to toe in Anna Sui. Piling my hair loosely on my head, I'd left just the odd wisp or two free to curl softly round my face. I'd even pushed the boat out and worn full make-up:

foundation, lip liner, lipstick, mascara – the works, and even a touch of eyeliner which to my amazement gave me a slightly Audrey Hepburn in *Breakfast at Tiffany's* look. If only Tyrell could see me now. The thought came unbidden. But, like the rose that's born to blush unseen, sadly, I too seemed destined to waste my fragrance on the London air.

"So? You gals all set, then?" As Orla and I nodded in tandem, Maurice rose to his feet, gave one last reassuring pat to his toupee, and possessed himself of his car keys, which Lilly the Malaysian maid appeared with bang on cue. Those oriental women certainly train up well! No wonder they're in such demand as wives! I made a mental note to check how things were going with Sophie and Brigitte. "Right then, let's go." Gallantly he held out an arm to each of us and a few moments later found us comfortably ensconced in his six series BMW and heading for the river.

The Oxo Tower restaurant was everything Orla promised and more. Ambience, views, food, everything was perfect and a far cry from the daily drudgery of my life at *Vets 4 Petz*. Still, for the most part, I found myself content simply to sit there, listening to Orla and Maurice making plans for their future and, when pushed, adding a comment or two of my own, toying absent-mindedly with my food because, suddenly, despite all the grandeur, the clothes, the make-up, I felt emptier than I'd ever felt in my whole life before. It was almost a relief when Maurice finished off his second large helping of tiramisu and, bill settled, with an extravagant tip for the waiter, we left for the concert. Ricky Martin couldn't fail to cheer me up. Just one look at his trousers and I'd be ecstatic, two and I'd be raised to celestial heights not yet achieved by even the most accomplished yogi.

* * *

"Right, we're here!" Orla announced, swinging round to look at me as the car eventually drew up in front of the imposing London Arena. "Now, Gemma, promise you won't get mad! Promise you won't go into one."

"What?" Startled, I sat bolt upright on the back seat. "What do you mean? Why on earth should I get mad when God is in his Heaven, Ricky Martin is on stage and all's right with the world?"

Orla looked more than a little anxious. "Well, because I lied." She hurried to gloss things over. "Only a little lie, mind – and with the best of intentions."

Deliberately, I strove to keep my voice calm, uncomfortably mindful of that old adage about the road to hell being paved with good intentions. "O–kay, Orla. You'd better come clean. What exactly *have* you done?"

Imploring, Orla clasped her hands to her chest for all the world like a 1920s heroine about to be strapped to a railroad track. "But first, promise you won't get mad?"

"No," I said coldly. "I won't promise any such thing.

Now come on, spit it out! I'm sure it can't be that bad."

"Okay." Taking a deep breath, Orla suddenly capitualted. "It's not a Ricky Martin concert. It's not a concert at all, as it happens. It's a Rocky Cashel show!" The last came out in a rush. "A re-run of *Rotten to the Core* to be exact! In its new and improved version, if all the publicity hype is to be believed!

Oh Christ! I thought as the full impact of her words hit me like a sledgehammer in the face. It *was* that bad! It was worse than bad! It was bloody disastrous! "*Why*?" I screamed, wanting nothing more than to reach across and throttle the life out of her, letting go only when my fingers went numb and fell off at the knuckle. "*Why* would you lie to me like that? *Why* did you make me think we were going to see Ricky Martin?"

"Because I knew I'd never get you near the place otherwise, that's bloody why!" Shriving herself of all blame, Orla suddenly launched straight into battle mode. "Besides, it's your precious friends, Debbie and Sophie you should be mad at, not me! Debbie's over with Rocky for the show and Sophie and that Brigitte woman have come along for the ride and presumably they thought it might be nice for all of you to meet up and so they got in touch with me!"

My eyes flashed fire. "Well, why didn't they get in touch with me – you know, use the direct approach? Since when have any of us ever needed to use an intermediary?" Aggrieved, I pulled out a tissue and

440

dabbed violently at my eyes, which had grown very moist around the tear ducts. Bye-bye, eyeliner! Hello, Dusty Springfield! "It's the first I've heard about anyone coming over!"

Orla rolled her eyes. "Well, *dah!* Of course it's the first you've heard of it! This little reunion was meant to be a surprise. Read my lips, Gemma – a sur-prise! A *hap-py* surprise!"

"So why the Ricky Martin charade, then?"

"Oh, have a word with yourself!" Orla shook her head in disgust. "Like I've already said, I wouldn't have managed to get you within an ass's roar of the place if I'd come clean and told you the truth. Plus I *know* you've got the hots for Ricky Martin so in that respect you were guaranteed to be a bit of a pushover and, as you know, I'm all for anything that makes my life easier." She nodded earnestly. "Besides, you *have* to be at this show, Gemma, because Rocky's going to propose to Debbie live on stage and you wouldn't want to miss that, would you?"

"No! No, of course I wouldn't," I said, completely taken aback by this disclosure and genuinely delighted for Debbie, if a bit surprised by the speed with which things were happening on that front. "But why couldn't Debbie have told me herself?"

Orla gave the vocal equivalent of stamping her foot. "Would – you – stop – being – so – daft, Gemma! Debbie doesn't actually know. Sophie tipped me off on the QT and told me to pass it on to you. Debbie's got no idea of what Rocky is planning. She just thinks it would be a real laugh for you all to meet up together."

"Which, of course, it would," I began, "It would be great fun but –"

"Look," Orla jumped in, taking advantage of my obvious softening, "you don't have to have anything to do with Tyrell O'Neill. Yes, he's going to be there! Of course, he is! He's part of the whole shebang. But then, so are hundreds of other people going to be there. Just ignore him, can't you? Do it for your friends! Be there for Debbie."

"Well, I suppose I *could* keep a low profile," I said grudgingly, whilst a tiny egotistical part of me couldn't help but feel gratified that Tyrell O'Neill would get the chance to see me in all my long-legged, glossy-tighted, stiletto-heeled, look-but-don't-touch glory. What's that people said about the best revenge being to rub his face in it? "I wouldn't like to let Debs down."

"Of course you wouldn't," Orla enthused. "Now, come on. Let's go in and see your mates. We've got the best seats in the house, you know – practically sitting on the stage, we are! We'll be able to count the sweat-beads on their faces." Reaching behind, she slapped me hard on the knee. "Time was, Gemma Murphy, when you would have killed for a ringside seat at a Rocky Cashel show."

I nodded, a little sadly, a changed girl from the one who would have bankrupted herself for just such a chance. "I know and now it's going to kill me being so close."

"Nonsense!" Relief at having manipulated me made Orla bracing. "You'll be grand. We'll have a great time and it'll be an education for Maurice to see how the peasant classes enjoy themselves, won't it Mo?"

Maurice, who had tactfully maintained a low profile throughout the long altercation between Orla and myself, chuckled easily. "Oh, come now, Orla! We, the ruling classes, are not all just about *Last Night At The Proms*, you know. Some of us even have a thing about Britney Spears."

"Well, so long as it's just a *little* thing!" Orla pouted, then led the exodus from the car and into the Arena, with me, the condemned, reluctantly bringing up the rear.

* * *

"Gemma! Orla! Over here!" Waving furiously, Sophie beckoned us down to the front of the auditorium. "What kept you? We were getting worried you might not come."

"And so you bloody well should have been worried," I hissed as I dropped into an empty seat on one side of her. "I almost didn't come, you know! And just for the record, you *owe* me a Ricky Martin concert!"

"Fair enough but believe me, it was desperate measures – all in a good cause, etc etc. Besides, I know you'll forgive me before the night is out." Before I could argue the toss, she leaned backwards, to reveal the woman sitting on the other side. "By the way, Gem, this is Brigitte. I don't think you've met before."

Ah, Brigitte! Guy-the-Sly's ex-missus. Leaning across Sophie, I sketched a friendly salute, as a sophisticated version of Cher, all black leather and scraps of lace smiled back. "Hi, Brigitte! How's it going?"

"Great!" Brigitte, slipped a slender, perfectly-manicured hand into Sophie's. "It's going just great!"

"That's . . . er . . . great," I said, a bit weakly on account of feeling a bit out of my depth with all this lesbo-bonding and all girls together bit. "Er – where's Debs?"

"She'll be here in just a minute," Sophie said. "She's probably just backstage geeing Rocky up for his big performance tonight. Anyway, she's got the seat right next to you, and Orla and Maurice are next to her. So it's happy families all round!"

"Isn't it just!" I tried to sound happy but I was very conscious that of the group, I, alone, was flying solo.

"Hi, Gem!" With only moments to spare before the curtain went up, Debbie flung herself into the seat beside me. "It's great to see you. We were really worried you wouldn't show up. I mean, I know it's awkward – me being with Rocky . . ."

"And me being with neither Rocky *nor* Tyrell?" For Debbie's sake, I took a gigantic breath and resolved to put my best foot forward. After all, nothing should be allowed to spoil her big night. "Ah, don't worry about it! Besides, I'm with my two best mates and that's what counts. Whatever happens, we'll always stick together, won't we?"

"Course we will!" Debbie shot me a brilliant smile just as the lights went down, the curtains parted and Rocky, resplendent in 1840s poor-starving-Irish-person gear, prepared to strut his stuff. "Ooh, isn't he gorgeous!" she gasped, with the blind eyes of love, but I wasn't looking at Rocky. I was looking beyond him, my eyes pulled via a magnetic force to where Tyrell sat at the piano, darkly handsome beneath the spotlights, his eyes scanning the audience, almost as though he was searching for somebody. Honestly, as he gazed in my direction, I felt as though five thousand volts of electricity shot through me. If you'd hooked me up to the mains, I swear I could have powered Battersea Power Station. So strong was the sensation that I felt sick. I felt elated. I felt emotions I could put no name to, and then to the accompaniment of a hugely dramatic drum-roll, the music started up and he bent his head over the keyboard. The songs that followed were all familiar, dear to me, conjuring up as they did visions of a time when life was less stressful, less complicated, full of promise. A time when Rocky Cashel was just another out-of-reach pop-idol, to be lusted after from afar, a time when Tyrell O'Neill didn't even exist. Well, not for me, anyway! Tears in my eyes, I found myself croaking along to the chorus of each well-known, well-loved song and by the time the show drew to a close and Rocky was ready to make his public declaration of love, I was completely destroyed, weeping and wailing like a newly bereaved Jackie Kennedy.

"Right, ladies and gentlemen," Rocky announced as

the last haunting strains of 'Hunger' died away. "We've got a real treat for you now – something extra on the menu that you won't have heard before and which won't cost you a penny – something to warm the cockles of your hearts and put a smile on your faces as you go home tonight. Yes, siree! Never let it be said that lil' ol' Rocky Cashel don't give good value for money!"

Sniffing, I sat up straighter. This was it! This was Debbie's big moment! On either side of me I sensed rather than saw Debbie and Sophie sitting up straighter too. God, how I envied Debs! Oh, not the man! Heaven knows I'd long since gotten over Rocky – but the gesture. I envied her the big romantic gesture. How come nothing like that ever happened to me?

"All right! All right!" Rocky raised a restraining hand as, around us, the audience clamoured loudly for this unexpected treat, clapping wildly and stamping their collective feet into the ground. "Now hold on, y'all!" Obviously, he was still boning up on his *Young Guns* role. "Hold your hosses! Quiet! Quiet! Shut the hell up! Thank you!" As silence duly descended, he gave a slight bow from the waist and with a flourish of his hand worthy of a circus ringmaster stepped back revealing, much to my utter amazement, Tyrell, half-shrouded in darkness and sitting quietly at the piano. What on earth was going on? Seeking enlightenment, I glanced from Sophie to Debs and back again but they were both sitting bolt upright now, eyes focussed on the stage and yes, even in the semi-darkness I could see it, a great big stupid smile plastered across each of their faces. As the spotlight came on full and the last vestiges of shadow lifted, there was a sudden introductory tinkle of musical notes and, raising his face in the direction of my seat, Tyrell started to sing.

I'm looking at you, Gemma,
But you're looking right through
To somebody else, Gemma,
Who doesn't see you.
Well, he doesn't love you
But, darling I do,
He's looking at you, Gemma,
But he's looking right through . . .

Oh, my God! I'd been set up! The bitches had set me up! There was a rushing sound in my head, an overpowering awareness of the blood pulsing round and round in my body, a sensation of my heart struggling to burst free of its arterial anchors and launch itself into the heavens. Tyrell was singing my song. *My* song! The song he wrote for me. But that was in a different lifetime! A different place! A place called Nirvana way out in the wilds of Donegal and about as far removed from metropolitan London as it's possible to imagine.

As the last notes of the song died away, Tyrell stood up, came round front of the piano, and got down on one knee. "Gemma Murphy!" he called, as the house lights came on full and I found myself being hauled like a sack of potatoes to my feet, by Sophie on one side and

Debbie on the other. "Gemma Murphy, will you marry me?"

"Yes! Yes! Yes!" The excited affirmative came from all over the place as suddenly from amidst the crowd, a sea of heads bobbed up – heads with faces I recognised but would never have expected to see here, not in a thousand years. Aunty Kay, would you believe it, and Rob Kilbride! My mother and my boss, Martin Shanahan. Even my schoolteacher from infants' school! They were all in on it, the bastards!

On the stage, Tyrell chuckled. "Well, if you think I'm asking all of you lot to marry me, you've another think coming. There's only one girl in the world for me." Shining like stars, his dark eyes sought mine and suddenly, just like that daydream I'd had about Ricky Martin, everybody else just seemed to melt away. "So, what do you say, Gemma? Could you bear being married to a sheep-farmer? Could you bear being buried alive out in the wilds of Donegal, smothered in thermal knickers and reeking of turf smoke?"

Tears in my own eyes, I nodded with a certainty I'd never previously known. "I can bear anything," I said, shakily, cornily and with a good deal of feedback as somebody had pushed a dodgy mike into my hand. "Just so long as you're by my side." Corny it may have been but it was clearly the right answer as around us the crowd went wild and Tyrell, scrambling over the orchestra pit, the conductor, assorted muscians and a cello that he put his foot through, closed the distance between us. Pausing only to place a diamond ring on my finger, he took me in his arms and for the next five minutes it would have taken the combined forces of the Royal Marines and the US Navy to prise us apart.

* * *

Backstage in the greenroom, Rocky, with an imperious clap of his hands, called for silence. "If you could all cut the cackle for a minute, I'd like you to charge your glasses and drink a toast to the happy couple." Obedient silence fell. "Ladies and gentlemen," he said as all faces turned to where Tyrell and I were once more busily engaged in a spot of tongue-wrestling, "a toast to Gemma and Tyrell! May your joys be many and may all your troubles be woolly ones!" As everybody laughed, he raised a hand again. "*And*," he said heavily and with emphasis, "have I got an engagement present for you!" Glancing over at Debbie, he tipped her the nod and she scurried from the room, only to return a moment later with . . . shock . . . horror . . .Gretchen!

Well, if the combined forces of the Royal Marines and the US Navy couldn't part us, Gretchen managed it in seconds.

"No!" Jumping back I made a crucifix out of my fingers. "*Please*, not the Antichrist!" I was dimly aware that, beside me, Tyrell had sunk to his knees, and his eyes were both upturned and rolling in a manner that suggested frenzied bartering with the Lord. Neither the Lord nor our so-called friends appeared to be listening, however, as bending down (in an awkward fashion on account of the fact that her bump had suddenly sprouted) Debbie unclipped Gretchen's lead. Unused to such freedom, the dog looked confused for a moment, then, like a bullet from a gun she was up and running towards us at the speed of light, paws skittering and sliding over the polished floor, teeth bared in a death snarl. Leaping to his feet, Tyrell grabbed me in a kind of *Titanic* if-we're-going-down-then-we're-going-down-together-while-the-band's-still-playing way. Bracing ourselves for the impact we closed our eyes and then, after a few seconds, when nothing happened, slowly opened them again only to find Gretchen sitting at our feet, butter wouldn't melt, offering one tiny pink paw.

"It's just a ruse," Tyrell hissed. "You wait and see! She's got a chainsaw hidden in the other one. *Or* a tommy-gun. *Or* a machete. Be warned, poodles don't change their foul and filthy natures overnight!"

"Oh, rubbish," I said. "Just look at her! She's *so* sweet. Honestly, Tyrell, you've got to show a bit more faith." Bending down, I brought my face level with hers. "Hello, Gretch, you wretch," I said. "Wanna shake paws?" But Tyrell was right and a moment later it would have taken the combined force of the Royal Marines and the US Navy to prise her off my jugular. As the paramedics bore me off on a stretcher, I was dimly aware of yet another fracas taking place.

"Rocky Cashel!" Out of the mêlée an unknown, officious voice came loud and clear. "You are hereby summonsed to appear at Marylebone Court on December 21st on twenty-one counts of plagiarism, but specifically in relation to Tom Jones's 'Green Green Grass of Home'!"

"What?" In pain though I was and choking on my own blood, I could still hear the outrage in Rocky's voice. "But Tom Jones's 'Green Green Grass' is nothing like my 'Green Green Tumbleweed'! Ask anybody!"

THE END